Happy Reading!

Kathleen Irene Paterka

the other wife

Kathleen Irene Paterka

The Other Wife
Copyright © 2015 by Kathleen Irene Paterka. All rights reserved.
First Print Edition: 2015

ISBN-10: 0989283836
ISBN-13: 978-0-9892838-3-0

This is a work of fiction. Names, characters, places, brands, media, and incidents are either the product of the author's imagination or are used fictitiously. Any similarity to persons living or dead is purely coincidental. All situations in the books are products of the author's imagination. Any resemblance in situations to persons living or dead is purely coincidental.

All rights reserved. Without limiting the rights under copyright reserved above, no part of this publication may be reproduced, stored in or introduced into a retrieval system, or transmitted, in any form, or by any means (electronic, mechanical, photocopying, recording, or otherwise) without the prior written permission of both the copyright owner and the above publisher of this book.

For Cyndi, who lived it...

Also By Kathleen Irene Paterka

The James Bay Novels
Fatty Patty
Home Fires
Lotto Lucy
For I Have Sinned

Women's Fiction
Royal Secrets

Nonfiction
For the Love of a Castle

Acknowledgments

To my loyal readers, I owe an enormous debt of gratitude. Thank you for continuing to read my books and for telling me how much you enjoy them. Writing a novel can be a very lonely and isolating experience. Knowing you are out there waiting to read the next book keeps me on task. You make the difference.

I'm truly blessed to have the following people in my life. They've provided invaluable support and friendship. Virginia Conlon, Marsha Braun, and Claudia Guerra, readers extraordinaire, for their thoughts and commentary on the early drafts. Fellow authors and readers, Catherine Chant and Jackie Bouchard, for providing editorial input, pointing out inconsistencies, and rallying me on when my spirits were sagging. Dear friends and fellow authors, Jenna Mindel and Christine Johnson, travelers along the way. Long live the Queen of Hearts Club!

Researching for a new book is never easy. I am particularly grateful to the following people who helped me get my facts straight: Dr. Penny Visser, professor of psychology at the University of Chicago, for providing insight into the human psyche as well as the world of academia; Phil Alderks, of the Lake Forest Illinois Cemetery, for his information on funerals and burial arrangements; Duane Krauss, of Macy's Department Store, for allowing me to pick his brain and providing answers to every one of my *this-will probably sound-strange-but...* questions about the world of working retail; and Laura Potter, of the Charlevoix Public Library, for sharing her passion of books and children, and allowing me to sit in on a session of '*Miss Laura*' the Library Lady.

And finally, to my husband Steve. You keep me going, sweetheart, and I couldn't do this without you. With you, my heart is home.

Three may keep a secret, if two of them are dead.

~ Benjamin Franklin ~

Prologue

It wasn't much of a sound. Later, she would remember it as an odd sort of grunt. Still, it had been loud enough to wake her. Eleanor rolled over in their king-size bed, stretched out an arm, and nudged him. Richard's snoring had worsened in the past months. She lay there in the darkness, waiting to see if another nudge was necessary. Just the other day, she'd read how snoring could be a sign of sleep apnea, leading to other, more serious, health problems. Perhaps tomorrow, depending on what kind of mood he was in, she'd mention the subject over breakfast. Maybe she should insist that he see a doctor. Not that it would do much good. Richard rarely listened to her. For most of the thirty-eight years they'd been married, he hadn't listened to much of what she had to say. He'd probably give her his usual shrug, tell her to quit worrying.

Quit worrying. It wasn't until five hours later that she realized she'd had good cause to be worried. She should have known that sound was different. She should have stayed awake. She should have tried to rouse him. Instead, she waited another minute, surrounded by silence. Then, turning over, she laid her head back on the pillow and curled up in her spot, still warm from sleep, snuggling into the clean, fragrant smell of freshly laundered sheets changed by Martha the day before. Closing her eyes, Eleanor drifted off into the most pleasant dream... only to wake the next morning to her worst nightmare.

Richard, in bed beside her, was dead.

Chapter One

"Sorry if you think things are moving too fast, Mom," Jeffrey said from behind Richard's desk. "But we need to get the paperwork started."

"I understand." Eleanor nodded, pretending as if she were following exactly what her son was saying, though that couldn't be further from the truth. Why the hurry? Richard was dead and he wasn't coming back. She pushed away the thought of the gleaming black limos lining the curb of the church yesterday as they departed the funeral service, the dark, somber hearse as it moved through slushy streets lined with snowbanks. Chicago in March was often bleak, and the graveside service had been that and then some. Returning home for the mandatory gathering of family and friends hadn't proved much better. The men stood in loud, boisterous clumps throughout the house, warming themselves in front of the fire, enjoying the feast spread out by the caterers. They laughed and joked, and ate and drank, as if the reality of an untimely death of one of their own could be chased away by delicious food and Richard's best scotches and bourbons.

Women, however, were realists. Who needs food when you're being served drama? They crowded around her as she moved through the rooms, following her down hallways, seeking her out in every corner. *"What a tragedy, Eleanor. How terrible for you,"* they murmured, as if speaking such might convey upon them a special blessing and guarantee a similar horror would never touch them. Only one brave soul voiced the crucial questions all of them must have longed to ask but didn't dare.

"Is it true you performed CPR? Wasn't it horrible, putting your mouth on his, knowing he was dead?"

And her personal favorite: "What will you do now?"

Good question, Eleanor had thought as she wandered the rooms, numbly accepting hugs and words of condolence. What *would* she do now? First thing would be to put her house back in some semblance of order. The refrigerator shelves and every inch of the kitchen counters were crammed with dishes from the catered luncheon, and the house was filled with overripe blooms that had taken over like uninvited guests settling in for a long stay. The stargazer lilies were especially unwelcome, their overpowering scent wafting through the house, drifting into Richard's study. Maybe if she begged politely, Martha would take them home with her along with some of the leftover food. Then again, Martha lived alone. No one person could be expected to eat all that food. What was she supposed to do with it? Throw it out? It seemed a shame to let good food go to waste.

She shook her head, focusing back on the here and now. "There's quite a bit of ham in the refrigerator," she said. "Would you like to take some of it home? Genevieve and I will never be able to finish it."

"I'm a vegetarian." Genevieve shifted in the chair beside her. "I've been a vegetarian for years. That means I do not eat meat... including ham," she added with a cool stare for her mother, as if Eleanor were the one responsible for having butchered the pig.

"Knock it off, Vivi. We haven't got a lot of time, so let's focus. Okay?" Jeffrey raked a hand through a shock of thick hair that would have resembled golden wheat if it weren't such a drab brown. "I've asked Jim Kennedy to join us today." He glanced at his watch, gold and gleaming on his wrist. "He should be here soon."

Eleanor's eyes fluttered shut. Not only was Jim Kennedy their insurance agent and a confidant of Richard's, he and his wife Anne had been their close friends for years. They'd attended the funeral yesterday, returning to the house after the service. Jim had spent considerable time closeted in conversation with Jeffrey while Anne had been part of the group hovering around Eleanor, offering wine, sympathy, and a shoulder to cry on. Not that she'd needed one. Rather, she'd been the one moving through the downstairs rooms of her home, handing out tissues as she accepted condolences from weeping mourners. The doctor had assured her that her own tears would start once she recovered from the shock. Until then, the little blue pills would help her cope.

"For your nerves," he'd informed her as he pressed the bottle into her hand. "Trust me, you'll need them."

She'd accepted the prescription, though she had no intention of taking any pills. Doctors weren't necessarily always right, and she wasn't in shock. She simply needed time to absorb what had happened. It didn't feel as if Richard was dead and buried, but more like he'd suddenly departed on one of his frequent trips to the Middle East. If she hadn't been in bed with him, seen his fixed, glassy stare, felt the cold, rigid skin of his body under her hand, she wouldn't have believed it. She still found it hard to believe.

Though everyone else acted as if they believed it. Anne's tears and alcohol consumption had increased with each glass of wine Eleanor refused. Briefly she considered offering Anne one of those little blue pills, then thought better of it. One shouldn't mix alcohol and pills. By the time they left, Anne was in full-on grief mode and a smashed stupor, supported by Jim's arm as Eleanor escorted them to the door. She'd hate to be living in Anne's head today.

Bad enough she was stuck living in her own.

Jeffrey tapped a burgeoning file on the left side of the desk. "The funeral director provided me with copies of the death certificate."

The mere mention of the word *death* brought Richard back to mind. Richard, cold and unresponsive as she'd tried to rouse him that morning. A massive heart attack, his physician had informed her, occurring around the time she'd been woken from a sound sleep by the odd sound he'd made in the night. The *death rattle*, the doctor had called it. It was a sound she would never forget.

"I talked about Dad with Social Security this morning," Jeffrey continued.

"Do we need to discuss this now?" Eleanor tugged at the waistband of the skirt pinching her middle. They still

The Other Wife

hadn't settled the question of the leftover ham cramming the refrigerator shelves. Maybe she should send it home with Jeffrey, no matter how much he objected. Lord knows she didn't need it.

"Sorry, Mom, but this is important." His voice sliced through the thick, reeking odor of lilies and grabbed her attention. "I'm afraid it's not good news."

"What's wrong?" More bad news was the last thing she wanted to hear. And something was wrong; definitely wrong. She could tell from the look on Jeffrey's face. Somber and pale, she was suddenly reminded of the little boy who had once cuddled at her side as they read aloud bedtime stories, nudging ever closer when they reached the sad parts, patting her cheek when she invariably started to cry.

Would his news make her cry?

"As Dad's wife, you're entitled to receive death benefits."

"I understand. And that's fine." Richard had handled the finances in their family, and she'd never had any cause to worry. She wasn't worried now, either, especially since Jeffrey was in charge. Their son, an accomplished attorney, had been in private practice for more than three years. She was in good hands. "I trust you'll handle the paperwork for me?"

He cleared his throat. "I'm afraid it's not that simple. Dad was sixty-two, but you're only fifty-seven."

Something about the way he moved his head, the way his gaze suddenly shifted away, caused her heart to knock about in her chest.

"Is that a problem?" Eleanor finally asked. She hated

the way her voice quivered, hated that she'd been forced to be part of the conversation. She'd much rather be outside, puttering in her garden. Or sitting in the sunroom, relaxing in one of the cheery chintz-covered chairs, enjoying the spring sunshine. Or upstairs in her bedroom, curled up with a good book. But the garden was littered with muddy snowbanks, the skies had been gray and overcast for weeks, and she couldn't even recall what book she was currently reading. Not that it mattered, for she was sure the words wouldn't make sense. Nothing made sense. Since *that day*, as she'd come to think of it, her mind wasn't cooperating. The world wasn't cooperating. And as for her bedroom? She hadn't set foot inside since that horrible morning when the EMS crew crashed through the doorway, departing with Richard's lifeless body on a stretcher, leaving her standing speechless and alone in their wake. Sometime in the hours afterward, she didn't know when, Martha had removed her clothes and personal items, switching them to the guest room. God bless her, Eleanor had thought, upon finding them there. Somehow Martha had known she wouldn't be able to enter that room, let alone sleep in the bed where Richard had died.

Not that she was doing much sleeping. Would she ever be able to sleep again?

"For God's sake, Jeffrey, quit being so dramatic." Genevieve sat forward, perching on the edge of her chair. "What's the problem? What did the people from Social Security say?"

"They weren't very encouraging."

"Meaning?" She shot out the word in an exasperated sigh.

"Meaning," he said, his voice tightening, "that Mom won't be eligible to draw survivor benefits until she reaches the age of sixty."

"Why should we care about that?" She sniffed slightly, stroking her blond hair, which was pulled back in a smooth chignon.

Eleanor eyed her slim, beautiful daughter. Genevieve had inherited Richard's patrician nose as well as his self-assured air of authority and grace. Her flawless comportment had been present even as a child. But how or from whom she'd learned it, Eleanor couldn't say. Certainly not from her.

"Besides, it's not as if she needs the money," Genevieve added. "Daddy had plenty. She'll be fine."

But would she? Eleanor wasn't so sure, especially since Jeffrey wasn't quick to rebuff his sister's assumption. Plus, that little telltale tic in his brow above his left eye had started up again. She watched it with a curious distraction as it twitched—up, down, up, down—and she straightened in her chair. Under her heavy hips, she felt the springs bounce. She winced as her skirt pulled around her waist, cutting into her stomach along with the fear. Maybe she wouldn't be fine.

"Who cares about Social Security? It's a nonissue. Everyone knows the government is broke." Genevieve shrugged. "I thought we were here to talk about Daddy's will... So let's get on with it, shall we? You might have all the time in the world, but I have to catch an eight-o'clock flight out of O'Hare tonight. They expect me back in New York tomorrow. We have buyers coming in from all over the country next week, and I'll be working round the clock to catch up. This... this..." Genevieve's voice broke suddenly, her body struggling to contain an involuntary shiver. "This *event* has already cost me five days away from my desk."

Richard was dead, and his daughter begrudged him a few days out of her life? Eleanor's mouth twisted against the unspoken rebuke, even as her mother's heart opened to protect her own. It was obvious that Genevieve was still suffering. She'd put away the tissues, but her eyes were red rimmed, smudged with dark shadows despite the makeup. Richard had loved playing the role of her hero. Father and daughter had always been close.

Unlike their own relationship. Genevieve had banished her to the dungeon of disillusion and disappointment long ago. Having her daughter back in the house again for these past few days had made Eleanor want to take to her bed and bury herself under the covers.

Except Richard was the one they had buried.

"Dad's will is pretty straightforward," Jeffrey said. "I can read it if you like, but it would be a waste of time. Since Mom is still alive, there's no estate to disburse." He cleared his throat, glancing between the two of them. "However, the will contains a provision we need to discuss. Dad made a bequest for each of his children. That bequest is effective regardless of who died first: Mom or Dad."

"What kind of bequest?" Genevieve asked.

"Each of us is to receive ten thousand dollars cash."

"Ten thousand dollars," she said, mulling it over.

There was no surprise in her voice, no breathless awe at her father's generosity. Her daughter's words were calm and cool, as if she'd already made plans for how to use the money. Had Richard mentioned the bequest to Genevieve at some point in the past, Eleanor found herself wondering. She wouldn't put it past him. He and Genevieve had always been close, to the point that sometimes she herself had felt shut out, even as his wife.

Yet she'd thought they'd agreed that their wills would be confidential.

She'd thought they had agreed upon a lot of things.

Such as Richard slowing down and taking better care of himself. He was under constant stress with his frequent flights in and out of Afghanistan and Iraq. As an independent contractor working with the U.S. government, his structural-engineering consulting firm was a thriving business that kept him constantly occupied. He'd laughed off her concerns when she told him it was dangerous. Richard had thrived on danger. He'd relished the thrill of exposing himself to the daily hazards and risks associated with his job, of placing his life in jeopardy. No amount of money is worth a life, she'd argued. Why hadn't she insisted he take better care of himself? That he slow down, perhaps take on a partner. Someone younger, someone to share the worries, the burdens, the travel.

She should have insisted, Eleanor caught herself lamenting. She shouldn't have backed down when he laughed off her concerns. She never should have let him ignore her, run roughshod over her. Maybe if she'd stood up to him, things would have turned out different.

Now it was too late.

"I knew Daddy would remember us," Genevieve said. "Ten thousand isn't much, but at least it's something."

A cold disdain washed over Jeffrey's face. "You would say that."

"I don't have to sit here and take that from you." She threw him a haughty glance and rose to her feet. "I'm going upstairs to pack."

"Sit down, Vivi," he said in the same voice he might use with a client he suspected was guilty. "We still have some things to discuss."

"Things?" She glared at him. "What kind of things?"

Perhaps they could begin with why her daughter didn't like her given name, Eleanor mused. It had taken a full three days after Genevieve's birth before she'd finally managed to convince Richard to name their firstborn daughter after her maternal grandmother. Eleanor had always thought it a beautiful name, and her mother had been so pleased. Obviously, Genevieve didn't agree.

"The bequests, for one," Jeffrey said. "I can't make the payments."

"Why not?" Vivi demanded. "Can't you find the checkbook?"

"Try the bottom left-hand drawer of his desk," Eleanor wearily suggested. "I think that's where your father keeps the checkbooks." The bickering between her children was making her dizzy. Or maybe it was the thick, cloying fragrance of those horrid stargazer lilies. She'd never cared much for that particular flower, and now her entire house reeked with its overpowering presence. Much of her life right now was beyond her control, but not those flowers. She was determined they'd be gone from the house before the day was over, even if she personally had to throw each and every one of them in the trash.

"I found the checkbook, Mom. That's not the problem."

Her son's strained voice put her in mind of the afternoon years ago when Jeffrey had fessed up to his parents and admitted he hadn't been accepted at Northwestern University, Richard's alma mater. The news had been a crushing disappointment to Richard, but she hadn't minded. No doubt Jeffrey would be accepted at another university and eventually make something of himself... which he had. It was simply a matter of having confidence in oneself. She'd always had confidence in her son's abilities. Whatever the problem, Jeffrey could handle it.

Genevieve sank back in her chair, cool and chic in an elegant beige pantsuit that complemented her like a second skin. If she herself were to try wearing an outfit like that, Eleanor was certain she'd end up looking like a bleached stork.

"What's the problem? Daddy appointed you personal representative. Write the checks."

"I can't. There's a problem with the bank."

"What kind of problem?" Vivi pressed.

"For one thing, there's not enough money in the account to cover the checks."

Vivi shrugged. "So make a transfer from one of his other accounts."

"Unfortunately, it's not that simple."

"What are you talking about?" Her brown eyes—Richard's eyes—blazed to life. "Daddy was loaded. What about his savings? What about his stocks?"

What a mess. The two of them sounded no different today than they had when they were children bickering over their toys. Who cared about stocks and bonds or their savings account? All of this was merely a financial hiccup. Jeffrey would sort things out. He was making the phone calls Richard would have made. He was taking care of matters Richard would have seen to. He was sitting in Richard's study, behind Richard's desk, and he was doing it all without being asked. Probably because he assumed she couldn't do it herself.

And he was right.

She couldn't think about anything but Richard. It felt as if she'd been sleepwalking through her life for the past five days. How could he be gone? When he'd been home a few weeks ago, he'd been so alive, vibrant, so *Richard*: grumbling about the stock market over dinner; fussing over his graying beard and salt-and-pepper hair in the bathroom mirror at night. Richard, ever the perfunctory husband, off on another of his numerous business jaunts to the Middle East, taking leave of her with a dutiful kiss. And though she worried about him constantly, nothing ever happened. He chided her regularly, admonishing her not to upset herself about things over which she had no control. Everything would be fine. He'd be home when his business was finished. And over the years, though she'd grown accustomed to being alone, she'd never quit worrying about him. Richard was her husband. She loved him. She missed him. He was often gone for weeks at a time—but he always came home.

Except this time. When he'd left the house this time, it had been on an ambulance gurney, which eventually was traded out for a black hearse.

This time, Richard wouldn't be coming back.

"There's not much money," Jeffrey said.

"You must have made a mistake," Genevieve insisted. "Daddy has a huge stock portfolio."

"Leveraged through bad accounts." He shook his head. "I talked with his stockbroker this morning. The recession pretty much wiped him out."

"This is unbelievable." Genevieve whipped her head around and glared at Eleanor. "Simply unbelievable."

Eleanor nodded. Unbelievable? For once, she and her daughter were in complete agreement. In fact, this whole week had been unbelievable. She tried her best to look serious, though she found it hard not to laugh at the outraged accusation on Genevieve's face. Did she really believe that her mother was the financial doofus responsible for providing Richard with bad advice? He never listened to a word she said; why would he have consulted her about their investments?

She closed her eyes, turning a deaf ear as her children continued squabbling. There was no point in listening. Things would eventually work out. They always did. Everyone had their priorities, and so did she. Get rid of those horrible flowers. Find someone to take that ham. And make sure Genevieve boarded that plane tonight. That, above all, was priority number one. She needed the house to herself again. She longed for peace and quiet, for the serenity and privacy she'd come to treasure; something which had been nonexistent in the past few days, especially with Vivi around.

"Mom, are you listening? Did you hear what I said?"

Eleanor's eyes blinked open as her face flushed a guilty crimson. Glancing up, she found Jeffrey staring at her with an odd mixture of frustration and pity. Poor

Jeffrey. And poor Genevieve too. She didn't blame them for being upset. True, she'd lost her husband, but they had lost their father.

Perhaps they could both benefit from that unopened bottle of little blue pills still sitting on a shelf in her medicine cabinet.

"I know this has been horrible for you both," she said. "Genevieve, you're so busy with your job in New York. And Jeffrey, I'm sorry you and Susan were forced to cut short your vacation. I know how much you were looking forward to getting away." Someone—exactly who, she had no idea—had made an emergency phone call, summoning Jeffrey and his wife home from Hawaii.

"For God's sake, Mom, of course we came back. Did you think we wouldn't?"

"Well, I appreciate everything you've done." She watched as he ran a finger under his shirt collar, straining the soft roll of flesh pudging around his neck. How long had it been since he'd had a physical? Jeffrey needed to take care of his health. Cardiac issues ran in the family. Richard's father had died of heart complications, plus both her parents, and now Richard too. Jeffrey was only in his early thirties, but you never knew. That little paunch settling around his middle might have already shaved a few years off his life.

No leftover ham for Jeffrey, Eleanor decided, making a mental note as the doorbell rang. A few moments later, a somber Martha ushered Jim Kennedy into the room.

Her husband's old friend quickly made the rounds with a firm handshake for Jeffrey, a consoling hug for

Genevieve, and an affectionate peck on the cheek and pat on the shoulder for her.

"I still can't believe he's gone." Jim sank into a seat in the one empty chair left in the room. His forehead was lined with a few new wrinkles, his face pinched with a peculiar look of there but for the grace of God. "The two of us played golf a few weeks ago, and he told me he'd recently had a complete physical. The doctors found him in perfect health." He shook his head. "Unbelievable, that someone his age could..."

Die? Eleanor found herself supplying the word in her head. Why couldn't anyone, including her, say the word aloud? She knotted her hands together in her lap. There was no getting around the truth of what had happened. Richard had died. If he hadn't, the four of them wouldn't be sitting in his study today, discussing the terms of his will and the dry details of his life insurance policy.

"You asked for a copy of the death certificate." Jeffrey slid a crisp white paper across the desk. "For the insurance files."

Genevieve shifted in her chair, gazing at Jim with an expectant look. "Did you know or have anything to do with Daddy's estate? My brother just informed us that the money seems to be gone."

Jeffrey's face reddened, and he shot her an angry glare. "I already told you I'll deal with the bank. Jim's here to discuss Dad's insurance policy."

The sober smile—what little there was of it—disappeared from the insurance adjuster's face. Snapping open his briefcase, he rustled through a thick stack of papers and drew out a file.

"I'm sure the three of you are aware that your father—Richard, that is"—he corrected himself with a deferential nod for Eleanor—"had a life insurance policy in place. The policy is current and quite substantial. It's worth several million."

Millions? Eleanor blinked to the beat of Genevieve's delighted laughter. But that couldn't be right. What had she missed? She couldn't recall them having such large policies in place. She would have remembered if Richard had mentioned wanting to change their policies. Plus, wouldn't something like that require her signature? Then again, she'd grown used to him constantly presenting her with papers to sign. Thick stacks of paperwork filled with legal jargon and run-on paragraphs that blurred before her eyes. Official company policies, shareholder meetings, affidavits, trust documents. "Nothing for you to worry about," he'd assured her time and again. "Sign on the dotted line." After a while, she'd gotten tired of trying to decipher things. After a while, she simply signed.

Jim cleared his throat. "As I mentioned before the funeral, the autopsy was necessary due to the facts surrounding his death. But the results confirmed that he died of natural causes."

"Meaning...?" Genevieve quickly prompted.

"Meaning that his insurance policy is a valid claim."

"Wonderful." She flashed Eleanor a brilliant smile. "See, Mother, now all your problems are solved. Even if Jeffrey is right about the stocks being worthless, Daddy still provided for you. You'll have plenty of money. And personally, I don't mind waiting for my inheritance check." She glanced at Jeffrey. "You can wire transfer the funds into my account once she receives the insurance settlement."

"I'm afraid it's not that simple." An odd note lingered in Jim's voice. "You see, the policy was changed four years ago."

"Changed?" Eleanor frowned. "But that's impossible. Who would have changed it?"

His face flushed a dark crimson, and he crinkled the paperwork in his hand, as if consulting it would make it easier to share the news. "Richard."

She swallowed down a sudden swell of fear. Richard had changed his policy? Without telling her? How could he have done that?

"What do you mean, *changed his policy*?" Jeffrey asked. "What exactly did Dad do?"

Jim cleared his throat again, adding to Eleanor's rising panic. She didn't like the sound of that harrumph, or the sudden ruddy complexion of his face, an odd consortium of grief and guilt. And she definitely didn't think that she was going to like what she was about to hear.

"He changed his primary beneficiary."

"I... I don't understand." A sour bile rose in the back of Eleanor's throat as a yawning gap filled her stomach. Part of her comprehended what Jim was saying, but the other part—the one that had been married to Richard for thirty-eight years—was free-falling in complete denial. This had to be a dreadful mistake. "I'm his wife. Shouldn't I be the primary beneficiary?"

Isn't that the way things worked? Isn't that the way things were supposed to be?

"I don't believe it," Genevieve said. "Daddy wouldn't

have done that. Why, the two of them have been married…" She halted, turning to her mother with a questioning look.

"Thirty-eight years," Eleanor supplied in a faint whisper.

"Did you hear that?" Genevieve's voice was like a knife, slashing through the twisted knots and tangles of a financial misunderstanding. "They've been married thirty-eight years. Of course she's his beneficiary."

Jim drew a deep breath. "I know this must come as a shock."

"Damn right it is," Jeffrey said. "Look, Jim, you told me yesterday there was an issue with the policy and we needed to talk. But this… this is unbelievable." He shook his head hard, in flat-out denial. "Dad never would have done something like this."

"I understand how you feel," Jim replied. "And I'm sorry you had to hear the news from me. But unfortunately, I can't change the facts. I have a duty to the policy owner. Whoever owns the policy has the right to name whomever they choose. And since Richard was the owner of his policy, it was in his discretion to choose his beneficiary. For many years, that was Eleanor. But four years ago, Richard came to me and said he wanted to make a change. I tried to talk him out it, but his mind was made up. I had no choice but to do as he asked. The policy changes have been in effect since then."

He turned to face her, his faded blue eyes offering no hope. "I'm sorry, Eleanor. I wish I had better news."

Silence settled over them like a shroud, and Eleanor tugged her sweater tighter around her shoulders. This room was so cold. Why didn't someone turn up the heat?

Their house had always been drafty in the winter. It was a stately home, handsome and elegant, with high ceilings and large, spacious rooms. She'd tried her best to warm things up with plump, cushioned chairs and floral prints. But Richard's study, all sharp angles and hardwood floors, had never been cozy. He'd resisted her efforts to switch out the sober, serious furniture, told her it didn't matter, that she should concentrate her efforts on something else and leave his study alone.

"Who is the beneficiary?" Eleanor suddenly heard herself ask. At least she thought the sound emitted from her. The small, tinny, faraway voice sounded nothing like her, but more like an echo from some distant tunnel.

"I'm afraid I'm not at liberty to disclose that information."

"Excuse me?" Genevieve shot from her chair, five foot ten inches of outraged indignity glaring down at Jim. "You can't refuse to tell us who's going to get his money. Daddy's policy is worth millions, and that money is ours. We're his family. We deserve it."

Jim swallowed hard, his Adam's apple straining against his neck as he met her challenging gaze head-on. "Ethically," he said, his eyes never wavering, "I'm authorized to release that information only to the beneficiary and the personal representative."

"You weasel." She whirled and aimed a deadly stare at Jeffrey. "You're Daddy's personal rep. You knew about this all along and you didn't tell us?"

"Hey, back off." He lifted his hands, splaying his fingers in an attempt to hold back her ire. "I had no clue. Dad never discussed it with me."

"He's right," Jim said quickly. "Jeffrey didn't know. I couldn't share the information until I had a copy of the death certificate." All of them watched as he slipped the official document into the burgeoning stack of papers comprising Richard's file.

"Well, since you now have what you need, there's no longer any reason to keep us in suspense. So tell us: who's the lucky beneficiary?" She slid a lethal glance in her brother's direction. "Is it Jeffrey?"

"No."

"Oh." She gathered a soft breath and tilted her head slightly. Pondering a moment, she suddenly brightened. "Well, if Daddy didn't leave his money to Jeffrey, did he give it to me?"

"Vivi, you are a disgusting human being, you know that?" her brother said. "Why don't you shut up?"

Eleanor closed her eyes, blocking out the ugly sight of sibling rivalry. She couldn't believe she was sitting there listening to her children squabble over their father's money. *Their* money. *Her* money.

"He didn't leave it to any of you," Jim admitted. "I haven't contacted the primary beneficiary yet."

"Wait a minute. Let me get this straight." Jeffrey tiredly rubbed his forehead. "You're telling us that Dad left his money to someone else? Not to Mom, not to either of us, but to someone else? And that he has no idea he's inherited millions?"

"*She* has no idea."

She? Eleanor shivered, uncertain whether she'd heard Jim correctly. She shook her head as if by doing so she could dislodge the words rattling around in her brain like loose pennies that somehow had ended up in the bottom of her purse. *She?* She was certain there must be some mistake. Richard never would have left his money to another woman.

Would he?

"Let's stop the bullshit," Jeffrey said. "We're his family, Jim, and we have a right to know. You said you could release the name to Dad's personal rep? Well, you're looking at him. And I'm telling you right now, in my legal capacity as his personal representative: I want to know. I demand to know."

Genevieve's eyes narrowed. "Me too."

"Eleanor?" Jim's voice was a soothing stream of quiet concern. "Are you all right?"

What a stupid question, she thought to herself as she pulled her sweater tighter around herself. Of course she wasn't all right. She'd had the oddest feeling when she'd woken that morning that today wouldn't be a good day. Jim's revelation was all the confirmation she needed to officially pound the last nail in the casket. Richard's casket, so to speak. And now, if it wasn't too much to ask, all she wanted was to be allowed to crawl back into bed, burrow down in the blankets, pull the covers over her head, and go to sleep. And maybe, when she woke up, she would discover all this had simply been a horrible nightmare. Richard would come strolling in the door, as he had countless times in the past, returning from yet another extended trip to the Middle East, his rolling suitcase filled with dirty socks and underwear, and a world-weary look about him. And after planting a kiss on her forehead, he would head upstairs where he would collapse in their bed, once sleeping for nearly sixteen hours straight, before he finally woke. Yes, that would be the way of it. She'd go upstairs and sleep off this nightmare. And when she was awake again, this ghastly business would have drifted away, leaving only mists of misery as a remembrance.

"Mom? Are you okay?"

Eleanor couldn't remember hearing Jeffrey's voice sound so distraught save for the day he'd returned from Hawaii, the day after Richard's death. He'd broken down when he saw her, collapsing in her arms and crying unabashedly like he'd done as a little boy. She'd done the comforting when he was small, and she'd been the one to provide the comfort last week too, never questioning whether he'd been grieving over the loss of a father to whom he'd never been close or the lost opportunity to put things right between them. It hadn't mattered then, and it didn't matter now. Somehow she managed to summon the willpower to open her eyes and discovered the three of them staring at her.

"I'm fine." Eleanor pulled in a deep breath. Much as she didn't want to hear Jim's news, she knew in her heart that she didn't have a choice. "Jeffrey's right. We need to hear the truth."

Jim's face was a cacophony of ethical concern versus friendship, and for a moment, she wondered if he would respect Jeffrey's command and abide by her wishes. But thirty-plus years of friendship with their family finally won out.

"He left the money to a woman named Claire Anderson," Jim finally admitted.

Claire Anderson? Eleanor frowned. The first name

meant nothing to her, but the last name certainly did. It was the same name listed on her own driver's license. She'd been Eleanor Anderson since she and Richard had exchanged wedding vows at the Fourth Presbyterian Church in Chicago thirty-eight years ago last month.

Claire Anderson. She couldn't recall ever hearing Richard mention that particular name. He'd been an only child, so she couldn't be a niece. A long-lost relative? A distant cousin? But if that was the case, surely he would have told her. Wouldn't he? After all, she was his wife.

Correction, Eleanor reminded herself dully. She *had* been his wife. She was the one he should have turned to. All those years they were married. You'd think he would have told her something as important as this. She hung her head, hugging herself close, trying to remember the last time Richard had held her close.

On second thought, maybe he wouldn't have told her.

On third thought, obviously he *hadn't* told her.

"Claire Anderson?" Jeffrey's voice cracked through the black void, trapping her like a clap of thunder. "Who the hell is Claire Anderson?"

"Yes. Who is Claire Anderson?" Eleanor echoed to no one in particular. Though, if Richard happened to be listening from beyond the grave, she would appreciate him providing some answers. She rubbed her forehead, sifting through the memories of those who'd crowded the funeral home, who'd followed them to the cemetery, who'd paid their respects at the house afterward. So many people, so many faces. The crush was overwhelming, yet she couldn't remember seeing anyone she hadn't known.

No woman she didn't know.

"I've never met her." Jim shifted in his chair, his face impassive. "I'll be able to tell you more once I speak with her. She lives in Hyde Park. From what I understand, she's a professor at the University of Chicago."

"Why would Daddy leave his money to some dull old professor?" Genevieve's bottom lip jutted out in a pretty pout, a trick Eleanor recalled her daughter perfecting as a toddler. "Who is she? What's her connection to Daddy?"

"I don't know," Jim admitted.

She rolled her eyes and turned to her mother. "Do you know her?"

Eleanor shook her head. She couldn't imagine what Richard had been thinking. Why would he change his insurance policy? They were his family. She was his wife. "No."

"This is ridiculous," Genevieve fumed. "I can't believe no one knows her."

"Obviously, Dad did," Jeffrey muttered.

Genevieve slumped back in her chair, her arms forming a barricade across her chest. "Someone had better figure out who she is. I have plenty of questions for her."

Eleanor stared wordlessly at her daughter. For once, the two of them were in complete agreement. Meanwhile, she had a few questions of her own.

Beginning with who exactly was Claire Anderson, and what kind of hold did she have on Richard?

Chapter Two

Chicago was definitely living up to its nickname as the Windy City, Claire thought as she hurried across the quad, struggling against the blustery headwinds. Everything bowed to the forces of nature, including the swaying trees bursting into bud, the springtime flowers with their scattered petals, and the birds swooping and soaring on the gusty winds blowing through campus. Undergrad students swarmed around her, eager to escape the biting chill and make their next class. One of them, a painfully thin young man with a burst of fuzz on his chin, paused at the entrance to Stuart Hall and held the door for her. Claire scooted past him with a grateful smile, recognizing him as a student from one of her undergrad classes. He always chose a front-row seat in the lecture hall, and he never missed class.

"Thank you," she said, racking her brain in a vain attempt to remember his name. She'd known it once upon a time.

"No problem, Dr. Anderson." His voice was young and hesitant, a student's voice tinged with respect, but his eyes and expression spoke a different language. It was the same look Claire sometimes saw on her husband's face when she caught him watching her. The slight tilt of his head, the hint of an admiring smile.

Claire pressed through the crowded hallway, heading for the stairs and her fourth-floor office. Her student-who-unfortunately-must-remain-nameless pushed ahead of her, blazing a trail through the crowd of swarming bodies. She tried to keep up, her heels clicking in quick staccato. Today definitely had not been the day to break in a new pair of shoes.

"Thanks again," she said as they reached the staircase, wishing she could remember who he was. Too many students, too little time. For months she'd been promising herself she was going to slow down, get her act together, but she still hadn't done it. Lately, it seemed, she was forgetting everything. She'd even forgotten today was Dickie's treat day at Lab nursery school. He'd been a puddle of tears, howling his heartbreak as only a four-year-old can. His outburst had set off sweet little Sophie, who up until that point had been content in her high chair, daintily plucking dry cereal from a flowered plastic bowl. Sophie's sympathetic sobs filled the kitchen as her big brother started to cry. Claire had suddenly felt like crying too.

"I'm sorry, sweetie. Mama forgot." She crouched next to Dickie, feeling like the world's worst mother. How could she have forgotten? Hadn't it been on her to-do list? Then again, did she know where today's to-do list was? Had she left it on the cluttered bathroom vanity? She'd always prided herself on her organizational skills, on being the person everyone could count on to be in charge, the one person who never let anyone down. How and when had that person disappeared? Maybe while she was rushing around, trying to juggle all the balls, keeping up with the demands of the university and her students while singlehandedly running a household and mothering two small children. A person could only spread themselves so thin; eventually the jam jar would run empty and the toast would taste dry and bland... exactly how she felt at times.

Claire rubbed Dickie's sturdy little back with small, circular strokes. "Don't cry, sweetie. I promise to make it okay." She glanced up at Hallie, who was busy releasing Sophie from her high chair. "Do you have time to swing by the bakery and pick something up?"

"Sure thing." With a flourish, Hallie scooped Sophie onto her hip and joined her at Dickie's chair. "Hey, buddy, did you hear what your Mama said? We'll stop at the bakery on the way to school, and you can pick out whatever you want. Won't that be fun?"

"Thank you," she silently mouthed to Hallie.

The young woman was worth every penny they paid her and then some. Part-time-nanny-housekeeper-grad-student-and-friend, the children loved Hallie. She was calm, competent, and in control. *She reminds me of me*, Claire ruefully thought, *when I was her age*. Organized, relaxed, not at all the way she was now. How had her life morphed into this mess?

Dickie sniffed, smearing a snotty trail of tears across his cheeks. "Promise?"

"Double-heart promise," Claire swore, crossing herself in a swift movement. She planted a swift kiss atop his head, surprised to find his hair had turned from soft, fine blond strands into thick, brown straw-like big-boy hair. When had that happened? How could she not have noticed?

With a last kiss for him, she stood, vowing to herself that starting today, things were going to be different. No more rushing about. She had to slow down. She needed to start living her life rather than simply hurrying through the hours, making promises she had no time to keep, only to collapse into bed exhausted at the end of each day. And for what? To be woken by a shrill alarm, forced to roll out of bed, bleary-eyed and suffering from lack of sleep, and start all over again.

Something had to give... if not, it would be her sanity.

Damn, where had she put that to-do list? She had to find it. It was her life.

"Bye-bye, my babies. Mama has to go to school now. Be good for Hallie."

"Okay, Mama." Dickie had been all smiles as she'd smothered him with kisses, but Claire doubted his brightened mood was due to motherly love. More likely the thought of bakery cupcakes with colorful sprinkles and swirls of frosting. When Hallie made a promise, she always delivered. Claire knew better than to make promises she couldn't keep. Her life revolved around schedules, and her world was ruled by a clock. Sometimes it felt as if she'd sliced herself up into such tiny pieces there were hardly any crumbs left for anyone, including her.

Mother, teacher, wife. She was failing at all three. Somehow she needed to find time, to make time, to be a better mother to her children, a better teacher to her students, a better wife to her husband. If she could manage those things, the rest would follow. She would become a better woman... for herself.

Unlocking her office, Claire stepped through the door, dropped her bag on the desk, and sank into her chair. She kicked off the offensive new shoes and wiggled her toes, relishing the welcome release of unencumbered freedom. A fleeting pleasure, unfortunately, for as usual, she was running late, due in class in fifteen minutes. Students weren't allowed to go barefoot and she assumed the rule applied to professors too.

Massaging her feet with one hand, she flicked the mouse, causing the computer screen to jump to life. Bypassing her e-mail, she opened her calendar, cringing as she spotted the day's rundown. Two undergrad lecture classes followed by a round-table discussion over lunch with departmental staff to brainstorm upcoming curriculums. A meeting with her grad assistants that afternoon to discuss their ongoing research projects, followed by a one-on-one with Sarah, the newest of the bunch. The first-year grad student had had difficulty all year trying to adjust. If today proved anything like their last few sessions, it would not be pleasant.

Claire could already predict exactly what would happen. Sarah would start by offering numerous excuses as to why she was having problems and why the goals she'd set for herself hadn't been met, only to eventually break down all teary-eyed, the way she always did. Sarah was passionate in professing her love of psychology, and Claire didn't doubt her commitment. But sometimes people just didn't get it. How she wished things were different and that Sarah were different. Defensive and belligerent,

Claire could handle. Anger, she could handle. It's easy to admonish someone who pushes your buttons. But Sarah wasn't like that. Smart as a whip, but the young woman was also soft, sensitive, and susceptible to the extreme. All the book learning in the world couldn't teach certain things, and she had the sinking feeling that Sarah might not be cut out for a career in psychology. She should have sat down with her weeks ago, talked about Sarah's future in the department, this field of study, but she'd been dreading the conversation. The girl was already an emotional puddle. To make matters worse, Claire liked her. How do you tell someone that they're not good enough? What right did she have to kill Sarah's dreams?

Sometimes she hated her job.

The University of Chicago was a revered institute of higher learning. Claire had been on staff eight years, and it was a place she'd come to call home. But while the campus was lovely and the lecture halls and buildings spacious, in no certain terms could they be called modern. The same applied to her office, an odd assortment of fixtures and furniture inherited from other departmental personnel who'd retired, been removed, or fallen by the wayside. A scratched filing cabinet stood sentry against one wall, flanked by a high bookshelf crammed with textbooks and research materials. A large window unencumbered by blinds overlooked the quad, offering a bird's-eye view of the world of academia. Her metal desk, industrial and indestructible, was a large expanse with plenty of space for her current files, keyboard, and the oversized monitor that had finally been delivered to her office after months spent wrangling with the acquisitions department. Dickie and Sophie's smiles burst from a colorful frame next to the monitor, a photo taken on a Michigan beach last summer during a quick weekend escape from the city heat. And the true dichotomy of her life: her sweet babies' faces mere inches from a cloudy glass jar atop her desk, containing a specimen of an actual human brain.

A bright red glow on her phone reflected through the glass, announcing the presence of voice mail. Claire gave it a cursory glance. No time to check her calls. She was due in the lecture hall soon. Fifty students were waiting, expecting her to provide them with valuable insight into the workings of the human mind.

She shot one last look at the photo of Dickie and Sophie playing in the sand, recalling the promise she'd made to herself that morning. What if it was Hallie, calling to say there was a problem? What if Dickie had hurt himself? What if Sophie needed her?

Her students were waiting, but so was her life. Besides, they couldn't start class without her. Claire placed the phone on speaker and punched in her private code to access voice mail. An unfamiliar male voice, strained and somber, flooded the office. The message was brief. The matter was of particular urgency. Though his name was unfamiliar, she recognized the insurance company he claimed to be with. A national firm, respected, well known. Grabbing a pen, Claire scribbled down his number. Then, slipping on her shoes, she headed for class. Whoever this Jim Kennedy was, he would have to wait.

But even as she took her place behind the podium to face her students, a part of her separated from the sea of faces and the lecture she was about to give. Even as she began speaking, a part of Claire wondered why the man had called. Glancing at her notes, she tried concentrating on that day's topic, focusing on the discussion and questions sure to follow. But even standing before fifty students, her mind was elsewhere. He'd said it was urgent; *imperative* the actual term, that she contact him today.

And he'd mentioned her husband.

But why would he be calling about Richard?

"What's with this guy?" Tulie slouched in the plastic chair across from Claire's desk, peering at her over gaudy rhinestone cat-eye reader glasses. Petulia by name, she was a Tulie at heart, and every bit as hip and easy as the swinging 60s. "Are you going to call him back?"

"I don't know," Claire said, twiddling a pen between her fingers. "I suppose I should. He said it was urgent. Plus, he called again while I was in class." She decided not to mention Jim Kennedy's third message, the one delivered while she'd been meeting with her grad students about their current research project. Three times he'd phoned, leaving voice mails stressing the urgency that she return his calls. Part of her wanted to know what was up, but another part didn't.

Why did he want to talk to her about Richard? The logical part of her argued that it couldn't be bad news. If something terrible had happened, she would have known. Richard had left ten days ago, and she didn't expect him home for at least another week. His work as an independent infrastructural engineer contracting with the U.S. government had him flying in and out of various parts of the world much of the year. Bahrain, Iraq, Afghanistan. Troubled hot spots with American interests to protect. He was gone more often than not, and she missed him. Sometimes she didn't think he realized exactly how much she missed him. It wasn't the life she would have chosen, but once she'd met him, she'd had no choice. She'd known from the start what she was getting into, that she would have to accept Richard for the man he was and the life he led. Her friends and colleagues were thoughtful and understanding, though she knew they probably thought her marriage and family life unorthodox. For the most part, she didn't care. Every marriage had its own peculiarities. She and Richard were no different. He simply wasn't home most of the time. Meanwhile, she handled things as best she could. It was the children she worried about most. Sophie was still so little; she didn't understand what it meant when Daddy packed his bags and nuzzled her cheeks with farewell kisses. Dickie, however, was another matter. He adored his daddy and was old enough to realize that when Richard said good-bye, it meant Daddy was off on another trip and wouldn't be coming back for a while.

It was hard on Dickie. It was hard on her. Living a life with an absent husband was hard all around. But what choice did she have? She loved him.

"I'll bet he wants to talk about your policy," Tulie predicted. "Remember, Claire, the guy is in sales. Car, life, or home insurance, it's all the same. He's probably looking to make some money."

"I don't think so. Richard takes care of all of that."

Tulie shrugged. "So let him deal with it when he

gets back. Save yourself some grief. You have enough to handle."

"I suppose you're right."

"Darn tooting, I am," she said, flashing Claire a smile that instantly made her feel better.

What would she do without Tulie? Her cohort, confidant, and co-professor in U of C's psych department had been hired in from Northwestern two years ago. With her office two doors down from Claire's own, it hadn't taken long for the two of them to bond. Tulie's intellect was off the charts, her emotional savvy hot-wired in all dimensions, and her friendship a blessing. With a quick wit, vivacious laugh, and flair for the dramatic, Tulie was a welcome burst of color in Claire's life. Her living room walls would never be that stunning shade of red if Tulie hadn't convinced her they needed fresh paint.

"I hate insurance salesmen. They're always looking to sell you more coverage. And why? More money on the policy means more money in their pockets." Tulie rolled her eyes. "Buying life insurance is crazy. It's like betting against the odds that you're not going to die. Except that eventually you do. It's a fact of life. Sooner or later, everyone dies."

Claire shrugged, listening only with one ear. She didn't want to think about dying. No one wants to think about dying.

"Richard took out the policy around the time Dickie was born." Claire vaguely remembered him mentioning some sort of policy... not that she'd paid much attention at the time. She'd been sick throughout much of the pregnancy and on total bed rest the last two months before Dickie's birth per doctor's orders. Maybe Richard had increased the terms of the policy, concerned that something might happen to her. He was very detail oriented, obsessed with the fine points that would never snag the attention of the average person. Claire assumed it was partly the engineer in him. But it was also partly the man whom she'd fallen in love with five years ago.

"Insurance isn't a bad thing. He probably wanted to make sure that our children would be taken care of."

"He's a good dad, I'll grant him that."

"That's all?" Claire's mouth twisted in a smile.

"You want more?" Tulie's green eyes sparkled. "Okay, obviously he loves his kids. Plus he adores his wife. And he's a great provider. Honestly, Claire? That house he bought you is insane. It could be on the cover of *Architectural Digest*. And let's not forget the fact that the guy is pretty hot... for an older man, that is."

Claire felt some of the day's earlier worries slipping away as she started to laugh. Being around Tulie always helped her relax. From the first time they'd met, her friend had had an uncanny ability to make her laugh. It was one of the reasons Claire loved her. Being with Richard was exactly the same. He was in his sixties, but he still had what it took to make a woman happy... to make *her* happy. Maybe he wasn't home as much as she would like, but he made up for it during the times that he was. Richard was attentive to their children, helpful around the house, and one hundred percent committed to making their relationship work. Some of her friends had tried to warn her off before she married him, telling her she was crazy to tie herself down to a man thirty years her senior. The classic Oedipus complex, they'd argued good-naturedly. Richard was old enough to be her father. But Claire couldn't have cared less. *Who cares how old he is?* she'd bantered with them, knowing any argument they threw at her wouldn't change her mind. How could she deny herself anything to do with Richard? He was affectionate, affirming, attentive.

Not to mention extremely good in bed.

Tulie squinted up at the Tweety Bird wall clock perched high on the wall above Claire's computer. "I should get going. I'm supposed to be meeting a guy in twenty minutes." She didn't budge but instead slumped farther in her chair.

"Marie set you up with another hot date?" Claire guessed.

"Some prof from the economics department," she confirmed with a curl of her lip and roll of her eyes.

Claire smothered a smile. Marie, the one ever-constant member of their department's revolving support staff, was the resident romantic of Stuart Hall. "She has your best interests at heart. And who knows? He could be a great guy. He might turn out to be the love of your life."

"An econ professor? Are you serious?" Groaning, Tulie unfolded her limbs and hobbled to a stand. "I can predict what the next two or three hours will involve. Sitting in a crowded restaurant listening to some guy with ear hair and a wrinkled shirt spouting economic theories till my brain is ready to burst. I'll eat too much pasta, drink too much wine, and wake up tomorrow morning with a blistering headache." She grimaced. "Next time Marie tries to set me up, I'm saying no. I don't need this. I'm thirty years old. Why do I keep submitting myself to this torture?"

"Good question," Claire agreed. "Perhaps we should conduct some analytical research."

"Very funny." She flashed her a dark look. "Most of us aren't lucky enough to have a man like Richard waiting at home."

"Touché," she conceded, though she knew full well Richard wasn't at home waiting. He was off in some unknown region of the world. She hadn't heard from him in nearly a week. He wasn't even answering his cell phone. Resolutely, Claire made a silent vow to try him again one more time before she returned Jim-Kennedy-whoever-he-is-insurance-salesman's phone call.

"Call me after you talk to the insurance guy," Tulie said as she headed for the door. "I want to know what he has to say."

"You'll be the first to know," Claire promised.

The first after Richard, that was.

"Thank you for agreeing to see me on such short notice," Jim Kennedy said. He sat perched on the edge of his seat on one of the two couches in her living room. He craned his neck, taking in the scarlet walls, the plump, upholstered furniture in creamy shades of white, the various pieces of artwork collected by Richard on his travels around the world. "You have a lovely home."

"Thank you." Claire settled on the couch opposite him and eyed the bulky briefcase at his feet. How she wished Richard was home to facilitate the meeting. *Correction.* How she wished Richard was home to *take* the meeting. In fact, he *should* be home to handle it. A sudden surge of resentment flared within her. Normally she tried not to allow herself to be too concerned at her husband's absences. She was a capable woman and could handle most things, even the nearly century-old house they lived in. Built in the twenties, it had the normal creaks and persnickety characteristics one would expect from a structure that age. A leaky roof? That's what contractors were for. A dripping faucet? Call the plumber. And with Hallie on speed dial, even child care was relatively simple. Dickie came down sick at preschool? Hallie rushed in to save the day.

A super-structured life Claire could deal with, thanks to the terrific support system she had in place. Ninety-nine percent of the time, she was able to handle things. But when it came to legal paperwork, banking, or insurance, she gladly abdicated responsibility. They were not her forte, and she had no desire to be in charge.

And she still didn't understand why all this insurance business couldn't wait until Richard returned. He was the one who'd set up the policy. But there'd been no putting Jim Kennedy off when she fielded his fourth phone call just before leaving her office for the day. *It's urgent,* he said, so Claire reluctantly suggested he meet her that evening in her home. Now, with the man a solid, unmovable presence on her couch, she regretted her decision... and resented Richard for being absent and forcing her to deal with this alone.

"How can I help you?" It was late, she was tired, and she still had a paper to edit for one of her grad students. Why couldn't they get down to business? Why was he so busy looking around? She followed his gaze to the mantel and the array of framed pictures showcasing her family:

her and Richard when they'd visited Paris; Dickie and Sophie as babies. His eyes lingered on a recent photo from last winter, Richard and the children building a snowman in the park. Funny how a simple photo, a moment frozen in time, could capture a piece of your heart.

It had been one of those gorgeous January days, the sun glistening against gleaming white snowbanks that sparkled like a field of diamonds scattered from the brilliant blue skies. Little Sophie, bundled up in her bulky pink snowsuit, had barely been able to walk. Richard had tossed her in the air, caught her in his arms, laughing and kissing her burnished red cheeks. Afterward, at home, with Sophie down for a nap, he and Dickie had played a mean game of checkers with Dickie crowing his delight as he emerged the victor. Hours later, after dinner, their children safely stowed in bed, she and Richard had spent a lovely evening together on the floor in front of this very fireplace. Surrounded by pillows, warmed by wine, he'd let his eyes roam her body. "You are so beautiful," she remembered him whispering as he moved to take her in his arms. Emboldened as always by his encouraging gestures, she made the first move, unbuttoning his shirt, brushing her lips in gentle kisses upon the soft chest hair she found nestled there, which disappeared past his belt buckle in a delicious downward direction. His touch was tender as he slowly undressed her, covering every part of her with fervid kisses that grew more urgent until finally the two of them lay naked together. As always, Claire had opened her arms to him, offering him both her body and soul.

No photos existed to memorialize that night; only memories that lingered in her heart. Claire blinked back sudden tears. *Where was he*? She missed him. Why wasn't Richard answering his phone?

"Are you certain you wouldn't care for something to drink? Coffee?" She would have loved a glass of wine, but she wasn't about to offer alcohol to some strange man in her home.

"No, thank you." His eyes linger on the photos lining the mantel. "You have children?"

"Yes. Dickie is four and Sophie just turned two."

His face blanched an odd sort of gray. "Richard never mentioned them. I didn't expect children."

And Claire didn't expect his remark. It was none of his business how many children they had. Then again, he dealt with insurance. Car, home, life insurance. She thought of Tulie's remarks about insurance salesmen, increasing policy limits, upping their commission. Perhaps there was a good reason he'd decided to make her children his business after all.

"How long have you and Richard known each other?" she asked.

"A number of years," he said. "More than I care to admit."

He knew Richard personally? That counted for something. Claire settled against the pillows, regarding him with a cautious smile. "I don't remember Richard mentioning you."

"We're business associates." The veil slipped down to cover his face again. "Hyde Park is a lovely area. Have you lived here long?"

"Eight years," she said, "though not all of them in this house." She and Richard had shared an apartment before they'd bought the house. Working at the university, she preferred living close to campus. It was an easy walk. Her eyes narrowed as she watched his gaze once again stray to the mantel. She didn't like the way he continued examining the pictures. It was odd and unsettling, as if he was taking inventory; not of their possessions, but rather, of their lives. If she had the nerve, Claire suddenly thought, she'd scoop up the photos and shove them in a drawer. She was beginning to feel like her family was nothing but a commodity on some oblique insurance list generated by his company.

"I understand you're a professor in the psychology department."

"Yes."

"Eight years now." He nodded. "Impressive."

And his point? Claire's lips tightened, forming a thin line. Had Richard told him, or had he read her bio page? The university website focused strictly on her professional profile, but her personal life remained her own, thanks to a conscious decision she'd made years ago. She was much too busy to interact in social media. She didn't have a Facebook page, and while she texted, she had no interest in tweeting. Her private life was strictly that: private.

"Richard and I bought this house several years ago, shortly after we were married."

"You're married?" His eyes widened, then narrowed and darkened as he shifted in his seat, putting Claire in mind of their visit to the Shedd Aquarium a few weeks before. Jim Kennedy reminded her of one of the black reef sharks. Sophie, in her stroller, had been more impressed by the pink plastic juice cup with the turtle imprint they'd purchased at the gift shop, but Dickie had been mesmerized by the sea life surrounding them. He'd exclaimed in delight as they strolled through the halls and cavernous rooms, tugging his daddy forward as Richard pointed out the various aquatic creatures. The sharks, sleek and swift, had cut through the water, dead eyes watching, ready to strike.

But why should this Jim Kennedy be on alert? If he'd known Richard as long as he'd said, their marriage should come as no surprise.

"We've been married a little over four years now," Claire said. She'd been three months pregnant when they eloped to Las Vegas. Some women dreamed of a big church wedding, but she'd never been one for grand gestures or sentiments. It didn't seem to matter, especially with both her parents gone and a baby on the way. Plus, Richard hadn't wanted to wait. He insisted it was important they make things right, that their child deserved the best, including a set of parents who loved him... parents who were *married*.

A sudden memory rushed through her as she remembered how she'd buckled herself into her seat on the plane, nauseous from the pregnancy, panicky and sweating. Was she doing the right thing? She wasn't even thirty years old, and Richard was pushing sixty. What would their lives be like in another thirty years?

Would she regret it, this rash decision made in haste? Jetting off to Las Vegas, tying herself in an emotional, financial, and legal knot by marrying a man she barely knew. Yet how could she not marry him? Claire argued with herself. Wasn't she in love with him? Then Richard had grasped her hand and pressed it to his lips, kissing each of her fingertips as he smiled that special smile that never failed to melt her heart. Somehow he'd sensed her fear, caught a whisper of how worried and nervous she was. And in that one delicious moment, any doubts she had about what they were doing dissolved. Marrying Richard was the right thing to do. The *only* thing to do.

You didn't think twice when you were in love.

Claire cleared her throat. "Mr. Kennedy, I agreed to meet you because you said it was urgent. How can I help you?"

Nodding, he reached for his briefcase. Drawing out a thick accordion file, he placed it on the coffee table between them. "When was the last time you spoke with Richard?"

"Five days ago." He was still in Afghanistan and their conversation had been brief. *I'll be here at least another week*, he'd said.

"You haven't heard from him since?"

"I've tried to reach him, but his voice mail is full. But that's not unusual," she hurried to explain. "The reception can be terrible when he travels overseas. Sometimes he isn't able to accept or receive calls. It depends on what part of which country he happens to be in."

His eyebrows arched at a queer angle. "That's how he explained it?"

The shark was circling at the scent of blood. Claire didn't like it, and suddenly she didn't like this man. She didn't like the way Jim Kennedy was looking at her, the kind of questions he was asking, or the suppositions and assumptions he was raising in her mind. Most of all, she didn't like the question she was about to ask. But she couldn't stop herself. She had to know.

"What do you mean?" she demanded. "What do you know about Richard?"

"Richard isn't in Afghanistan," he said. "He might have been, but not anymore. He came back to Chicago over a week ago."

"That's impossible." She perched forward, suddenly intent on making her case. "He would have told me if he planned on coming back early. But he hasn't called, and he hasn't come home. He's not in Chicago."

Richard would have told her. She knew without a doubt he would have told her. They never kept secrets from each other. Even the day she'd discovered she was pregnant with Dickie, he'd known right way she was holding something back. She'd thought about not admitting it, not wanting to make him feel as if he'd been trapped. But he wouldn't let it go; he'd insisted—demanded—that she tell him the truth.

The truth. But the truth is often difficult to hear. Sometimes, after hearing the truth, you wish the words had never been spoken, that you'd left things alone, that you were still stumbling about in blissful ignorance.

Claire had an unsettling feeling that this was going to be one of those times.

"I know how difficult this must be." His voice softened as he glanced at the mantel again, circling in on the photos of the two of them, of their children, of their family. Lifting his head, he turned to face her. "But he did return to Chicago. And he *was* home."

"I'm sorry but you're wrong. What you're saying

doesn't make sense." Her heart pounded against the walls of her chest. "*This* is his home. Obviously, he's not here."

"Dr. Anderson." He halted. "Mrs. Anderson," he said, correcting himself. "I'm afraid I have bad news."

She wanted to clap her hands over her ears. She didn't want to hear what he had to say. She wanted him out of her house before he ripped her world apart. But all she could do was stare at his feet. He wore black wing tips, the kind of shoes older men wear when paying formal visits they'd rather not make. As if the polished, high-gloss leather would bolster them up and carry them down paths others dared not go.

And she wasn't wearing shoes. Claire felt the numbness settling upon her like a shroud, a cold dread drawing from her head to her bare toes. Her feet were cold. Her feet were always cold. But she'd been so eager to kick off those new shoes. She never should have worn them today. She should have known better. She should have worn them around the house and broken them in before walking the five blocks to school and back. All day long on her feet, all day long in those shoes.

"I'm sorry to be the one to tell you, but Richard is—"

"No. Don't say it. Please don't say it." Somehow she found herself on her feet. Her toes spread against the smooth, polished hardwood floors as she wrapped her arms around her chest and hugged herself tight. Why was it always so cold in this house? It was a late spring, but the chill remained. She should start a fire in the hearth. Richard loved fires. When he came home, there would be one waiting for him.

She turned to Jim Kennedy and found those dead,

sharklike eyes filled with compassion. "It's cold in here. Do you think it's cold in here?"

He lumbered to his feet. "You shouldn't be alone. Is there someone you would like me to call?"

Claire stared at him, conscious of her heart racing, a curious dichotomy when timed against the mantel clock slowly ticking away the seconds as her world collapsed. She thought of her children upstairs—sweet little Sophie, tucked in her crib, and Dickie, asleep in his big-boy bed. Her children. Richard's children.

And suddenly she found her voice. She had to know. If not for her sake, then for theirs.

"Where is he?" She clutched his arm, pulling at his sleeve, desperate for news. When did it happen? How did it happen? Had Richard been targeted by some militant group in Afghanistan? Had he been taken hostage? She thought of all the times they'd discussed the possibility of this very thing happening. Richard might still be alive. Where was he? Claire knew, with utter certainty, that Jim Kennedy had the answer.

But how could a stranger know more than she did? It wasn't fair. She was Richard's wife.

"Was he hurt? Is he in a hospital?" she demanded. "You said he's in Chicago. How long has he been here? Why didn't anyone tell me?"

"Because we didn't know."

"But how could you not know?" She heard the voice of some lunatic shrieking, wild words ricocheting off the walls, filling the red walls of the room with resentment and rage. She lashed out, pummeling his chest with her fists, fighting against him as he grabbed her and held her tight against him, preventing her from doing either of them harm.

"I'm his wife, damn you! How could you not have known?" From some distant place, Claire realized the frenzied screams were coming from somewhere down deep inside her. And her cheeks were wet. When had she started to cry? She never cried. Even when she and Richard had been married, even when their babies were born, she hadn't cried.

But this time she did cry, though her shrieks were gone and her voice was barely above a whisper. "I want my husband. I want Richard." She wept against his chest, crushing herself to him. "Tell me where he is. Please. I want to see him."

"I'm sorry." He held her tighter. "Richard is dead. They buried him yesterday."

Chapter Three

"You should call the bank again," Eleanor said. "Someone made a mistake. This can't be right."

"I don't think so, Mom."

"Call them," she insisted. "You'll see."

Jeffrey sighed and settled back in his chair. "It won't make any difference."

Eleanor fumed to herself. Normally she enjoyed visiting her son in the small suite of offices where he practiced law. Located on the ground floor of a converted brownstone with lofty ceilings, hardwood floors, and mullioned windows overlooking a quiet street, his offices were a calm oasis where legal matters were peacefully resolved. Upstairs, he and Susan had made a comfortable home for themselves and their son Richie. *My* grandson, Eleanor thought to herself. *Our* grandson, named after his grandfather.

A grandfather named Richard who—according to Jeffrey and the bank—had refinanced her home four years ago.

"Talk to the bank," she repeated. "Tell them to recheck

the paperwork." She'd been thinking about it all night. Thinking came easily when you couldn't sleep. Or was it the other way around? She couldn't sleep because she kept thinking. But the longer she thought about it, the more she continued thinking about it, the more she was convinced that all this was a dreadful mistake. Richard never would have done this. He never would have mortgaged their house. It had been paid off for years.

And as for all that nonsense about Richard changing his life insurance policy to benefit some woman none of them knew? Eleanor sniffed in disdain. No doubt that would prove a mistake too. Eventually the truth would come out and things would make sense.

Jeffrey opened his mouth to speak, but she raised her hand, effectively silencing him.

"That is my house we're talking about," she reminded him, remembering how her parents had given them the down payment as a wedding gift. Their home in Lake Forest has always been her sanctuary. "*Our* house," she continued. "Your father and I have lived there since the day we were married."

"Mom, I'm sorry. I know how hard this is for you. Believe me, I wish like hell none of it had happened."

Eleanor nodded. Her thoughts exactly. None of this should have happened. It was wreaking havoc on the whole family. She took in Jeffrey's face, noting how the skin under his eyes was puffy and red, underscored with deep circles. Even as a child, he couldn't sleep when something troubled him. Now this foolish thing his father supposedly had done was keeping him up at night. But Jeffrey couldn't afford to worry about her. He had his own family and his own problems.

"Things will work out. You'll see. Call the bank and talk to them." She forced a bright smile, though she felt like crying. Funny how you managed to find it in your heart to do things for your children that you'd never do for yourself. Lord knows she'd cried an ocean of tears since Richard's funeral. Until that day, she'd never believed a person could cry so many tears.

But what was she really crying about? Was it Richard or something else? That one thought alone kept her awake more than the others combined.

"There's no mistake." He waved his hand at a thick stack of papers covering his desk. "The house is mortgaged. Like I told you last night, Dad refinanced four years ago." He removed a clip from the top sheaf of papers and slid them toward her. Flipping to the end page, he pointed near the bottom. "Do you recognize this? It looks like your signature."

Eleanor stared at the spidery script in faded blue ink. It certainly appeared to be her signature. Yet she didn't remember signing the document. She took a harder look, her heart falling in pieces as she stared at the truth. If she had to swear in a court of law, she would have to admit it was her handwriting. Richard had mortgaged their house for five hundred thousand dollars and had gotten her to sign off on the paperwork. How could she not have known? And she was certain they'd never talked about it. She would have remembered that conversation. Five hundred thousand dollars was an enormous sum of money. She shook her head as if the action might stir up some sense, some faint recollection hiding in her brain. Richard was always talking about investments. Had he needed the extra money for a business loan? But why mortgage their financial security? And how could she forget signing off on something as important as refinancing their house?

Yet the evidence was right in front her nose. Richard's signature was on one line, with her own directly underneath.

Everything was legal, notarized, and binding. Four years' worth of monthly payments on a house she'd assumed they owned. Four years' worth of *Don't worry, Eleanor, I'll take care of it*. Four years ago? How was she supposed to remember what happened four years ago? Four years ago seemed like forever. Four years ago she'd taken over as director of volunteers for the children's wing of their local library. Four years ago Jeffrey and Susan had been expecting their first baby, and she'd been caught up helping Susan decorate the nursery. Four years ago she'd been pulled in all directions, barely able to concentrate.

She could barely concentrate now.

"You know your father, how he always took care of the money. Maybe he needed it for an investment." Eleanor's voice trailed off. "I don't remember."

But would she? Though Richard had been dead nearly a week, staring at his signature, scrawled in that familiar bold, steady stroke of his pen, suddenly spooked her. It felt as if he were in the room, as if he'd returned to challenge her for questioning his decision. But she never argued with Richard. There was no use arguing with him once his mind was made up.

Suddenly she was furious with herself. How could she have been such a fool? How could she have allowed herself to be put in this situation? She *should* have argued with him. Why hadn't she stood up for herself? Why hadn't she told him he was gambling with their future?

Because she'd trusted him. She'd always trusted Richard. Their mothers had been best friends, and she'd grown up hero-worshipping him from afar, never dreaming that someday he would actually propose. And yet he had. True, his offer of marriage had come as a surprise, but how could she refuse him? She'd loved him all her life. Richard was all she'd wanted.

Her mother had been thrilled, but her father had warned her not to marry him. "He's on the rebound." He'd been referring to Richard's on-and-off again fiancée who'd jilted him time and again, only to finally have married someone else months before. "Are you sure about this? He won't make you happy," he'd said, warning her even as she waited on his arm at the back of the church. Eleanor placed a tender kiss on her father's cheek. How could he think Richard wouldn't make her happy? They weren't even married yet, and she already was delirious with joy. Then the organ music swelled, the bridal march began, and she stepped out, pulling her father down the aisle to the altar where Richard waited.

She'd be the perfect wife, Eleanor had promised herself thirty-eight years ago as Richard stood beside her in the church filled with their family and friends, promising to love and honor, to cherish and protect her. Hearing him recite his vows, she loved him more than she thought possible. She'd make him forget about that other woman. To be cast aside must have been a crushing blow to his ego. Richard wasn't used to women refusing him. At least she'd never held any grand illusions about herself. When you don't have high expectations, you're grateful for anything that comes your way.

She'd kept the vows she'd made when they married. She'd loved him, honored him, cherished him. She'd even obeyed him and held her tongue when he insisted he knew what he was doing, that he'd run his company the way he thought best. Hadn't she kept her opinions to herself as they raised their children, even though she'd thought he was too hard on Jeffrey and too easy on Vivi? Hadn't she sat back and kept the peace, even when she hit menopause and often felt like telling him to go to hell?

How could she have lost herself in such an unhealthy relationship? How could she have not seen him for the selfish man he was? True, part of that had always been Richard's personality. She'd known that since she was a young girl. But if she was being honest, his arrogance, his self-assuredness, his blithe disregard for society's rules, had been part of his appeal. She'd admired him not only for his good looks and charming manners but also for the brash, *what the hell, you only live once* way he seized every moment and lived his life.

To honor and cherish, all the days of our lives. But this didn't feel like she'd been honored or protected, cherished or loved.

The paperwork blurred before her eyes. How could he have done this to her? How was she going to pay off the mortgage? Eleanor pressed her fingers against her forehead, trying to rub away the pain. Richard was the only man she'd ever loved, the only man she'd ever slept with. She'd given him thirty-eight years of her life, and what had he left her in return? Brokenhearted... and broke.

Not to mention him switching his insurance beneficiary and leaving the money to some professor at a university, a woman none of them knew. What had he been thinking? For one blissful moment when she'd woken this morning, all this—Richard's death, the funeral, the financial mess he'd left behind—had been merely remnants of some horrible dream that Eleanor was sure would fade into nothingness as the day progressed. She'd drifted for a while, enjoying her slumber... until she finally opened her eyes and saw the bedroom in which she slept.

Not her room. Not their room.

Not a nightmare, but reality. Richard was dead, and the nightmare continued.

"What about our stocks and bonds?" she asked.

"Most of them are gone," he reminded her. "Wiped out in the recession."

"And his business? Can't we draw from that?"

"Going through the company assets will take time. As for the rest?" Jeffrey shook his head.

Eleanor could feel Richard's presence slipping from the room. *Traitor*. Alive, he hadn't had the nerve to confess what he'd done. In death, he didn't have the courage to stick around and listen, to acknowledge his mistakes, to apologize for what he'd done.

"There's something else you need to know." Rising, Jeffrey came around the desk and sank into the chair beside her. "It's not good."

Eleanor grimaced. How could things possibly be worse than they already were?

Taking her hand, he squeezed it gently. Spotting the tears welling in his eyes made her swallow hard. She dragged in a deep breath and prepared herself. Whatever it was, it had to be bad. Aside from when he'd gotten off the plane after Richard's death, she hadn't seen Jeffrey cry since his son Richie had been born.

"I don't know how to tell you this," he said in a halting voice. "I spoke with Jim Kennedy this morning. He went to see Claire Anderson last night."

She tugged her hand from his, turned her back slightly. "I don't want to know."

It was better if she didn't know. If she didn't think about her, the woman couldn't hurt her. And she hurt too much already. How much could one woman's heart be expected to bear?

"I'm sorry, Mom, but you have—"

"Jeffrey, please. I don't want to hear it." She tugged her sweater closer around her shoulders. The gray cashmere cardigan was one of her favorites, and she'd worn it for years. But even with the soft comfort of an old friend, there was no escaping the chill seeping into her bones at the pity she saw sketched on her son's face, the apprehension in his eyes, and the sorrow in his voice as he began to tell her things she had no desire to hear.

"Dad didn't use the money for investments. He bought a house."

"A house?" Eleanor blinked as if that could clear away the sudden confusion. "Why would he do that? We already have a house."

Jeffrey hesitated, then finally spoke. "He bought it for her."

"Oh, Richard." Her eyes fluttered shut. Who was this horrible woman? Who was this Claire Anderson, the benefactress of her husband's benevolence, the beneficiary of his insurance policy? What kind of hold did she have on Richard?

"He was having an affair." Her voice, bitter and biting, sounded unfamiliar, and she hated herself for speaking words that should never be mentioned between a mother and child. Jeffrey was a grown man, but he was still his father's son. She wanted his memories of Richard to be good ones, not tainted with the messy details of whatever sordid deeds his father might have committed while alive.

"No, Mom." His voice broke as his fingers tightened around her own. "Dad wasn't having an affair."

No? Something lifted inside her, and Eleanor found herself wondering if the stirring could be hope. She'd felt so numb these past few days she no longer trusted what she was feeling. But perhaps she was the one who'd been mistaken. Maybe all this was nothing more than a simple misunderstanding. Maybe things weren't as bad as they seemed. Richard hadn't betrayed her. Richard never would have betrayed her. He loved her. She knew he'd loved her. Hadn't he told her so every night as she stood at the door of his study before she went up to bed?

"Then why?" Her eyes fluttered open and she studied Jeffrey's face. "Why would your father buy her a house? Why would he leave her all that money?"

Jeffrey bowed his head, closed his eyes for a moment. Then finally he faced her.

"He married her. He bought the house shortly after

they married. She was pregnant. They were married in Las Vegas four years ago."

They were married. The words floated between them like the tiny dust motes caught in the sunbeams shifting in the late morning light, settling on the faded Persian carpet beneath their feet. Eleanor stared at the carpet as if she could scoop up his words, sweep them in a pile, throw them in the trash. *They were married?* How could they be married?

"But he's already married." She stared at Jeffrey. "He's married to me."

He swiped away his tears with the palm of his hand. "I'm sorry, Mom. I wish to hell I wasn't the one who had to hurt you like this."

"But you didn't," she whispered. "You weren't."

Jeffrey wasn't to blame. None of this was his fault. But something he'd said. Eleanor tried to concentrate, but her thoughts were jumbled. Nothing made sense. Something he'd said. What was it? *Something.*

And then her heart plunged, the bottom dropping out of her stomach as she suddenly remembered.

"She was pregnant?" Her words were a ragged whisper.

He nodded. "They have two children."

He and Claire had children. Eleanor closed her eyes, absorbing the blow. Not one but two children. It felt as if someone had suddenly grabbed hold of a giant vacuum cleaner and turned it upon her, sucking away all the hope, the trust and confidence she'd built her life upon, destroying the foundation of the way things had been and how they would be. "How old are they?"

"A boy, four years old," he said, "and a little girl just turned two."

Her husband, married to another woman? Her husband, father to another woman's children? Richard had a little boy who was four years old? But Jeffrey's son Richie was four years old. Richard had become a grandfather around the same time another woman had given birth to his son.

Oh, Richard, what have you done?

"Thank God your grandmothers aren't alive. This would have killed them." She twisted her wedding ring between her thumb and forefinger, worrying it round her knuckle. Thirty-eight years she'd worn the ring with its antique diamond setting. A treasured family heirloom, it had once belonged to Richard's grandmother. He'd slid it on her finger, a circle of eternity, and promised her the world.

What had he promised Claire Anderson when he slid a ring on her finger?

"How could he have done this?" she whispered to herself. She'd known women with husbands who had cheated and found themselves mixed up with an unwanted pregnancy. Mistakes happened. Such was the way of life. But people used to handle things differently. It wasn't like when she was younger, or when her parents were growing up. Back then, a woman who found herself in a family way disappeared for a few months. Everyone knew why, of course, but it was never openly discussed. Neighbors whispered between the sheets flapping outside on the line to dry. Husbands cheated, and wives suffered the consequences. It had always been the way of the world. But she'd never thought it would happen to her.

Perhaps if it had been only one child, Eleanor decided. She might be able to understand. Anyone could make a mistake. But two children? One child meant a couple with a baby. Two children made a family.

Richard had had a family with that woman.

Eleanor clasped a fist to her chest. Poor Jeffrey. And poor Genevieve. How would her children live with the shame?

"I don't understand how your father could have done this," she repeated.

"I know," he said.

"And that woman." Something shifted inside her, something hard and fierce. Something so intense it frightened her. "Claire Anderson." The name tasted sour on her tongue, like milk that had sat too long. "What kind of woman does something like this? She turned his heart against me."

"We don't know that."

"You're taking her side?" Her eyes flew open in an accusatory stare.

"No, of course not." His voice softened as he laid a hand on her arm. "Mom, listen to me. None of us know what happened. At this point, we don't know what Dad did or what he told her. Jim said she was shocked. Supposedly she didn't know about you, or Vivi and me. She had no idea Dad had another life."

Eleanor clapped her hands to her head, covering her ears. She couldn't bear to hear anymore. Who cared about that other woman, that Claire Anderson? Jeffrey, of all people, should be able to understand what she was going through. Didn't he know that she'd had another life too? A life with her husband.

My husband, not hers.

She'd thought nothing could be worse than that morning when she'd woken to find Richard dead in bed beside her. But she'd been wrong. This was worse.

This was reality.

This was betrayal.

"Why don't you go upstairs for a while? Susan will make you a cup of tea, and you can lie down and rest."

"I don't want any tea." She didn't want anything except the impossible: she wanted her life back. Gathering her purse, she stumbled to her feet.

"Where are you going?" Jeffrey rose, blocking her exit.

"Home."

"Don't go. Please, Mom? Not like this. We want you to stay."

Just the way he said *we* was a dead giveaway. Susan already knew. Yet how could she blame him for sharing the news? Jeffrey and Susan had been together for years. They had a close marriage. Eleanor shuddered slightly. She'd always assumed that she and Richard had had a close marriage.

"Susan knows, doesn't she?"

Jeffrey hesitated and finally nodded. "I told her this morning, after Jim called me."

So she wasn't even the first to learn that she was merely Richard's first wife. Not his only wife. His *first* wife. There was another.

The other wife.

Turning, she started for the door.

The Other Wife

"You shouldn't be alone right now," he insisted.

"I can't stay." While she loved Susan, the last thing she felt like doing was talking. These past few days had been filled with talk; so much talk buzzing around her that she felt as if she'd been attacked by a swarm of bees. Her eyes were puffy, her ears were ringing, and her head felt as if it might explode. Didn't they understand what this week had been like? Her world had collapsed. A person could only handle so much grief. She felt ragged and torn, as if she might be on the verge. Her nerves wouldn't take much more.

She barely recognized herself. One minute she felt numb, wanting nothing more than to climb into bed, pull the covers over her head, and lose herself in the blissful, black nothingness of sleep, only to be consumed by a sudden anger and resentment, a raging river of swirling emotions that threatened to sweep away all the good parts of her life that should have been left to her. It was horrible and frightening. She wanted peace and quiet. She wanted her things around her. Her books, her house, her space.

But there was one thing she didn't need. Not anymore.

The ring didn't give easily. Her knuckle was swollen. Too many years, too much heartache. Thirty-eight years she'd worn his wedding ring. She'd never taken it off, not even to do the dishes. *He put a ring on another woman's finger.* She gave it a fierce tug, yanking it free. It raked across her knuckle, leaving a scraped, red sore. Eleanor tossed it atop the stack of Richard's papers that lined the desk.

"What are you doing?" Jeffrey's face fell. "That's your wedding ring. It was Grandmother's ring."

Eleanor lifted a shoulder and shrugged. "Keep it," she said. "Give it to Susan. Throw it in the trash. I don't care."

"But Mom, you can't—"

"I can do anything I want." Her eyes narrowed. "Wait and see what I can do."

And with that, Eleanor walked out the door.

Chapter Four

They were all up early, at first morning light. Dickie was first, as was his routine. Definitely her son, a bleary-eyed Claire thought as he wandered into the bedroom and tumbled onto Richard's side of the bed, curling up beside her. She wrapped herself around him, cradling him in her arms. His breath was soft against her cheek as he tucked in closer. Her little boy, oblivious to the horror that life had tossed in their path. Things were going to change for Dickie. Things would change for all of them.

The room was quiet, and she felt his little chest rise and fall as he stilled beside her, drifting into a light sleep. The faint scent of baby shampoo lingered in his hair from his bath last night, and she held him even closer, inhaling the trace of innocence about him. At four, Dickie was caught in that time warp between babyhood and little boy. His legs had lost their baby fat, and he'd moved beyond that selfish, stubborn, *I want it and I want it now!* stage she expected Sophie would soon enter.

Claire lay there in the semidarkness, Dickie drowsing

beside her, her mind running full tilt as it had through the night, replaying the same filmstrip over and over: Jim Kennedy's visit, the ungodly news of Richard's death, the staggering blow of his ultimate betrayal. It was simply unbelievable. Things like this didn't happen to people like her. Her heart started racing, pounding in her chest as it had all night. She clenched Dickie closer in her arms. What if, just like Richard, she were to suffer a heart attack and die? Part of her wanted to die right now. Wouldn't that be better? Easier? At least she wouldn't have to bear this heartache, endure this terrible grief.

But if she died, who would take care of the children? How could she leave her babies behind?

Soft sounds from the monitor at her bedside alerted her to Sophie, in the next room, stirring in her crib. She hadn't yet mastered the art of climbing the railings, but it wouldn't be long. Only when the babbling turned to wailing did Claire finally lift herself from the bed and pad to the other room. After changing Sophie's diaper, she carried her daughter back to bed with her, which was where Hallie found them when she showed up on schedule at eight a.m.

"You're still in bed?"

Hallie sounded incredulous, and Claire didn't blame her. Usually by the time Hallie arrived, she was up, dressed, and ready to bolt out the door for school. Propping herself on one elbow, Claire stared at her through bleary eyes. "I'm not going in."

"Yay! Mama's staying home today." Dickie giggled and began tickling Sophie, who kicked and frolicked against her brother. Claire winced and shifted away from them. Her mind's confusion, the children's commotion, the world's chaos, was all too much to bear.

What was she going to do? And how would she do it without Richard?

And then the thought that had plagued her all night returned once again: how could this be true? How could Richard have done this?

To her? To them? To their children?

"Let me take them." Hallie moved forward, pulling Sophie from the bed, holding out a hand to Dickie. "Come on, you crazy monsters, let's go have breakfast and let Mama rest." She glanced at Claire, cautious concern etched on her face. "Can I get you something?"

Can you wind back time? Can you give me back my world?

"I'm fine, thanks. I'll be down in a bit. I... I just need a few minutes."

A few minutes? Furthest thing from the truth. What she really wanted was to pull the pillow over her head, burrow beneath the blankets, and never emerge. How could she face the world after what had happened?

Facing the truth that Richard was dead. He was gone, leaving her alone to deal with her grief. Utter, complete, overwhelming grief... and no one to talk to, nowhere to put it.

Grief... and betrayal.

How could he have done it? How would she live through it? How would she live without Richard? How would she live with herself?

All her life, she'd thought she was so smart. A brilliant woman, her professors confirmed, a rising star in the world of academia, her postgraduate credentials affirmed. Highly regarded, sought after by prestigious schools, she'd accepted an offer from the University of Chicago and had had no regrets—until now. Her days spent as both an undergrad and grad student at an Ivy League school out east had taught her how easily people could be caught up in the trappings of esteem and social prominence. When the time came to choose her own path, she'd returned to her roots. She'd grown up in the Midwest, and the friendly feel of the U of C campus and the easy flow of symbiotic relationships between students and faculty appealed to her.

How could she go back? How could she face everyone?

How could she have allowed herself to be duped by a man?

And not just any man. Richard was in a league all his own.

They'd met at the courthouse, two strangers summoned for jury duty, seated next to each other during the process of *voir dire*. He'd trailed her into the hallway after the judge called a midmorning break from jury selection. "Buy you a drink?" he'd asked in a slightly teasing tone as they halted in front of a drinking fountain. Claire remembered rolling her eyes at the slick come-on, though he soon had her laughing in spite of herself. Back in the courtroom, Richard was quickly dismissed on a peremptory challenge. He threw her a quick wink, gathered his coat, and with a whispered "See you later," headed for the door. Fifteen minutes later, dismissed for cause, Claire departed the courtroom and found Richard lounging in the hallway, waiting for her.

"But how did you know they would dismiss me?"

she'd asked him over lunch, only to see him counter with a smile. "No lawyer in his right mind would want you sitting on a jury," he'd answered. "You're much too pretty for a courtroom. You'd be a distraction." It was corny and sappy, a come-on line that she would have automatically dismissed if anyone else had said it. But coming from Richard, it hadn't mattered. Richard was like that: able to toss off the most inane things and make you believe them.

Exactly the kind of man she'd always feared... and immediately been attracted to. She'd hesitated when he asked her to marry him. Richard was arrogant and self-centered, flamboyant and outspoken, but he had a way about him that made her love him anyway. She'd entered the relationship with both eyes open, yet found herself in love with him before the end of their second date.

Loving Richard was crazy and impulsive, like nothing she'd ever done in her life. He was impetuous, reckless, and definitely not the man for her, Claire constantly admonished herself. It would never work. They came from different worlds, with nearly thirty years separating them. Yet she found herself helpless to let go and feared for them both when she agreed to marry him. What had she been thinking?

And yet, when it came to Richard, all logical thoughts flew out of her head...

"I can't believe you're still available," she'd confessed one night in bed amid tousled sheets after a particularly amorous lovemaking session. "Are you sure you don't have an ex-wife or two lurking in the background?" She'd been teasing him at the time, but if only she'd known.

"You worried?" he asked.

"Not worried, exactly. It's just that I find you so…"

"Desirable?" He finished her sentence, pinning her down with his weight, his mouth and lips traveling up and down her body, delivering deliciously wicked kisses in all the right places. "No ex-wife," he promised. "No children either."

It didn't require a degree in mathematics to follow the law of statistics. She knew the odds were against them. He had thirty years on her. What kind of a future did that promise them? He probably wouldn't live to see Dickie graduate from college or settled with a good job and a family of his own.

She'd known it wouldn't be an easy life, but she'd married him anyway. The age difference alone should have been enough of a deterrent, not to mention the additional strain placed on him by his work and constant travel, which kept him away much of the time. Claire had known from the start it would be up to her to carry the load, to keep things together and ensure there was something for him to return to. When he was gone, she found herself longing for him, craving him like an alcoholic shivering outside the corner bar on a Sunday morning, waiting for the rumble of a lock and its doors to fling open. Stupid, foolish, she berated herself, leading up to the day of their marriage, but she hadn't been able help herself. She'd let go of all the rules she'd lived by, tossed aside the safe reality of logical, precise thinking. For once in her life, she'd allowed her heart to rule her world. And despite the fact of a complicated pregnancy and her ending up on bed rest the weeks leading up to Dickie's birth, they'd gotten through it. Richard's business concerns normally kept him gone three weeks out of four, but he'd made her a promise that he would be with her when Dickie was born. True to his word, he'd had been at her bedside, holding her hand, the day Dickie kicked and screamed his way into the world. Richard was there, telling her how much he adored her, how he would love her to his dying day. Two years later, Sophie had surprised them by making an appearance. They were no longer a couple, plus baby makes three. With Sophie, they became a family.

But their family had been shattered. One of them was gone. The head of their family—or so she'd thought—the one who truly never belonged. Whatever had happened in the past, she needed to make sure the three of them survived. Claire hung on to that thought. She needed to keep it close. She needed to keep her babies close. They were all she had left from the wreckage of the past.

She couldn't lie there any longer. The children were already up, and Hallie was moving around in the house. Morning had arrived with its harsh brilliant sunshine, shedding light on the remnants of her life. Plucking her phone from the bedside table, she made a quick call, informing the staff she wouldn't be in that day. Slipping out of bed, she threw on a pair of jeans, socks, and the first sweatshirt she grabbed from her closet (*The University of Chicago – Where fun comes to die*). Staring in the mirror, the irony of the statement wasn't lost on her. For a moment she considered changing but then decided the shirt was entirely appropriate. After all, Richard had died. Their life together was dead. She might as well be dead too.

Dragging a comb through her hair, Claire stumbled down the narrow back stairs that opened into the kitchen.

"I made you some tea." Hallie placed a steaming mug on the granite countertop before her. "It's mint, nice and soothing. It will help settle your stomach."

"Thanks." Claire slid onto the ultra-stylish kitchen stool, curling her toes around the cool steel rungs. Sleek and modern was fine and good when the world was running the way it was meant to. But sometimes a person needed comfort and support. Something to lean on. This morning was one of those times. Richard was the one who had insisted their kitchen should be a gleaming showcase. He'd been the one who dealt with the interior designer. He'd been the one who made all the choices, who insisted the faded oak cabinets and tired appliances be replaced by the gleaming stainless steel now surrounding her. Richard chose what they would live with. Now he was gone, and she was left to live with the aftermath of his decisions.

But what did they have? What kind of life had he left her with? Two children, a house, and—if Jim Kennedy's revelations were true—a life built on lies.

Claire's stomach lurched sideways, and she pushed away the tea. "I don't think I can drink this."

"Maybe some toast," Hallie suggested. "We bought apricot jam at the grocery yesterday."

"Mmm," Dickie said, steering his little toy car along the edge of the counter to bounce against Claire's arm. Up over her hand he drove it, zooming across her forearm, rounding the curve of her elbow, reaching the soft skin under her upper arm, approaching her heart.

"No, sweetheart." She brushed him away, something she normally never did, taking him by surprise. He peeked up at her, the beginning of a frown capturing his eyebrows.

"Why don't you take your cars out on the sun porch?" Hallie suggested. "You can play out there."

"It's all right," Claire murmured. "Go play."

Dickie stared at her a moment, his brown eyes round and curious, as if he'd suddenly realized something was amiss. Toys were rarely allowed on the sun porch, a small enclosed area off the kitchen.

"Can I take my garage?" he asked hopefully.

"Yes," she said, waving him away. Anything to keep the peace. He stared at her another moment, then scrambled from the kitchen. When he returned, he was lugging his newest toy, a present from Richard a few weeks earlier. The plastic garage was four stories high with an elevator shaft in the middle and garish colors no self-respecting garage owner would dream of painting his building. But Dickie loved it, just as he loved playing on the sun porch. Why deny him? Today of all days he needed something to love.

Claire felt her eyes begin to fill with unexpected tears. Today she needed something to love. She blinked hard. No tears. Richard hated tears. If she started now, she'd never stop.

Hallie wiped Sophie's face and freed her from the high chair. "Take your sister with you," she said to Dickie. "Let her play too."

Sophie toddled toward the garage with a greedy grin.

"She'll break it," he said with a wary glance at his sister's pudgy outstretched fingers.

"Then we'll buy you a new one." Claire's voice floated between them, like an auto repairman assessing the damage. Accidents happened, even in a garage. Isn't that what car insurance was for?

Accidents happen. Isn't that what life insurance was for?

"Take Sophie and go play." Hallie's voice offered no choice, and Dickie didn't protest.

Watching as her babies disappeared, Claire suddenly no longer had the strength to hold herself up. She sagged against the counter, folding her arms on the hard, cold surface, and laid her head down.

"Claire?" Hallie's voice floated beside her, soft as a tissue ready to wipe away any tears. "What's wrong?"

How could she tell her? From the moment she'd opened the front door last night and allowed Jim Kennedy into her house, everything had gone wrong. Her world had disappeared. Why had she invited him? From the beginning, she'd had the uneasy feeling he would bring bad news. *Urgent*, his numerous voice mails had told her. *Urgent*, he'd reiterated when she'd eventually taken his call. *Urgent*, her heart had whispered through the night as she lay awake in the darkness, curled up in the spot where Richard normally slept. The bed sheets had been changed since he'd left on his last trip and smelled only of fabric softener. There was no lingering scent of her husband, nothing left of the man she'd known and loved.

Come back to me. Come back.

"Claire, are you sick? Do you want me to call a doctor?"

Yes, she was sick. Heartsick. And no doctor would be able to cure it.

"Are you going to school today?"

She shook her head, some distant part of her mind

racing through her schedule. She'd made the phone call to the university without even thinking about what day it was. Wednesday? Yes, that was right. And Wednesday meant no classes. Thank God for small favors. No way in hell would she be able to manage standing in front of a classroom, let alone lecturing students on some inane psychological theory. She'd barely made it out of her bed and into the kitchen. Claire lifted her head, eyes still closed, trying to visualize her office calendar. Meetings? Appointments? What did it matter? How could it matter?

Nothing mattered.

A swish of fabric slid against her skin as Hallie claimed a seat on the stool beside her. "Is there anything I can do?"

She couldn't tell her. Saying the words out loud would give them truth. And the things she'd learned last night simply couldn't be true. Richard couldn't be dead. It was unimaginable, thinking that when he'd kissed her a few weeks ago before walking out the door, it had been his last kiss. Never again would they chat about their children, or their house, or the getaway trip they'd been planning to Saint Lucia. Never again would she feel his arms around her. Never again would she hear him playing with the children, feel his breath soft against her cheek, hear him whisper that he loved her more than anything, above all else, more than anyone else.

But had he ever said that? Claire struggled to remember. He'd always said that she was the love of his life. But had he ever said that he loved her above all others?

He had another wife.

She twisted the simple gold wedding band round and round on her finger. Another woman wore his wedding ring. After she'd shown Jim Kennedy the door, after she'd turned the deadbolt and locked out the world, she'd gone straight to her desk, opened her laptop, and typed in Richard's name. The lengthy list of Internet links opened: professional references, various mentions, journal articles linking him to numerous jobs around the world. And there at the top of the Google page was the most recent mention, the one reference she couldn't ignore.

Richard's obituary.

Anderson, who died suddenly at his Lake Forest, Illinois, home, is survived by his wife, Eleanor; son Richard (Susan) Anderson of Chicago, daughter Genevieve Anderson of New York City, plus a grandson, Richard.

She'd stared at the words on the screen until they dissolved into nothing more than a fuzzy blur. Richard was lost to her forever. She wasn't even allowed to claim him as her own. He'd left behind another wife. A woman named Eleanor. And children. Two children. Seeing their names—Jeffrey and Genevieve—had brought goose bumps popping on her arms. And the little boy, Richard's grandson. How old was that little boy? He shared the same name as Dickie, their own son.

Her husband Richard, the father of her children, was a grandfather? Even this morning, the grief was inconceivable. Claire pressed her fingers against her eyes, bringing vibrant starbursts flaring and pain radiating beneath her fingertips. If only she could smudge away the words she'd seen last night, smear them from her memory. The stark words, crawling over the page in black and white for the world to see, made her feel as if she and the children had been erased, as if they'd never been there.

It was as if when she'd opened her laptop and brought up the obituary, she'd tumbled into a parallel universe. A universe that didn't include them.

Where did they fit into this world? Where did she fit in? Where was their mention?

Richard left behind a beloved wife named Claire. He is survived by two children, two babies, Dickie and Sophie.

But the truth was they didn't fit in. They didn't belong. They didn't exist.

They'd never existed.

"Claire?"

She looked down, surprised at the cool touch of Hallie's hand on her own. From the next room came the soft babbling of children at play. A normal sound, such an ordinary thing on an extraordinary day. How she wished there was a way to protect them from the horror, but she had no choice. They were young, but they had to be told. But not yet. Let them have today. Give them one last chance for the normal life they'd always known. After today, everything would be different. It was already different; they simply didn't know it.

Tonight, at bedtime. She didn't think she could summon the courage to do it before then. Tonight, after their baths, once they were in their pajamas, she would wrap them in her arms, cuddle them close to her heart, and then she would tell them. Maybe it wouldn't be as difficult as she imagined. They were accustomed to Richard being gone. Maybe if she used simple words, she could explain that Daddy had gone on another of his trips... and that this one was so far away, all the way to heaven, that he wouldn't be coming back. Never again.

God, how would she manage that conversation? The mere thought made her stomach heave. Her poor babies. They were so young. They had no clue their world had ended. She would never scold them again, Claire promised herself. She would never make them unhappy. They could play on the sun porch whenever they wanted. She would feed them cookies, chocolate, and cupcakes instead of carrots. She would smother them with kisses and tell them they were loved. Every single day, she would remind them how much they were loved and how much their father loved them.

Because he would no longer be around to tell them himself.

And suddenly the realization was too much to hold inside. Claire slid from the stool and bolted for the small bathroom off the kitchen. Sinking to her knees, she hugged the toilet, her stomach roiling and retching as she heaved up everything inside her. The sour, acrid taste brought tears springing to her eyes, but still she didn't cry. She clung to the stool, praying for strength to make it through.

Hallie crouched behind her, gathered Claire's hair, and smoothed it away from her face and the foul odor of vomit. "Claire?" she asked softly. "Are you pregnant?"

Sputtering, Claire swiped her mouth with the back of her hand. The irony of the statement wasn't lost on her. Her husband was dead. There would be no more babies.

"No, I'm not pregnant."

How she wished she were. More than anything else, she wished that was the reason why she felt sick today.

"Then what is it?" Hallie wrapped her arms around Claire, hugging her close. "What's wrong?"

Claire rested her head against the young woman's shoulder. Much as she felt like hiding from the world and the truth, she knew she had to face things... and right now, she had to face Hallie. There'd be no putting her off. She was here every day. Claire slumped against the sink. "It's Richard." Her voice echoed around the tiny room with its celery-green walls, bouncing off the black and white floor tiles. "He's gone."

"Gone?" Hallie frowned slightly. "Gone where? When's he coming back?"

Claire lifted her eyes to face her. "He's not."

Somehow they made it through the next few hours. Claire blindly followed instructions, allowing Hallie to take over in her usual effortless style, shepherding them around the geography that made up the house, maneuvering them through the morning maze. They got through lunch with the children and put them down for early naps. Sophie went quickly, but Dickie protested, stating that since he was in school, he no longer needed a nap. His budding masculine ego was somewhat soothed when Claire eventually promised he didn't need to sleep, but could play quietly in his room.

"Have you thought about what you're going to do?" Hallie asked after both the children were safely upstairs.

"What do you mean?" Claire asked, though Hallie's question was all she'd been thinking about last night, and all this morning. Why hadn't she seen it coming? Her entire professional career was based on understanding the working of the human mind, but her own brain was currently not cooperating. The facts did not compute. How could Richard be dead? How could he have died in his sleep? In bed with another woman, who supposedly was his wife?

She was his wife.

"This situation... this whole thing." Hallie gathered a deep breath as if she'd been pondering how to put it. "Claire, I think you need to talk to someone. Do you have a lawyer? You need some advice on how to handle things."

"I don't want to talk to anyone."

As if on cue, her phone began to vibrate across the glass coffee table. She stared at it, mesmerized by its dance across the polished surface. Maybe it would skitter to the edge and fall to the floor. Maybe it would break. Maybe she could sit on the couch forever and never need talk to anyone again.

Hallie grabbed the phone and scanned the screen. "It's Tulie."

Claire shook her head. She didn't want to talk to anyone, not yet. She wasn't ready. She didn't think she'd ever be ready. Hallie, however, didn't ask her permission. Touching the screen, she made the connection, then wordlessly handed the phone to Claire.

She lifted it to her ear. "Hi."

"Claire?" Tulie's voice filled the void between them. "Hey, you. What's going on? I've been calling and texting for hours, but you haven't been answering."

She pinched her nose, pressed her fingertips against the corners of her eyes, pushed away the instant tears. "Sorry," she said. "Something came up."

"God, you sound terrible." Relief and a nervous laugh

rushed through the phone. "Are you sick? Is it the kids? Are they okay?"

"They're fine. We're all fine," Claire said, though nothing could be further from the truth.

Tulie's energy vibrated through the phone, acting like a vacuum, threatening to suck away every ounce of strength she had left. "So why aren't you at school? Didn't Hallie show up?"

"No, that's not it. I mean, yes, she did." She glanced at the receding figure headed for the kitchen, leaving her with her privacy. "Hallie's here."

"You don't sound right." Tulie hesitated. "What's wrong? Is Richard home?"

God, if she only knew.

"No," Claire whispered. "He's not."

"All right, that settles it." Tulie's voice was firm. "I've got a meeting with a grad student in a few minutes. After that, I'm coming over."

Forty minutes later, Tulie's face was the exact vile shade of green Hallie's had been after hearing Claire's confession in the bathroom.

"I can't believe it," she mumbled. "Are you sure there's no mistake?"

Claire stared woodenly at her best friend, seated in the exact spot where Jim Kennedy had sat last night.

"It's true," she said, remembering how she'd felt viewing the bleak black-and-white words of Richard's on-line obituary. What was that tongue-in-cheek statement, that whatever you saw on the Internet must be true? If ever there was cause to think someone was playing a joke, a cruel, monstrous joke, then this would be it. But

April Fools' Day was still a week or so away. Plus, the website link had been courtesy of the *Lake Forester News*, a division of the *Chicago Sun Times*. Newspapers, even online newspapers, were in the business of printing news, not lies.

Why run an obituary if it wasn't true?

Why print the name of another woman as Richard's wife if it wasn't true?

But *she* was Richard's wife. They'd been married four years. They had two children.

Tulie drained the rest of her wine in one long swallow, then shook her head, muttering underneath her breath. Claire decided it probably was a good thing she couldn't hear what her friend was saying. Reaching for the bottle, Hallie had opened before she left, she refilled Tulie's glass, upending the bottle to coax out the few remaining drops.

"It's unbelievable." Her gaze darted from the glass to Claire's face. "I'm so sorry, Claire. About Richard, and…"

Claire knew exactly what she meant without Tulie even speaking the words. Sorry about Richard. Sorry that he'd died. And *oh by the way, so sorry to hear that he had another wife.*

"What are you going to do?"

"What can I do? Have some more wine, and try not to think about it," Claire said, knowing it was a moot point. As if another drink could wipe away the thoughts pouring through her mind. She'd already had one glass and didn't feel the slightest bit different. Rising to her feet, she padded to the dining room and Richard's treasured wine rack where his precious award-winning vintages were stored. Claire had no illusions or pretensions of having a discriminating taste for fine wines, and normally could not have cared less what she was drinking. But today was different. Today, it mattered. Squatting on the floor, she ignored the top shelves of American domestics to concentrate on the bottom row of bottles nestled on their sides. That was where Richard kept his most expensive wines, the best of show, the ones he saved for special occasions.

Today seemed appropriate. It wasn't every day you discovered your husband had died. It wasn't every day you discovered your husband had lived another life... or had another wife.

Searching the rack, she eventually found the bottle she wanted. Its appearance was deceiving, merely a small gold-embossed label pronouncing the brand. Richard had exclaimed in delight upon discovering the bottles of rare vintage during their visit to the small winery in France. They'd shared the first bottle the night Sophie was born. Today seemed fitting to crack open the other.

Tucking it under her arm, Claire grabbed a corkscrew and padded back into the living room. She popped the cork and began to pour. Richard would have been aghast that she hadn't let it breathe. But what did it matter? He'd been the wine connoisseur in the family, not her. Claire shrugged. Screw it. She watched as the rich red liquid spilled into Tulie's glass. Topping it off, she refilled her own.

"Not bad," she said. Not bad at all for a bottle that had cost hundreds of dollars. But Richard had always insisted on the best. It seemed fitting that his best wine be sacrificed on this day of all days.

Turning to Tulie, she lifted her glass. "Shall we share a toast? To Richard. To my husband."

To *her* husband.

Claire swallowed a good third of the glass without pause. Richard had been right. This *was* good wine. The rich ruby liquid went down smoothly, warming her senses, chasing away the chill of death. Too bad only one bottle was left. She could drink the rest of the day and night away. Anything to bring a sweet sense of oblivion. Anything to release her from the reality of what she might—*would*—be facing. Dragging in a deep breath, she curled herself into the couch pillows, wrapped her hands around the glass, and took a few more sips.

Tulie crossed to the couch and perched beside Claire, resting her hand on her forearm. "Claire, listen to me. I'm here for you, sweetie. I'll always be here." She squeezed her arm. "Whatever you need, you've got it. How can I help?"

"I don't know." It was an honest answer. Her brain wasn't working. Not that she cared, Claire thought, as she sipped her wine.

"Is there anyone you want me to call?"

"I don't think so." Who was there to tell? If her parents weren't already dead, this would probably kill them. *We don't understand what happened to Claire. Our daughter, a psychology professor at a prestigious university, trained in the workings of the human mind... deceived by a man who had another wife?*

No, never in a million years would they have understood. She'd been their change-of-life baby, the child they'd given up on having by the time she made her unexpected arrival when they were nearing fifty. An only child, beloved and precious, Claire had always been acutely aware that she carried all their hopes and dreams. Her father had managed a hardware store, and her mother had worked full time as a school secretary to provide their family with health insurance. They'd been kind, decent people who'd worked hard to give her a better life than they'd had. There hadn't been a lot of extra money in the household budget. Every penny they could sock away had gone toward her education. "That's the ticket to a better life," her dad had always told her. "A good education will take you where you want to go."

It was a good thing her father had no idea where it had taken her, Claire thought. The minute she'd met Richard, every rational thought in her head had disappeared. She'd been captivated by his good looks and quick wit, by his throaty laugh and the wicked sparkle in his eyes. Most of all, she'd been charmed by his intelligence. She was surrounded at the university by male colleagues, some of them with more education and experience than she could ever hope to have. But none of them—at least not the ones who were single and available—had appealed to her. None of them moved her, made her breath catch or her heart bump and skip a beat, the way Richard had the day he strolled into her life. He had that certain something, an easy way of interacting with people that made you feel as if you were the only one in the room, the only one he cared about. He was gifted and articulate, but he was also vain and arrogant. Most of all, he was a man who appreciated women. Richard had loved women. He had loved her.

"You have bewitched me," he'd confessed one night

over dinner soon after they'd met. "God help me, because I can't help myself. I've fallen in love with you."

How could she help but fall in love with him?

God help them all. But how could she have known? Richard had never told her. He'd never given her the slightest clue that he had another life… that he had another wife.

Claire stared at her empty glass. What kind of woman was she, anyway? How could she have fallen in love with him? How could she have fallen in love with another woman's husband?

How could she have married another woman's husband?

Leaning forward, she reached for the bottle.

Tulie's hand stopped her. "That's not going to help," she said softly.

Claire shook off her hold. "I'm finding it a tremendous help." She'd never been much for drinking, but alcohol, when used properly, was an excellent means of helping one forget. Which was exactly what she intended to do. She wanted to forget everything that had happened. She wanted to play at being San Francisco, floating through an existence in a lovely fogged-out sort of world. And she had no desire to contemplate the future. It was a future without Richard… and a future that involved a woman named Eleanor.

He'd been married to Eleanor for thirty-eight years, Jim Kennedy had informed her. Claire had no reason to doubt him. He'd spoken with such authority. And he'd known them as a couple, he'd told her, both he and his wife Anne. They'd seen Richard and his wife socially. He knew Eleanor. He knew her children.

And suddenly Claire realized something else. Eleanor's children were Dickie and Sophie's half-brother and sister.

She steeled her nerves. There was no way in hell that the two of them were going to meet. No way in hell, she determined. She was certain Eleanor would want to meet, especially once she learned that Richard had switched the beneficiary on his life insurance policy. That news was the one thing that hadn't come as much of a surprise. Richard had always made sure he took care of them, of her and the children... and so he had, in life *and* in death. He'd left enough money that, if invested wisely, Claire would never have to worry again in her life. But she didn't want the money. She'd gladly give it up if it meant she could have a do-over, if it meant she could have Richard back again.

But he wasn't coming back. Meanwhile, she would be receiving millions of dollars; money that Eleanor had rightfully expected was hers. Eventually she would come looking for Claire. And Claire had no doubt that Eleanor would come looking. That's what she herself would do if their roles were reversed.

How long would it be before she showed up?

How would she handle it when Eleanor showed up?

Claire grabbed the bottle and filled her glass. Some spilled over the brim, splashing onto the hardwood floor. She stared at the red liquid puddled at her feet. "Oh."

"Let me get it." Tulie moved quickly, mopping up the mess before it resulted in an ugly stain.

"I'm sorry." Claire shook her head. Three glasses of wine and she'd turned into a sloppy drunk. If Richard had been here, he would have taken the glass from her hand, kissed her lightly on the lips, teasing her that there would be terrible punishment involved if she ruined his floors. He'd taken such pride in these floors, original from when the house had been built. A vomit-green shag carpet had greeted them when they'd first toured the property, but Richard had suspected—correctly, as usual—that once the carpet was pulled back, they would discover the original wood. Now polished and buffed to a high-gloss shine, the floors were a stunning showcase for their living room, directly off the entry. The floors were perfect. The house was perfect. Their life was perfect.

Their life *had been* perfect.

Claire moaned to herself. How could this have happened? She drained the rest of her wine.

"Enough now," Tulie declared, removing the empty glass from her hand, placing it far from her grasp. "The kids will be up soon. You don't need this."

"But I do," Claire insisted, for the lovely limits of San Francisco were receding even as they spoke. Such a beautiful city. She'd visited it once with Richard. How she wished they could return. She wanted to luxuriate in the feel of his arms wrapped around her, feel his breath warm against her neck, listen as he crooned the lyrics of the famous song softly in her ear.

A gasp of laughter bubbled up from somewhere deep inside her, surfacing into a full-blown chortle. Richard had been gifted in many things, but singing definitely had not been one of them. Dickie always made a point of plugging his ears whenever Richard broke out in song.

"Something funny?" Tulie asked.

"It's... it's something I remembered about Richard."

"That's the way to handle it, Claire. Keep remembering the good things."

Hold on to the good things, she reminded herself as the giggles subsided and her smile faded. They'd be important in the days, weeks, and months to come. She had no doubt that plenty of bad things were headed her way. She felt her face crumple. The threat of hot tears prickling behind her eyes returned. Claire tried her best to hold them back. What would Richard say if he saw her tears?

And then she remembered the reality that was now her life. He was no longer around. No one cared if she cried. No one cared what she did. From now on, everything in her life would be up to her... including that conversation with their children tonight. How was she going to tell them their father was dead?

She turned a sober face to Tulie. "I don't know if I can do this. How am I going to get through life without him?"

"You will," she assured her. "I know it doesn't feel like it now, but you will. You're a strong woman, Claire. You've always been strong."

"But I don't feel strong. I... I feel like..." She halted, realizing there were no words for how she felt inside, for the nothingness that encased her, the weary numbness, the overwhelming grief. With Richard gone, everything was different. Everything she'd thought true had been nothing but a lie. A horrible, deceitful lie. How was she going to live with the reality of what he'd done to her? How could she believe anything—trust anyone—after this?

She couldn't. She wouldn't. Claire bent forward, folding herself inward. She was conscious of arms slipping around her, warm and comforting as if it were her own mother. But it was Tulie, who had no maternal bones in her body.

"We'll get you through this," she murmured. "I promise you, Claire. We'll get you through this."

"I don't know if I can do it," she moaned.

"You can," she insisted. "You have the kids, you have Hallie. You have friends."

"Not for long," she predicted, raising a bleak face. "Not after they find out the truth about my marriage."

"Screw 'em." Tulie shrugged. "If that's the way they think, they weren't your friends in the first place. And I'm not going anywhere. Like it or not, you're stuck with me. We'll get you through this. We'll get you through this... together."

Claire searched her friend's face. There was no pity, no scorn, no *how could you have been so stupid*? She saw only compassion, empathy, and love mirrored in Tulie's eyes. That and a promise that things would be better.

It was too much to bear, and Claire could hold back no longer. Finally, her tears started.

Chapter Five

If life was like a box of chocolates, she'd definitely ended up with the wrong box, Eleanor decided. Where were all the gooey caramels, yummy nougats, and rich, velvety creams? It felt like someone had switched things out and snatched the goodies while she wasn't looking, leaving only bitter chunks littered with nutshells. And she never ate nuts, not after she'd cracked that filling last year. Then again, did she really need chocolate? Mirrors didn't lie, and neither did the waistbands of the two pair of slacks she'd discarded on the bed. She'd barely managed to struggle into them, let alone close the zipper. She was getting pudgy. No, *pudgy* wasn't the word for it. She was getting fat. She was still wearing the five pounds or so she'd gained over the winter, plus the few extra she'd put on in the past several weeks.

Rooting through her closet, she finally unearthed an old pair of navy-blue slacks featuring a comfortable eat-all-you-want expanding elastic waist. No more comfort foods, Eleanor warned herself as she struggled into them. No more evenings huddled in front of the TV with her two favorite men, Ben and Jerry. No more puttering around the house with a sack of salty pretzels. No more afternoons spent in her big sunny kitchen, baking cookies and cupcakes and all things sweet and delectable. *No more.* She stood in pants and bra before the guest bedroom's full-length mirror. *I can do this*, she assured herself, striking a bodybuilder's pose and flexing her arms. *I am strong. I am capable. I am woman.*

A woman with bat wings. Good Lord, when had that happened? She recoiled in disgust at the sight of the fat dangling under both arms. Who was she kidding? She couldn't zip her pants, she had flabby arms, big boobs, and a waist growing thicker by the day. She was a woman, all right... a woman in dire need of a do-over. She hadn't visited her hairdresser since before Richard died, and her roots were in desperate need of a touch-up. More than a touch-up, Eleanor noted, leaning in toward the mirror and fingering a few strands. She'd read once that tragedy could turn a person's hair white overnight. What if that happened to her? She still had some color left, but how much came from a bottle and how much was hers? She squinted, inched forward, examining her head closely. Was it her imagination, or did her hair seem thinner?

What if she was going bald?

A knock on the half-opened door pulled her back from her reflection.

"You decent?" Martha's voice drifted from the other side.

"Decent as I'll ever be," she said, quickly buttoning her blouse. "Do you think my hair is getting thinner?"

Martha brushed past her, empty laundry basket in hand,

toward the unmade bed. "I think you need to quit worrying about your hair and things you can't control."

Easy for you to say, Eleanor opened her mouth to speak, then wisely decided to keep quiet. Martha's hair was as thick and glossy as a thirtysomething, despite the fact her sixtieth birthday had come and gone years ago. And it was obvious Martha didn't bother with monthly visits to a hairdresser. Then again, Eleanor decided, if she knew for certain that her dull brown mop would turn out that lovely shade of glorious white crowning Martha's head, she'd let her hair go in a heartbeat.

Martha plucked the discarded slacks from the heap atop the blankets. "Do these go back in the closet, or are you donating them to Goodwill?"

Good idea. If she gave them away, they wouldn't be around, taunting her from their hangers. "Maybe I should, seeing as how they don't fit." Eleanor flopped into one of the matching chintz-covered armchairs nestled under the window. "Maybe I should go shopping."

"Maybe you should quit eating so much." Crouching, Martha plucked a few chocolate wrappers from the floor that had missed the wastebasket last night. "Then you wouldn't need to go shopping."

"I know." Eleanor sighed. Her defense was weak, and so was her willpower. But there was no getting around Martha's logic. As always, she was the voice of reason. She'd been with them for years, since Jeffrey had been a baby. She showed up every Monday and Friday, regular as clockwork, always willing to put in more hours if needed. Martha also had no qualms about opening her mouth and firing off an opinion if she saw something amiss. Richard found her abrasive and wanted her fired, but Eleanor refused to let her go. Martha could be temperamental, judgmental, and quick to say what was on her mind, but their housekeeper also had a heart bigger than a laundry basket, and arms willing to fold towels and tidy up emotional messes. Eleanor didn't know how she would have survived without Martha around these past several weeks. She'd coddled her since Richard's death, serving as a ferocious watchdog, guarding her privacy, protecting her from snooping so-called friends seeking to confirm if the rumors they'd heard were true. Martha had taken up patrol as her personal phone policewoman, shielding her from unwanted calls... even from Genevieve, who'd begun calling on a daily basis, despite the fact that her normal modus operandi was pretty much *never*. After Vivi's fourth call one week—the second on that particular day—and listening to Eleanor's weak answers to her daughter's persistent questioning about the inheritance promised her, Martha had stepped in, pried the phone from Eleanor's hand, and ordered Vivi to back off and give her mother a break.

Eleanor hadn't heard from Vivi in three days, and she wasn't complaining.

With a few brisk movements, the bed was stripped and the laundry basket full. Martha did not believe in wasting time. Hands on hips, she turned to face Eleanor. "What's on your agenda for today?"

Did she dare admit the truth? Eleanor contemplated her housekeeper from her comfy spot. Martha was so energetic—sometimes it wore Eleanor out, watching her work. And with the bed stripped, there was no chance to do what she really wanted, which was to crawl back under the covers and hide. There might even be a few of those chocolates left in the box beside the bed.

"I don't know," she finally admitted.

"Last week you mentioned wanting to start sorting through his things, If you're serious about donating to Goodwill, maybe you should start on the closet."

Sort through Richard's things? Eleanor hadn't expected that particular suggestion. Was she ready to do it? It had been three weeks since his funeral, but Richard's clothes and personal effects still remained untouched in the bedroom they'd shared. One part of her was content to leave it that way... maybe forever.

Sometimes it felt as if he weren't really gone but merely departed on another of his long trips abroad. Why not leave everything exactly as it was? Then again, how long could she put off facing reality? He'd died in bed next to her. She'd been the one who'd called 911. She'd attended his wake service and funeral. She'd been at the cemetery when they lowered his coffin into the ground. There was no earthly reason to keep any of his suits. Jeffrey might want to have some of the ties, but the rest would be of no use to him. Father and son had been opposites in stature and size. The thought of going through Richard's clothes, gathering his neatly pressed shirts in their plastic bags fresh from the drycleaners, collecting his shoes, cleaning out his drawers, tossing his underwear and socks in the trash, gave it all such finality. Was she up for it? Could she do it?

Then she thought about last night, and the drama in her life once the drama of *Masterpiece Theater* had ended.

She'd had nothing to do but flip through channels filled with inane programming, and contemplate another week of utter nothingness sprawled out before her. Before she'd realized what she was doing, Eleanor found herself in Richard's study, at his desk, logged on to his computer and the University of Chicago website. It hadn't taken long, merely four clicks, to find her.

Claire Anderson. Professor of Psychology, the faculty website read. Eleanor sat there a moment, staring in surprise at the small grainy image on the screen. She hadn't been sure what to expect. A femme fatale, perhaps. A beautiful blonde or a ravishing redhead. Richard had always had a thing for redheads.

What she *hadn't* expected was the woman with a mop of curly brown hair pulled back from her face and eyes that crinkled in a friendly smile staring out from the computer screen. And there was something else about her… something familiar. Eleanor leaned in closer, hoping for a better look, but clicking on the photo wouldn't enlarge it. She sank back in the chair with a sigh. Granted, Claire was attractive. Most women in their late twenties and early thirties were. But nothing about her screamed *homewrecker*! In fact, she'd looked like someone who'd be more comfortable puttering around at home rather than dallying on the arm of a married man. She didn't look threatening, Eleanor had decided as she continued staring at the photo. Not threatening at all… but rather nice.

Like someone she'd like to know. Someone she might be friends with.

Like *that* was going to happen!

Eleanor x'ed out of the website and shut down the

computer without even following the link to Claire's bio. Who cared about her credentials or how many degrees and academic accolades the woman had to her credit. Claire might think she'd fooled the outside world, but Eleanor had the inside scoop. She knew her for exactly who and what she was: a Rottweiler in disguise. Claire Anderson was smart and savvy, and she'd stolen Eleanor's husband.

Claire Anderson had stolen her life.

Damn them both. She didn't need the grief. Struggling to her feet, Eleanor headed for Richard's closet.

"Donating to Goodwill is a great idea," she said. "Let's start with his suits."

"It's nearly one o'clock," Martha said. "How about I make us some lunch?"

Eleanor, exhausted and beyond hungry, didn't put up an argument as Martha disappeared through the bedroom door. Standing alone, she surveyed the results of their three-hour marathon sprint. Who knew cleaning out closets could be so cathartic? Richard would be appalled at seeing his precious suits, his shirts and slacks, his three-hundred-dollar shoes, clumped in heaping piles on the bed. Everything goes, she'd insisted as they began. Martha had obeyed with a quiet vengeance, ruthless from the start as she rifled through his closet racks and drawers. Eleanor started with the same resolve, which quickly crumbled as the sorting brought her face-to-face with items that had memories of Richard clinging to them like a lingering hint of his signature cologne.

There was his favorite yellow silk tie, the one Vivi

had brought him on her first trip home after beginning her executive career in fashion and marketing for Grayson's department store in New York City. There in the far recess of his closet were the nondescript clothes and fatigue jackets necessary for his trips to Iraq. There was the bathrobe he rarely wore, the one with the ship's logo she'd purchased on impulse during their cruise to the Southern Caribbean some years before. She'd thought he would love it, that it would remind him of their time together on board, the tranquil blue waters, the balmy night breezes, the leisurely breakfasts spent dining on the balcony of their suite.

But it was the soft wool sweater with the suede elbow patches she'd bought him for Christmas a few years back, around the time Richie was born, that nearly brought her to her knees. Memories flooded through Eleanor as she remembered how Richard, in that sweater, had sat in front of their fireplace as Jeffrey had placed his newborn son— Richard's first grandson—in his arms. She swallowed over the growing lump in her throat, recalling how proud he'd looked as he'd cradled Richie in his arms, stroked his soft little cheek, placed a kiss upon his forehead. So different than when Jeffrey and Vivi had been babies and he'd treated them like porcelain dolls. But with Richie, Richard had seemed to know exactly what he was doing and had no fear. Perhaps the years had mellowed him, she'd decided, for it seemed Richard was a natural, as if he'd been born to play the role of grandfather.

Or perhaps had had some recent practice. That was when she remembered the other little boy who'd been born around the same time. Another baby. A little boy named Dickie.

Not Richard's grandson, but his son.

His son.

Her son.

Eleanor grabbed the last remaining armful of clothes from the closet and dumped them on the bed. Who cared if his suits were wrinkled? It wasn't as if he'd be wearing them again. Stomping to the door, she slammed it behind her. After lunch, she decided as she headed down the stairs, she would spend the afternoon collecting boxes so the stuff could be packed up and transported across town. The sooner his things were out of the house, the better. She felt the frustration churning in the bottom of her stomach like a bitter acid.

Good! Anger burned calories, and she was swimming on a wave of resentment guaranteed to burn off unwanted pounds.

The sun-splashed kitchen brightened her mood as Eleanor took her seat at the antique table they'd inherited from Richard's mother. She'd always loved that table, with its sturdy matching chairs and cozy circular design. Richard's complaints that it was old and shoddy and should be replaced had started when the children were babies. Though he'd continued to complain throughout the years, she'd never given in. Resting her hand on the surface, Eleanor traced one finger over the lines where a six-year-old Jeffrey had used his pencil to carve a tree, earning a rare spanking from his father. One person's junk was someone else's treasure. To her, the worn table was priceless, its well-polished surface heaped with memories. Her babies were gone now; how could she let go of her memories too?

"Eat," Martha ordered, sliding a plate in front of her.

The turkey sandwich on rye with ruffled lettuce leaf tasted like spongy cardboard and stuck to the roof of her mouth. She washed it down with a chaser of coffee laced with milk and plenty of sugar. "What happened to the mayonnaise?"

"Mayonnaise is fattening," Martha said, sliding into the chair across from her. "You told me you wanted to watch your calories."

It was one thing to say something; it was something else entirely to have it thrown in your face. Besides, what was wrong with mayonnaise? She liked it. Then again, Martha was merely doing what she'd asked. She watched as the housekeeper polished off her own sandwich, mayonnaise and all. The woman was a tough old bird with a wiry body and no need to lose weight. She was constantly moving, just like her tongue.

"Jeffrey phoned while you were upstairs. He wants you to call back. He said it's urgent."

Urgent. Once upon a time, she'd loved chatting with her son, but she was beginning to dread it. They used to talk about good things, like how Richie was doing in preschool, how Jeffrey's law practice was thriving and he might take on a partner, how he planned to surprise Susan on their anniversary with that special necklace she'd been wanting. But those lighthearted calls had died the morning she discovered Richard cold and stiff in bed beside her. Jeffrey had morphed into her personal prophet of doom, with every phone call relaying yet more difficulties, more obstacles, more financial trouble. Why couldn't things go back to normal? Why couldn't everything be the way it used to be? Life shouldn't have to be so hard.

It wasn't fair, Eleanor thought, choking down another bite of her sawdust sandwich. *At least let me have my mayonnaise back.*

How was she going to get through this? How did other people do this? She eyed Martha, popping the last bite in her mouth. "Do you like living on your own?"

"Are you kidding?" Martha chuckled. "Once those divorce papers were signed, I never looked back. It's been thirty years, and I don't miss him one bit. Anything is better than living with a deadbeat drunk."

Eleanor tucked away the sobering reminder. Everyone had their struggles. Martha's alcoholic husband had refused to put the cork in the bottle, and eventually Martha had refused to put up with him.

"Personally, I like living alone," Martha said. "There's no one around telling me what to do. I'm in charge of my life. Maybe it sounds selfish, but I like it that way. Being on your own, you can do as you please, sleep when you want, eat what you want—"

"Except mayonnaise," Eleanor couldn't resist adding, which put a quick smile on the other woman's face.

"Being alone isn't so bad. You get used to it after a while."

But she was already used to it. She'd grown accustomed to being alone years ago. After Jeffrey moved out and Vivi left for college, she'd rattled around by herself in the big empty house. It was lonely without them, especially with Richard gone so much. Business in the Middle East kept him away for weeks at a time.

Or had it? All those times she'd assumed he was traveling the deserts of Saudi Arabia or conducting business in Abu Dhabi, he might have been worlds away... or merely miles away. He might have been in Hyde Park, Illinois.

With *her*.

"Are you worried about living alone?"

Eleanor lifted her head at Martha's question. "I don't know."

It was an honest answer. How could she tell her how she felt, with things changing from one minute to the next? Sometimes she thought she knew what she was doing. Filled with resolve, she would promise herself that she was going to do something productive. She always had good intentions—until the mail was delivered. Sympathy notes from friends and Richard's business associates still arrived on a daily basis. Everyone was so kind, so compassionate. They offered their condolences, their support. *Please let us know if there's anything we can do.* They all thought of her as the grieving widow.

Little did they know Richard had left behind two grieving widows.

How would she handle it when people found out? How could she face them? No doubt they'd be sympathetic, Eleanor assumed, showering her with kind, supportive statements of obligatory outrage. Yet what exactly was obligatory in a situation like this? Bad enough she'd be forced to suffer the humiliation of knowing *they* knew what Richard had done. And once they discovered the truth, she knew their comments would be thoughtful and tactful. But what about their unspoken questions? What about those things they'd be whispering behind her back?

Poor Eleanor. Can you imagine? Her husband married to another woman. A younger woman. And with children! Little ones! How could she have not known? How could she have been so stupid? Then again, Eleanor never was that smart... or that attractive. I always wondered why he married her in the first place.

That was usually the time she gave up, wrapping herself in a cozy comforter and blocking out the chattering voices in her head by surrendering to her books and chocolates. Once, when things had been particularly bad, she'd even tried one of those little blue pills the doctor had prescribed. It had done a wonderful job of blocking things out, but she hadn't liked the way she felt when she woke up in the morning. Better to give up the pills and face things on her own than to feel sluggish and drained. It was hard enough getting out of bed in the morning. Every day seemed to bear great tidings of yet more bad news.

And Jeffrey's news today was the worst yet.

"The accountant and I have been going over Dad's business assets." His voice on the phone was strained. "There's some money available, but we have to take the outstanding debts into account. Once we pay those off, I'm not sure how much will be left."

Eleanor paused, struggling to accept the notion that Richard might not have been as astute a businessman as he'd portrayed himself to be. "What exactly are you saying?"

Silence sat between them like an unwelcome visitor.

"I wouldn't count on there being much left," he finally said. "I'm sorry, Mom."

Her heart sank. She was sorry too. Sorry about a lot of things. "It's not your fault."

"There's more," he added.

Eleanor knew from his tone that *more* wouldn't be good.

"I talked to the bank again this morning. They're willing to give you another thirty days to work things out."

"Work what out?" Phone in hand, she wandered through the spacious living room and foyer, outside onto the front porch. She closed the door behind her. Poverty needed privacy, and there was no need for Martha to hear any of this. She stared out over the lawn, wondering if she was shivering because of the abnormally cold spring they were experiencing or the topic they were discussing. "What exactly am I supposed to work out?" she repeated.

"The mortgage on the house. The payment hasn't been made since before Dad died. It's more than thirty days past due."

"How much are we talking?" The words stuck in her throat, but she forced them out. She had to know. There was no way around it. Even mayonnaise wouldn't help this situation.

"Three thousand dollars, plus another three due next week."

"Three thousand..." Her voice caught, blown away in a gust of cold air that whipped her words across the porch and lawn. She must have heard him wrong. There was no way that amount could be correct.

"The house's mortgage is three thousand a month," he said softly. "And there's no escrow."

"What's an escrow?" she asked, though she didn't want to know.

"The amount doesn't include taxes or insurance."

Three thousand dollars a month just to stay in her own home? Three thousand dollars to live in the house that had been hers since her parents had helped them purchase it nearly forty years ago? How was she supposed to come up with three thousand dollars?

"I don't have that kind of money."

She used to, but not anymore. Now *Claire Anderson* had the money.

"I don't want you to panic. I'm working with the bank. They're aware of your situation," Jeffrey said. "Hopefully we can get something worked out. Meanwhile, Susan and I talked it over last night, and we want to help you out with—"

"No. Absolutely not." Eleanor felt her shoulders stiffen. Some things were sacred. She didn't care how much she owed the bank or how desperate things were, she refused to take money from her son. It went against the natural order of things. Parents give; they do not receive.

"Mom, we have to be realistic. Susan and I are both working. We can afford to help. Let us help you out... at least for now."

"The answer is *no*. You're sweet to offer, but I can't take your money. I'll figure something out."

"How?" His voice turned suddenly steely, marching over the phone. "How do you plan to come up with six thousand dollars by the end of next week?"

Good question. Unfortunately, one for which she had no answer. Closing her eyes, Eleanor whispered a silent prayer. *Lord, help me.* God knows, someone needed to.

"Let us do this for you." His voice dropped, becoming gentle and wheedling. "I promise it won't break us. Plus, it'll give you some breathing room."

Eleanor gazed out over the sweeping lawn and gardens as if seeing them for the first time. She'd always been so proud of their home and the manicured grounds surrounding it. The house sat on a huge lot, nearly an acre, and a lawn-maintenance service took care of all the mowing and mulching. The crew showed up every week. They fertilized and pruned, they trimmed the hedges, leaving everything looking neat and tidy. But at what cost? Until today, she'd never given it a thought. But then, she'd never had to. Richard had taken care of the bills. She had no idea how expensive the lawn-care company might be. Would she be able to afford their services? Maybe she needed to cut back, ask them to come twice a month rather than once a week. That would save some money.

Then again, how could she pay their bill, when she couldn't even pay the mortgage?

"Mom? Are you there?"

She felt her resolve crumbling. Ever since he'd been a little boy, Jeffrey had known how to get around her. His offer was sincere, and his heart was in the right place. And what about that prayer she'd just sent winging its way to heaven? God answers all prayers. What if Jeffrey and Susan were the answer to her prayer? Accepting their loan wouldn't be the most terrible thing in the world. And it wasn't as if they intended to buy the house. They were simply helping her get back on her feet.

No, they were helping her *find* her feet.

"All right," she said, swallowing over her sorrow at the strange situation she'd found herself in. Two months ago, she'd strolled into Grayson's department store at the nearby mall and purchased a gorgeous silk scarf for Martha's birthday without even glancing at the price tag. Now, in merely a matter of weeks, she'd been reduced to one of those women who subsisted by accepting handouts from her children. "Thank you, Jeffrey. Once everything is settled, I'm going to repay you in full."

"Let's not worry about that."

She heard the relief in his voice. They'd dodged a bullet, and both of them knew it.

"I'll call the bank as soon as we hang up and transfer some funds. That will take care of things. And try not to worry. We'll get through this. I promise."

"I love you, Jeffrey."

"I love you too," he said, hanging up.

Eleanor stood on the porch another moment. Jeffrey had tossed her a life preserver, provided some breathing room while she found her way to the end of the pool. But she'd never been much of a swimmer. Somehow her bottom always weighed her down and she'd start sinking, without a clue as to which way was up. Jeffrey and Susan had come to her rescue this time. But what if they hadn't been there to help?

And what would she do next month? And the month after that? How would she pay her bills? What was she going to do?

Eleanor dragged in deep gulps of cold air, shivering as the wind whipped round her, nipping at her ankles, biting her cheeks. She should go inside, she thought, back to the kitchen. She should sit with Martha and have another cup of tea.

I should do lots of things.

Spinning around, Eleanor headed back inside. She strode through the hallway, kitchen, and mudroom. Martha eyed her as she reappeared, pulling on her jacket and snatching her purse from the chair.

"Where are you going?" she asked.

"To get some boxes." Eleanor didn't like lying, but she wasn't about to admit the truth. And at the moment, boxes were the furthest thing from her mind. Forget all that nonsense about donating Richard's clothes to Goodwill. She needed to raise some money, and fast. Maybe she'd have a yard sale. How much could she get for one of his suits?

Meanwhile, there was someone else out there with Richard's clothes hanging in her closet. Eleanor wanted to see this woman who'd wreaked havoc in her life.

She was going to see *her*.

Chapter Six

Richard had loved going to the mall. *A jaunty journey through the teeming masses*, Claire remembered him teasingly calling out each time they passed through the doors, causing her to roll her eyes. Hoisting Dickie on his shoulders, and her close beside him, pushing Sophie's stroller, he would march forward, leading them on yet another adventure. There was the jungle-safari store, he'd point out to Dickie as they passed Sharper Image with its display of binoculars crowding the window. There was the store run by gypsies, he'd hiss in a menacing whisper, causing Dickie to hold on tight, eyes wide agog as they sauntered past the tattoo parlor, a controversial new addition to the mall. There were the boutiques for social butterflies, the grandma stores with their matronly dresses, the shoe stores where the wannabe sports stars shopped.

And finally, with sacks and bags hanging from the stroller, they'd arrive safely at their ultimate destination, their family's favorite shop. Out would come Richard's wallet, which he always pretended was empty, much to Dickie's delight. *Silly Daddy!* he would crow, causing

Richard to laugh and suddenly discover some money after all. Soon they were snacking on soft twisted pretzels fresh from the oven. They would laugh and joke, relaxing on the blue cracked-vinyl chairs lining the corridor in front of the booth, indulging in the simple sport of people watching, sharing sips of Dickie's orange juice.

A simple Sunday afternoon spent at the mall, yet Richard had made it fun. He'd made it exciting. He'd made it special.

But it wasn't special anymore. In fact, it was downright hideous, Claire thought as they pushed through the mall doors. Coming here had been a bad idea, a huge mistake on her part. But Dickie needed new shoes, and she needed to get out of the house. She'd been hibernating at home, slinking around the corners of her kitchen and the garden, hiding from everyone save Hallie and Tulie. Even worse, she'd been hiding from her grad students. She'd have to make a decision soon about what she was going to do. She couldn't leave her students hanging. It wasn't fair to them. She'd always taken pride in her work, and they deserved a professor who was involved in their studies and in their lives. But how could she assist them, critique and review their work, give them guidance, when she herself was caught in the shadowy existence of a sadness that never seemed to lift.

They never should have come to the mall. Every corner they turned, every store they passed, was a reminder of everything they'd lost. Retail therapy wouldn't work.

She couldn't buy her life back.

She couldn't buy Richard's life back.

Sophie, in her stroller, strained forward, bumping her

sippy cup, which tilted, rolled, and hit the floor. Claire scooped it up and stuffed it in her bag, causing Sophie to wail, making Claire feel like crying too. Her daughter was too young to comprehend what had happened, but Dickie knew. He'd understood that first night when she'd tried to explain about heaven being such a long trip for Daddy that he wouldn't be coming home anymore. Dickie pulled at the stroller, his scowl spreading as he tugged her forward, past the jungle-safari shop, now simply an electronics-equipment store. His eyes darkened and his frown deepened as they passed the tattoo parlor. With Richard gone, there were no more gypsies at the mall. Only an odd assortment of ragtag shoppers on a Monday afternoon... including them.

Especially them.

She purposely picked a giant retail store they rarely frequented. Fewer memories to chase away. Fewer ghosts haunting each aisle. She steered toward the shoe department, intent on finding something quickly so they could leave. But Dickie refused to cooperate.

"No." With a swift kick, off came the Velcro sneaker she'd struggled to slip on his foot. "Don't like it. Don't want it."

He grabbed the grungy gray fireman sneaker he'd worn all winter and scrambled to jam his foot back inside. "Don't want new shoes."

Claire sat back on her heels, wishing she were anywhere but where she was. Poor little guy. She didn't blame him for being mad.

"Your feet are growing," she said, trying to reason

with him. "If we don't buy you new shoes soon, your toes will pop out. You don't want that to happen, do you?"

His lower lip trembled and the thundercloud that had been racing across his face finally exploded in a furious roar. "Don't want new shoes!"

With a violent swing, he flung one of the sneakers across the aisle, hitting the arm of an elderly woman passing close by.

"I'm sorry," Claire said over Sophie's shrieks and Dickie's shouts of protest. "Are you all right? He didn't mean it. He's... upset."

The woman's lips pursed and her eyebrows rose. Turning sharply, she whipped her cart around and hurried away as if they'd contaminated the aisle. She hadn't said a word, but it hadn't been necessary. Women are excellent at nonverbal communication, and the elderly woman had a doctorate. But Claire had her own PhD and knew exactly what the woman was thinking... and she didn't blame her. If she'd stumbled across some whacked-out woman and her out-of-control kids, she'd be thinking the same thing too. *What is wrong with this woman? Her children are little monsters. What kind of mother is she?*

But her children were *not* monsters. They were simply upset. They were all upset. Claire grabbed Dickie's arm, tighter than she intended, which instantly increased the intensity of his howls. Immediately she dropped her hold. What was she doing? She was the worst kind of mother. *She* was the monster.

"I'm sorry, sweetheart." Claire reached for him again, but instead of falling into her arms, he cringed and pulled away. God, what had she done? He was wearing his sporty spring jacket, so it was impossible to see if she'd left a bruise or mark. The mere thought of hurting one of her babies made her stomach slide sideways in a queasy lurch. She pressed the palm of her hand against her forehead, trying to push away the ferocious headache suddenly throbbing between her eyes. How could she have done it? Dickie's face was blotchy, his nose red. Tears spilled across his cheeks as he rubbed his arm. His brown eyes, normally so open and trusting, were filled with fear, anger, and accusation. She hated herself, and she hated the way he was looking at her. It was a look she was coming to recognize more and more in the past week or so as he began to realize how much their lives had changed, that Daddy was gone, that she was all that he and Sophie had left.

They were stuck with her.

Dickie's wails were gone and his lower lip trembled. He stared at her another moment, searching her eyes, then suddenly threw his little-boy body against her, collapsing in her arms. He buried his head against her shoulder. "I wanna go home."

"Okay." Claire pressed him gently against her, taking care not to hurt him as she rubbed his back. She felt his warm little body, so precious and vulnerable, his thin little shoulder blades under her hands. She held him close, grateful that he didn't resist and pull away.

"I'm sorry, Dickie," she whispered. "Mama is sorry."

She was sorry for them all.

The large, roomy SUV buffered them against the blustery

wind as she made the final turn toward home. The streets of Hyde Park were notoriously narrow, and the crowded on-street parking made for a navigational nightmare. Claire maneuvered her way past nearby homes filled with unknown neighbors, finally reaching their house in the middle of the block. With a driveway and detached garage, it sat on prime real estate, mere blocks from the university.

What must her colleagues and students be saying? Everyone must be wondering what was wrong with her. No one knew what had happened. She hadn't even told the dean. He only knew there'd been a family emergency and she needed some time.

How could she tell them? What was she supposed to say? No doubt they would have been full of condolences, wishing to share her grief. They would have wanted to attend the funeral.

What a joke. *She* hadn't even attended Richard's funeral.

Claire yanked the wheel and pulled into the driveway. The SUV bounced against the uneven pavers lining the path, bumping a memory of a discussion she and Richard had had. He'd wanted to have them replaced last fall, but she'd talked him into waiting until the spring snows melted. Why hadn't she listened to him when he wanted to do it? Why hadn't she indulged him? Now it was too late. The muddy snowbanks had finally melted, but Richard was gone.

Parking the car near the front porch, she unsnapped Sophie from her car seat. Dickie had already managed to unlock his seatbelt and scramble out of the car.

"Wait for me," Claire called as he scurried across the

sidewalk toward the porch. As she turned back to Sophie, she noticed movement inside a car across the street. The older-model Mercedes was parked at an odd angle. A woman sat behind the wheel. Even from a distance, Claire knew the driver was watching her. She didn't recognize the car, or the woman, either. But something about her, the intensity of her face, the unrelenting stare, made Claire suddenly uneasy. She swung Sophie into her arms and closed the car door with a hard bump of her hip.

"Dickie," she called out sharply over her shoulder, "stay where you are. Stay on the porch and wait for me."

The door of the Mercedes opened. The woman swung one leg out of the car.

Who was she? What did she want? Claire didn't intend to hang around and find out. She scurried up the front steps, juggling Sophie in one arm, her purse and keys in the other.

"Get in the house," she urged Dickie as she fumbled with the lock. "Now. Go!"

Shoving him inside, she was right behind him. Slamming the door, she bolted the lock. She threw herself against the door, pressing her back against it, praying that when she turned around, the woman and her car would be gone.

Who was she? A reporter who'd somehow discovered her secret? It was a lurid tale, exactly the kind of story the press loved. A hidden love nest in Hyde Park. A respected professor, schooled in the workings of the human mind, duped by a man. She rested her head against the door, closing her eyes, cursing herself for having been so stupid.

How could she have allowed herself to have fallen under his spell?

He'd pressed her to marry him when he'd found out she was pregnant.

"I won't take no for an answer," Richard had said. "So don't let that analytical mind of yours start running full-tilt, dreaming up all sorts of reasons why marrying me is a bad idea. Because it's not a bad idea... and we *are* getting married, whether you like it or not. Though you *will* like it," he added. "I promise you will like it."

She remembered him running his hand slowly up her arm, lingering against her throat, lifting her chin with one finger, tilting her face, forcing her eyes to meet his.

"Marry me, Claire. I promise you will never be sorry."

Oh, God. Was she sorry? There'd been so many good times. But this? This wasn't good. This was horrible. Richard—the man whom she'd thought was her friend, her confidant, her lover, her husband—had allowed them to live a lie. Their life together had been nothing but a lie.

How could he have done it?

"Mama?" Dickie tugged at her arm. "Mama, what's the matter?"

Opening her eyes, she looked down and forced a smile for her son. How could she tell him the truth? She'd already injured him once today. It would be wrong to hurt him a second time, simply to indulge herself. She was the grown-up. It was her job to protect him from the big, bad, scary things in life. But she was scared too. She wanted to run away, to hide, to be left alone. And she didn't want visitors. She didn't want curiosity seekers. And she certainly didn't want publicity. She cared nothing about herself, but she did care about Dickie and Sophie. Bad enough this had happened. She refused to allow it to destroy their lives.

"Nothing's wrong, sweetheart. Nothing" She plastered a bright smile on her face. "Go play with your trucks. Go play on the sun porch," she urged as Sophie wiggled from her arms. Claire pushed her toward him. "Take your sister and go play."

He opened his mouth, but she cut him off before he could protest. "Pizza tonight," she promised. "Pizza tonight if you go play right now."

Dickie's eyes brightened and he grabbed Sophie's hand without a whimper. Claire waited until they disappeared down the hallway and out of sight. Sinking against the door, she silently began to pray. She prayed harder than she'd ever prayed in her life.

Let her be gone. Please, please, whoever she is, let her be gone. Make her go away.

She stood there, her stomach sliding sideways as she waited to hear the knock on the door. Her hands trembled, and her purse slipped from her grasp, falling to the floor. It settled by her feet on the gleaming hardwood stained with sunlight. Her heart pounded inside her chest, and she dragged in a ragged breath, trying to calm her nerves, steady her breathing. What if the woman was on the porch? What if, when she turned around, she found the woman staring at her through the beveled glass? What would she do then? Did this qualify as an emergency? Could you phone 911 in case of an emotional emergency? And this certainly qualified. She felt as if she were in the middle of a breakdown. She'd always prided herself on being a strong, capable woman, competent at managing things on her own. Her marriage to Richard never would have worked if she hadn't been able to manage on her own.

Claire crumpled against the door. Her marriage to Richard? How could she be married to a man who was married to someone else? She wasn't a widow. She was nothing but a fool. Richard had played her for a fool, and their so-called marriage was nothing but a sham, a fraud. She'd been hiding out for days, but she couldn't hide any longer. Whoever she was, the woman outside knew her secret. If she didn't do something, the world would know too. She had to do this. She had to face her. She had the children to protect.

Somehow her brain connected with her feet, and she found herself moving. With a deep breath, Claire turned to face the door. Her heart raced as she forced herself to look.

No woman. No face glaring at her through the beveled glass. The porch was empty. Claire glanced across the lawn, the street. The Mercedes was gone.

Her legs gave out, and she slumped against the wall, sliding to the floor. She sat there, breathing heavily, thinking about what had happened... what could have happened... what probably would happen.

How long before the woman showed up again?

Chapter Seven

"It would be for a few days," Susan suggested, glancing at Jeffrey, who nodded. "Or as long as you want. It's no inconvenience. We have that spare bedroom, and you could stay until you get your feet on the ground." Her face softened. "We're worried about you."

"You are both loves," Eleanor said, looking up from her dinner plate. The two of them were so kind and generous, already loaning her money to pay the mortgage, inviting her to join them for dinner as often as she wished. This offer to stay with them had touched her beyond belief. How could she turn them down without seeming ungrateful? She loved them both, but the last thing she wanted was to move in with them. She wanted to be by herself, in her own house, surrounded by her things. She needed time alone to nurse her wounds, to overcome this horrible sensation, this absolute certainty that she'd done something wrong... that Richard reaching out for someone else, for another woman, had been her fault. Everyone understood, on some basic instinctive level, that death eventually would come calling... but no one ever expected it when it happened. Richard's heart had been fine. He'd experienced no symptoms of cardiac distress. There'd been no warning signs. The last thing she'd expected to find when she woke up that spring morning was him dead in bed beside her.

And she'd never expected his death to wreak an aftermath of tragedy—emotionally, financially, psychologically, physically—such as she was experiencing.

Eleanor pushed a piece of chicken breast around on her plate. "I went to see her the other day."

"Went to see who?" Jeffrey asked.

Honestly? Did he need it spelled out for him? She felt the tug of frustration inside, like a silver thread that might snap at any minute.

"You know... that professor." Eleanor couldn't bear to use the other term. Claire didn't deserve it. It wasn't a legal marriage. *"Her."*

Jeffrey's mouth fell open as he dropped his fork. It clanked against his plate. "You did what?"

"I wanted to see her," she said. It probably hadn't been the best idea she'd had in her life, but it wasn't as if she'd done anything wrong. Besides, why should anyone care? If anything, *she* was the one who had been wronged. She'd done nothing to deserve what'd happened to her life. Yet she was the one forced to live with the shame.

Stabbing another piece of chicken breast with her fork, Eleanor calmly chewed another bite. No wonder Jeffrey was putting on weight. Susan was a wonderful cook.

"Swear to God, Mom, sometimes I don't understand you—"

"I wanted to see what she looked like. Why is that so difficult to understand?"

And why should he care? It wasn't as if she'd pulled a gun on the woman. Although surely it would have been justifiable homicide. What judge or jury wouldn't be sympathetic to a woman who'd found herself betrayed by her husband after thirty-eight years of marriage? Anyone would understand. Yes, they probably would have found her guilty, but Eleanor doubted they'd have sent her to prison. Perhaps a mental institution for a little rest. But would that be so bad? A bed to sleep in, meals served on a regular basis... and no mortgage to worry about. Yes, she was certain no one would have blamed her if she'd gone to see *that woman* with criminal intent. But she hadn't. Instead, all she'd done was taken a little drive.

"I wanted to see what she looked like," Eleanor repeated, not that she thought it would sway Jeffrey's thinking. "I wanted to see what Richard saw in her."

"And did you?" Susan asked from across the table.

Eleanor nodded, keeping the secret locked away in her heart. When she'd checked out the university website, she'd thought Claire had looked vaguely familiar. But the picture had been grainy and outdated, and she hadn't been able to place her. Up close and personal, Eleanor had immediately recalled the face from her past.

No wonder Richard had been attracted to Claire. Tall, lithe, with a swag of brown curls framing an open, angular face, she bore a striking resemblance to Richard's former fiancée.

Eleanor picked at her chicken, chewing on the memory that she hadn't been Richard's first choice. His mother,

Julia, had been best friends with her mother, Genevieve, since they were young girls, and their families had grown up together. Eleanor couldn't remember a time she hadn't known Richard. He'd always been in her life. But the five years between them made a difference when they were growing up, and Richard had rarely given her more than a passing glance. He'd always been polite, making it a point to mind his manners and treat her nicely, especially when their mothers were around. She remembered him always rushing with somewhere to go, friends to see, or to pick up his date.

And back then, Richard had plenty of dates. The girls loved him, and it was little wonder. He was handsome, with thick glossy hair, dark, flashing eyes, and a cleft in his chin that gave him a delicious devil-may-care look that had the girls flocking round him. If he were any other young man, mothers would have warned their daughters. But Richard was Richard, and his mother was Julia Anderson, of the Rockport Andersons, an old and established family. Everyone loved Julia, and no one questioned the motives of her son. Especially not Eleanor.

Even as a little girl, she'd found Richard amazing, and with no trouble could recall the first time she'd thought of him in *that way*. She must have been eleven, for that would have made him sixteen and old enough to drive. Car keys jingling in one hand, he brushed a swift kiss against his mother's cheek, and with a round of good-byes for them all, off he went in his tennis whites for a late-afternoon game with the cute young thing who happened to be his girl-of-the-moment.

With Richard, there were always girls. Young girls,

older girls. Eleanor sat on the sidelines, yearning to grow up faster so as to catch his attention. While she loved her books, she would have willingly dropped them on the floor to grab her tennis racket and play a game with him. She lived for the thrill, hoping and praying that someday Richard finally would notice her. Then he went away to university, where he met a girl. *The girl*. And all the other girls faded from Richard's radar.

"It's serious," Eleanor remembered Julia confiding to her own mother. Curled up on the couch with her nose in a book, she wasn't noticed and kept on listening. "They're in love," Julia continued. "He asked her to marry him, and she accepted. A wonderful girl; perhaps a little flighty, a little pretentious... but from a good family. They're to be married right after graduation. Richard doesn't want to wait, but her parents insisted," Julia added. "A long engagement, but at least they'll have time to plan. It will be a grand wedding."

Eleanor slipped quietly from the room, out into the garden. Tucking herself under a tree, she hugged her knees, buried her face, and wept for what she didn't have and never would. Richard was marrying someone else. He'd be lost to her forever.

But fate has a funny way of twisting and turning what one would assume is a smooth path lined with fragrant rose petals. As it turned out, his fiancée wasn't nearly as interested in Richard as he was in her. Graduation came and went; the engagement was called off, then they reconciled. Eleanor watched and waited as the years went by and still he wasn't married. And then she was a college student herself.

"What will you study?" everyone wondered. "Social work" was her automatic reply, thinking them silly to even ask the question. She would dedicate her life to working with the poor and disadvantaged in south Chicago. Working with the underprivileged... wasn't that what privileged people were expected to do? But the racial riots of the late '60s left Eleanor terrified and rethinking her decision. She wasn't the kind of girl who got involved in radical protests, dabbled in psychedelic drugs, or embraced free love. She had no desire to be a part of the social-activist movement of the '70s, either. She'd been raised to be a good girl, to follow the rules and not let loose.

Her decision to teach came as a relief to her parents and Eleanor as well. There was nothing threatening about teaching elementary school, and her first-grade classroom was a safe haven, a sea of milky-white faces, squirming little boys and girls wriggling in their seats exactly like she had twenty years ago. Her school, in a neighboring suburb only five miles from the house where she'd grown up, was convenient and safe. Eleanor was an adult, earning her own income, but sometimes it felt as if she hadn't left her childhood behind. Then again, that might have something to do with the fact that she was still living in her parents' home.

Then somehow, someway, she and Richard ended up together. She was never sure how or why it happened, but when to her—and everyone else's—great surprise, he asked her to marry him, Eleanor accepted without hesitation. After all, wasn't that what she'd been waiting for all her life? To grow up and marry Richard? She'd always loved Richard and she always would. Within six months, they were married and settled in the Lake Forest home her parents helped them purchase as a wedding present.

Being with Richard gave her courage, strengthened her self-assurance that she was someone of worth, someone who could make a difference in the world. She was proud to be the one he'd chosen. So what if she'd been his second choice? What did it matter that he'd proposed only after being thrown aside by his college sweetheart? She, Eleanor Anderson, was the one who would wear his wedding ring and carry his name. She was the one who would comfort him, who would see to his needs, who would bear his children. So what if she chose to give up her career? Many of her friends did the same. True, others kept their jobs and managed to raise a family too. But when the children came along, Richard insisted she was needed at home more than in the workforce.

At first, she disagreed. But as the months went along, his argument made sense. Jeffrey was a colicky baby. She spent most of her nights on her feet, cradling him in her arms as she walked the floors with a screaming newborn. Even after Martha was hired to help out, things didn't get easier. Jeffrey fussed and screamed whenever he was put down. "Quit babying him so much," Richard advised time and again, socking a pillow in frustration as the whimpers evolved into cries, then full-blown screams from the nursery down the hall. "Let him cry it out; he'll get it over it." But she couldn't do it. The mere sound of her son crying created an anxiety that brought panic rising in her throat every single time. What was she doing wrong? Why was she such a horrible mother?

Every night was the same, and by morning her nerves

were frazzled and her energy exhausted. Up all night with Jeffrey, then struggling to keep up with a class of energetic first graders. By evening, she was at the end of her rope, and by the close of the school year, she gave the school her notice. Then Vivi was born, and with two little ones underfoot, her time was suddenly no longer her own. Richard liked her being home with them, and it seemed easier to go along with what he wanted.

Besides, there was nothing wrong with being a homemaker, in putting her needs aside to provide a warm, loving environment for her husband and children. Wasn't that what being a wife and a mother, a woman, was all about? She and Richard had grown up in a similar fashion. Neither of their mothers had worked, and both of them had seemed content and fulfilled as women.

Although, sometimes being the mother of two small children scared the bejesus out of her. How could she be sure she was doing things right? What if she made a mess of things? Her babies were healthy, but would they be happy? Would they grow up to be kind, generous, loving individuals? Productive members of society? The kind of people who made a difference in other's lives? Wasn't that what a successful life was all about?

And carrying it further, what kind of difference was she making in people's lives? She'd never doubted it while in the classroom, teaching little ones, helping them to learn their numbers, to make sense of jumbled words on the page. At the end of the school day, she felt as if she'd accomplished something. Once, shortly after Vivi was born, with both children down for their afternoon naps, she broke down and confessed her fears to Martha.

The Other Wife

Hunched in her seat at the kitchen table, Eleanor sobbed like some strung-out teenager instead of a woman in her late twenties who should have her life in order and know what she was doing. Bless her heart, Martha never said a word, but simply made them both cups of tea, then sat and listened, patting Eleanor's hand, making her feel better.

Yet sometimes she'd found herself with a restless longing for something more. She hated herself for having those feelings. Didn't she realize how lucky she was? She was married to the man she'd always adored. She was Richard's wife, mother to his children. They shared a beautiful home where she was surrounded by fine things, living a life most women only dreamed of.

But sometimes, in the still of the night, especially after they'd made love, she would lay there open eyed, staring at the ceiling, listening to the sound of Richard's quiet breathing beside her. And as she listened, she would wonder, asking herself: *Why me?* Why *had* he married her? Richard could have had anyone he wanted. She would think of all the girls who had been a part of his life, and she would remember the one girl who had tossed him aside. Richard wasn't accustomed to being tossed aside. He was the chosen son and everyone's favorite. For years, he'd been that girl's favorite, only to fight, make up, and then fight again. Eventually she'd returned his ring; then, much to everyone's surprise, she'd married someone else a few months later. Richard never spoke about it, and Eleanor loved him too much to question him, to bring up something from the past that would hurt him. He wasn't used to being second in someone's life. Cut adrift, he'd returned home for some TLC.

Why had he married her? Maybe because she knew how it felt to always finish second. Maybe because he had an inherent need to be number one in someone's life. Maybe because he'd known that, with Eleanor, there'd never be a question of whether she loved him or if she would leave him.

If anyone would do the leaving, it would be Richard.

"Did she see you?" Jeffrey asked, snapping Eleanor from her reverie. "Did you talk to her?"

"No. I never got out of the car." Though she almost had, Eleanor remembered, reliving the scene from yesterday. She'd gripped the steering wheel, said a quick prayer for strength, then swung her legs out of the car, with every intention of marching up the sidewalk, onto the front porch, and confronting her. But in the end, she hadn't. The startled look on the woman's face had stopped her, as had her quick, wary movements as she pulled her children from the car.

Her children. *Richard's children.*

Eleanor slammed away the thought, just as Claire had slammed the car door and scurried onto her porch. She'd been afraid, Eleanor realized. In some ways, the two of them were alike. She was afraid too. Richard had two other children... children he obviously had loved very much.

"All finished." Richie pushed away his plate and scooted off his chair.

"What do you say?" Susan asked.

"Ex-coose me, please," he said, his tongue sticking against the rough spot where his missing tooth should be. He jutted his chin, flashing his other teeth and showing off with the healthy attitude of a child secure in the knowledge that he's surrounded by adults who love him.

Jeffrey and Susan exchanged glances, rolling their eyes.

"Go on then," Susan said. "You're excused."

Richie slid Eleanor a cheeky grin, causing her heart to swell with love. Her grandson had already lost a baby tooth, most of his baby fat, and was growing taller every day. Soon he would be lean and lanky, like Jeffrey had been as a little boy. He scooched toward her, allowing her to cuddle him with a quick hug and kiss. Then he was gone, darting from the dining room like any self-respecting four-year-old who had toys to play with, books to read, and worlds to conquer... worlds which didn't include grown-ups.

Jeffrey lifted the bottle of merlot and tipped it toward his mother, but Eleanor shook her head. He poured another glass for himself, but instead of drinking, slumped back and stared straight ahead.

She recognized that look on her son's face. It was the one he always wore when something was wrong. She glanced at Susan, who averted her eyes. Something was up. Eleanor straightened in her chair. "What's wrong?"

He ran a fingertip around the edge of his glass, then finally looked at his mother. "I had a phone call from Vivi today. She wants to know when she can expect her check."

"Excuse me?" She felt like Richie, asking permission to state the obvious.

"She wants her money." Jeffrey downed half his wine in three quick gulps. "The money Dad left her in his will. She wants to know when you're going to pay her."

Susan had the grace to look embarrassed. Eleanor had no clue what her own face looked like, but she was certain it couldn't be half as bad as how she felt inside. Her heart pounded like the steady clang of a hammer slamming against an anvil, her thoughts racing in concentric circles that never intersected, and her stomach swirled in a wild mix of nostalgia, nausea, and bits of chicken breast. It took a few moments before she managed to compose herself.

"What did you tell her?" she finally asked.

"That she has one hell of a nerve." There was a sharp edge to his voice that Eleanor rarely heard. "That I'm embarrassed to be her brother. That she ought to be ashamed of herself, bringing up the question of money. You're going through a difficult time. She has no right."

"Your father left her the money." Eleanor struggled to keep her voice level. "He left both of you money. In fact, he left *all* his children money."

"You can't be serious." Jeffrey sat back, his eyes wide. "You're not thinking about paying out an inheritance to those other kids? They weren't named in his will."

"He never named any of you," she reminded him. "He simply said, *each of my children*. And unless you plan to try and prove otherwise, they're also his children. The money also belongs to them."

How could she do it? She hated the thought, and she didn't want to do it. Yet, according to the provisions of Richard's will, those two little ones she'd seen the day before were each due ten thousand dollars. How could Jeffrey not understand that? She wasn't a lawyer, but even she knew that a will was a binding legal document.

Eleanor thought for a moment, considering the

ramifications of what she was about to do. Jeffrey would be mad. Vivi would be furious. *Are you crazy? Don't be stupid.* How could she do it? She barely had enough money as it was. Yet her heart told her it had to be done. If those children she'd seen belonged to Richard, giving them the money was the right thing to do.

"I want you to contact... her." Try as she might, Eleanor couldn't say the name aloud. "Let her know about the provision in your father's will."

"We do not want to do that," he countered in a firm voice.

"Why not?"

"Because it would be conceding the point. If I contact her, as your attorney, and provide her with a copy of the will, we'll be admitting liability and you would owe her children money. It would be a debt you'd be obligated to pay."

"I intend to pay it." Hopefully there'd be some money left from Richard's business. In any case, it didn't matter. Things would work out.

"Why are you being like this?" He stared at her, shaking his head. "I don't get it. It's crazy."

But it wasn't. Knowing what he'd done, that Richard had had another family out there, was like having a sore tooth. She'd suffered from a toothache the previous winter and done her best to ignore it. She hated going to the dentist and had put it off as long as she could. But the ache was constant. Worse, she couldn't keep her tongue from straying to the sore spot. She'd gingerly test it, only to discover that, *yes*, it still hurt. It hurt every day. Eventually she'd made a dental appointment and had the tooth fixed, bringing instant relief.

How long before this ache went away? Maybe Jeffrey was right. Maybe she couldn't fix the situation by throwing money at it, as she'd done with a simple visit to the dentist. Maybe the tooth should be yanked.

Jeffrey hunched forward. "Mom, stop and think what about you're saying. It's ridiculous."

"Your father's will—"

"For Christ's sake, forget the damn will. They weren't even married. For all we know, they're not even his kids."

Oh, but they were. The minute she'd laid eyes on that little boy yesterday, looking so like her grandson Richie, she'd known they were Richard's children.

"Jeffrey, why are you bringing that up again?" Susan asked quietly.

"Because the whole thing stinks." He glared at his wife, then back at his mother. "Look, I'm your attorney. It's my job to protect you. As your attorney, my advice is to do nothing. The less involvement we have with her, the better. And I further advise that we do not provide her with a copy of the will."

"I'm sorry, Jeffrey, but I disagree." Eleanor's heart pounded. The last thing she wanted was to battle with her son. "Send her a copy of the will. Let her know that we'll be in touch about the money."

"Do you realize you're talking about twenty thousand dollars?" He stared at her a long moment. "You give her that money, and you'll be wiped out."

Eleanor nodded numbly.

"Great. Just great." He threw up his hands, and turned

to Susan. "Would you please try and talk some sense into her? She listens to you."

"I think you should honor your mother's wishes." Rising, Susan stacked the dinner plates. "It's her money and her life." She snatched up the silverware and threw it atop the plates.

The clinking put Eleanor in mind of tiny tremors in the massive family earthquake she was causing. Weren't things bad enough? Did she have to create a rift in her family too? Now Jeffrey and Susan were arguing, with her son talking about her as if she weren't even there.

Jeffrey's face darkened from a bright red to a deep shade of purple as Susan disappeared into the kitchen. "Great," he muttered. "First Vivi and now those damn kids." He turned to his mother. "This is an ugly mess that's getting bigger every day."

Reaching out, she laid a hand atop his, squeezing gently. "But it isn't your mess," she quietly reminded him. "It's mine."

His hand tightened around her own. "We're in this together, Mom. You got a raw deal." He shook his head. "After what you've been through? You shouldn't have to be dealing with something like this. What Dad did? Dammit, it's not fair."

"Life isn't fair, not for a lot of people. I never expected it to be fair," she said, knowing full well it was a lie. The truth was, she'd expected, assumed, that her life would be perfect. For years, it had been. Yes, there'd been difficulties, but she'd learned to deal with them. She'd turned a blind eye to Richard's working so hard, to his being gone so much of the time. She'd learned to lean on people like Martha, turning to her for help around the house and also her personal needs. And once her children had left home, her life had begun to revolve around books and her volunteer work at the library. Even when Richard was home, those rare occasions that the two of them coexisted in the house for days at a time, she'd learned not to count on him. He wasn't the kind of man you could hold on to. If you tried too hard, he'd suddenly be gone, leaving behind disappointment and heartache. So she'd learned how to let go, how to offer up a cheek for him to kiss good-bye as he departed on yet another of his frequent trips.

Their marriage hadn't been perfect, but it had worked. For thirty-eight years, she'd made sure it'd worked. Now all she had left was a burgeoning pile of troubles growing higher every day.

Eleanor suddenly felt soft lips grazing her cheek. She searched her son's face as he drew away, her heart melting with pity as she recognized his pain. How could Richard have been so uncaring and neglectful? Hadn't he given any thought as to how his alternative lifestyle, his financial decisions, would affect Jeffrey and Vivi? He'd loved his children.

"I feel so damn sorry for you," he said. "You were a good wife and a great mother. You don't deserve this."

Poor Jeffrey. He didn't deserve it, either. Leaning into him, Eleanor wrapped him in a soft hug. "Don't worry," she said. "Everything will be all right."

But even as she said the words, she knew that wouldn't be the case.

Chapter Eight

"This is a rather awkward situation." Maximilian Vilbrandt, department chair of U of C's psychology department and her direct superior, cleared his throat and eyed Claire over a steaming mug of tea.

She nodded across the table, contemplating her own tea. At her request, they'd met off campus, but she still felt fragile and exposed in the little corner café where they sat, mere blocks from the university. It'd been weeks since she'd been on campus. Probably everyone knew the truth by now. The spring quarter was nearly finished, and the summer session would be starting soon. Part of her mourned the thought, knowing she wouldn't be there. She'd always relished the few months of summer when the university emptied out and only grad students roamed the quad. With no classes on the calendar, it was a time to sit back and contemplate courses, pore over theses, collaborate about upcoming research projects.

But not this year. Not this summer. How could she face her students and fellow professors when she couldn't bear to face the truth herself? She'd purposely avoided straying anywhere near campus on the off chance she might bump into someone she knew. She didn't feel up to answering questions.

"Rather awkward," she agreed.

In the few years he'd reigned over their department, she'd found Dr. Max to be honest and fair, though a bit distant. For someone trained in the workings of the human mind, he could be oddly detached from evoking human emotions. Did he have any idea how awkward she felt, sitting with him, facing the facts? Facts not of her own making, but facts that couldn't be denied.

"I'm sorry to have put you in this position," she added. "I'm sure it's been difficult, trying to find someone to cover for me. But everything happened so fast, and I... I didn't know how to cope."

His dark face reddened, and Claire realized she'd embarrassed him. Did he think she was trying to play on his sympathies? The mere thought embarrassed her, as did the realization of where they were meeting, huddled in a dark corner of a coffee shop blocks from campus. Weeks ago, she would have chosen a prominent spot at a window table overlooking the world and the steady stream of people hurrying past with things to do and places to go. Not long ago, she'd been one of those people, filled with energy and plans. Now all she had was regret and remorse.

He cleared his throat and put a hand to his head, smoothing back his graying dreadlocks. Milli Vanilli, Claire thought, remembering the wisecrack Richard had made behind Dr. Max's back when she'd first introduced them. But Dr. Max did resemble one of the aging pop stars involved in some music scandal back in the '80s.

And while his hair was manageable, his hand constantly strayed. Did Dr. Max realize he did it? How many people react in a subliminal fashion, oblivious to what they're doing?

Claire gathered a deep breath. Wasn't she guilty of the same? How could she have been blind to the fact that Richard was keeping such an enormous secret? How could she not have known? How could she have been so stupid?

"I think any of us would experience the same reaction." Dr. Max clasped his hands together, pointing his fingers upward in a perfect arch, resting them under his chin. His dark eyes held their usual somber expression as he stared at her. "Have you made any plans? Do you have any idea what you intend to do?"

"Not yet," she admitted. "It's been difficult, trying to adjust. My first priority has been the children."

"Yes, naturally." He nodded in sympathy. "How are they?"

"They seem to be coping," she replied, grateful for that small favor. Children were resilient and took things in stride. Perhaps it was because so much of the world was beyond their control. "They were used to Richard being away. I doubt Sophie notices much. She's still a baby. But Dickie is four years old. He knows."

Claire paused, thinking of her son. Such a smart little boy and growing smarter by the day. More than once he'd caught her crying, though she'd tried to hide it. He recognized the silence in the house. He knew things had changed. He knew their world had shifted. "Dickie understands that Daddy isn't coming back."

"What about you? Are you coming back?" Dr. Max asked.

The question caught her by surprise. "I... I don't know."

"Summer session is starting soon. You won't have any classes to teach. I'm sure we can work something out to accommodate your needs."

"That's... that's very generous," she stammered. "Thank you."

"I don't mean to sound presumptuous," he said quietly, "but if there is anything the university can do to help..."

"No, I'm fine." Claire rushed to reassure him. "Financially, things are fine. He left us... he provided for us quite well."

The house was paid off, and she had a comfortable salary. Plus, with the insurance proceeds from Richard's policy, there was—or soon would be—money in the bank. Enough money to cover all their needs for many years to come.

"If you decide you want the leave of absence, we can make that happen. I'll arrange to have the paperwork drawn up. But I'll need an answer about the fall semester."

"I understand." Claire cupped her hands around her mug as if the tea could provide comfort and warmth. *A leave of absence.* Is that what she wanted? Could she do it? Walk away from her students, her classes, her research? A few weeks ago, those things had encompassed a huge part of her life.

A few weeks ago, Richard had been a huge part of her life.

"Do you have any idea how long it might take you to make a decision?"

Dr. Max was asking for answers she didn't have. It had taken her a half hour to pick out her clothes that morning. Her thoughts were random, a constant cacophony swirling through her mind. Her world had shrunk to the basic essentials. Her children. Fresh food to keep them fed, clean clothes to keep them warm. As for the rest? It would have to wait.

"I'll try to have an answer by the end of the week," Claire said, noting as he glanced at his watch. Their conversation was finished. He had places to go and things to do, while she had nothing more important than to head back home. Her time was her own, stretching out before her like waves lapping against the shore of Lake Michigan, washing across her toes as she stood on the edge of the sand, scanning the horizon. But the storm had already arrived, and the waves were building, crashing in a great crescendo that had swept her out to sea, her body and soul tossed and battered, bruised and broken.

And the storm wasn't over. Eleanor was out there somewhere.

It wasn't over by far.

Claire watched as Dr. Max left, winding his way between the crowded tables and out the door, headed back to the university, to his classes and his students, to the kind of life that recently had been hers. After he disappeared, she sank back in her chair, more depressed than when she'd arrived. Would it always feel like this? Gray skies and dark water ahead? She was accustomed to brilliant blue landscapes and the glorious radiance of hot sunshine beating against her skin. To the sound of her children's laughter. To Dickie's exuberant shouts of "Mama, watch me!" as he climbed higher on his swing, and Sophie's delighted crowing as she discovered the spring blooms in their backyard, plucking them, one by one, presenting Claire with a lopsided bouquet.

Where have all the flowers gone?

"You need this chair?"

She glanced up and found five students staking a claim on a nearby table for four. One young man had his hand on the chair recently vacated by Dr. Max.

"Do you need the chair?" he repeated.

"No, go ahead."

But he was already in motion. Grabbing the chair, he hauled it away and joined his friends.

"No one is using it," Claire added under her breath.

She sat there another moment, watching and listening as they sprawled out in comfort, laughing and chatting amongst themselves. Loud and noisy, their energy spilled around the room, spurred on by the excited exchange of ideas and an overload of caffeine. *Once upon a time*, she mused, *I used to be like that.* Sometime in a former life, she'd been one of them.

When had she exchanged her beloved coffee for a soothing cup of tea? When had she stopped sitting in a window seat and started lurking in the shadows?

More important, how would she find her way back?

"You need professional guidance, Claire. You're not thinking clearly."

Daniel Mitchell had a reputation as an excellent attorney, or so Tulie informed her when Claire had told her about the letter she'd received. Hadn't her family been through enough? Did she want to put herself through what could prove a long and public courtroom battle?

Under protest, she'd made the appointment, though she'd privately dithered about keeping it. But Tulie's words on the phone last night had led her to the attorney's office today.

"I love you, Claire, and I'm worried about you. You can't go on like this. You need help."

Did she need help? Maybe with the children, Claire conceded. She'd been forced to bring them to the appointment since Hallie had an exam scheduled and was unavailable. Then her scheduled appointment time had come and gone with Mr. Mitchell's receptionist apologizing for her boss's tardiness, citing a prolonged court hearing. Though every instinct urged her to grab her babies and bolt, Claire had forced herself to sit there, playing with Dickie and Sophie as they awaited his arrival. Finally, an hour later, he'd blown into the office, cursing the court system in one breath and introducing himself in another as he ushered Claire into his inner sanctum.

"You're the first client I've had in this particular situation," he commented as she finished leading him through the facts as she understood them. "Quite unique."

One dead husband and two very-much-alive wives. *Unique?* An understatement, if she'd ever heard one.

Through the closed door to the outer office, Claire heard the muted strains of children's chatter. Why hadn't she thought to arrange for a babysitter? The receptionist, an older woman with twinkling eyes and a kind smile, had offered to keep an eye on them, and Claire had reluctantly agreed. Hopefully Dickie and Sophie weren't making a mess and wreaking havoc or the receptionist would hate her.

If I were her, I'd hate me too.

Mr. Mitchell cleared his throat. "You do realize that if all this had been discovered while he was still alive, he would have been guilty of a felony."

"A felony?" She swallowed around the raw edges of fear rising in her throat.

"Bigamy is considered a felony in the state of Illinois. It's punishable by up to three years in prison."

"They would have put him in jail?"

Richard had been so fastidious about the way he dressed. The thought of him in orange prison garb made her stomach flip in a queasy yawn.

"Obviously, that's no longer an issue."

She couldn't bear to witness the guilty verdict written on Mitchell's face. What had Richard been thinking? He'd committed a crime. People had been wronged. Lives had been shattered. Their children would be forced to live with the shame for the rest of their lives. How could he have done it? Had he actually believed he wouldn't be caught?

But he hadn't. He'd escaped, scot-free. For four years, they'd lived together as husband and wife. Now he was gone, and she was left alone to deal with the aftermath of his sins. But what choice did she have? There were Dickie and Sophie to consider. She was all they had left. Her poor babies. What kind of lives could they look forward to? One parent, mortally accused of wrongdoing, and the other, guilty of stupidity and naiveté.

"What about me?" If there were any possible ramifications, she had to know now. She had the children to protect. "Am I also guilty of a crime?"

Mitchell's eyes narrowed and he hunched forward, regarding her with a stare so intense it made Claire squirm. Behind him on the wall, a sleek, modern pendulum clock ticked away the minutes. "He never told you he was married?"

"No." She shook her head emphatically. "I had no idea."

She'd taken Richard at his word. She'd trusted him. He'd never given her reason not to. She'd been inexplicably captivated by him from the moment they'd met. Her field of study was confined to academia, but Richard's field of study encompassed the world. He was well-read, well-traveled, and he'd offered a life filled with promise and hope, excitement and adventure, passion and romance. He'd given her all that, and more. He'd been a good man.

He'd been a good liar.

"If what you're saying is true—"

"It is," she assured him. "I didn't know."

"If you believed he was free to marry you, then you committed no crime. You're a victim, the same way she is."

The statement confused her. Did he mean Sophie? But what about Dickie? Her little boy was involved in this too.

"Have you had any communication with Mrs. Anderson?"

But I'm Mrs. Anderson.

And then the obvious returned, slipping in to take the seat beside her. Claire's spirits sank. How could she have forgotten? There was another person involved in this scandal. Another woman. Another wife.

Claire shook her head. "No, we haven't spoken."

"Don't assume that will continue to be the case."

She felt the frown tugging at her forehead. Why would Eleanor Anderson want anything to do with her? They meant nothing to each other. "You think she'll try to contact me?"

"I'm sure she's been advised against it, but there's no telling what she might do. If there's one thing I've learned in my years practicing law, it's that you can never predict how a person will react, given a certain set of circumstances. She might fade away and you'll never see her face... or she could go ballistic and be all over you." He sat back and eyed her thoughtfully. "Has anyone been around?"

"I... I don't know." Yet even as she spoke, Claire's thoughts returned to the woman she'd spotted in the parked car outside her house that day. At the time, she'd thought her to be a reporter looking for an exclusive, bent on exposing lurid details about Richard and their children. Yet she'd never approached the house, never knocked on the door. Claire found herself wondering, had that been Eleanor? Had the woman been Richard's other wife?

"Regardless, I expect you'll be hearing from her attorney."

"I already have." Fumbling through her purse, Claire pulled out the creamy envelope. The crisp, embossed letterhead in the left-hand corner still made her stomach clench as tightly as the day she'd spotted the envelope when it arrived in the mail.

Jeffrey R. Anderson, Esq. *Richard's son.*

She slid the thick envelope across the desk, then sat back and waited.

Mitchell briefly scanned the letter, then flipped to the attached legal document. He studied the pages, paying particular attention to the same paragraphs Claire assumed were the ones that had caught her eye. Some minutes passed before he finally glanced up.

"If this will is valid, it would appear that each of your children stands to inherit some money."

Claire nodded. "That's what I thought. But the tone of the letter is so cold and impersonal. He makes it sound as if I'm some horrible woman who stole his father's—"

"Don't worry about him." Mitchell dismissed her comments with a quick wave of a hand. "It's Legal Maneuvering 101."

"But he's also her son," she pointed out, remembering the terse two-paragraph missive. Succinct, noncommittal, yet with a menacing undertone. It wasn't hard to read between the lines. Jeffrey Anderson was daring her to try to collect the money. "It made me nervous. He makes me nervous."

"I'll send out a letter advising him to back off. Meanwhile, try not to let him get under your skin."

"I don't want my children hurt." Dickie and Sophie would always be her number-one concern. She could afford to take care of herself, but she couldn't afford them to be hurt. "I'll do anything to protect them."

"Anything?" He sat back in his chair.

"Anything," Claire vowed fervently. "Anything."

"You do realize they'll probably fight you on this."

"I'm not sure I follow." She halted, suddenly confused by his line of questioning. Richard's will—at least the part addressing bequeaths to his children—seemed simple and straightforward. "The will states that each of his children is to receive ten thousand dollars. And Dickie and Sophie are his children—"

Mitchell shrugged. "It's your word against theirs. They could—and in all probability, will—choose to dispute the fact. Since you weren't legally married, there's no proof they're his children."

"But that's ridiculous!" She gripped the arms of her chair. "Of course they're his children. Richard is listed as their father on their birth certificates."

"Excellent," he said smoothly. "But who filled out the paperwork?"

"What do you mean?"

"Information for the birth certificates. Someone provided it to the authorities. Did he?"

Claire halted, suddenly realizing the meaning behind his words. "No," she admitted. "I did."

He nodded. "You see my point. Just because you named him as the father doesn't mean it's true. They'll use any legal ramification that works in their favor."

She blinked rapidly to force back the tears pricking behind her eyes. "Richard is their father."

"I believe you. But I want you to be prepared if they choose to force the issue. You could be facing a proof of paternity suit."

"Proof of..." She sputtered into silence. Richard would

be appalled to know his children's names were being dragged through the mud by another of his children.

No, not his son. Not Jeffrey Anderson. There was no doubt in Claire's mind as to who was responsible. It was Eleanor, the other woman. *She* was to blame.

"Granted, this is merely supposition on my part," Mitchell said, "but I suspect they'll take you to court if you attempt to collect on your children's inheritance. If they decide to push the paternity issue, each of the children would need to submit to blood testing."

"You can't be serious." Some meddlesome nurse poking for blood from her babies' arms? Both of them hated needles, especially Sophie. She'd screamed for what seemed hours after her last booster shot. Claire couldn't imagine subjecting her, or Dickie either, to that kind of torture simply to prove something she knew was true.

"On the contrary, I'm dead serious," he said. "The will is not specific. It simply states"—he flipped through the document, halting to trace his finger along a line mid-page—"*and the sum of ten thousand dollars to each of my children.*" He glanced up. "Notice that it does not name names."

Claire's gaze strayed to the wedding ring on his finger. Did Mitchell have children? How would he feel if this had happened to him? What if his wife had had an affair, gotten pregnant, then lied and told him that the child was his? How would he know if it was the truth? How did anyone know about the things that people did in their lives? Things from the past that couldn't be undone. Mistakes that were made.

My children are not mistakes.

"If they don't intend to honor Richard's bequest, why did they send me a letter and a copy of his will?"

"I don't know," he admitted. "It doesn't make much sense."

"I don't care about the money," Claire said firmly. "I don't need it, and I don't want it... especially if it will cost my children pain. I will not allow those people to make a mockery of them and what their father and I had together."

"That's your decision. But you might want to think it over before we provide them with an answer."

"Didn't I make myself clear?" Her voice caught. "I don't want the money. I don't need the money. And I especially don't want my children involved."

"Unfortunately, they're already involved." Pulling the green file toward him, he consulted it for a quick moment. "You're named as the sole beneficiary of the life insurance policy. Is that correct?"

The words brought a chill running up Claire's spine. "Yes."

"A policy worth millions," he added.

She nodded. Any words she had were caught in the vise grip of fear that had hold of her throat, relentless and unforgiving.

"Regardless what you do about your children's inheritance, don't be surprised if she comes after the insurance money."

"But... but that money was left to me. Richard wanted me to have it. It was meant for our children, to help them have a better life."

And they deserved it, every penny. Their lives would be a mess, thanks to the secret life Richard had led. She scrambled to recall exactly what Jim Kennedy had told her that night he'd visited the house. "The insurance agent said that the money was mine, regardless of... of the legal situation."

"I understand. But let's consider her situation." Consulting the green file, Mr. Mitchell pointed to the printout of the online obituary Claire had provided him. "She was married to the man for thirty-eight years. They had a house. They had children."

"But we do too." Her words rushed out like a spent balloon, zipping round the room, splashing against the brilliant spring sunshine flooding his office. "Richard and I have a house. And children," she added, straining for sounds of Dickie and Sophie in the following room. But all was quiet. Had the receptionist found coloring books for them to play with? Sophie was still in the crayon-eating stage. Hopefully Dickie had enough sense to keep an eye on his sister.

"We have"—Claire stopped, correcting herself—"we *had* a life together. Richard and I were married for four years."

"No, you weren't," he said bluntly. "Whatever he told you, whatever you may have thought or believed at the time, your marriage is invalid. There's only one Mrs. Anderson. She's his widow, and she's the one entitled to any benefits."

Didn't the man have any compassion? How could he be so unfeeling? Clutching the arms of the chair, Claire started to rise. "I think today was a mistake—"

"Wait." His eyes softened. "Sorry, I didn't mean to offend you. You're upset. And I'm being a jerk. My wife's always telling me I need to slow down and think before I speak."

Something in his voice, the way he looked at her, knowing he had a wife that he listened to, gave Claire pause to reconsider. Slowly she sat down.

"Good." He blew out a strained breath. "Look, I realize this is difficult for you. It's a terrible situation. He's dead, you have children. Naturally your first concern is for them. But my job is to help you understand the law. According to the state of Illinois, you were not legally married."

He pushed a box of tissues toward her, but Claire ignored them. She was beyond tissues and tears.

"I understand," she said, though it was a lie. Because she didn't understand. She didn't understand how any of this could have happened. She didn't understand how she could have believed him. Was she that stupid?

It had all been a lie. Their marriage, their family, their life together. Had Richard thought she would never discover his secret? Had he assumed he'd get away with it forever? Or perhaps he'd planned on introducing them at some point. His first wife and his second, meeting over coffee, or perhaps a glass of wine. No, something stronger. "This calls for a slug of whiskey," her dad would have said. Claire closed her eyes, trying to ward off the pain of remembering her parents and how much they'd loved her. They'd been so proud of her and had had such hopes and dreams for her life and for the difference they'd believed she would make in the world.

"You okay?" Mr. Mitchell came around his desk and perched before her on one corner. His eyes were a stark, brilliant blue, filled with care and concern.

"Yes." If at first she'd thought he was judging her, she no longer did. She had nothing to fear from this man. He was her lawyer. He was on her side.

"All right, that's it, then." He stood, started toward the door. "Let's keep in touch."

But there had to be more. Claire gathered her purse, tucked it under her arm, rose from her chair. "What do I do now?"

"Go home and think about everything I said." He reached for the door with a quick, open smile, but his face did not follow. His eyes were somber and his tone serious. "Meanwhile, let's see what they do next. If anyone tries to contact you, tell them they need to speak with your attorney." He offered his hand, signifying their session was finished.

"And if they do?"

"Contact me, and I'll take it from there."

Claire nodded, wondering which side would make the first move.

Let the waiting game begin.

Chapter Nine

"Life turns on a dime," her father had been fond of saying. Eleanor had always thought it an odd phrase. How could you fit your life on the thin edge of a dime? And why a dime? Why not a quarter? But given the recent circumstances of her life, she'd discovered it was true. Give a dime a good spin and it'll twist and flicker so fast you barely have time to notice before it flips and falls to the floor. And so it goes with life. One minute someone had been taking care of her, and the next thing she knew, she was flat on the floor.

A dirty floor, especially since Martha would no longer be around to mop it.

"I'll miss you." Watching Martha load the special cleaning supplies in the canvas bags she'd brought from home was painful. Not that Eleanor begrudged Martha carrying away the items. Most of them belong to her. Martha had always preferred to clean with the products she purchased from an eco-friendly online company run by one of her neighbors. "I wish I could afford to keep you on," she added, "but it's not possible."

"Don't worry about me." Martha tucked the bottles in her bag. "I already picked up another job. I'll make out fine."

Martha might, but Eleanor wasn't sure about herself. Not only was she losing her housekeeper, she was losing her house. *What's done is done, and there's no way around it*, so Jeffrey had informed her a week ago when relaying the news she'd been both expecting and dreading. The bank intended to call in the note on the house. There was nothing to do but to let it go. She couldn't afford to keep it.

Life turns on a dime. She'd need plenty of dimes—millions of dimes—to buy back her old life.

Martha heaved the last tote onto the counter and turned to face her. "That's it, then."

"Stay and have a cup of tea?" They'd always shared a cup of tea after Martha finished her tasks. Eleanor was loathe to see her go. She'd been a part of her life for more years than she could count. Every Monday and Friday, and sometimes more often if they'd had something planned and people coming in. But her entertaining days were long gone. Once Martha walked out that kitchen door, Eleanor would be alone.

Martha sank into one of the kitchen chairs with a weary oomph. Beads of sweat popped across the bridge of her nose. Pulling a tissue from her pocket, she mopped her face. "It's going to be a warm one today. Make sure the filter on the central air unit is cleaned and working properly before you turn it on."

"I'll have someone take a look at it," Eleanor promised, though she had no intention of doing so. Why bother telling her the truth? No more central air-conditioning for her. One more bill she didn't have the money to pay. Besides, there was no telling how long she'd be staying in the house. Jeffrey had been in contact with a realtor who was coming tomorrow with the paperwork to list the property. *It's easier to sell an empty house*, Jeffrey had told her. Who knew what would happen? She could be gone as early as next week.

"I know it's none of my business," Martha blurted out, "but if you ask me, this whole thing stinks. You're a good woman. You don't deserve this."

"I suppose none of us really know what's going to happen in our lives, do we?" She stirred a little sugar into her peppermint tea, then added a bit more, watching it dissolve into the fragrant brew. The teaspoon clicked softly against the flowered bone china that had belonged to her grandmother, along with the antique buffet which housed the rest of the set. Eleanor used the china on a daily basis and handled it with loving care. Amazing that it had survived the years without a single chip or crack. It was exactly the type of thing people marked as a true find at an antique consignment shop. Even better, it would probably fetch a pretty price on eBay.

What was she thinking? Eleanor recoiled, realizing how far her thoughts had wandered. The thought of letting her grandmother's china go to a stranger made her sick to her stomach. She quickly dumped another heaping spoonful of sugar into her tea. God knew her life could use a little sweetening.

"Have you made any plans?"

"Sell the house." That had to be her number-one

priority. The longer it sat on the market, the higher her debt grew. And according to Jeffrey, she was drowning in debt. Not a good situation for someone who'd never been a strong swimmer. She was treading water as best she could, floundering in the deep end of a pool not of her own making.

"This is a big house. I can't see you packing it up by yourself. Give me a call when you're ready. I'll help. And you don't need to worry about paying me," Martha added. "I'll do it for free, on my days off. We'll have a regular gabfest."

Eleanor swallowed hard over the sudden lump in her throat at Martha's generous offer. Their relationship had evolved throughout the years over many cups of tea from an employer and hired help to a deep, enduring friendship. Martha had been with them since the children were small, and she'd never hesitated to speak her mind, something that irritated Richard to no end. S*he has no business interfering in our lives,* he'd fumed one day years ago over some trivial matter regarding the children that Martha had remarked upon. *Why don't you get rid of her?*

Instead, Richard was the one who was gone.

"Thank you, Martha," Eleanor said softly. "I appreciate it."

She bobbed her head. "We'll get it done."

"It will take a while. There are lots of things that need to be packed."

"What about the kids? Genevieve coming home to help?"

"I don't know." Thinking about her daughter introduced

a sour note to the sweetness of the moment. "She isn't happy about the house being sold."

Vivi wasn't happy about a lot of things, including chatting with her mother, it seemed. Their telephone conversation the night before had ended with Vivi hanging up without even so much as a good-bye. Eleanor couldn't understand it. She'd done her best to be polite. She'd talked at length about the steamy weather New York was experiencing, inquired as to how her daughter's job was going, asked Vivi about her recent trip to Europe for the following spring inventory. She'd even gone so far as to broach the subject of the man in Vivi's life and how she hoped they could someday meet. Isn't that what a mother should say? Isn't that what Richard would have done? Then again, Richard had probably already met him.

So much for the close mother-daughter relationship she'd always hoped to have. Some things simply were never meant to be. At least Susan didn't find her an utter bore. Thank God for Jeffrey's wife. What a blessing in her life.

"There's nothing to do about it. Jeffrey says I don't have a choice. I'm out of money and out of options."

Never had she imagined she'd be reduced to this. Somehow her life had morphed into the plot for a Lifetime TV movie—a poorly written one at that. Too bad she couldn't sell her story to Hollywood, Eleanor mused. She could use the money. She needed to find something, some way, to support herself. And when the house sold, she'd need a new place to live. That wouldn't come cheap. She'd have to find some way to pay the rent. She'd need to find a job.

"I'm so depressed."

"You need to find some balance in your life," Martha said firmly. "When's the last time you were at the library?"

"I don't remember." She'd always been an avid supporter of their public library and loved her job as director of volunteers for the children's section. She especially loved her role as "the Library Lady." Every Tuesday morning for the past four years, she'd spent an hour reading to the children who came to visit. But she hadn't been to the library in weeks. Their friends and neighbors patronized the library. How could she face them? By now everyone must know what Richard had done. How he'd played her for a fool and how naïve she'd been. How she'd never had the slightest clue about the other woman in his life... his other wife.

"They must miss you. You did that work for years."

Eleanor grimaced at the irony behind Martha's statement. Yes, she'd worked, but as a volunteer. Now her time was no longer her own. She couldn't afford to give it away for free.

"Something wrong?"

She shook her head. "Just thinking to myself."

"Know what I think?"

Eleanor was almost afraid to ask. "That woman needs to keep her opinions to herself," Richard used to say when one of Martha's homespun platitudes threw him into yet another fit of frustration. "Why doesn't she just dust and then go home?"

"I'm glad I'm no longer working for you."

Eleanor's mouth gaped open. Martha was glad to wash

her hands of her? How could she say that? Here all along she'd thought they were friends.

"Don't look at me like that. Listen, if I were still working here, I wouldn't feel right saying what I'm about to say. But now it doesn't matter. You might not want to hear it, but maybe it's time you did. I think you need to quit feeling sorry for yourself. It's been nearly two months, and you're moping around like you're the one who's dead and buried. Yes, you got a raw deal. What that man did to you was beyond cruel... not to mention illegal. But you can't let what he did pull you down. That was his mistake, Eleanor, not yours. You're stronger than that. You're better than that."

Was she? Eleanor found herself wondering.

"And that woman he married? If I were you..." Martha's eyes narrowed and she clamped her mouth shut.

"You'd what?"

"Let's just say she wouldn't be sitting pretty like she is right now," Martha finally said, clucking her tongue with disgust.

Eleanor chuckled to herself. Martha hadn't been shocked when Eleanor confessed about the drive-by she'd done. And yet Eleanor had to admit there'd been a certain thrill at spotting Claire, seeing her so spooked. Maybe she should do it again.

Then again, maybe she shouldn't.

What was wrong with her? She'd always taken pride in her ability to keep her emotions in check. But she no longer trusted herself. One minute she felt calm and in control, and ten minutes later would be dissolved in a puddle of tears, wondering how she'd face the days, weeks, months and years bleakly stretching out before her.

Maybe if she were still in her thirties, or even her forties, it wouldn't seem so scary. But she'd be fifty-eight in a few months, with the big sixty looming around the corner. They say you're only as young as you feel. Today she was feeling every single one of her years.

"Never mind. That woman will get what's coming to her in the end," Martha said. "Meanwhile, remember that everyone has problems. Some people don't talk about them. One of my friends has a sick grandchild with chronic asthma. That poor baby is in the hospital on a regular basis. Her parents both work, but they don't have medical insurance. You don't hear them whining and complaining. And my neighbor lost his wife, Effie, to cancer last year. They'd been married over fifty years. No children. After she died, he was all by himself. He has the macular degeneration thing going on in his eyes. It was hard on him, learning to get around without her. But eventually he started making a new life for himself. He goes to the senior center, plays cards twice a week. He even joined the low-vision group. And he's got a girlfriend now... at eighty-five years old!"

A sly grin spread across her face. "That old geezer has turned into quite the dapper gentleman. He told me Effie made him promise he wouldn't sit around moping after she was gone. He took life and grabbed it by the balls. Maybe that's what you need to do to."

"Me?" Eleanor's laugh caught in a strangled sob. "How am I supposed to do that?"

"You can start by giving yourself some credit."

Reaching across the table, Martha took her hand. "You're a smart woman, Eleanor. You're kind and decent, and generous to a fault. Everyone loves you."

She could no longer hold back the tears. It had been so long since anyone had said anything nice to her. She needed to hear the words. Richard hadn't loved her or he never would have done what he did.

But Richard hadn't known the real her. And she needed to be reminded of who she was.

"Don't make it harder than it has to be." Martha clutched her hand and squeezed it hard. "You'll get through this. You're educated, you have family and friends. I know things seem bad now, but it will all work out. You have your whole life before you to figure things out."

Maybe Martha was right, Eleanor decided. Maybe she could do this. Maybe with the help of her family and friends, she could pull herself through.

But she wasn't ready yet.

First, she needed to figure out how to grow herself a set of balls.

Chapter Ten

Claire held herself together with a Band-Aid and a prayer by staying detached and focusing on her family. There was a comfort to be found in the minutia of daily life that children offered. Surrounded by Matchbox cars and juice boxes, following schedules built around morning trips to the park, afternoon naps, and nighttime rituals of reading fairy tales, it was easy to fall into a make-believe world that had a semblance of reality. But a part of her—the cognitive part she couldn't shut down—knew it wasn't true. That would be faced soon enough, when—or if—she returned to campus. Everyone at school would want to enfold her, circle the wagons round her, pull them tight, protect her at all costs.

But what if she didn't go back? There was no need, at least for now. The money had arrived. Three million plus, after taxes. She remembered how her hands had trembled a few days earlier when she'd taken delivery of the envelope that held the insurance check. What did people do with that kind of money? "You have to secure the children's future," the financial advisor she consulted had advised. For now, the majority of the funds were invested in securities and government bonds. Against his advice, she'd held back a few hundred thousand and placed it in the bank. It was accruing minimal interest, but it comforted her to know the money was readily available should the need arise. Dickie's tuition for the upcoming year at Lab nursery school was due soon.

Though whether she could convince Dickie to go remained to be seen.

"Not going!" he hollered, landing a swift kick against the sleek black leather ottoman that Richard had loved. "Stupid school."

"Quit being such a silly-billy," she said, trying to tease him into a better mood and tamping down the fear rising in her throat as she witnessed his explosion. It was Dickie's official second temper tantrum of the day. He'd always been a good-natured little boy. But as time passed with the days stretching into weeks following Richard's death, the cheerful little boy who used to live at their house had grown moody and sullen, his normal sweet smile replaced by a scowl.

"You love school," she said. "Of course you're going."

"Am not!" he shouted, giving the ottoman another kick. "No school!"

Sophie, snuggled in Claire's arms, regarded her brother with an owl-like stare and popped a thumb into her mouth. Gently, Claire pried Sophie's hand away from her face, kissing her fingers one by one. They'd broken her of the pacifier habit long ago. She never sucked her thumb anymore. "No, Sophie. You're a big girl now. Big girls don't suck their thumbs."

"No school!" Dickie shouted, kicking his bare feet against the floor. "Won't go!"

Claire took a deep breath. "But everyone goes to school. Daddy went to school, Hallie goes to school, Tulie goes to school—"

"You don't," he said, his eyes dark and accusing.

She opened her mouth, then snapped it shut. What Dickie'd said was true. How could she be expected to set an example for her son when she hadn't been to school in weeks? There were probably cobwebs in the corners of her office.

Sophie fought against Claire's grip on her fingers, then threw back her head and began to howl. Wearily Claire gave up and let go. She didn't have the strength to fight both her children. Immediately Sophie's wailing ceased— it was impossible to cry with a thumb in your mouth. She stiffened against her mother as she noisily sucked her fingers, her big round eyes brimming with leftover tears as she watched Claire with a suspicious stare.

Claire felt like crying too. She didn't blame her daughter or Dickie either. Her children no longer trusted her, just like she no longer trusted herself. But she didn't dare break down. Her tears would come at too great a price. Her children depended on her, and they looked to her for support and strength. She was the adult. She was the one who was supposed to be in charge.

"I have an idea." Without looking, she grabbed an oversized children's book from the basket beside the chair. "Let's read for a while. Reading is fun."

"Not fun!" Dickie shouted, giving the ottoman another kick for emphasis.

Claire flipped through the well-thumbed book of favorite nursery rhymes. Sophie snuggled closer and after a few pages, pulled her fingers from her mouth, plastering them on a particular bright image.

"Mary had a little lamb." Claire slowly pronounced each word. *"Whose fleece was white as snow. And everywhere that Mary went, the lamb was sure to go."* She swallowed hard, took a deep breath. She could do this. She could get through this. *"It followed her to school one day—"*

"Not going to school!"

But Dickie's voice wasn't as strident as before. Claire ignored him and kept reading. After finishing the tale of Mary and her lamb, they flipped through another few pages of bright images and familiar verses, Sophie choosing her favorites and Claire happily giving in to her demands. She read about the three blind mice, and her voice grew stronger. It climbed in strength and tone as the itsy-bitsy spider crawled up the water spout. Dickie crawled on his belly, kneeling in front of her rocking chair. By the time she finished Sophie's next choice, he'd crawled into the chair with her. Claire scooted to make room for him and, for the first time that day, allowed herself to breathe. Closing her eyes, she cuddled her children, inhaling the fragrance of baby shampoo as she kissed the tops of their heads. She could do this. It would be all right. Concentrate on each day, on each hour, each moment. One day at a time.

"More stories," Dickie said, grabbing the book and flipping through it.

Sophie's wet finger smudged a page, landing on top of

The Other Wife

the fat little man with the bright bow tie, round egg face and body to match. "Dis," she demanded.

Claire glanced down at Dickie. Though he couldn't read all the words, he was smart and knew the rhyme. "Want to read it to us?"

Wriggling in the chair, he held the book high and straightened his back with an air of self-importance. *"Humpty Dumpty sat on a wall,"* he chanted. *"Humpty Dumpty had a great fall. All the king's horses and all the king's men couldn't put Humpty together again."*

Sophie pulled her fingers out of her mouth and beamed. "All bwoke."

"That's right. Humpty broke." Claire patted Sophie's chubby little thigh and squeezed Dickie's shoulder. "Good job." He was growing up so fast. He already knew all his letters. Soon he'd be able to put them together and read the words too. Claire planted another kiss on his head, but he turned his back on her.

"Hey, sweetie. It's okay." Laying a hand on the small spot between his shoulder blades, she began to rub his back. His sturdy little body grew rigid under her touch.

"Dickie, what's wrong?"

Finally he turned, lifting a solemn face toward her. His brown eyes were troubled. A small frown replaced the eager childish smile of moments before.

"Humpty is just like Daddy," he said. "Daddy broke too."

Just as she'd thought she'd finally begun to breathe again, the air whooshed from her in one heavy gasp. She tried to find a way to breathe around the pain. Her children stared at her with big round eyes, waiting for her response.

She had to say something. She had to make it right. They were her babies. She was their mother. She was the one who was supposed to have all the answers.

But what did you say when you were searching for the answers too?

"You're right." She finally managed to find her voice. "Humpty broke into pieces because he fell off his wall."

"But Daddy didn't have a wall," Dickie reminded her. "Why did he break?"

She sifted through her thoughts, frantically scrambling to find the right words. This was the first time since Richard's death that Dickie had spoken of it without screaming or crying. Finally she decided to go with the truth.

Taking Dickie's small hand, she raised it, placing it upon his chest. "Do you feel that?"

Stilling for a moment, he cocked his head and listened, then stared up at her with big round eyes. "It's like a ticktock inside me."

Claire nodded. "That's your heart beating. We all have hearts inside us. You, me, Sophie—"

"Did Daddy have a heart?"

Did he? She'd thought so for the longest time.

Oh, Richard. How could you have done it?

Her own heart was breaking, but she didn't dare surrender to the sorrow and the memories of the life they'd shared and the pain she still felt every time she thought about the life he'd shared with Eleanor. It was too great a hurt. If she allowed herself to give in to the grief, it would overwhelm them.

Steeling her resolve, Claire forced a bleak smile.

"Yes, Daddy had a heart too," she said. "Everyone has a heart. That's what keeps us going. But sometimes, for no reason, they just... stop. That's what happened to Daddy. His heart broke."

Dickie sat for a moment, quietly pondering her words. "The king's men tried to fix Humpty," he finally said.

"The doctors tried to fix Daddy too." No matter all the trouble Richard had caused, she didn't want her children thinking he'd gone down without a fight or that he'd voluntarily chosen to leave them. No matter what kind of a man Richard had been, what sins he'd committed, or why he'd chosen to do the things he did, one simple truth could not be denied. He'd loved his children. He never would have done anything to cause them pain.

"The doctors did their very best," she said, "but Daddy's heart was too broken to fix."

Dickie nodded. "He was like Humpty. They couldn't put Daddy together again."

"That's right, sweetie." Claire nodded. "Just like Humpty."

Sophie crowded across her lap and pulled at the book. Flipping the page open to the next rhyme, she shoved the book into her mother's hands. "'Nother," she demanded.

Claire stared at the colorful images swirling on the page: the little boy with metal pail in hand and the little girl with the golden curls trudging up the hill beside him.

Jack fell down and broke his crown, and Jill came tumbling after.

Richard had fallen off his wall, and there'd be no putting him together again. But what about her? Was she doomed to always feel like this? Like she was about to spill down the hill and come tumbling after?

She couldn't read anymore. She no longer trusted her voice.

Claire closed the book. "I think we've had enough stories for now."

Squirming out of the chair without protest, Dickie headed for the Matchbox cars scattered haphazardly around the room. If Richard had been there, he would have joined Dickie on the floor, sprawled out beside him. Though he hated clutter, Richard had never lost his patience when it came to the children. He would have spent time with Dickie, zipping the cars along the gleaming floor into what would eventually become an orderly replica of a racetrack, neatly parking them in a garage. Dickie never would have realized they were cleaning up a mess.

But Claire didn't care. If it kept him happy, Dickie could build racetracks all around the house. He could make all the messes he wanted. Who cared what he did as long as he was happy?

Somehow she needed to find the road back to happiness too.

Sophie yawned and then, popping her fingers back in her mouth, snuggled close to Claire. Tucking her chin atop her daughter's head, she closed her eyes and began to rock, allowing her thoughts to drift.

Humpty Dumpty sat on a wall. Humpty Dumpty had a great fall. For more than four years, Richard had sat on that wall, balancing between two lives, two wives, two families. Somehow he'd manage to keep his secret and keep them all ignorant of the man he was. Hadn't he realized that sooner or later he would be found out? That people would discover his secret? Or had he assumed he was above it all? Had he thought he could manage to live a double life with one family in Lake Forest and the other only forty miles away?

How could he have done it? And *why* had he done it? That was the cruelest thing of all... the missing part of the puzzle, the piece that had fallen through the cracks. It was something she'd have to live with for the rest of her life.

Why had he done it?

She would never know.

Chapter Eleven

"I thought I'd stop by after work and see how things were going." Susan, in a creamy yellow buttercup suit totally appropriate for her job as a creative consultant for a marketing firm in downtown Chicago, looked cool and composed despite the scorching heat of the early summer day. She glanced around with interest at the rows of tables set up inside the garage. "Can I help?"

"No, but I'd love the company." If Jeffrey and his wife hadn't told her they were pregnant, Eleanor would have had no clue. Susan didn't have the slightest hint of a baby bulge, but the news that another grandchild was on the way had lifted Eleanor's spirits. It was as if their family had been given a chance at a new beginning. "Have a seat. I'm nearly done."

Her garage sale started the next day at nine a.m. sharp, and she still had a number of things to tag before the customers arrived. *If* they arrived. She loved antiquing, but she'd never shopped garage sales, and she'd never held one in her life. She'd been worried all week. What if no one showed? What would she do then? She'd finally given up and tried to quit thinking about it. No matter how much she fretted and worried, she couldn't control the outcome. She'd put up the signs and placed ads in the papers. Tomorrow would bring what it would. At the moment, she wanted nothing more complicated than a nice long soak in the bath, followed by a quick bite to eat, then climbing into bed. All day long, she'd been moving from table to table, pricing items, grouping assortments of pieces together. It was exhausting. How did people manage to work jobs that required them to be constantly on their feet?

"You're selling this?" Susan lifted a fragile vase from the table, running a finger across the delicate porcelain, touching the gold rim and elaborate roses entwined around its body. "But you've had it forever."

"All the better reason to sell it." Eleanor thumbed a piece of masking tape on another item. One more piece of her former life for sale. "I'm sick of looking at it."

"But it's beautiful. And it looks like it might be valuable. I don't know much about antiques, but are you sure you don't want to keep—"

"Richard brought it back from Iraq." Lifting her head, she eyed her daughter-in-law across the table. "I don't want it anymore."

"Oh." Susan's voice softened in sudden understanding. "Oh. I see."

"You can have it if you like. Take it home with you," Eleanor offered. "In fact, take anything you want." She waved her hand around the garage. High time she got rid of these things. The less she had sitting around to remind her of Richard, the better off she'd be.

Susan stared at the vase in her hands, then gingerly replaced it on the table. "Thanks, but I don't think so. It's probably better if you sell it."

"I hadn't realized there would be so much." Eleanor glanced around the garage, her gaze sweeping across the long rented tables crowded with items from her past. Martha had stopped by to help for a few hours that morning, but she'd been on her own all afternoon. She was proud of how much she'd accomplished. Amazing how productive a person could be, given the proper motivation. *No more Richard*.

"I hope people come." She swiped some loose hairs from the sweat beading across her forehead. "It would be terrible to have done all this work for nothing."

"I don't think you need to worry about that," Susan predicted. "Everyone knows you have nice things. And you know how people are. Everyone loves a bargain."

"Let's not forget *nosy*," Eleanor said, returning the smile. "They want to see how I'm coping. Am I a crazy woman bent on revenge? Have I dissolved into some old hag who throws herself a daily pity party? Well, let them come over and see for themselves. And while they're here, I hope they buy something. They're welcome to it... all of it." She swept a hand over the tables. "My life—or what's left of it—reduced to a tag sale."

"Are you sad, seeing it go?"

"Not anymore." She might have been sad once upon a time, but she'd moved on. "I suppose *reflective* is a better way to describe how I feel. I can't say I'm happy about the situation, but I'm coping."

The Other Wife

Susan's eyes shone with admiration. "I admire you so much, Eleanor. You're such a strong woman."

"Me?" Her cheeks flamed at the unexpected praise. It was a good thing Susan hadn't been around to witness her meltdown last night, when she'd collapsed in bed and indulged in a good long cry. It was the first time in days that she'd broken down. Yet overwhelmed and exhausted by how much she had to do, she'd been helpless to stop herself. "I'm not strong."

"That's not true. You *are* strong... and I think you're very brave. I can't think of any woman I know who would have handled herself in a similar situation with such grace and style. If it were me, I don't know what I would have done. That horrible woman..." Susan shuddered. "How could she do that to you?"

Eleanor shrugged. She didn't want to go there and think about that. "It takes two," she reminded her daughter-in-law. Claire might be partially to blame, but so was Richard.

"When I think about her over there in that house he set her up in, with all that money that rightfully belongs to—"

"Stop," Eleanor said. "Please stop. I don't want to talk about it."

"I'm sorry. Of course you don't." Susan drew in a deep breath.

"The realtor said that a house shows better for prospective buyers when there aren't lots of personal things cluttering up space," Eleanor said, changing the subject. "Besides, I'll have to move eventually. And when I do, there won't be room for everything."

Still, she hadn't been willing to part with everything. Some things were precious. The antique grandfather clock she'd inherited upon her marriage had stood in their foyer, guarding the sweeping staircase for nearly forty years. The massive mahogany bookcase with beveled glass doors had belonged to her father. And as for the overstuffed, overpriced Victorian chaise lounge she hadn't been able to resist upon discovering it years ago in an antique shop? She'd had it reupholstered in a cozy floral chintz and placed it in their bedroom despite Richard's protests. He hated floral patterns, he hated chintz, and he especially hated *that hideous chaise lounge*. Eleanor smiled to herself. All the more reason to keep it.

A muffled car engine caught their attention. Together they watched as a sleek convertible pulled into the driveway and up the long paved path. Eleanor tamped down a surge of frustration as the driver cut the engine and opened the door. What was the matter with people? The sign out front specifically stated that the sale wouldn't start until nine a.m. No early sales. Whoever it was, they'd have to come back tomorrow.

"Uh-oh." Susan dragged in a ragged breath. "Look who's here."

Eleanor shaded her eyes against the brilliant afternoon sun and squinted at the blonde behind the large black sunglasses emerging from the car. There was no mistaking the patrician nose, the scowl on her face, the haughty disdain.

"Uh-oh," she said, echoing Susan as she watched her daughter stride toward them.

"So it's true." Vivi yanked off the designer frames and glanced around the garage. "When Carolyn e-mailed me about your ad in the paper, I told her there was no way my mother would stoop so low as to have a garage sale. But after she forwarded me the link, I decided to fly out and see for myself."

Whipping around to face her mother, she leveled Eleanor with a glare hotter than the sun beating down on their heads. "You never said a word," she said, her voice full of accusation.

"I hadn't realized you'd be interested."

"And why would you think that?" Vivi spit out the words. "You're selling our things."

My things, Eleanor thought, then decided it was wiser to keep her mouth shut. She was feeling braver than she had in weeks, but not brave enough to battle her daughter's fury.

"It never occurred to me that you'd be willing to come all the way from New York to help with a garage sale. I'm sure you have more important things to do." She leaned forward to give Vivi a kiss but missed the mark as her daughter yanked away.

"No, Mother, I did *not* come to help. I came to make sure you didn't sell anything valuable." She tossed a sideway glance at her sister-in-law. "Hello, Susan."

"Welcome home."

"But it's not really home anymore, is it?" Vivi jerked her head toward the realtor sign prominently displayed on one corner of the lawn. "I still can't believe you're selling the house."

Eleanor sank onto one of the folding chairs and fanned her face with one hand, trying to blow away some of the heated words. Their mother-daughter relationship had always been contentious. Why had she thought things would be better once Richard was dead? He'd always served as a buffer.

But that wasn't exactly true. More times than not, it had been two against one. Vivi had always been able to convince her father to take her side of things. With Richard gone, Eleanor suddenly realized Vivi was stuck with her. The thought didn't leave her much hope for their future. Their daughter had the benefit of an excellent education, plus she'd inherited Richard's gift for the powers of persuasion. If she'd come looking for a confrontation, Eleanor had no doubt who would end up the victor.

"I had no choice about selling the house," she said quietly. "I thought you understood that I don't have the money to keep up the payments. I'm out of options."

"I think it's time I went home." Leaning over, Susan brushed Eleanor's check with a kiss. "See you tomorrow."

"Bright and early," she reminded her, trying to sound chipper. She had a strong hunch tomorrow would dawn anything but bright... especially now that her personal little storm cloud had made landfall and taken up residence.

Eleanor sat a bit longer, trying to gather her wits, which had been in a jumble since Vivi's convertible roared up the driveway. Vivi hadn't been home since Richard's funeral, and the two of them rarely spoke—especially now since Jeffrey was the one dealing with her demands for the money left her by her father.

Money. Is that what had brought her back? Certainly Vivi had more important things to do than worry about her mother's garage sale. What about her job? And that boyfriend of hers Richard had mentioned? Had he met the man while visiting Vivi during one of his frequent layovers in New York? She regretted never having followed up with Richard, never having questioned him as to whether this man was good enough for their daughter. Now it was too late. Dead men don't tell tales, and Vivi wasn't talking. Then again, why would she? Mother and daughter had never been close.

Maybe it was time to try. Eleanor watched as her daughter strolled around the garage, lingering at the folding tables, discarding some things, scrutinizing others.

"Take anything you like," she offered.

Vivi sniffed and moved on to yet another table. "It's mostly junk."

Junk? Eleanor straightened. Granted, most of the items weren't expensive pieces, but every single thing meant something to her... and she'd never thought of any of it as junk.

"You're selling this?" Vivi lifted the same vase that Susan earlier had plucked from a table. She turned to her mother with an accusatory stare. "Daddy brought this back from Iraq."

"Yes, I remember." It'd been one of those trips where he'd left promising he'd be gone a few days—a week at most—which had morphed into nearly a month instead. When he finally returned, he'd presented her with the vase as a token apology. She'd treasured it until the day she discovered his deceit. Where had he been? In Iraq, or forty miles away, shacked up with his girlfriend in Hyde Park?

Damn it. How could she have been so blind? She should have known something was going on. She should have realized Richard was involved with someone else.

She should have smashed the damn vase.

"I can't believe you're selling it."

Finding her legs and voice, Eleanor joined Vivi at the table. "I already said you could have it." Her words sliced through the heavy air between them. "Take it."

"I will." Tight-lipped, Vivi cradled the vase in her arms as if it were a treasured relic rather than some cheap Mideast curiosity Richard had probably picked up at a bazaar. "I'm going upstairs to unpack."

She spun through the kitchen door, making sure to give it a good hard slam behind her. Biting her tongue at her daughter's haughty departure, Eleanor turned back to the items still needing tagging. Not much had changed since Vivi was a teenager. Even then, she'd been accustomed to stalking through the house, shouting and sulking when things didn't go her way. Eleanor had thought Vivi's terrible two's and her teenage years had been bad enough, but Vivi-the-adult put her former selves to shame.

The hell with it. Let the rest of the things sit until tomorrow, Eleanor decided. She was done. Everyone else got to do what they wanted... why not her? She'd worked hard all day. She deserved some pampering. With her thumb on the button, she hit the remote and closed the garage door. She intended to go inside, head upstairs, and indulge in that well-deserved soak in the tub that she'd been promising herself all day. She deserved it. She needed it.

And maybe before heading upstairs, she'd pour herself a nice big glass of wine. Something strong to fortify herself. She would need that too... especially now that Vivi was back in town.

Chapter Twelve

"Any particular reason he's stacking the pepperoni into towers," Tulie said, "or is it some random thing he likes to do?"

Claire glanced down at Dickie and found her son in deep concentration, his little fingers arranging the spicy meat slices into one neat little pile.

"Don't play with your food, sweetie," she said softly, though mainly for Tulie's sake. She couldn't have cared less if he ate his pizza or not. Let him build his little pepperoni tower. At least he was being constructive and working on his fine motor skills. Who knew? Maybe he would grow up to be an architect or an engineer like his daddy.

But for today, he was merely a little boy without a daddy... and a mother who was falling apart.

"You aren't eating, either." Tulie eyed her across the booth with a troubled frown. "I thought you liked pizza."

Claire stared at the congealed mass of gooey cheese and thick, golden crust on her plate. "Guess I don't have much of an appetite tonight.

"At least someone's enjoying her food." Tulie nodded toward Sophie in her wooden high chair. Her little fist was filled with pieces of crust, her chin and cheeks smeared with pizza sauce.

"You, little miss, are a mess." Grabbing a napkin, Claire leaned over to wipe her daughter's face, only to have Sophie shriek and squirm away. Several people at nearby tables glanced in their direction, and she quickly decided it wasn't worth it. Slumping back in the booth, she watched Sophie cram more crust in her mouth.

"Looks like Mama has lost round one," Tulie said.

"I never said I was a contender," she mumbled.

"You're in a mood tonight. What's wrong? You were the one who wanted to come here."

"Dickie and Sophie like it." She glanced around the kid-friendly pizza parlor not far from their house. "And we haven't been here in forever. We used to bring them here all the time."

The words rolled out of her mouth before she realized her mistake. *We* used to bring them. But there was no more *we*. There was only *me*. The strong scent of Italian spices wafted through the air, and she pushed away her plate, uncertain if it was the pizza that was making her queasy or the pills the doctor had prescribed that she'd finally begun taking a few days ago. He'd said they would keep her calm, but she'd been counting on them to take away the feelings. She wanted the pain to go away, for everything to quit hurting so much. The pills were working to some degree; she hadn't morphed into zombie-mode, and she was still functioning. But she also still felt things.

Emptiness. Sadness. Like her life was over.

The soft light of the lamp hanging above their table caught the rhinestones on Tulie's glasses, making them sparkle. She looked as if she were a wise prophetess, someone with the answers. Claire sat, fascinated. God knew she could use some answers... or something. Maybe what she needed was hope.

"Promise you won't laugh if I tell you something terrible?"

"I would never laugh at you." Tulie's face softened as she reached across and grabbed her hand. "You're my best friend. I love you."

Claire bit her lip. It was one thing to have a running internal dialogue constantly chattering in her head. But confessing the truth, even to her best friend, would take every bit of courage she could summon.

"Part of me thinks I'm going crazy," she finally admitted. "I can't stop thinking about what happened. One minute, things were fine, wonderful... then suddenly, they weren't."

But was that the truth? She'd begun to wonder if she could trust her memories. Had her years with Richard been as pleasant as she remembered? Before she'd met him, her life had revolved around schedules. She'd built her world on a solid rock of rationalization. He'd changed all that. He'd taught her how to loosen up, to not be so rigid, so strict and inflexible with others... especially with herself. And she'd thought—she'd believed—that was a good thing. She'd let down her guard, allowing him to fill up the space inside her heart. How could she have not noticed what he was doing? She'd surrendered her detached observer status and let him lead her into a gorgeous haze of happily-ever-after framed by gilt-edged mirrors. *He showed me exactly what he wanted me to see.* How could she have allowed herself to have been manipulated like that? She knew better. She was a trained psychologist. And yet...

"I still miss him," she admitted. "Even after everything he did, all the horrible things he did, I miss him. I miss him every day." She lifted her chin, searching Tulie's face. "Is that crazy or what? Am I certifiable?"

"Claire, for God's sake, of course you're not crazy. After what you've been through, anyone would feel the same."

"Want to know the worst part? I don't feel like me anymore." She shook her head, her eyes beginning to swim with tears. She quickly fingered them away before they spilled over onto her cheeks, before Dickie noticed his mother was crying. "I thought it would get better. I thought I would quit thinking about him."

"It hasn't been that long," Tulie reminded her. "Two months, Claire. Give yourself some time."

"I know," she said, nodding in agreement because Tulie probably expected it. But the truth was she no longer knew what to do... how to act. It was a terrifying thing, realizing that you no longer trusted yourself. And that was what scared her most, the one thing that kept her awake at night, that finally drove her to seek out a doctor and beg for pills that would make the doubts and despair disappear.

"Frankly, Claire, if I found out that a man had done something like that to me, I don't know how I would handle myself." Her jaw clenched, a little quiver ticking off the beats of anger. "When I think about how he cheated on you, and the lies he—"

"Stop. Please. Just... stop." Even though everything Tulie said was true, even though the same thoughts kept tumbling through her own head, she couldn't bear to hear it. Especially not from Tulie—someone she knew and loved and trusted.

"Claire, don't you understand? No one blames you. We all thought he was terrific. The two of you were perfect."

Her eyes welled with more tears. They *had* been perfect.

"Do you understand what I'm saying? He wasn't that guy, Claire. None of us saw it coming. And what we hate most, what *I* hate most, is knowing how he treated you."

"He treated me like a queen. That's what's so confusing." She pressed her hands against her chest, as if she could stop her heart from splintering into smaller pieces. "I never thought for one minute, for one second, that anything was wrong—"

"But that's my point. You didn't see it because he didn't want you to see it. He wouldn't *allow* you to see it. It's a classic case, Claire, right out of a Psychology 101 textbook. Richard was confident and charming, he was witty and articulate. And he certainly was never at a loss for words, right? He always managed to convince people to do things his way. There's a psychological term for people like that. We call them sociopaths."

"Don't say that," she whispered, trying to shush her friend before Dickie overheard. But he was oblivious to the conversation, having given up on his pepperoni tower and turned his attention to scribbling with crayons on his paper placemat.

"He fit the profile," Tulie continued ruthlessly. "He thought the rules didn't apply to him. He thought he could get away with things normal people wouldn't dare."

She had a point, Claire conceded miserably, remembering Richard's recklessness and his casual disdain for other people and their boring lives. At the time, she'd assumed his attitude was due to his work and the constant peril he put himself in while in the Middle East. After Dickie's birth, she'd begged him to step back, to delegate some of his responsibilities and allow someone else to put themselves in harm's way. But he'd laughed off her concerns, reminding her that she'd taken him on for better or worse.

"Aren't you content?" he'd asked. "You already have the better part of me." And a part of her, understanding the logic behind his reasoning, had quieted. If he'd done as she asked, if he'd pulled back and stayed home, it would have changed things. He wouldn't have been the man she'd fallen in love with. She'd known from the beginning what he was like. He thrived on danger. How could you ask someone to become something they weren't? She'd fallen in love with a man who was impulsive, reckless, charming and clever. She'd fallen in love with his constant energy and his sexual charisma.

Yes, yes, yes! Everything Tulie had said was true.

"Everyone thought Ted Bundy was quite a charming guy."

Claire drew in a sharp breath. "Richard was not a serial killer!" she hissed.

"True," Tulie agreed, "but consider what he did: he divided his life into two separate halves. Two wives, two families... and no regard for the consequences. He never considered how it would affect you."

"We don't know that," she whispered. "He loved me. I know he loved me."

"I'm sure he did."

"And I can't believe that he didn't think about telling me the truth."

"But he didn't, did he?" Tulie's face softened. "And what about her? Did he tell her the truth? Do you think she knew about you before he died?"

"No," she admitted, barely able to speak the word. She'd first learned of Eleanor Anderson's existence from Jim Kennedy. And from what he had told her, the first Eleanor was aware of Claire was when she discovered Richard had changed his primary insurance beneficiary.

"He was a sick man, Claire. A sick man who needed help, and no one knew."

"But I should have known!" Her voice shook with sudden fury, surging from somewhere deep inside her. Dickie looked up from his coloring. The sight of his round eyes and the sudden fear on his face made her heart catch. What had she done? She'd scared her son.

She'd scared herself.

"It's all right, sweetheart," she assured him. But was it? Claire wondered. Would things ever be all right again?

"People love you, Claire. They care about you. They're concerned. We're all concerned."

"Don't you understand? I can't think of him like that. He was their father."

"I know."

But Tulie didn't know. No one knew. Everyone thought they did, but they couldn't understand how she felt, and they never would. But that was reasonable. It wasn't their problem. They hadn't been through it. She was all alone in this. No one could understand.

No one... except a woman named Eleanor.

She might simply fade away and you'll never see her face... or she could go ballistic and be all over you. Daniel Mitchell's words haunted her. *If anyone tries to contact you, tell them to speak with your attorney.* Up until now, that hadn't been necessary. But she was starting to see shadows behind every corner. Was it her imagination, or was Eleanor out there, waiting to strike? How would she know?

What did Eleanor want? What more could the woman possibly want? Eleanor had everything. Her house, her reputation, the life she'd led with Richard. And what did Claire have? Nothing except the money.

The check arrived and she reached for it, but Tulie covered it with her hand. "I've got this."

"No, let me," Claire said. "You're by yourself, but there are three of us. Besides, I can afford it."

There was a reason they called it *filthy lucre*, and she had plenty. Had Richard truly believed that the money he'd left her would soothe things over and make it right? That the millions safely stashed away in her bank account would make up for the rejection and pain he'd caused? What he had done was horrible and hideous, not to mention illegal. Once upon a time, she'd thought he was the most intelligent man she'd ever met. Funny that he'd never realized money can't buy you peace of mind. Money can't assuage guilt. Money is impersonal, and it changes nothing. If anything, it creates a new set of problems.

Including greed.

And that one thought kept her awake every night.

Exactly how greedy would Eleanor Anderson be?

Chapter Thirteen

"Why don't I declare bankruptcy and get it over with?"

Declaring to the world that she was broke, her credit dead and buried, couldn't be worse than what she'd faced a few months ago, discovering Richard's lifeless body in bed beside her. And she was tired of trying to play catch-up. That wasn't the way she'd been raised, and not the way she was used to living. Why not call an end to it all? Call it *quits* and start over again?

A new beginning. A new life. A life without Richard.

"You're getting ahead of yourself." Jeffrey finished the last of his turkey sandwich and swiped his mouth with a napkin. "Bankruptcy is a last resort. Your situation isn't that desperate."

Not yet. The unspoken words hung between them like cold wet sheets flapping in the wind, but Eleanor wasn't about to yank them off the line and fling them in his face. Jeffrey was doing the best he could. It wasn't his fault the house wasn't selling. The recession had hit everyone hard. The market was down, and—according to the realtor and

Jeffrey—so was she. Upside down, that is, whatever that meant. Property values had dropped, and the loan Richard had taken out four years ago when refinancing their house was now higher than the house was worth. How could that make sense?

She glanced around the sun-splashed kitchen where the two of them sat. She loved her kitchen with its gleaming hardwood floors, warm wooden cupboards, and plenty of counter space. True, the countertops weren't granite like so many people fancied nowadays. Richard had been pressing her to do a remodel, but she'd resisted. Why spend the money? She loved the house exactly the way it was. It was a beautiful kitchen, a beautiful home. People should pay extra for the privilege of living in it. Some had booked appointments to view the property and had toured with the realtor, but so far there had been no offers. The fact thrilled her, but also scared the hell out of her. She didn't want to sell, but she couldn't afford to stay. And even if by some miracle they managed to sell the house and—joy of all joys—realized their asking price, it still wouldn't be enough to cover her daily living expenses.

Things weren't looking good. She had to do something.

Starting with Vivi. Her daughter was becoming a royal pain in the patootie. "I've taken a few days' vacation," Vivi had informed Eleanor when she'd burst upon the scene before the garage sale. But vacations were supposed to be fun, pleasant flings, meant for relaxing. Life with Vivi underfoot was no vacation. The garage sale had been a disaster, something she'd suspected would be the case long before the first customers arrived. Sometime between dinner and dawn, Vivi had taken it upon herself to remove most of the upscale items advertised in the weekly shopper, pieces that Eleanor had counted on to bring in quality shoppers with disposable cash. Eleanor had held her tongue as her daughter stood guard over the tables, scowling as their family treasures disappeared. She didn't like what Vivi was doing, but she couldn't blame her. She herself had been lucky enough to inherit everything from her parents. There'd be no such inheritance for her children. Richard and his stupid paramour had seen to that. By the time Vivi departed at week's end and flew back to New York, Eleanor was miserable. But it wasn't grief holding her heart hostage as she kissed her daughter good-bye.

Mothers weren't supposed to be happy to see their children leave.

"I know you're busy dealing with the house," Jeffrey said, "so I've been trying to handle some things without getting you involved."

The strained look on his face wasn't encouraging. "What is it?"

"You know I've been working to wrap up Dad's business affairs. I wanted to get it done sooner rather than later, but I'm afraid that's not going to be the case." He hesitated. "His work was primarily through government contracts, but dealing with all the bureaucratic paperwork is complicated. And some of his clients weren't from this country. We're talking contracts with vendors from the Middle East. It's going to take time to sort it all out."

"That's all right," she assured him, hoping he wouldn't notice the fear on her face. "I'll get by."

"There's more," he admitted. "I don't want you

counting on something that might not pan out. There might not be much money left when this is over. There might not be any money at all."

He leaned forward, propping his elbows on the antique wooden table that had seen their family through so many breakfasts. Pancakes smothered in syrup and plump little sausages lining the plate. She'd always made sure to drain the grease from the sausages. None of them needed the extra fat. Not good for your heart, Eleanor thought, sobering as she remembered Richard's cardiac arrest. Obviously she hadn't done a great job draining off the grease. Maybe she never should have served sausages.

Maybe she never should have married Richard.

"We have to figure out a way to trim your monthly expenses."

Eleanor turned her head, hoping he wouldn't catch the hot flush rising on her face. How embarrassing. A child shouldn't have to deal with their parent's financial misfortunes.

"I've been going over your monthly bills. I think there are some cuts you could make that would help. First, I suggest increasing your insurance deductible on the house." Pausing, he eyed her across the table. "In fact, I think it might be a good idea if you switched insurance companies too."

"Switch companies?" The beginning of a frown wrinkled her forehead. "Why should I do that?"

"To pick up a cheaper rate. I've done a cost-comparison analysis. The price savings are significant."

"But Jim Kennedy has handled our insurance for

years," she reminded him. "We've always carried our coverage through his company."

"It's business, Mom. Strictly business."

"But how can I do that to Jim? He's our friend." She and Richard had spent many evenings with Jim and his wife, Anne. The two couples had always been friends. Good friends. The best of friends.

Yet when was the last time she'd spoken with Jim? It had to have been at least two or three weeks, maybe even a month. And as for Anne? The two of them used to get together and chat over lunch every few weeks. When was the last time she'd seen or heard from Anne?

She'd faded away, like so many other so-called friends. Oh, they'd phoned for the first several weeks following Richard's death, with sympathetic overtures. But the calls quickly dropped off as people learned the truth about the scandal surrounding her marriage. Not that she minded. She'd always been content with herself for company. Perhaps it came from being an only child. She'd learned at an early age how to keep herself amused. She'd always been a private woman. And she was smart. She'd never felt the need to surround herself with other women buzzing in her ear, telling her what to do.

Then again, maybe she wasn't so smart after all. A smart woman wouldn't have allowed herself to end up like this. Isolated in a house no one wanted, abandoned by her friends. The one friend she could count on was Martha, bless her heart. As for the rest of them? Once they'd learned the truth, they wanted nothing to do with her. Bad enough she was a widow. Now everyone knew what Richard had done, and they knew her for what she was.

A fool. A total fool.

Richard and that woman had made her into a fool. And while Richard was dead, Claire Anderson was alive and well, less than forty miles away. An easy car ride, if you didn't hit rush-hour traffic.

She should know. She'd driven the route once already... and so far had managed to resist the urge to do it again.

"Let's talk about your cable coverage," Jeffrey said. "You're paying for premium services you don't need—"

"I am not giving up *Masterpiece Theater*," she warned. "I don't care about the other channels, but I refuse to give that up."

"You can keep PBS," he replied with a fast smile.

"Good," Eleanor said, slightly mollified. But only slightly. Sometime in the past month, she'd taken to spending her evenings in the sunroom. It was smaller and cozier than the living room, and she enjoyed curling up in one of the overstuffed chairs with the TV remote, randomly flipping through the stations. When Richard had been around, she'd retreated to their bedroom most evenings, to spend time reading. But now that he was gone for good, she could claim the whole house as her own. It was hers to do as she wished, for as long as she still lived here. She could spread out, throw her clothes around (not that she would ever do such a thing), or even cover every chair in a colorful chintz fabric if she liked (not that she could afford it).

"Let's drop the speed of your Internet connection. Dad had the fastest available, but you don't need it. You're wasting your money."

"But I use the computer," Eleanor said. Not much, but

she liked to surf the Net. It made her feel as if she were connected to the rest of the world. She didn't understand all the social media or those apps the television ads constantly touted. And she had no use for the ridiculous game requests people constantly sent her. *Frustrated Farmers*? *Angry Animals*? What were those about? Until recently, she'd thought people were foolish for wasting precious time playing stupid games that didn't make sense. But then one night last week, she'd logged on to the computer and found out for herself. Maybe the games weren't so silly after all. In fact, some of them were downright entertaining. Before she knew it, an hour had disappeared. Better an hour spent playing on the computer than sitting around drowning in her own misery, playing the Pity Poor Me game. She'd actually liked some of those games.

And she'd used the computer in Richard's study. *Her* study, now.

"Dropping the Internet speed won't affect you much," he promised. "It's not like you're streaming videos, downloading apps, or playing lots of games."

Eleanor swallowed hard. She supposed she could learn to live without *Frustrated Farmer*. In the past several months, she'd learned to live without lots of things. She was a survivor.

"All right," she agreed, watching him soberly tackle the row of numbers on his sheet. What had happened to that lighthearted little boy she'd known and loved? Maybe she should introduce Jeffrey to the fun she'd found on the Internet. Maybe a few games of *Frustrated Farmer* would lighten him up.

He cleared his throat. "I know how important it is for a woman to have her hair done."

"You can't be serious." Eleanor touched a hand to her head. She'd been coloring her hair for nearly thirty years. She had a standing appointment every four weeks, with her visits to the salon booked months in advance. Lucky Richard, with that wonderful salt-and-pepper color that some older men were blessed with. She'd no doubt that if her own hair was allowed to go *au naturale*, it would quickly morph into an ugly mix of messy gray and yellowing white.

"I can't believe you want me to quit coloring my hair."

"I didn't say—"

"You certainly implied it." She glared at him. "What do you expect me to do? Buy a box of dye at the drugstore and dump it on my head?"

"I'm sorry. I didn't mean to upset you." Jeffrey's face flushed a fierce shade of red that Eleanor doubted had ever seen the inside of a salon bottle. "Susan warned me not to bring it up. She said you wouldn't like the idea."

"Obviously your wife has more sense than you do. I suggest you listen to her more often."

"I'm not saying you need to stop visiting the salon. Spread out your visits. Make them last a little longer. Now, let's talk about your grocery account."

"Honestly, Jeffrey?" She couldn't hold back the sigh. "I realize I could lose some weight, but I *do* have to eat."

Her levity lifted a smile to his face. "I'm talking price, not giving up food. You buy your groceries at Daly's, right?"

"You know I do." The small, exclusive, family-owned

store mere blocks from their home had been in business for over sixty years. She wouldn't dream of shopping anywhere else. Daly's Deli had the choicest selection of meats and the freshest produce. They featured thick, crusty homemade breads—wheat, rye, sourdough, all made daily by Daly's!—and a bakery that served up decadent desserts to die for. Plus, they delivered, a service she'd taken full advantage of in the past several months. Daly's was an essential part of their neighborhood, a meeting place where people gathered to shoot the breeze and—as her Dad would have put it, *chew the fat*—while Daly's butcher trimmed the fat from their prime cuts of beef. Everyone shopped at Daly's Deli.

Everyone who could afford it, that is.

Eleanor turned her face away so she wouldn't have to witness the sympathy she knew she'd see on her son's face, that anguished look that was slowly morphing into *I'm sorry as hell and I wish it hadn't come to this Mom.* She didn't want to see it. She couldn't bear to see it.

"Do you know how long I've been shopping at Daly's?" she choked out. Her mouth felt as dry as if she'd been eating stale crackers. The kind of crackers you found in a box on the shelves of a discount grocery store.

"I know you love the place, but their prices are—"

"Since the day your father and I were married, that's how long," she said. "Your first birthday cake came from Daly's. Every one of your cakes, every one of Vivi's; they all came from Daly's."

Some things were sacred. Asking her to give up shopping at Daly's was like asking her to find a new church in which to worship, a church in a run-down section of town. But she was a member of Daly's congregation. She had her regular seat and she knew the hymns by heart, the same way she knew the layout of the narrow aisles. Just like she knew that her favorite cashier, Penny, the pretty one with the blond corkscrew curls who was always so pleasant and chatted nonstop while she rang up the groceries, was pregnant. "It's a girl!" Penny had whispered excitedly to Eleanor last time she'd been in the store, "and we're naming her Michelle." Giving up shopping at Daly's would mean finding a new store. It would mean cutting coupons. It would mean learning how to comparison shop.

Eleanor blinked away hot, sudden tears. How much was she expected to give up without cracking? First her hair, then her TV shows, her computer games. But Daly's Deli? They were famous for their plump geese at Christmas, for juicy honey-baked hams at Easter, and succulent Thanksgiving turkeys. She'd had a standing order with Daly's for over thirty years. No more gourmet cheeses, no more yummy desserts?

"I thought about the lawn-care service, but—"

"Don't bother. I canceled it last week," she muttered, her thoughts still shuffling through Daly's aisles and the checkout counter. She wouldn't even get to meet baby Michelle. It wasn't fair.

"You canceled the lawn service? Why?"

"Because you said I should try to cut costs." She stared at him. Why did he look so flabbergasted? Jeffrey was the one who'd told her she needed to save money.

"I appreciate your efforts, Mom, but I don't think that's such a great idea."

Watching him hesitate was as bad as feeling the

stinging needles of irritation sliding under her skin. What was wrong with him? Didn't he realize she was doing the best she could? One by one, she was losing all her little indulgences. Did he intend to take away her pride too?

And she wasn't about to let that happen. When all was said and done, a person didn't have much in life except their honor and self-esteem. She still had her honor, but the other had been shattered when she'd learned about that horrible woman. It had taken some time to get over the initial shock, but she'd weathered it well, all things considered.

Except for her hair. With all the stress she'd been under, it probably would turn stark white overnight if she quit the salon.

"I couldn't believe it," she said, "when the man from the lawn service told me it cost two hundred dollars. *Per month*? I asked him. Granted, I might have shouted. I'm not sure. And he wasn't too happy with me after that. In fact, he was downright huffy. Well, he said, of course that included the price of mowing, pruning, and fertilizing, plus trimming the trees, and the spring and fall cleanups." Eleanor shook her head. "Can you imagine? That company was charging me more than two thousand dollars a year to pick up some leaves and mow the lawn. I told him it was ridiculous and to take our house off his customer list. That's one bill I don't need."

Jeffrey pulled in a deep breath. "Actually, you do. The house is on the market, remember? It has to look its best for potential buyers." He slumped back in his chair. "I'll call them today and tell them to resume the—"

"No, you will not." She straightened in her chair. "I'll mow the damn lawn myself."

"Since when did you start swearing?" One eyebrow lifted as a crooked smile broke across his face. "Come on, Mom, be realistic."

"You think I can't do it?" She pushed aside her half-eaten sandwich. Why did they all think she was helpless? Everyone assumed she couldn't handle things on her own. Richard had always thought so; even her children, when they were small, had thought so. That's the way things had always been, and they probably assumed it would never change. But she could no longer afford to let them think that way.

She could no longer afford to allow herself to think that way. She wasn't the same woman she'd been three months ago. It was time she took control of her life... and her lawn.

"I love being outside. I love working in my garden."

"This house sits on nearly an acre of land. And what about the hedges? The trees? Taking care of a lawn is different than weeding a few flower beds. Besides, you don't even own a lawn mower," he reminded her.

She tamped down the frustration at knowing he was right. Her gardening tools were stored in a special spot in the garage: trowel and pruners, bucket, fork and spade. But last time she'd looked—had she bothered to look?—there was no lawn mower in the garage. No lawn-care equipment of any kind.

"It's no big deal. Meanwhile, let's hope the house sells before summer is over. Then there won't be any need for a fall cleanup." Jeffrey grabbed his suit coat, which was slung over the back of his chair, and shrugged into it. "I've got to get back to the office." He knotted his tie, which he'd loosened during lunch. "What are your plans for the afternoon?"

Eleanor paused. She had a busy few hours ahead, but she had no intention of telling him what she planned to do. "Just a little shopping."

"Stay out of Home Depot," he warned with a smile. "I don't want to see a lawn mower in the garage next time I'm here."

"Ha-ha." She followed behind him as he headed out of the kitchen and down the hallway into the foyer.

Halting at the front door, he turned and planted a quick kiss on her cheek. "I'll be in touch. Love you."

"I love you too," she said, closing the door behind him.

Stay out of Home Depot? That promise she could keep. But Jeffrey didn't need to know everything. He was already involved in her business affairs. He knew the exact balances of her checking and savings account. He knew the type of groceries in her cupboards, the premium TV cable channels she subscribed to, the price of the clothes hanging in her closet. He was a good man, a good son, and he didn't judge. But some things were private.

Jeffrey didn't need to know everything about her... especially about her plans for the rest of the day. He definitely would not approve.

Good thing her Mercedes was already paid for or he might have insisted she give that up too. And she needed that car, especially this afternoon.

No, if he knew where she was headed, Jeffrey definitely would not approve.

Chapter Fourteen

She went in under the growing cover of darkness, striding through the slumbering stillness of a Saturday night on the quad. With the spring session winding down, the campus was quiet, and understandably so. Once upon a time—had it only been ten years? It seemed like a lifetime—she'd been one of them: students reveling in one last fling before the mandatory knuckling down, before that final swing plunging them into the deep abyss of studying for final exams. But all that was yet to come. They'd deserted the quad to party in corner bars, downbeat dorms, and off-campus apartments. They were knocking back beers, cheap wine, and watered-down drinks in a boozy attempt to forget their responsibilities. They were celebrating the tradition that the young of each generation held fast as their own: the right to enjoy themselves, each other, and life. Tomorrow would dawn soon enough.

But for her, tomorrow had already arrived.

All the king's horses and all the king's men couldn't put Humpty together again.

There was no going back. Richard was dead. If she didn't move on, she'd be dead too.

Claire hurried across the quad courtyard, heading for Stuart Hall. The trees sheltering the great stone building cast gloomy shadows in the pale moonlight, and she quickened her pace. It had been months since she'd been on campus, and she'd deliberately chosen to return on a Saturday night. With campus deserted, her privacy was guaranteed. No students asking awkward questions and her fumbling for answers. No staff members offering condolences, prompting a need for an awkward response. No passersby sneaking furtive glances of curiosity, pity, and contempt, which she would have to pretend not to notice.

But she noticed everything. That was the problem.

Off to the left, something stirred. A rustling sound, near the trees. The sound of footsteps? Claire, nearly at the steps, halted, cocking her head to listen. She'd never been one to be easily spooked, but she had the sudden uneasy feeling that she wasn't alone.

Reaching the heavy door, she grabbed the massive handle and pulled, praying it was unlocked. The rich light poured out, surrounding her with its warmth. She rushed inside, glad to have the darkness behind her. Taking a deep breath, she had a little laugh at herself as she headed for the staircase. Her father had always said she had a wild imagination. Even so, if there *had* been someone outside, it no longer mattered. Stuart Hall was familiar territory, and she wasn't far from the safety of her fourth-floor office.

She'd reached the top of the first-floor landing when she heard the dull thud of the mighty door below. Her heartbeat took off like a racehorse flying around the track with nostrils flaring, breathing heavily. The muffled sound of footsteps grew nearer and her hand gripped the railing. She'd taken a class in self-defense years ago because she'd thought it was important. Women should know how to defend themselves. The course had given her a sense of empowerment. And while she didn't remember much from the six-week class, she thought she could protect herself if it came right down to it. Though she had no intention of sticking around to find out.

Whoever it was would soon be at the bottom of the steps.

Claire bounded up the stairs, fingers barely touching the railing as she took the steps one, two at a time. Past the second floor, up and around the landing, flying past the third floor and one final landing with one flight left to go. She skidded onto the landing of the fourth floor and grabbed for the door, as from below came the sound of hurried footsteps nearing. Whoever it was, they'd quickened their pace. Heart racing, she yanked open the door and ducked into the long narrow hallway. Her office was at the far end of the hall, and she cursed the distance as she hurried down the corridor, frantically groping through her bag for her keys. *Stupid, stupid.* She should have had them ready. Then her fingers connected, gratefully closing around jangling metal as she reached her office.

A door banged at the far end of the hall as she yanked the keys from her bag. Fear clutched at her throat. Why had she come here alone tonight? Claire snatched a quick moment to glance over her shoulder and saw a figure emerging into the hallway. The sight filled her with the kind of dread that made your knees go weak and your stomach pitch in free fall.

A woman. It was a woman.

But why was she surprised? She should have known. Hadn't she been warned to be on guard?

She might simply fade away and you'll never see her face... or she could go ballistic and be all over you. A strange woman had already showed up at their house. And while she had no direct proof, Claire was nearly one hundred percent certain that woman had been Eleanor.

Was Eleanor here on campus tonight?

Her fingers trembled as she fumbled with the key. Exposed in this hallway, alone and vulnerable, she didn't have much time. Claire struggled with the lock, anxious to get inside. For all she knew, Eleanor could be delusional and deranged. No wonder Richard had turned away from her. Who could blame him, wanting to free himself of a madwoman? And there was no telling how she'd reacted to his death or the news about his other life. Had it pushed her over the edge? What if she'd gone fanatical and was intent on getting rid of her?

What if she had a gun?

Claire wriggled the key harder, frantic to get the door open, then lock it securely behind her. Once she was safely inside, she'd call campus police.

Heavy footsteps rapidly closed the distance between them. She sucked in a deep breath as she continued fighting the door. The lock was stiff. Why wasn't the key working? She could do this. She had to do this.

A hand fell on her shoulder.

Claire screamed.

"Dr. Anderson?" The girl shrank against the wall like a wounded animal, her eyes wide with fear.

One look at Sarah's pudgy face and Claire felt the sudden whoosh of breath rush out of her like a balloon deflating. She had nothing to fear from the first-year grad student except a barrage of questions and an enthusiastic embrace that would be difficult to escape. If she'd learned one thing about Sarah in the months they'd worked together, it was that the girl was needy. She needed assurance, assistance, and most of all, advice. And, from the fresh set of pimples landscaped across Sarah's forehead and cheeks, she could also use the name of a good dermatologist.

"I'm sorry," Sarah stuttered, her face flushed and red. "I didn't mean to scare you."

"That's all right," Claire said. "I thought I was alone."

"I was coming back from the library when I saw you." She shrugged the bulky backpack from her shoulders, dropping it with a heavy thud. "I know I shouldn't have followed you, but... but I've been trying to contact you for weeks. I never heard back from you."

Claire hesitated. She hadn't been around and she hadn't been checking her e-mail. The university had a protocol for use in case of emergencies. Someone would have gone into her account and set an automatic forward to someone else in their department. But what had everyone been told?

She hadn't thought to ask Dr. Max what type of story he'd concocted about her sudden departure when she met with him in the coffee shop. How much did her colleagues and students know? Just that her husband had died? Or did they know the sordid details? Probably the latter, she realized with a sinking heart. Despite being located in a major metropolitan area, the U of C was its own closed community. News traveled fast; especially the kind of scandalous story she was involved in. The gossip must be rampant. *Poor Dr. Anderson, supposedly so smart, so well versed in psychology… how could she have been so stupid?*

Were they laughing at her all over campus? Was her sorry situation the joke of the week? The month? Was she the object of pity or scorn?

"I've taken a leave of absence." Claire stumbled through the words. How did you discuss your husband's death, especially when he wasn't your husband after all?

"I was so sorry to hear about your husband. Everyone was shocked when we heard what had happened."

Claire bowed her head. Sarah and her friends weren't the only ones shocked to learn of Richard's death. "Thank you for the sympathy card. I was very… touched."

"I felt terrible for you. A bunch of us wanted to attend the funeral. We asked, but no one seemed to know any details."

"That's all right. And truly, it wasn't necessary. Your heart was in the right place."

What if she admitted the truth? What if she told Sarah that she herself hadn't even attended his funeral; that she hadn't even known Richard was dead until he was already buried.

"We all miss you. I miss you." Sarah bit her bottom lip, eyes wide and watchful. "You're the best teacher I've ever had."

"Thank you. I appreciate that." It was exactly what she needed to hear. Validation that she'd done a decent job with her students, that she was good at what she did.

That she could still be good at it. All she needed was the courage to try again.

"I can't imagine what you must be going through." Tears welled in Sarah's eyes. "You didn't deserve it. No one deserves something like that. It isn't fair."

"Life isn't fair," Claire replied, "but that doesn't mean we don't go on." Even as the words slipped from her mouth, she regretted them. Who was she to be spouting off like some ancient Greek philosopher? Her life these past few months hadn't been filled with *going on*. Rather, more like *getting by*. "Things happen," she added. "You learn to deal with it."

But had she? Could she? She was barely functioning.

"And your children. They're so young." Sarah swiped away a few tears. "Both my parents are still alive. I can't imagine not having my dad around."

Claire quieted. She and Richard had known when Dickie was born that there was a possibility—a very real possibility—that Richard might not survive to see their son grow into adulthood. The odds were against them. Some would have called their attitude fatalistic, but facts were facts and couldn't be ignored, especially given the law of statistics. Richard had been thirty years older than her. Not to mention the routine dangers he faced on his frequent business journeys in and out of the Middle East.

Yet in her heart, she'd held on to the naïve hope that the years would pass and things wouldn't change; that even if Richard survived into his nineties, he would still be at her side and sleeping in her bed each night. Perhaps he would have sported hearing aids and shambled slowly with the assistance of a walking cane. But he'd been such a vigorous, energetic man. She couldn't imagine him having succumbed to that slow descent into old age or having been beaten down by the ravages of dementia. And she would have loved him no matter what, hearing aids and all. He would have remained her Richard. In her heart, she'd never lost hope. What was life without hope?

She knew the answer to that one now. Her hope had dissolved the night Jim Kennedy showed up on her doorstep.

But even if her own hope was lost, Sarah was young. She deserved hope. And despite the girl's neediness, Sarah had always been one of her favorites.

"What are you doing here on campus?" Claire made an effort to smile. "It's Saturday night. Why aren't you out with your friends?"

"I was at the library catching up on some things. You know how it is; there's always something. But it's okay. I'll be okay."

One look at the girl's face and Claire knew that wasn't the case. Sarah wasn't okay. She was floundering. When she was Sarah's age, she'd been driven and focused, impatient and full of herself. Perhaps too full of herself, too confident of her abilities. Her natural tendency was to rush about and get on with the business of life. Sarah, however, was a messy mix of churning emotions and desperate bravado. Granted, she was smart; if she wasn't, she never would have been accepted into U of C's doctorate program. And despite her apprehensions and fumbling efforts, Sarah sometimes displayed moments of sheer brilliance, stammering to the forefront as she presented her theories about a particular hypothesis, even against fierce arguments from her classmates. Claire loved her for that. The girl was gifted with a brilliant mind, but most of the time it was bogged down like a muddy street puddle. Things clogged together, swirling beneath the surface. If anyone needed help, it was Sarah. And it didn't look like there would be a street cleaner coming to her rescue anytime soon.

Claire turned to the door. As if by miracle, the key worked this time. The door swung open. Stepping aside, she waved her hand, inviting her inside. "Come on in. We'll talk."

She snapped on the overhead light as they entered the room. It was still her office, and everything looked the same, but somehow it felt different, as if she were an interloper. There was her prized Tweety Bird clock, a gift from Richard and baby Dickie, directly above her computer where she'd hung it herself three years ago while perched in stocking feet atop her desk. There were her bookshelves, crammed with textbooks, professional journals, and research materials, and the scratched filing cabinet adjacent to the big blue plastic water cooler. There was the brain-in-a-jar atop her industrial metal desk, in the exact same spot where it had been the day she'd walked out.

And there, in the middle of the desk, in front of the monitor, sat an oversized coffee mug half-filled with a milky liquid, as if someone had been there, then gotten up and wandered off, expecting to return. Her photos of Dickie and Sophie playing on the beach had been pushed aside, half-hidden behind a stack of papers. Sticky notes marched down the side of her computer monitor, scrawled reminders in an unfamiliar handwriting of things too important to be forgotten or overlooked.

Claire stared at the unmistakable signs of an intruder. Someone had taken over her personal space. Someone had been sitting at her desk, using her computer. Someone had been using her office.

But what did she expect? She'd deserted the campus, her colleagues, her students. Richard had died. Life moved on.

She grabbed for the armchair behind her desk. Her legs no longer had the strength to support her. If she didn't sit down, she'd be on the floor. Sooner or later, she needed to make a decision about what she was going to do. But not now. She couldn't think about it now. Claire sank into the chair before her legs gave out. Her ears were ringing and her mind was fuzzy. Black and white spots danced across her line of vision. Closing her eyes, she took a deep breath. She'd never fainted in her life, but there was a first time for everything.

"Dr. Anderson?" Sarah's voice filtered through the hazy space between them. "Are you okay?"

"Give me a moment." Bending over, she put her head between her legs and forced herself to take deep, calming breaths. In, out. In, out.

A cool nudge of something wet bumped her forearm. "Drink this."

Opening her eyes, she glanced up and saw a paper cup in Sarah's hand.

"Drink it. You'll feel better," the girl said.

She didn't have the strength to argue. Taking the cup, she forced herself to down the water in tiny sips. Somehow she managed a weak smile. "Thank you."

Wordlessly, Sarah refilled the empty cup and Claire

obediently drank. By the time she'd finished, the ringing in her ears had disappeared and the dizziness had faded.

"The color's starting to come back in your cheeks."

"I feel better," she admitted. "Thank you for helping me."

"I fainted once." Sarah perched on one of the chairs in front of the desk. "I was playing on the monkey bars at school. You know how kids like to goof off. I lost my balance and fell. It wasn't far to the ground, probably about five feet, but I landed at a funny angle directly on my arm. I heard it snap beneath me. The pain was instant and white-hot, and I knew it must be broken. I remember kids circling around me as I lay there on the sand, and then I heard a girl scream. I looked down and saw that the bone had broken through the skin and was poking up at a jagged angle. That's the last thing I remember. When I woke up, I was in the hospital. The surgeons had put a metal plate in my arm to hold it in place while it healed."

Claire shuddered. She had an instinctive aversion to anything remotely connected with blood or broken bones, with ill health and hospitals. "It must have been horrible."

"Seeing the bone sticking out like that was gross, but the rest wasn't so bad. They cast my arm and I had it in a sling for two months. And since I'm right-handed ..." Sarah lifted her hand and wiggled her fingers, a crooked smile on her face. "I wasn't able to do my homework. My teachers gave me a free pass while I wore the cast. Thank God, or I would have flunked out of math class. We were studying geometry. To this day, the mention of an obtuse angle or an isosceles triangle makes me break out in a cold sweat."

Claire laughed. She'd never much been one for

mathematics either. Settling back in her chair, she gingerly fingered the nasty coffee mug, then placed it on the floor. Whomever it belonged to, they could claim it later. Until she resigned—*if* she resigned—this was still her office.

"How are things?" She studied Sarah's face.

The young woman shrugged. "Okay, I guess."

But things weren't okay. She'd been around the world of academia long enough to recognize that drawn look on a student's face. It was the one they wore while clinging to the last visage of hope, before they surrendered to the defeat of knowing they'd never be good enough, that they were surrounded by others far more competent, and that the best thing to do was to remove themselves from the equation before their ambitions were sliced, diced, and divided between peers infinitely more qualified.

"Is it one of your classes? Are you having problems?" She couldn't imagine Sarah having a difficult time with the bookwork involved. The girl could memorize facts and theories before other students had finished reading the page.

She paused. "No, it's not that."

But it was something. Definitely something.

"What about your research project?" Claire guessed. All first-year grad students were expected to immerse themselves in the world of clinical research: propose a hypothesis, collect data, explore empirical statistics. Each student was assigned to a specific professor. Up until Richard's death, she'd been the one responsible for supervising Sarah's progress. "How is that going?"

Sarah's face fell and she bowed her head.

"What's wrong?"

"Oh, Dr. Anderson, it's such a mess." The words

spilled out in a torrent, gushing between them like a river gone wild, overflowing its banks in a spring flood. "I've tried and tried, but I can't figure it out, and I don't know what to do. I'll never finish it before spring quarter ends."

"They assigned you to someone else, didn't they?"

"Yes." The words were long in coming, and the drawn-out tone didn't offer much hope. "I'm supposed to be working under Dr. Vilbrandt, but..."

Claire waited a moment, but the words weren't forthcoming. "But?" she prompted.

"But he's not you," Sarah finally admitted. "Most of the time I don't understand what he's talking about." She sighed. "It's got to be me, because it can't be him. Dr. Vilbrandt is brilliant."

Poor Sarah. No wonder she looked defeated. Being placed under the direct supervision of the departmental head, a man who had difficulties finding time to manage his own duties, let alone manage his staff and students, would confuse anyone. Especially someone like Sarah, who suffered from low self-esteem.

"I've been thinking about leaving," she mumbled. "I don't belong here."

"You can't leave. That would be a mistake." This was her fault. Sarah had tried to contact her, but she hadn't been around to take the calls. She'd been needed, but she'd made herself unavailable to her students.

"Listen to me," Claire said, waiting until the girl lifted her head and met her gaze. "Don't be so hard on yourself. Maybe things aren't going well right now, but that doesn't mean you can't turn it around. You have the brains, and you have the heart. All you need is a little..."

"Faith?" the girl whispered.

"Exactly." Claire's head bobbed in a furious nod. "Faith in yourself and that things will get better. And they will. I know they will. Maybe tonight isn't a good night, but I promise you things will look better in the morning." Reaching out, she extended a hand. "Tell me how I can help."

Sarah's face brightened, and a spot of hope lit her eyes, then quickly flared out. She shook her head. "No, I can't ask you to do that. It wouldn't be right, not with everything you're going through—"

"You didn't ask. I offered."

The girl hesitated. "Are you sure?"

Claire nodded, even though she wasn't sure about anything except the certain knowledge that she couldn't desert Sarah. The girl needed help, and she needed it now. Maybe if she phoned Hallie and asked her to stay with the children a bit longer than they'd planned, she could spend some time working with Sarah. She'd be able to help.

While it might not be a proven psychological theory, she'd always believed in the positive cause and effect of karma. Maybe, if she helped Sarah, she might end up helping herself in the process. And God knew she could use it.

Grabbing her cell phone, Claire touched the screen for Hallie's number, turning to Sarah with an encouraging smile. "How about some coffee?"

It could be a long night.

Chapter Fifteen

"The touch screen makes it very easy," the saleswoman said, demonstrating with a flick of her finger. "When the customer is ready to purchase, you simply tap the button labeled Make a Sale"—she clicked on a link at the top of the screen, instantly producing another layer of screen upon screen—"and use your scanner." She snatched the plastic handheld device that reminded Eleanor of a clunky black gun, seized a sweater discarded by a customer moments before, and hovered the scanner over the bar code. A tiny ping registered on the computer.

"See that?" she pointed out the display to Eleanor. "It does all the work for you: registers the full price, applies the discount, if any, plus adds the tax. Like I said... it's easy."

Eleanor nodded, though it didn't seem easy. She and machinery weren't exactly friends, and this one seemed complicated. Would she get the hang of it?

"You'll get the hang of it," the woman added. "Any questions?"

She had so many questions she didn't know where

to begin. She was already having doubts about having taken this job. How would she learn to become as fast and efficient as the woman training her?

"Fold this and put it back on the shelf." She handed the sweater to Eleanor. "Remember, you're responsible for assisting customers and ringing up sales, but you're also expected to keep the inventory stocked and neat. You wouldn't believe what a mess people can make. They don't think twice about pawing through things, especially when we're having a sale." She rolled her eyes. "Women are the worst. Some of them are like pigs rooting through a barnyard, trying to sniff out the best deals and leaving us to clean up their mess."

Eleanor reddened, remembering all the times she'd shopped in this store because of a sale. Had she straightened up after herself, or had she left it for someone else? God forbid she'd been one of those women they thought of as pigs.

"And don't forget to check the fitting rooms."

"Right." One more thing to add to the mental checklist she'd been making during their training session and hour-long tour of the woman's retail department.

"You'll have lots of clothing to put away. Most people don't bother. When something doesn't fit, they either leave it hanging, or sometimes on the floor. They expect us to take care of everything. What are we, their mothers?"

Eleanor kept quiet. She'd taught her children to pick up after themselves at an early age. Jeffrey had learned fast, but Vivi still treated her clothes the same way she lived her life, strewing blouses and suits as freely as her emotions, leaving others to deal with the mess.

"If you have any questions, I'll be over in jewelry."

"You're leaving?" Her heartbeat quickened at the thought of being left alone to face the crowds. So much for the pledge given her by the young woman in Grayson's Human Resources department. Three days training assisted by another staff member, she'd assured Eleanor. Empty promises, she thought to herself. But what did you expect from someone barely old enough to have graduated college, let alone be heading up an HR department? The girl had been young enough to be her own daughter... or granddaughter.

"Don't worry, you'll be fine. Tuesdays are usually slow unless we're having a sale."

Eleanor watched in dismay as the woman breezed away, rounded a corner, and disappeared from sight. Turning, she glanced around the sales floor, trying not to panic as she took in the racks of colorful summer sweaters, silky polo shirts, and cropped capris. Her first day on the job and they expected her to handle things alone? She hadn't even been on the clock two hours.

She eyed the sleek digital register with its vivid green display. It seemed to wink at her, as if daring her to just try to ring up an order. *You'll do it wrong!* Her mind raced to remember what came first. Why hadn't she thought to write things down? What if she pushed the wrong button? What if she rang up the wrong amount? What if she gave the wrong change? What in the world had she been thinking? She'd never worked a day of retail in her life.

Yet she hadn't hesitated when she'd noticed the ad for help in the store window. Why not? She needed the money. She'd marched in and asked for an application, only to be chided by a snooty young girl in a size-zero dress with a size-twenty-four-plus attitude. Online applications only, she'd informed Eleanor, who for once in her life had put pedal to the metal and broke the speed limit driving home. She had the application filled out and submitted via email to HR before even taking off her coat.

Three hours later, she'd been back at the mall, sitting for her first interview at Grayson's request. Despite her lack of retail experience and the fact she hadn't worked in over thirty years, she'd been hired on the spot.

And she'd done it herself, something she took immense pride in. She'd been tempted to list Vivi as a reference while filling out the application. What would be the harm in it, Eleanor argued with herself. At her age, she needed every advantage she could get. Mentioning her daughter's name and her high-profile career at Grayson's corporate headquarters probably would have guaranteed an automatic *you're hired*. But *don't do it!* had triumphed over desperation. Her mother's intuition warned her that nothing good would come of it. While she loved her daughter, there were times she didn't particularly like her. Even if it meant she didn't get the job, she'd rest easy knowing she wasn't beholden to Vivi. Better to be hired based on her own merit.

That, and her Grayson's elite charge card, which granted her premier gold-pin member status, entitling her to exclusive sales and benefits most customers couldn't afford. Not that she could afford them, either. Not anymore. She hadn't used the store's charge card in months. She didn't dare. No new charges, Jeffrey had warned once the balance was paid off. Cut the card up in little pieces so it doesn't tempt you, he'd urged, but she hadn't been able to bring herself to do it. It remained safely tucked away in her wallet. She'd lost so many things, but she didn't want to lose that too. Her Grayson's card was a reminder that, once upon a time, she'd lived a different life. A life where things were easy, credit came cheap, and bills were paid on time.

Not that she could afford anything in this store, even with the employee discount they offered. She was earning minimum wage, and that didn't stretch far. It barely covered her groceries. She wouldn't earn any commission on sales until she'd been with Grayson's for thirty days. And she needed those commissions. First and last month's rent plus security deposit on an apartment—even the tiniest of apartments—would stretch her budget to the point where it snapped.

Eleanor bent to retrieve some folds of wrapping tissue that had slipped from beneath the counter and floated to the ground. The irony of the situation put a twisted smile on her face. Ground floor, that's where she was now. That old adage about starting from the ground and working your way up applied to her.

"Excuse me?" A nasal voice filtered through the distraction of her former life. "I need some help."

Glancing up, Eleanor found her first customer of the day standing before her. The woman, whom she guessed to be slightly older than herself, held out a pair of floral capri slacks.

"I tried them on, but they don't fit." The woman shoved them across the counter. "I don't understand why they're too small. They're my size."

"Let me see." Taking the slacks from her hand, Eleanor carefully examined them. The soft, silky fabric was sporty and fun, outrageous with splashes of bright summer colors. Even more outrageous was the $150 price tag dangling from the waistband. She blanched at the sight. Six months ago, she wouldn't have thought twice about buying a pair of slacks such as these. The print was divine and exactly the type of thing she would have worn... *if* she'd had the nerve, not to mention the figure to go along with it. Women her age had no business wearing pants like these... especially women sporting a rear end as large as hers.

And the woman across the counter looked even bigger. Size ten? Eleanor double-checked the tag. No wonder they hadn't fit. The woman had to be at least a size fourteen, if not a sixteen.

"You must have mismarked them," the woman insisted. "I want to try on another pair. I wear a size ten."

Eleanor hesitated, glanced at the tag, then back at the woman. "Are you sure? I wear a fourteen, and we look about the same size."

"Excuse me?" Her eyes popped. "I don't remember asking you for a commentary on what size I am. I told you I wear a ten." She snatched the slacks from Eleanor's hands with an icy stare colder than the arctic blast of air-conditioning chilling the sales floor. "I'll find someone else to help me."

"No, wait," Eleanor pleaded. "I'm sorry, I didn't mean to insult you. Let me see what I can do." *Don't panic*, she thought. There had to be a polite, professional way out of it.

Not. Ten minutes and four pairs of pants later, the

woman stormed off, muttering dire predictions about the cheap clothing manufacturers from China and their mismatched sizing, and the incompetent help Grayson's department store was hiring nowadays. Eleanor watched her go, both dismayed and delighted. True, she'd lost a sale, but at least she'd been saved from having to do battle with the cash register.

She lost herself in straightening inventory, checking the fitting rooms, making sure the sales floor was neat and tidy. There wasn't much to do. Just as the saleswoman who'd trained her had promised, Tuesdays were notoriously slow. Hopefully things would improve after lunch. A few shoppers trickled through her area, pausing to finger some of the merchandise before moving on. Then her mentor was back, informing her it was time for a break. She pointed toward an inconspicuous door.

Eleanor headed for the break room, relishing the idea of being able to sit and massage her feet. And it was thrilling to be a part of something bigger than herself, to be admitted entrance into the exclusive world of Employees Only.

The break room was sparsely furnished with two round tables, a groaning refrigerator, and a long utility counter containing a half-empty coffeepot, some Styrofoam cups, and a white microwave that looked as if it had seen better days. A lone woman sat at one of the tables. Eleanor had a smile ready, but the woman never glanced up. Head bowed, eyes down, she was engrossed in the e-reader before her. Eleanor passed in silence, allowing the woman her privacy. Everyone needed downtime, and it was nice to see someone reading. *Once a reader, always a reader*, she liked to say at the library. A pang of regret stirred in her heart as she realized it was Tuesday. That was her day to be at the library and read to the children.

Not anymore. Her Library Lady days were done.

Heading for the counter, Eleanor poured herself a cup of thin brown liquid. She grimaced as she took a sip. This wouldn't have passed for coffee in the restaurants she usually frequented. Then again, she didn't go to restaurants anymore. And at least the coffee was hot. She tore open a packet of creamer and added a dollop of sugar, then another. What was the harm in a little indulgence? She could afford it. She'd lost a few pounds, and her skirt wasn't as snug as it used to be. Besides, it was her first day on the job. That demanded some type of celebration, didn't it?

Crumbs and dirty paper plates from a half-eaten coffee cake littered the second table. Eleanor stared at the mess. The table hadn't been wiped down. What was the matter with people? Didn't they know how to clean up after themselves? Placing her cup on the edge of the table, she grabbed a few plates and headed for an overflowing trash can in the corner.

"I wouldn't do that if I were you."

"Excuse me?" Eleanor halted, then turned to face the woman holding the e-reader.

"Do it once and they'll expect it. Then you'll be stuck cleaning up all the time." She waved a hand toward an empty seat at her table. "Sit here if you want."

"I don't want to bother you."

She shrugged. "I'm leaving in a minute."

"Thanks." Eleanor dumped the plates in the trash can

despite the woman's advice to ignore the mess. That wasn't the way she'd been raised. Heading back to the sink, she briskly washed her hands, thoroughly drying them with a paper towel. Perhaps she should begin carrying hand sanitizer in her purse. One couldn't be too careful. You never knew what type of germs you might encounter from being around other people. And despite Grayson's being an upscale department store, the break room looked like it belonged in some bargain-basement outlet mall. Someone needed to give it a good cleaning with some industrial-strength sanitizer.

"You look familiar. Do we know each other?" the woman asked as Eleanor took a seat across from her. Removing her glasses, she examined Eleanor closely. A slow surprise spread across her face. "Miss Taylor?"

Eleanor blanched. No one had addressed her by her maiden name for nearly forty years.

"It *is* you." She shoved the e-reader aside. "I'd recognize you anywhere. You're Miss Taylor." Her smile widened into an outright grin. "You were my teacher in second grade."

Not in this life, the response bubbled up in Eleanor's throat, though she didn't say it. She might be old, but she wasn't *that* old. The woman, with a sagging neckline, crow's-feet lining her eyes, and a deep groove of wrinkles carved across her forehead, had to be at least in her mid-forties. Eleanor quickly did the math. Yes, she'd taught elementary school for a few years before marrying Richard, but there was no way in hell she'd been this woman's teacher.

"Missy Moran." The woman's face beamed like a

lighthouse beacon, intent on showing Eleanor the way. "Back then, everyone called me Missy... everyone except you, that is. I've never forgotten how you always insisted on calling me Melissa. You said it was a beautiful name and that I should embrace it."

Eleanor squinted at the woman's name tag. "Welcome to Grayson's!" it read. "My name is Melissa."

My God. She *did* remember. Missy Moran had been a little squirt of a thing, all knobby knees and shrill voice, darting around the classroom.

"I can't believe we're sitting here together," Missy said. "I mean, it's been, what? How many years? I must have been about seven at the time, which makes it—"

"Many, many years ago," Eleanor cut in. The last thing she wanted to participate in was a *let's count the years and see how old we are* discussion. And she couldn't believe Melissa wanted that, either. The years hadn't been kind to her former second grader. Missy Moran had been small for her age, with wispy golden-blond hair flying in every direction, while the adult Melissa had grown into her body and then some. Or perhaps *exploded* would be a better description, she thought, eyeing the ample bosom and the set of buttons straining across Missy's blouse. And though her hair still qualified as some type of blond, dark roots edging the hairline hinted that a bottle of color was definitely involved.

How could she have let herself go? Missy wasn't that much older than Jeffrey, yet she looked like she could be his mother. Well, maybe not his mother, Eleanor conceded, but a much older sister.

"How long have you worked here?" Missy asked.

The Other Wife

"Today's my first day." Eleanor tugged off first one shoe, then the other, wriggling her toes with a small groan of pleasure. At one point that morning, she gladly would have given an hour's pay for the chance to perch on a chair or stool, even for a minute. Being on your feet all day was hard work.

"What made you decide to quit teaching school and start working here? Did you get tired of kids mouthing off and decide to retire?" Missy shot her a quick smile. "Never mind, I shouldn't have asked. It's none of my business."

"That's all right," Eleanor replied. "I haven't taught in years. I gave it up after I was married."

There'd been no need for her to work, remembering how she'd given notice at the elementary school where she taught. Richard always took care of everything. He would take care of her too. It wasn't as if they needed the money from a second income. Richard always had a knack for being in the right place at the right time.

The first year she'd been fraught with worry, living on the edge as he gambled with their future, taking chances yet always succeeding. But that was life with Richard. Taking advantage of an unexpected opportunity, he'd started his own company... thanks to a hefty sum of financial backing from her parents. Within six months, he'd turned what could have been a dicey proposition into a successful financial endeavor and repaid her parents in full. Thank God for that. Eleanor hadn't liked the thought of his having borrowed money from her parents—especially since he'd never mentioned it to her. Only when her mother let it slip over lunch one day did Eleanor discover the truth. She'd been furious with Richard. Why hadn't he discussed it with her first? Probably because he knew she would have said no. But her parents could afford it, he'd argued with her later that night in bed. What was the problem? Besides, she was an only child and would someday inherit everything they had. She'd simply received some of it a little earlier than expected, he'd soothed her. And, as usual, she'd given in. She'd never been able to resist him, especially when he smothered all her well-thought-out arguments with passionate kisses that reduced her to senselessness. She loved every minute of being in Richard's arms. When he made love to her, she felt cherished and blessed.

Out of all the women in the world, she was the one he'd chosen. Eleanor never allowed herself to forget it. She clung to it as the years of their marriage unfolded like a silk fan, gently brushing away the covetous glances of other women. He could have had any woman he wanted, yet she was the one he'd taken for his wife. And while other marriages crumbled around them, littering the floor like stale bits of crackers to be swept up and thrown in the trash, their marriage survived. There even might have been other women—probably *must* have been other women. Richard had certainly had the opportunity, given all his travels—but she'd never wanted to know. It was easier to cope if you didn't know the truth. She turned a blind eye to anything that might have happened away from their house, clinging fervently to what they did have: their children, their home, and a life together.

She never worried about her husband straying. She'd been obsessed with him her whole life, and both of them knew it. Just as both of them knew that she loved him more than he loved her. Richard took full advantage of the power that knowledge gave him. He never offered excuses for his frequent absences, and Eleanor, in return, never complained. She hated herself for being so meek, for always giving in. But standing up for herself and her own needs might result in the unthinkable, which she refused to contemplate. Life without Richard was no life at all. How could she give him up? She couldn't. She wouldn't. She'd loved him all her life. And it wasn't as if her life wasn't fulfilling. She had her books, her gardens, her volunteer work, and her stint each week as the Library Lady. Small rewards, but satisfying in their own ways.

And she was the one Richard returned to at the end of his trips. She was the one who kept the bed warm. Things were good between them those first years, even during those middle years.

Until one day, when they weren't.

Until one day, when she suddenly realized that everything had stopped. How and when had it happened?

Until one day when she woke up in bed and found him dead beside her.

She still wasn't sure which had been worse: Richard's death or the discovery afterward that he'd fallen in love with another woman.

In love enough to marry her.

And if that hadn't happened, he never would have switched his insurance beneficiary. He wouldn't have refinanced the house, putting her home in jeopardy. That horrible Claire Anderson was to blame. What kind of evil spell had the woman cast over Richard? She'd destroyed everything. If it hadn't been for her, Richard never would have made the decisions he had, decisions for which

Eleanor was suffering now. Cutting back on expenses. Putting their house on the market. Being forced to find a job.

"Wish I didn't have to work," Missy said, bringing her back into the present. "But with three kids in school, every dollar counts. And my husband lost his job last year when his company was downsized. It hasn't been easy."

Eleanor nodded. She knew exactly how Missy felt. In a way, she'd been downsized too.

"What about you?" Missy asked. "Are you planning to work full time, or just picking up some hours for a little extra cash?"

Goodness, she was getting personal. Why hadn't someone taught her the niceties of polite conversation? Eleanor fumbled for her wedding ring, something she'd used as a touchstone throughout the years, worrying it around her knuckle when anything troubled her. But her ring finger was empty. She looked down in surprise, then abruptly remembered that day when she'd yanked off the ring and thrown it on Jeffrey's desk. A foul memory, returning like rotting garbage someone had forgotten to toss out.

Quid pro quo. When he'd married that other woman, Richard had tossed *her* in the trash.

"My husband died a few months ago."

"Oh." Missy's face reddened. "I'm sorry. I didn't—"

"It's fine," Eleanor assured her, though *fine* was the furthest thing from the truth. But she wasn't about to spill her guts in this dingy little break room. People didn't need to know everything. Especially Missy, who, from what

Eleanor recalled, had been the class blabbermouth, even in second grade. "I thought a job might help me…"

"To cope?" Missy nodded fervently. "My mom did the same thing after my dad died last year. It was the best thing she could have done. It helped keep her mind off things, you know? There's something to be said for keeping busy."

If only that were the case and all she needed: something to keep herself distracted. But it was more than that. It didn't sound as if Missy had heard the stories circulating about Richard's dalliance with that woman. Good, let her think what she wanted. Let them all think what they wanted. Meanwhile, she'd play the part of a recent widow who asked for nothing more than to be allowed to grieve in her own way. A widow who'd decided she needed to spend some time among others, away from the house. It wouldn't be so hard. Not really. Not at all.

Yes, she was grieving, but not for Richard. She was grieving what she'd lost. The ability to trust her friends, to believe in others. To keep her head up, and look people in the eye. To go where she wanted, when she wanted, without worrying about people whispering behind her back. Her friends had deserted her, her house was on the market, and her self-respect had tanked.

Damn Richard for putting her in this position. If she'd known about his relationship and marriage to Claire Anderson when it occurred, he would not have died in bed. He wouldn't have had the chance, Eleanor thought. She would have put him in the grave herself. And she wouldn't have a job at Grayson's selling retail to ungrateful customers. Instead, she'd be sitting in a cozy cell with a bed and three daily meals, courtesy of the Cook

County Penal System once they'd pronounced her guilty for murdering her husband.

How hard could it be to murder someone? You'd have to be careful. Then again, if you didn't care about getting caught, there was no need to be careful.

"I work Home Décor. China patterns, Waterford crystal, scented candles, and picture frames," Missy said. "But it's better than Bedding and Bath. They had me over there for a while last month, covering for an associate on sick leave. Talk about boring." She rolled her eyes. "All that folding towels and stacking throw pillows? No thanks. Not for me. And steer clear of the kids' section. What a mess. If it's not screaming babies in strollers, it's kids tearing down the aisles, grabbing for the stuffed animals and knocking into displays. Their mothers ignore them. I don't get it. My kids weren't raised to act that way. This is a store, not a kid's personal playground. And grandmothers? All money and no brains. They come in here, paw through things, looking for the perfect color and right size. And if they do buy something, nine times out of ten, they're back a few days later to return whatever it was because it didn't fit. Swear to God, grandmothers are the worst."

Eleanor stayed quiet. How many times had she shopped at Grayson's children's section for Richie, uncertain of the proper size, unable to make up her mind? The saleswomen had always been so patient and friendly, even when she left without buying anything or returned the next day for a refund on the item. Now she found herself wondering if the sales staff had secretly been laughing at her.

"What department have they got you in?"

"Women's Clothing." She took a cautious sip of her

coffee, grimaced, and forced herself to swallow. She'd throw some tea bags in her purse before she left the house tomorrow. Anything would be better than this horrible brew.

"That's not so bad. But watch out if you see a group of women coming in together."

"Why?"

"They'll waste your time." Missy nodded knowingly. "They try things on and expect you to keep hauling things into the dressing room for them. They're rude and demanding and complain about everything. And they usually leave without buying a thing. Trust me, when you see a group of women headed into your department, you might as well kiss your commission good-bye."

Eleanor shuddered, thinking of the floral-capri customer from earlier that morning. She hadn't been particularly friendly; in fact, she'd been downright rude. The only thing worse than waiting on that woman would have been waiting on her and a group of friends.

"You were a great teacher. Don't you miss it?"

"I... I suppose I do." The question caught her by surprise. It seemed like forever since she'd been in a classroom or discussing her own children's educational issues during parent-teacher conferences. Neither of their children had given them cause for concern. They'd grown up and had good jobs. Satisfying careers. Sometimes it was hard to remember when Jeffrey and Vivi hadn't been adults. Neither of them needed her anymore. Ironic, how the years had passed and the tables had turned. She was the needy one now.

Missy glanced at her watch. "Oh, God, I'm late. Sorry,

I've got to go. The china patterns are calling." Rising, she flashed Eleanor a bright smile. "I'm sure we'll see each other again. It was great catching up with you. Good luck, Miss Taylor."

"Thank you." Eleanor watched her go with mingled relief and reluctance. She felt as if for the past five minutes she'd been tiptoeing through a verbal minefield littered with live bombs ready to explode. Yet she'd safely reached the other side with no casualties.

Miss Taylor.

Or maybe not. Her life had been reduced to working shoulder to shoulder with former students, fetching clothes for women of privilege. Women with money, who took everything for granted, who had the kind of life she used to have.

The kind of life that was lost to her now.

She was no longer Miss Taylor. That life had disappeared long ago, and so had her life as Mrs. Anderson. And as for starting over in a new career? What made her think she had the skills? She'd taught for a few years, then sunk into a comfortable life as a stay-at-home mother, raising two children. Now she found herself alone, disgraced and ashamed, facing a mountain of debt. How would she find her way through the foothills, scale the peaks, reach the summit?

She couldn't. Not when she was competing with women like Missy, or her own daughter, Vivi, or women with fancy Ivy League degrees like that horrid Claire Anderson who'd stolen her husband. How could she compete with any of them? She was fifty-eight years old. Starting over was impossible. Who was she trying to kid?

She'd never felt as old as she did at this moment.

Eleanor blinked hard, forcing away the sudden tears. She clutched her coffee cup, rose, and pushed in her chair. She must have been crazy to have felt sorry for Claire Anderson. Granted, Richard's death had left the woman with two small children to raise on her own. But so what? She'd get through it. She was educated, she had a successful career. Claire Anderson wasn't stuck selling capri pants to overweight women in some overpriced department store. She'd never find herself swilling lousy coffee in a shabby break room, grateful for five minutes off her feet. She had a good job at one of the finest universities in America.

And let's not forget, Eleanor reminded herself, that thanks to Richard and his sneaky insurance setup, the esteemed Professor Anderson was financially set for life.

Maybe she should phone Jeffrey tonight, tell him she'd decided to take his advice and nix her original idea of gifting Claire's children with the money from Richard's estate, and that he should put a stop payment on the bank's checks. They didn't need it. Claire had enough. She had enough for all of them. Claire was the one with all the money... money that rightfully should have been hers.

Claire Anderson probably thought she was above it all, that she could do as she liked. What made her think she had the right to steal another woman's husband? To steal her house and her security? Claire had stolen everything that had been right in her world and her life. *She* was Richard's widow, Eleanor thought, not that stupid thirtysomething know-it-all. Any court in Illinois would back her claim as his legal heir.

Though not when it came to the insurance money. There

was no way around the switching insurance beneficiaries. She wouldn't be able to wrestle that money from Claire.

Two more hours, Eleanor consoled herself, and her day would be done at this stupid store. She could go home, bury her head in a pillow, and shut out the world. Until then, she could do this. She had to do this. Thanks to Richard, she had no choice.

Eleanor dragged in a deep breath and exhaled, trying to release some of the rage building inside her. She'd be late if she didn't get back on the sales floor. That wouldn't do, especially on her first day. She didn't want her new employers to have the wrong impression. She'd always been a punctual person, and she liked to keep things neat and organized. Life was easier that way. Less confusion equaled less disappointment. That's the way it always had been and the way it should be.

Including in a marriage.

Eleanor poured her cold coffee down the sink and dumped the dirty cup in the garbage. Too bad she couldn't dump her resentments as well. The coffee had left a bitter tang in her mouth. She hated feeling this way: vindictive and nasty, wanting a taste of revenge.

What goes around comes around, her mother had liked to say. A grim smile lit her face as Eleanor headed out the door. If there was one thing she'd learned about old adages, it was that they usually proved true.

Someday, Claire Anderson would be sorry.

Very, very sorry.

Chapter Sixteen

The house was closing in on her, and she couldn't bear it. Not for another month, another week, not even another day. Not if she wanted to keep her sanity... what little there was left of it.

Everywhere she turned, every room she entered, reminded her of Richard. The spacious living room and the beautiful artwork, collected during his world travels, that graced the scarlet walls. The gleaming original hardwood floors throughout the downstairs rooms; flooring he'd insisted the contractor save (damn the expense!) rather than pull up when they'd discovered the dry rot. The kitchen and its sleek granite countertops.

Even the cozy laundry room with its sterile white walls, utility cabinets, and functional washer and dryer, was no shelter from memories of Richard. He'd had her right there in the laundry room, stealing up behind her one cold frosty morning a few weeks into the new year as she sorted towels fresh from the dryer.

"What are you doing?" she'd whispered as his arms

wrapped around her and his lips pressed against the nape of her neck.

"What do you think I'm doing?" He'd laughed in response as his hands cupped her breasts and he turned her to face him.

"The children will hear us," she sputtered, common sense struggling against the instant surge of desire flooding through her.

"They're in the backyard making a snowman," he countered, breath hot against her ear. His nimble fingers quickly had her blouse unbuttoned and her breasts tumbling free, spilling into his hands. Bending his head, he took them in his mouth, his tongue teasing and tempting as she arched her back and closed her eyes. "They'll never miss us," he whispered. "But I miss you."

And in the end, she had no choice. He gave her no choice. He took her, right there in the laundry room, propping her atop the dryer, insisting that she yield and submit to his demands, though he never spoke a word. He didn't have to. His hands and lips did all the talking. And the minute he touched her, the minute she felt that familiar tug in her tummy, she knew she would give in. She couldn't deny him. She could never deny him. She wanted him as much as he wanted her. More, perhaps. There'd been a few men in her life, but none like Richard. He knew exactly how to please a woman, and she was like a drunk when it came to his touch, helpless to resist the powerful primal urges and the pleasure she found each time they came together. And Richard loved it. He reveled in the power of knowing he could make her body sing. He knew her, every intimate inch of her.

That midmorning tryst and the stolen moments they'd spent in the cramped space that smelled of bleach and fabric softener had been one of the most erotic moments of her life. Following that morning, she'd never minded doing laundry again. Memories of Richard and their lovemaking erased any thoughts of the room as a place for chores.

Until now. Now, she couldn't care less if the dirty towels piled high in the hamper. She had no desire to run the washer or empty the dryer. Hallie took care of things, making sure the children had clean clothes. Claire didn't care if she herself wore the same shirt two or three days in a row. What did it matter? There was no one around to see; no one except Hallie, who would never say a word. And the children were too young to notice. They didn't care.

She didn't care.

Sometimes, not so much in the stillness of the night as in the bright, unforgiving light of day, when she passed the laundry room door, it was then that she feared for her sanity. Somehow she had to find her way back to caring or she would slip over the edge. What would happen to her then? What would happen to them all?

What if she remained lost forever? That was the thing that frightened her most. She had to do something.

"I'm thinking of going away for a while," Claire announced, shielding her eyes from the bright morning sunshine spilling into the kitchen. She'd been up for two hours and already had a headache from the constant cheeriness surrounding her. Some rain and gray sky would be appreciated. At least it would match her mood.

"Go away?" Hallie, intent on loading the breakfast

dishes into the dishwasher, glanced up, a dirty plate still in hand. "But where? Why?"

"Why not?" She sipped her coffee, cold now, then pushed it away. Why not, indeed? Summer officially had arrived. Though the thick, cloying humidity hadn't yet descended upon the city, it wasn't far off. Chicago temperatures had already broken through the nineties twice the week before, and the forecast promised more of the same.

"Are you taking the children?"

"Yes." She couldn't leave them behind. She wouldn't do that to them. Dickie and Sophie were all she had left. The children would be miserable in the coming heat. Why not get away? She could think of no earthly reason not to. She'd been concerned about Sarah, but the girl was gone now, instructed by Claire to go home for the summer and work on nothing more than getting a good suntan and showing up for her second year on campus with a refreshed attitude. Dickie was on sabbatical from Lab nursery school, with three full months of freedom and fun stretching out before him. She was on sabbatical, too, since the University had granted her request for a year's leave. God knows what she would have done if they'd refused and she'd been forced to make a final decision.

She still hadn't decided which direction her life would take going forward. She needed time to think. She needed to find a way to put herself back together. Life as she'd known it had slipped away in the night, just as Richard's life had slipped from his body and out of her world. Nothing was normal anymore. Not her life, not this house, not her family. Not anything.

Somehow she had to find a way to make a new normal. A new normal that no longer included Richard.

"Why don't you come with us?" she suggested. "I'd love the company, and so would the children."

Hallie plopped down on the stool next to her, lifting her thick blond hair off her neck and looping it in a ponytail high atop her head. "Getting away sounds great. Where are you going?"

Claire shrugged. "I don't know. I haven't thought much about it. It doesn't matter, now I have the time, and the... the money."

The words stuck in her throat. It seemed like a travesty, using Richard's money to escape this house and memories of him.

"Please say yes." Reaching across the counter, she cupped a hand over Hallie's fingers. "Naturally I'll pay you. But I'm not asking you along because of the children. I'm asking you for me too. As a friend."

Hallie's eyes softened. "I'd love to come along. But you don't have to pay me."

"No, I insist. You'll have your regular salary, plus expenses."

"Honestly, Claire, I don't want your money. I could use a vacation, and the children—"

"Not another word." She lifted a hand, halting Hallie's protest. "I can afford it, and I want to do it. We'll have lots of fun," she said, doubting the words even as she spoke. "I promise," she added for good measure, trying to reassure herself.

"You're right. Getting away will be good for us all.

And we will have a great time." Leaning forward, Hallie caught her in a hug.

Claire felt like a traitor as she returned the embrace. She had no business guaranteeing anyone a good time, not when she felt like she did. Poor Hallie. The girl had no idea what she was in for.

"Where do you want to go? Let's make some plans. How long do you want to be gone?"

Hallie's questioning left her exhausted. This whole thing had been merely a way to escape. Faced with planning and logistics, it sounded too hard to contemplate. "I don't know. A week? Maybe two?"

"Dickie would love Disney World."

"Florida in summer?" Claire wrinkled her nose. "Too hot. Besides, Sophie's too little. She wouldn't enjoy it." Neither would she. Strolling through the family-friendly theme park surrounded by crowds of people, husbands and wives, fathers and mothers, sounded like something straight out of a nightmare. She wouldn't be able to handle it, not even with Hallie along for support.

"Someplace easy and not far away." She didn't have the energy for packing suitcases and flying out of O'Hare to some distant location. "Let's take a road trip."

"What about Michigan? We could drive north, see where it takes us. Have you ever been to Mackinaw?"

"No."

"My parents took me years ago, when I was still in grade school. We visited the fort, drove across the bridge, and took the ferry to the island." Hallie's voice warmed with enthusiasm. "It was lots of fun. And it's not a bad drive; five or six hours from Chicago. There's so much to do in that area. The kids would love it."

Claire quieted. Maybe Hallie was right. Northern Michigan, with its promise of sunny days and crisp, cool nights, might provide the perfect escape. No one knew her up north. There'd be no need to be on guard, constantly watching over her shoulder. She would have a chance to clear her mind. And with Hallie along, she'd be able to relax, loosen up, let herself go. Plus, the children would have a good time. Mackinaw might be just the spot. Tourists loved it.

More importantly, it held no memories of Richard.

Her thoughts turned to the treasured beach photo atop her desk in Stuart Hall. She'd captured the image last summer, of Dickie, Sophie, and Richard playing on a sugar-sand beach on the shore of Lake Michigan. What a grand, glorious time the four of them had had together... and they nearly hadn't gone.

"You need to relax, Claire," he'd insisted when she resisted his spontaneous suggestion that they scoop up the children and whisk them off to Michigan for a weekend getaway.

"I can't." She had no scheduled classes during the summer session, but that didn't mean her workload was any less. Like her colleagues, she used her summers to catch up on all the things spilling over from other sessions. There were grad students to supervise, future courses to prep for, supervisory meetings to attend. Sometimes the obligatory duties seemed overwhelming, and she would find herself wondering how she would manage.

And with Richard gone so often, she was the one

responsible for keeping things going. She loved her husband and her family, her job and her life, but overseeing everything could be exhausting.

"You're working too hard," he said, brushing his lips against the nape of her neck, arms wrapped around her in a gentle caress. "It won't hurt to take a break."

"But I can't," she protested weakly, knowing he wouldn't listen.

"Yes, you can. The kids need you, and so do I." His breath was warm and heavy against her neck as his hands roamed her body, touching her in the familiar places that he knew she loved. She felt the familiar tug of awakening desire stirring inside her. She could never say no when he touched her like that.

"Let's go play in the sunshine," he urged.

As usual, she gave in. And, as usual, he was right. The quick getaway was exactly what she needed. She tossed some clothes in their bags while Richard made the arrangements. Within a few hours, they were in the car, headed north up the coast. His choice of lodging surprised her when they arrived. The quaint one-bedroom cottage nestled on the shore of Lake Michigan near Glen Arbor was clean and immaculate, but not the sort of place he normally chose. Traveling with Richard usually involved five-star hotels with spacious suites, plush bedding, and twenty-four-hour room service.

But by late that first evening, Claire knew he'd picked the perfect spot for a family getaway. She was as enchanted as the children with the tiny cottage he'd chosen. Dinner on the deck, a hastily thrown-together fare of hot dogs and potato chips followed by toasting marshmallows in the fire pit beyond the front steps on the beach. Come ten o'clock, as darkness finally descended, the children willingly went to bed. Dickie scurried into the top bunk and proclaimed his kingdom while they tucked Sophie in the bottom bunk, the floor beneath her padded with sofa cushions in case she tumbled out. Both of the children were asleep before she took Richard's hand and led him outside.

They stayed on the deck, perched together on the steps leading to the beach, close enough to catch the sound of a child's cry through the open window behind them. Overhead, the sky was brilliant with stars, and they opened a bottle of wine, spent an hour sitting in the darkness, watching, quiet together. More than a few times, they spotted a glimmering streak in the sky and would point heavenward at yet another shooting star.

"This is nice," Claire whispered, snuggling closer into him. "I'm glad we came."

He touched her cheek and smiled into her eyes. "You need to be more gentle with yourself. Be good to yourself. Promise me?"

And she quietly agreed, toasting her promise with the last of the wine before they went inside and made love.

"Be good to yourself," he murmured again as they lay there in bed, drowsy with lovemaking, drifting off to sleep. "You're too hard on yourself. Promise me you'll try."

She'd promised him that night. She would promise him the world if that's what he wanted.

It was a promise she had to keep.

Despite the fact that he'd betrayed her. Despite the fact that, all the time he'd been relaxing and playing with her and the children on the beach, he'd left another family, another woman, another wife, behind in Chicago.

And that woman, Eleanor, was no longer content to sit in the shadows. For weeks, Claire had had the eerie sense that someone was out there, studying her movements, waiting for the perfect time to catch her alone. No doubt people would think she'd gone mental if she spoke of it. They'd say she was crazy. Sometimes she thought she *was* crazy.

Was she being stalked by Eleanor Anderson?

There was no concrete evidence, no tangible proof to prove she was right, nothing to back up her suspicions, save for the one time the woman had shown up at the house, sitting in her car, studying Claire across the lawn. It hadn't happened again, not that Claire had noticed. But that didn't mean Eleanor wasn't out there some nights, her aging Mercedes parked halfway down the street, hidden in the shadows of the mighty oak trees lining their street. Probably sitting in her car, cursing Claire's life as she guzzled coffee or God knows what else.

Was the woman an alcoholic? Claire mused over the idea more than once. That would have been a good reason for Richard to have turned against her. But it still wouldn't have excused him of culpability nor released him from responsibility for the horrible thing he'd hidden from them both. He'd duped each of them into believing she was the only woman in his life. What he'd done had been cruel, not to mention criminal. If Richard weren't dead, he'd be sitting in a prison cell. He'd caused both of them immeasurable pain and grief. If Eleanor was an alcoholic, at least it would make the situation more plausible, more understandable. Claire was accustomed to dealing with logic and rationale. Richard had been an astute thinker and so sure of himself. He would have searched for any way out. But why not divorce? How could he have allowed himself to have been shackled to that woman for so many years? A woman he'd obviously no longer loved. A crazy woman who sat outside other people's houses in the still of the night, munching on candy cars to keep herself awake, biding her time as she watched and waited.

Claire knew it was Eleanor, she knew it in her gut. Eleanor was probably also the one responsible for the random phone calls she'd recently started receiving. The one-ring-hang-ups in the night came from a private number, with call return blocked the few times Claire attempted to call back. And then there'd been that night on campus. She'd been positive it was Eleanor pursuing her up the stairs of Stuart Hall. Though Sarah had been the one following her that night, it didn't mean Eleanor wasn't still out there, watching and waiting. Maybe she wanted the money back; money she'd given the children from Richard's will. But if that was the case, why had Eleanor honored the bequest in the first place? Eleanor had no legal proof that Dickie and Sophie were Richard's children. They hadn't even been specifically named in the will.

Claire had been surprised when her lawyer phoned to inform her that the checks had arrived. Would she have done the same had the situation been reversed? How would she have felt, knowing that her husband had another family, that he'd switched his insurance beneficiary to provide for a stranger, a woman she didn't know? That he'd left a bequest protecting children she didn't realize he'd fathered? Yet Eleanor had never demanded that Dickie and Sophie submit to blood tests to establish paternity. Thank God she hadn't been so crass. Was she finally having some regrets? If Eleanor wanted the money back, she'd gladly hand it over. She didn't need it, not with the money from Richard's life insurance. And her intuition told her that this wasn't over; that even if she instructed her attorney to return the money, it still wouldn't be over. The woman wouldn't stop until the two of them met. Eleanor was bound and determined to have her say.

That, and whatever else she wanted. Was Eleanor hoping to settle a score? To retaliate for having lost her husband to a younger woman?

How far would Eleanor go to extract her revenge?

"All right," Claire told Hallie with a grim smile. "Michigan, here we come."

Hopefully five hundred miles would put enough distance between them.

Chapter Seventeen

"I still can't believe you did it without telling us," Jeffrey said.

Eleanor sighed. *Enough already.* Attorneys were notorious for fussing over details, but frankly, she was sick of the fuss. The topic of her new job had taken up the entire discussion at dinner.

"There's no earthly reason for you to get a job," he continued.

"Maybe she wanted to." Susan reached for his plate, stacking it atop her own, and rose from her chair. "Did that occur to you?"

Blinking, he gazed up at his wife. "Why would she want to work? She's never worked a day in her life. Why start now?"

Eleanor bit back her irritation. If Susan hadn't showed up at Grayson's today in hunt of new bath towels, she never would have been found out. She wouldn't soon forget the sound of her daughter-in-law's cry of surprise at finding Eleanor crouched before stacks of boxes filled with silky duvet covers waiting to be priced and placed on the shelves.

"I had a career before you were born," she reminded Jeffrey. "I taught school."

"Yes, but that was different." He dismissed her words with a shrug. "It wasn't like you had a real job. You lived at home with your parents. You weren't supporting yourself or a family."

Eleanor sputtered into silence. Is that what he thought? That she'd never had any hopes and dreams of her own? No wish to be accomplished at something, to make a difference in people's lives? Neither of her children knew she'd gone into teaching to mend a broken heart. Neither of them knew how Richard's own heart had been broken after being dumped by his fiancée. At least she assumed they didn't know. Eleanor couldn't imagine him having shared that unsavory detail from his past. He'd been at his lowest when he turned to her, and she'd welcomed him with open arms. How could she refuse? She'd loved him all her life. Marrying Richard was probably her one shot at happiness. She took it and she never looked back. And she'd never told Jeffrey or Vivi the story of Richard's fiancée. Their father deserved to be treated with respect. At least she could spare him that indignity.

Just as she deserved to be spared any indignities. Richard had betrayed her with his death, leaving her to suffer a widow's grief as well as the unexpected burden thrust upon her when she'd learned about his illicit affair and subsequent marriage to Claire. Thanks to the two of them and their sneaking around, she'd lost everything. Disillusioned, humiliated, abandoned by her friends.

Not to mention, financially ruined. She wasn't bankrupt or destitute... not yet. But she would be if she didn't do something. She had to take care of herself. If she didn't, who would?

"I had no choice," Eleanor said. "Things are different now."

"Different how?" His face pinched in a tight furrow. "Honestly, Mom, sometimes I think Vivi is right and that you could use some professional help."

"Since when did the two of you decide that you should be in charge of my personal life?" She felt the irritation building deep inside, like the throttle on an engine about to burst, exploding in a spray of scalding-hot steam, scorching everything in its path. She was a grown woman and owed explanations to no one. She'd taken it from Richard for years, but she wasn't about to take it anymore, and certainly not from her children. Vivi's reaction wasn't a surprise, but she'd thought Jeffrey would see things her way. Then again, what did she expect? He was his father's son. A man who'd died, intentionally leaving his wife flat broke.

Bastard.

"I need the money. It's as simple as that," Eleanor said.

"Why didn't you come to us? I already told you that Susan and I are willing to help out."

Accept handouts from her children? She was tired of being the object of people's pity and derision. Her so-called friends were ashamed to be seen with her. At first she'd been bewildered, then angry, but she'd finally moved into a state of laissez-faire. None of them called anymore, not even Anne Kennedy.

Of all people, she'd have thought Anne would understand; Anne, who'd been nursing her own share of shame and embarrassment with her not-so-secret drinking. For years Eleanor had suspected her friend had a problem. She'd tolerated the daytime drinking, watching silently during lunch as Anne downed the first glass of wine, then another, and sometimes a third. She'd taken away Anne's car keys more than once. What could be so terrible in someone's life to cause them to turn on themselves like that? Eleanor had often wondered as she'd driven her friend home. Poor Anne and all her so-called problems.

Problems? Anne didn't know what problems were. And who the hell cared? She had her own problems to think about. She no longer could afford the luxury of wasting time worrying about someone who no longer wanted to be part of her life. She couldn't run and hide like her former friend. She was nearly sixty years old. It was high time she learned to take care of herself.

"We are done discussing this," she informed Jeffrey. "I took the job, and that's all there is to it. End of subject." Rising, she took her plate and headed for the kitchen.

Susan, at the dishwasher, turned and reached for the dishes. "Give those to me."

"No." Gently she nudged her daughter-in-law aside. "You should sit down and rest. You've been working all day."

"So have you," Susan pointed out.

"But I'm not pregnant," Eleanor said, taking in the sight of Susan's tummy, swelling in the early stages of her second trimester. Babies meant new life and new hope, something she desperately needed in her life right now.

She shooed Susan away from the counter. "Sit," she commanded with a pointed look for her daughter-in-law.

Susan slid into a seat at the small kitchen table under the window. "He didn't mean to upset you. Jeffrey means well."

Eleanor scraped bits of food from the stacked plates into the sink, then flipped the garbage-disposal switch. The machine jumped to noisy life, grinding away the leftovers while churning over the pounding of her heart. "I know."

"He's worried about you. We both are," Susan added.

"There's no need to worry." Lord knows she'd done enough of that for all of them. "I can take care of myself."

"Yes, but..."

"But what?" Eleanor whirled round. "You don't think I'm capable? You think I can't do it?"

Her face reddened. "I didn't say that."

"Then what *did* you mean?" she demanded even as she silently cursed herself. This wasn't Susan's fault. It wasn't anyone's fault, not really. And she didn't mean to be spiteful or cutting. But she was tired. Oh, so tired. It had been a long day, harder than they knew, and she was in no mood to be coddled. No one had any idea what she was going through. "I know what it's like to work. I taught school."

"I think you'd find things very different if you went back into teaching." Susan picked her way through the words. "The world is different. It moves at a faster pace. Sometimes it feels like there's no letup. Businesses expect more from their employees. *Work harder, work smarter.*" She sighed. "Sometimes I feel like I'm working so fast it doesn't make sense. There's always another job, another project, something else demanding my attention."

"You think I don't know that?" It wasn't fair. After what she'd been through today—especially today—it wasn't fair.

"No, I think you do. And so does Jeffrey. But he's worried..." Susan glanced up with a hesitant smile. "All right, I'll admit it: I'm worried too. We're concerned that all this might be too much for you. You shouldn't have to put up with it, not at this stage in your life. It isn't fair."

"Lots of things in life aren't fair." God, she'd hated hearing that phrase while growing up. She'd sworn she'd never say it to her children, yet here she was, repeating it. How had this happened? Hadn't she learned anything in her years as an adult?

Oh, she'd learned something all right. All those idioms they threw at you when you were young didn't carry merely a modicum of truth. They *were* the truth.

Life *wasn't* fair.

"We love you," Susan said, "and we hate seeing you going through this. What Dad did to you wasn't fair. I can't imagine how you must feel, knowing she was... was out there that whole time. And all those times when you thought he was away, hard at work, and instead he really was with her..."

Susan broke off as her tears started. Eleanor's heart softened at the sight of her daughter-in-law's sadness. She sank into a chair and reached for the younger woman's hand, covering it gently with her own.

"I want you to stop thinking about all this. You forget about that other woman." *Claire Anderson*. She refused to even say the name. "She means nothing to us. Do you understand?"

Susan nodded miserably, though she refused to meet Eleanor's eyes.

"I don't want you to worry about this anymore. You need to take care of yourself." She nodded at Susan's tummy. "Right now, the best thing you can do is concentrate on making sure that you and that little one stay healthy. I'll be fine." Eleanor nodded firmly, unsure which one of them she was reassuring. "Just fine," she repeated.

But in the end, it wouldn't matter whether Jeffrey and Susan approved. She was a working woman and she *did* have a job. But she wouldn't for long; today had taught her that. She needed to learn to pull her weight, and fast.

She'd been on the job less than two weeks and already the departmental sales manager—Miss Peg, a brusque young woman in a shot-silk suit and pointy-toe heels that looked like they might be a contributing factor to the pinched look around her lips—had pulled her off the sales floor and into her office.

"This type of work isn't for everyone." Miss Peg had settled in and reached for a thin sheaf of papers to one side of her desk. "You need to be fast on your feet, and you have to know the merchandise."

Good Lord, was she being fired? Eleanor straightened in her chair, hands clenched in her lap. "I'm sorry it's taking me so long to learn. This is all new to me."

"Some people aren't meant to work retail."

"I can do better," Eleanor said, even as she saw the grim truth settling on the woman's face. Her heart sank. Her career at Grayson's was finished.

In a way, it was a relief. Miss Peg was right. She wasn't meant to do this. She hated retail sales. But it wasn't as if she hadn't tried. She'd given it her best shot, done everything they'd asked her to do, to keep up with what was expected. The first few days hadn't been too bad. But as the crowds descended for the weekend sales, she'd been caught off her game, not that she'd had much time to develop a game plan. She'd squeezed her way through the crowded aisles, scurrying to fetch new sizes, clean out dressing rooms, and straighten stacks after people pawed through them.

The sales clerk who'd trained her had been right. Most people were rude, inconsiderate slobs.

But the Capri Slack Customer had taught her a good lesson. Eleanor had learned to keep a smile on her face and her mouth shut about what she really thought. It wasn't easy, especially being on her feet all day, hovering over customers, letting smooth compliments slip through her lips in the hope that a credit card would be slid into her hand so she could ring up a sale. She couldn't figure out which she despised most: fawning over customers or jostling for prime position with the other sales clerks in hopes of earning a decent commission, which she would qualify for once she'd been there a month.

Being fired could be a godsend. Lord knows part of her would be relieved to walk out the door and never come back. But the other part of her, the practical part, argued she had no choice but to fight for her job. How else would she pay the electric bill that had arrived in yesterday's mail? And what about all the other bills stacked in a neat pile on Richard's desk? If she lost the job at Grayson's, what would she do? She'd have to start job hunting all over again. And who would hire her once they discovered that she'd been fired? The thought depressed her more than anything that had happened since Richard's death.

She was a failure, a complete and utter failure. First, her marriage, and now in the workplace.

"It's not a reflection on you," Miss Peg added, not unkindly.

Eleanor nodded, contemplating the framed degree from Northeastern Illinois University prominently displayed on the wall. The same school Jeffrey had graduated from. It was off center, hanging at a crooked angle. Hadn't Miss Peg noticed? Just like their stupid policy of displaying stacks of towels. You could have the right tags, but if they weren't displayed properly, what did it matter?

"Give me another chance. I promise you won't be sorry," she pleaded, though she hated it when people begged. *No whiners in this house,* she'd admonished Jeffrey and Vivi when they were little. But sometimes life didn't offer a choice, and you had to do what you had to do. "I promise I'll do better."

"You spend too much time straightening things."

"But I thought that's what I was supposed to do." Eleanor had the sudden notion to spring up from her chair, march behind the desk, grab the frame, and adjust it to fit the proper dimensions of the wall. But she didn't dare move. Hadn't she been warned that it wasn't her place to straighten things? But that was part of the problem. Nowhere seemed to be her place anymore. "Don't you want things to look nice?"

The woman's eyebrows shot up. "Our merchandise is nice."

"Yes, I know it is. I shop here regularly." Eleanor halted, gathering her dignity around her like the comforting touch of a child's soft, faded nursery blanket. "Not so much anymore, though. But I used to shop here... before my husband died."

In that moment, she hated Richard more than she had at any time in their marriage or after his death. Damn him for putting her in this position. And damn that Claire Anderson, his so-called *other wife*, with her fancy university degree. No doubt the eminent doctor had employed every skill and trick known to women and psychology experts to finagle her way into his life. Tears and tirades? Whatever method she'd used, it had worked brilliantly. He'd switched his life insurance policy, made Claire the beneficiary, and left Eleanor with nothing but a big fat mess. None of it was fair, but she couldn't allow herself to think about that now. She needed to concentrate and fight, not only for this job but for her self-esteem. She'd do whatever it took. Forget about pride. Forget about the other woman.

There'd be plenty of time to think about Claire tonight.

"I need this job." Eleanor heard the firmness in her voice, felt the hard set of her jaw, and nearly laughed out loud. How strange she must look, strong and confident, when inside, her stomach swirled like a curdled puddle of melted butter left out in the dish too long.

"Please," she repeated. She refused to go down without a fight. There wasn't much left in her life to fight about. "Please. I need it."

Miss Peg, about to speak, hesitated. And suddenly

Eleanor realized that she'd been saved the indignity of gathering her purse and being escorted from the store.

"All right," Miss Peg said. "I don't know why I should give you another chance, but I will." She leaned back, contemplating her with a level gaze that made Eleanor want to shrink in her chair. "But no guarantees. You're still on probation. You have to learn to work faster and smarter."

"I will," Eleanor promised, relief flooding through her as she watched her thirty-years-younger-than-she-was boss shove the thin sheaf of paperwork—termination papers?—into a file on one side of the desk.

"I'm moving you to Bedding and Bath. You'll find lots of things to straighten there."

Folding fluffy towels and stacking throw pillows. Her colleagues had warned her about that department, but right now she couldn't care less. Bedding and Bath sounded wonderful. She'd keep the sales floor clean and tidy. She'd coordinate the colorful bedding. She'd do such a good job they'd never dream of letting her go.

"Thank you." Rising to her feet, Eleanor finally unlocked the brusque set of her jaw and risked a smile. "I promise you won't be sorry."

"Make sure that I'm not." Miss Peg swiveled in her chair to face her computer.

Eleanor stood there. She'd been dismissed. She should go. Still, she didn't move.

"Yes?" Miss Peg's voice held an icy edge of I'm-very-busy-why-are-you-still-bothering-me? Her gaze never strayed from the computer screen. "Is there something else?"

"Your diploma." Eleanor motioned to the wall. "Do you mind?"

Without waiting for permission, she moved behind the desk and reached for the frame. It was heavier than she expected, and her heart knocked against the wall of her chest as she realized she could drop it if she didn't take care. Then, abruptly, the frame straightened in her hands. Stepping back, Eleanor examined her efforts, then nodded. "There. That looks much better, don't you think?"

Miss Peg glanced at the diploma, then at Eleanor. An imperceptible glimmer of grudging respect appeared in her eyes. "Thank you."

"You're welcome." Eleanor nodded and slipped from the room. For now she was safe. And who knew? The possibilities were endless. Maybe someday, if she didn't mess up, she might find herself promoted to the lofty position of the person in charge of picture frames in Home Décor.

Chapter Eighteen

"Again! Again!" Dickie shrieked as he jumped up and down through the tide of rippling waves crashing against his legs.

"Not any farther," Claire said, eyeing the sleek powerboat idling not far from shore and the source of the growing wake. She put up a hand to ward off the sun, watching as the boat bobbed and weaved closer to them.

"Nice boat," Hallie said from under the beach umbrella.

"Nice and expensive," she replied. The annual Chicago to Mackinac Yacht Race was famous throughout the world. One needed only to check out the adult toys docked at the piers and moored in the harbor to realize there was some serious money in the area. If the renowned summer island resort community ever changed its charter and allowed cars on the island, Mackinac would be overrun with Porches and Lamborghinis racing its roads.

She sat a moment longer, one eye on Dickie splashing in the waves and the other on the scene playing out before them. Moments before, a water-skier had been jetting behind the boat, skimming the rough lake waters like a skilled, seasoned athlete, only to abruptly lose his momentum and disappear under the waves. She watched as the crew finally managed to haul the skier aboard. With a deafening roar, the driver of the powerboat gunned its engine, revving to full throttle, and shot across the waves.

"I wanna do that." Dickie flopped down on the beach towel beside her.

"Do what, sweetie?" Pulling him into her lap, Claire briskly began toweling sand from his legs. His sturdy little body was tanned all over, and his hair gleamed like burnished gold.

"Like that man." He pointed across the water where the water-skier was once again up on his board and riding the waves. "Can I, Mama?"

"Maybe when you're older." Finishing her task, she tried not to think about how fast he was growing. He barely fit in her lap anymore. It wouldn't be too long before he was grown and pushed her away, before he was no longer a little boy who sought his mother's permission before embarking on some new, thrilling adventure. Dickie was a daredevil, just like his father. No doubt his future would be filled with all sorts of things that would push the limits of his physical endurance and push her to the brink of a mother's sanity.

"There you go, mister." She slammed the door on the frightening thought of her babies all grown up. "Nice and dry. Go see what Hallie has for you."

Dickie brightened and wrapped his arms around her neck. His flushed little cheek nuzzled her own. "Ice cream?"

"No, silly-billy. You don't need ice cream." Ruffling

his hair, she planted a kiss atop his head, inhaling the delicious scent of coconut suntan lotion, baby shampoo, and radiant sunshine. "It's a juice box."

He pulled away, the beginning of a pout pulling at his face. "I want ice cream."

"Hey, little guy, it's grape." Hallie waved a juice box in his direction. "You said last week that grape is your favorite."

"Don't want a stupid juice box," he repeated crossly, kicking up a little storm of sand. "Tired of juice boxes."

Join the club, sweetheart, Claire thought. She was tired too. Not of juice boxes, but the whole thing. "We'll have ice cream after dinner," she heard herself promise, cursing herself even as she did so for relenting again. Giving in to her children's demands wasn't the smartest thing to do, but capitulating was easier than holding her ground. And sometimes—more often than not—it felt like the ground beneath her was exactly like the sand, constantly shifting and settling, with nothing guaranteed except lots and lots of grit in her shoes, clothes, hair, and towels. She was tired of sand. It covered everything, filling every crack and crevice. Nothing could be worse... except, maybe, the ripe smell of horse poop that permeated Mackinac Island.

They'd traveled to the island high atop a jet-stream ferry packed full of tourists just like them. Stepping off the boat was like stepping back in time. The charming little Victorian village was famous for its *No Cars, Only Horses-Buggies-and-Bicycles-Allowed* law. They rented a private carriage and driver, and settled back for a tour. They clopped past the Grand Hotel, with its pristine white rocking chairs lining what the hotel boasted as the largest front porch in the world. Renowned for its magnificent façade, elegant furnishings, and exquisite cuisine, the Grand was far too imposing and stately for her motley crew. Someday, when the children are older, Claire had promised herself as she registered the four of them at a small, exclusive beachfront hotel steps from downtown. Outrageously expensive and probably cost as much as the Grand. But Claire never wavered as she handed over her credit card and booked them for a week's stay. Who cared how much it cost? Thanks to Richard, she could afford it. She looked forward to the privacy and the leisurely pace that the island promised.

And for a few days, life had been lovely. Mornings they'd spent playing on the beach with toys, sand buckets, and beach paraphernalia sprawled out around them. Afternoons were saved for exploring. She and Hallie each commandeered bicycles with a child safely buckled into a study child seat perched behind. They did the five-mile roundabout touring the island, with Dickie waving at each passing cyclist and Sophie crying out in delight at the seagulls swooping and soaring high above their heads. Arch Rock, with its natural limestone arch, amazed them all. They visited historic Fort Mackinac, high on a bluff overlooking the town. Dickie was fascinated by the tour guides dressed as British soldiers with their colorful uniforms and snap-to precision as they marched to and fro across the yard during the rifle demonstration. But the deafening blast of the cannon fire startled Sophie, making her scream, and the four of them scattered in a hasty departure. It took five minutes for Claire to calm Sophie down enough to strap her daughter back into the bicycle seat. But it was a meandering ride down a pleasant, shady street one afternoon that forced a halt to any further exploration.

A regiment of soldiers marched purposely down the road, followed by a line of women dressed in eighteenth-century costume. Spectators on foot and bikes brought up the rear. Claire and Hallie joined the parade, keeping their bikes at a respectful distance as the soldiers trooped on. Eventually, the head guard halted in the middle of the street. Stopping, he turned and led his men under the fieldstone entry arch with its simple cross overhead.

Hallie weaved her bike over to stand beside Claire. "Do you want to watch from here or go in?" she asked in a low voice.

God bless Hallie for her patience and understanding, Claire thought as they watched the small crowd enter the Post Cemetery and gather around the troop. At a callout from the corporal, the soldiers saluted, snapping to order as they began some type of reenactment of a memorial service. Claire's eyes scanned the whitewashed fence ringing the sacred ground. She took in the small granite gravestones lined up on the green, mossy carpet in neat military precision. One of the smaller headstones had been fashioned with a sweet little lamb resting on top. Goose bumps marched across her forearms and up the back of her neck as she realized it was a child's grave. The air, its caressing warmth against her skin so welcome moments before, suddenly felt hot and cloying, stifling her efforts as she tried to breathe.

"Claire, are you okay?"

"No. I'm not." Gripping the bike, she yanked its

handlebars and pointed them in the direction of downtown. "Let's get out of here."

There would be no escape. Once again, even on this beautiful, pristine island, she'd come face-to-face with death.

That was the end of their exploring. From then on, Claire purposefully kept their little group near the shelter of their beachfront hotel and the safety of downtown. They trooped through countless souvenir shops. They licked countless ice cream cones in search of the perfect flavor. They sampled bits of candy, though none of it compared to the rich, creamy fudge and gooey chocolates they'd found at Aaron Murdick's Fudge on the mainland in Mackinaw City. She kept the bad memories at bay by indulging the children, treating them to whatever they wanted, and granting their every wish.

Hallie was on the receiving end too, protesting that she couldn't possibly accept the beautiful silver bracelet resplendent with crystals and Mackinac charms that Claire discovered one afternoon in a little shop tucked away on Market Street. But she insisted, and eventually Hallie accepted. She even treated herself to a flamboyant lime-green-and-pink above-the-knee shift, a dress she never would have bothered with in her previous life. The summer sheath was sinfully extravagant and not her style, but Claire tried it on anyway at Hallie's urging. She twirled before the mirror, modeling it for her little group with every intention of returning it to the rack. Instead, to her surprise, she walked out with it safely tucked away in a bag under her arm.

"You have to wear it tonight at dinner," Hallie said as they left the shop.

"I will," Claire promised, lighthearted for the first time in months. She barely recognized the feeling; it had been so long since she'd allowed herself to experience anything remotely pleasurable. She didn't deserve it. How could she? She was alive, and Richard was dead. Her unfailing logic, the result of years of psychological training, warned she was being too harsh with herself. There's a time for grieving, a time to mourn the things lost forever. But there also comes a time when you realize you must go on, that you have to go on, or you, too, will die. Claire wasn't sure she'd reached that point, but she didn't want to analyze the situation to death. And when it came time for dinner, she reached for the dress, pairing it with some strappy sandals and her favorite earrings. For a while, she nearly felt human again.

Could this be the beginning of getting better? she wondered. Had she begun to put the worst behind her? Could she move on and forget?

The next morning, after breakfast, the phone call came.

"Dickie, slow down and wait for us," Claire called to her son, already out the hotel room door with his beach paraphernalia. Hoisting Sophie against one hip, she reached for her beach bag. Her cell phone vibrated on the bedside stand.

"Oh, shoot." She glanced at Hallie. "Grab Dickie before he takes off without us, would you?"

"Sure thing." Hallie disappeared out the door.

Claire sank down on the unmade bed, Sophie beside

her, and leaned across to snatch her cell. She scanned the screen but didn't recognize the number. "Hello?"

A few sentences uttered by a deep, rumbling voice brought a sharp cry rising from her throat. She clutched Sophie, hugging her daughter close, barely able to give numb responses to the questions he posed. But she had no answers. None at all.

There was no answer for insanity. What had been done was the act of a crazy person, a crazy woman. She sat there a moment after the call concluded, dazed by what she'd heard. How could she have believed everything was settled? That the nightmare was over?

It wasn't over. Not by a long shot.

Her bottom lip trembled as she thought about what the police had told her. How could Eleanor have done it? And Claire had no doubt that's who was responsible. No doubt at all.

"Mama?"

The touch of a plump little hand cupping her face brought her eyes open.

"Oh, Sophie, I'm sorry." Tears welled in her eyes, and she smothered kisses across her daughter's forehead and plump, soft cheeks. Poor little baby. None of this was her fault. She was a victim too. Both her children were victims. *Sins of the father*. How could Richard have done it? How could he have subjected their children to this insidious curse that would haunt them forever?

Claire jumped to her feet. She refused to take this sitting down. In fact, she wouldn't take it at all. If Eleanor Anderson thought she was going to get away with it, she had another think coming. Jamming her cell phone in a pocket, she clutched Sophie in her arms and headed out the door.

Hallie and Dickie had already set up camp at their favorite spot, centered in the sand a few feet from shore. Hallie, perched Indian-style on a colorful beach towel, was busy smearing suntan lotion on Dickie's arms and legs. She glanced up with a quick smile. "Everything okay?"

"No." Reaching for the beach bag at Hallie's side, Claire began cramming towels and toys atop magazines, flip-flops, juice boxes, and pretzel sticks. "We're going home."

"What?" Hallie fumbled for the bottle as the suntan lotion slipped from her fingers. Her face scrunched in a frown. "I thought we had another two days."

Claire turned to her friend but couldn't quite see her. It was like looking through a washed-out mirror, as if the young woman was no longer there. Or maybe she herself was the one who'd disappeared. She blinked hard, swallowing the rush of fear collecting at the back of her mouth, draining down her throat.

"We have to leave today." Unbelievable that she could sound so cool and calm while inside, her stomach was twisting and turning and her heart slamming against her chest.

"That phone call I had? It was the police."

Hallie's eyes widened. "What's wrong?"

"Someone was at the house last night. The police figure it happened sometime in the middle of the night."

"They broke in?" Hallie clutched her arm. "My God, Claire, that's unbelievable. I thought you had a security alarm."

"We do." She halted, remembering how Richard had installed a state-of-the-art security system shortly after they'd moved into the Hyde Park residence. She'd argued with him over the expense. She was perfectly capable of protecting herself and the children. She didn't want the fuss and bother of setting an alarm every time she left the house. But he refused to accept her protests. "I'd feel better knowing you're protected." Eventually she gave in. What was the point in fighting about it? His logic made perfect sense. "Don't argue with me, Claire. I hate leaving you alone so much of the time. There are lots of crazy people out there."

Crazy people? He'd been right about that. There were lots of crazy people in the world... and topping the list was Eleanor Anderson, his first wife.

"The neighbors discovered it this morning. But they... she didn't break in. She vandalized the house with spray paint."

Claire closed her eyes, remembering everything the sergeant had told her. "She... she used a can of red spray paint and went after the front of the house. She covered it with horrible words."

But the words weren't true. They weren't true!

"She covered the front of the house... the walls, and windows, and the sidewalk too."

How many people had already seen and read those words? And what about her children? Dickie wasn't very good at spelling yet, but he knew his letters. He would sound them out and ask her what they meant. The thought of hearing those vile words trip from the tongue of her four-year-old son made her want to vomit.

"Claire?"

Opening her eyes, she took a deep breath. "We have to go home. I need to hire someone to get things cleaned up. The police want to question me about who might be responsible."

"I thought you said it was a woman. Did they catch her? Is she in custody?"

"They haven't arrested anyone... *yet*. No one saw her do it."

If Eleanor Anderson thought she could get away with this, then the woman was stupider than Claire had imagined. The ugly words spray-painted across the shingles and sidewalk were a dead giveaway.

"But who?" Hallie asked. "Who would have done something like that?"

"Who do you think?" A grim smile wandered across Claire's face. "The woman who thinks I'm a *bitch* and a *whore*."

Chapter Nineteen

"This is the last of it. We can put it over there." Eleanor nodded toward the growing pile of boxes stacked near the front door. "The movers can take it tomorrow with the other things."

The day she'd hoped would never arrive had showed up to smack her in the face. Someone had bought the house. She no longer had a choice. She had to move.

"Good Lord, what have you got in here?" Martha asked as the two of them struggled under the box's weight. "It feels like rocks."

"Books probably," she guessed, swiping beads of sweat from her brow with the back of her hand. She'd spent so much time these past few days packing up boxes, she'd forgotten what was in most of them. She probably should have labeled them. She should have put more items in the discard pile. But how do you decide what to keep and what's no longer necessary? A person accumulates a lot of things in thirty plus years. You keep what is precious. But so much of those years were precious. It was crushing to see the life she'd valued reduced to a heap of cardboard boxes in the front entry hall of a house she no longer could call her own.

Martha brushed the dirt from her hands as she eyed the box with a dubious look. "Books take up a lot of space. That storage unit you rented will be filled up before you know it."

"I'll find room. And if I have to rent a second unit, I will." She couldn't bear to part with everything. Her books were treasured companions, time-tested friends that had comforted her throughout the years. She'd already been asked to give up so much. She refused to give up her books.

But it wasn't just the books. Being forced to leave her home behind and move into the small, cramped bedroom on the third floor of Jeffrey and Susan's converted brownstone felt as if she were grieving another death. All her beautiful things, the special ones she couldn't bear to part with, had been packed up and put in storage, waiting until she found an apartment of her own. Her mother's good china, her antique sideboard, all her precious things; she wanted them close. She *needed* them close. They would remind her that, once upon a time, there had been good days. And hopefully, good days were waiting in her future. Because she couldn't see beyond today. Everything seemed grim.

"Want me to go back upstairs with you for a quick run-through before I leave?"

"Thanks, I can do it. I still have a few more things to do before I'm ready to go."

"You sure? I can stay longer if you like."

"No, I'll be fine," Eleanor assured her. It would be her last chance to be alone in the house, her final opportunity to indulge in one last walk through of empty rooms which now contained only faded memories of a family that had disappeared. She didn't want to share it with anyone. Not even Martha.

"When do the new owners move in?"

"They're picking up the keys from Jeffrey on Saturday. Other than that, I don't know and I don't care."

It was a lie. She did care. She cared desperately. But she couldn't afford the luxury of knowing the details. She needed to be able to simply walk away. It was easier that way. She'd even refused to allow Jeffrey to tell her about the new owners. They could be anyone—a single young man or an older, established couple. In her heart, she hoped it was that nice young family with the three small children who'd toured several times last month. The woman had loved the kitchen and garden, though the man had complained about the high ceilings. A monster to heat, she'd heard him murmur to his wife. Well, and he'd be right. The heating bills were outrageous, especially given the snowy winters in recent years. But perhaps his wife had talked him into it. Their little ones would love the garden and the spacious backyard.

A pang of regret swelled inside, filling up every available space in her heart. It seemed like only yesterday that Jeffrey and Vivi had been playing in that backyard. She was constantly breaking up their little squabbles. The sandbox near the garden hedge had been their primary battleground, with one or the other constantly laying siege to territory claimed by the other. Vivi hadn't been much older than Richie was now the day she'd flung a bucket of sand in her brother's face, necessitating a hasty trip to the emergency room to have Jeffrey's eyes flushed out. More than twenty years ago, but the memory was as vivid as the day it had happened. And, as usual, Eleanor had been left to deal with the crisis alone. Richard had been off on one of his frequent trips abroad. Or had he? Even when their children were little, had he been in the Middle East building his business and fortune by brokering deals... or had he been dallying with other women? Not Claire, of course, for she was much too young. But there must have been other women before the esteemed professor entered his life.

Damn the woman! She'd robbed her of everything. Eleanor held back a sob. She wouldn't cry. She refused to cry.

"I know it's hard, but you'll get through it." Martha reached for her hand. "You're a strong woman, Eleanor. You can do this."

"Can I?" She swallowed hard.

"Yes, you can. I have faith in you."

Thank God someone did. "I don't know what I'd do without you."

"That's what friends are for." Martha squeezed her fingers. "We take care of our own."

"I'll have you over for dinner once I find an apartment," she promised. "You'll be one of my first guests."

"Something will turn up soon."

Eleanor nodded, though she didn't share Martha's optimism. It wasn't as if she hadn't been looking. But the few places advertised in her price range had been depressingly small, not to mention filthy. And while dirt and grime could be scrubbed away by vigorous cleansing and strong disinfectant, it was important to have enough space around her that she didn't feel trapped. That much she already knew from her first night at Jeffrey and Susan's brownstone. She had to find something, and soon.

Martha grabbed her purse. "Call if you need me, even if it's just to chat. I'm always available."

"Thanks again." She hugged her former housekeeper. "Thank you for everything."

"I was glad to do it. You know I'd do anything for you, Eleanor."

"You take care."

Eleanor waved as Martha slipped behind the driver's wheel and started down the driveway. She closed the door, shutting out the brilliant sunshine and the glorious smell of her gardens in bloom. What was the point? After today, she would no longer to be around to enjoy them.

She shuffled across the hardwood floor and climbed the stairs. Starting at the top, she wandered through the empty rooms, her eyes and heart absorbing every detail of her children's rooms. Jeffrey's bedroom was done up in the warm blue hues that still covered the walls from when he was a little boy. Vivi, however, had been another matter. She'd insisted on redecorating every few years. Even at age five, she knew what she wanted and there was no changing her mind. Eleanor's mere suggestion that geometric squares might not be appropriate for a young girl's room and maybe they should look at pretty floral wallpaper had caused Vivi to explode with the force of a cat-five hurricane. So much for her daughter being a delicate bloom.

Eleanor halted in the doorway of the corner bedroom

she and Richard had shared. She hadn't slept in the room since his death. Venturing a few steps inside, she glanced out the window to take in the sweeping view of the front lawn and side gardens. Such a peaceful spot. The room had always been her sanctuary. Even after the children were grown and gone, even with Richard out of the country for weeks at a time, she'd never felt alone in the house when she was in this room. It was a place where she'd been able to retreat from the world and the solitary existence that was her life.

The antique bed frame, stripped naked of its mattress and springs by the movers, was shoved tight against a wall. Tomorrow the movers would haul it away. It was destined not for storage but the consignment shop. Someone would want it. It was a lovely piece of furniture and should fetch a pretty price. She had no choice but to get rid of it. It took up too much space. More importantly, she couldn't bear the memories taking up space in her heart.

How many nights had she lain awake on her side of the bed, hoping the distance between them would melt away, that Richard would reach for her, pull her into his arms, whisper how much he loved her? Sometimes it happened, but more often, not. And she'd learned not to beg. She'd been rebuffed more than once—enough times that she eventually lost her courage to try. A person could only handle so much rejection. But his dismissals still hadn't stopped her from caring about him. It had never stopped her from loving him, even as he slept beside her, even when he was gone.

Eleanor stared at the bed, remembering the lonely nights she'd spent in the darkness, wondering where he was, in what godforsaken country halfway around the world. Sometimes, especially after 9/11, her imagination got the best of her. She imagined him attacked by vicious strangers, horrible men who dragged him into dark, shadowy corners, beating and robbing him, leaving him for dead. Those were the nights that she lay there in the quiet of their bedroom, whispering prayers, making little deals with God, begging Him to keep Richard safe and bring him back to her.

She couldn't blame God. He'd kept his part of the bargain. Richard had always come back. Except, most of the time, he hadn't been that far away.

Not far at all. The other side of Chicago, less than forty miles.

In another woman's bed.

Gone in a heartbeat. Eleanor sank to the floor, back against the wall, and sat there some moments as she glanced around the empty room. It was all over now. Her life, her house, and her love for Richard. Everything was dead and buried, surely as he was dead and buried in the ground. And the worst part? She no longer cared. She was glad it had happened. Glad he was dead. He'd put her through hell while he was alive. She'd known what he was like, but she'd married him anyway, hoping he would change. One could always hope. What was life without hope? And she'd never given up... not even the day he'd died. She hadn't lost hope or given up until the day she learned the truth about his other life and his other wife.

She stifled a cry, burying her face in her hands. How could it have come to this? What kind of a woman was she? She'd been raised to be a gentle soul. Her parents had taken her to church where she'd been taught to embrace the fruits of the spirit: patience, kindness, tolerance. And if that was the kind of woman she'd always thought herself to be, how, then, could she be struggling with these awful, evil thoughts?

Hatred.

Jealousy.

Resentment.

And the most horrific of all: an overwhelming desire for revenge.

Chapter Twenty

"Illinois has a stalking order on the books. It's relatively new, signed into law in 2013. It's something we might consider once we establish the identity of the—"

"I already told you who did it," Claire insisted. "Eleanor Anderson is responsible."

Daniel Mitchell leaned forward, elbows propped on his desk, regarding her with a pointed look. "Unfortunately, we can't prove it."

She fumed at the challenge in his eyes and words. No wonder attorneys had such horrible reputations. The good thing about this particular attorney was that he was on her side... supposedly.

"It was Eleanor Anderson." She threw the stare right back in his face. "Believe me, she did this."

He pointed to the papers on his desk. "The police report doesn't indicate they found any evidence at the scene."

"I don't care what it says. I'm telling you she did it."

Mitchell blew out a deep breath. "Okay, so we go to court and petition the judge to sign an order for Stalking

No Contact. According to the law, the elements of stalking include two instances. First thing he's going to ask is, *where's the proof*? What do you suggest we show him?"

Claire felt her jaw clench. Why was he giving her such a difficult time? He was her lawyer. He was supposed to be on her side. "I want something done. The woman is unbalanced."

He merely stared at her.

"Why don't you believe me?" she sputtered. "Spray-painting someone's house isn't the act of a rational person."

"I understand," he said slowly, as if addressing a child. "But this doesn't seem like something that was done on impulse. First, she would have had to buy the paint. And if she is the one who—"

"Oh, she did it, all right," Claire muttered, feeling worse by the minute. Her gut instinct told her Eleanor was responsible, but without evidence, the authorities would do nothing. And if they did nothing, what was to stop Eleanor from coming after her again? Next time it could be worse... much worse. What if she showed up one night, threatening her and the children with bodily harm?

"Let's assume for argument's sake that we can prove the first case. What about the second?"

"I told you I saw her at my house once before. She was parked across the street, watching from her car." Claire barely recognized her voice—shrill and insistent—and realized she was close to losing it. She forced herself to take deep breaths. If she didn't get hold of herself, Mr. Mitchell might start thinking she was as crazy as Eleanor Anderson. "She's dangerous, and I don't trust her. The woman is a threat to me and my children."

"You said she was in a car. Did she get out?"

Had she? Claire forced her thoughts to return to that afternoon. The air had been scented with the fragrance of sweet spring flowers, the trees bursting forth in buds... and parked across the street was an older car with a woman behind the wheel, watching and waiting. Claire closed her eyes, overwhelmed by the memories of a car door opening and a woman's legs swinging onto the ground.

"Did she approach you? Threaten you in any way?"

It had all happened so fast, she thought, sucking in a ragged breath. Her first instinct had been to protect the children. She'd scurried up the porch steps and hustled them inside, then slammed the door and braced herself against it. Moments later, when she'd finally dared glance outside the window, what had she seen?

An empty front porch. A deserted street.

Eleanor had disappeared.

"No," Claire admitted. "She didn't come near us. She sat there, and then she drove away. But it was her. I know it was her."

It sounded petty and spiteful, and she knew it. What proof did she have that the woman had been Eleanor? But who else could it have been? That spring day had been a traumatic experience, and Claire would never forget it. She wasn't accustomed to feeling threatened and vulnerable. Other women might experience those emotions, but it simply wasn't her. But that day, she'd been like anyone else. She'd given in to her fears.

She hated herself for having done it... and she hated Eleanor for giving her a reason to fear.

"She was there," Claire insisted. "I know she was there. And I know it was her."

It hadn't been her imagination playing tricks on her. She wasn't projecting what she wanted to believe. It *had* been Eleanor parked in that car, out on that street. For whatever reason, Richard's first wife had come calling, then thought better of it. Whatever had caused her to show up, then drive away, didn't matter. It had been Eleanor. She might not have concrete proof, but Claire knew it in her gut.

"Would you recognize her if you saw her again?"

"Yes," she replied without a moment's hesitation, dismissing the potential consequences. She'd never met Eleanor in person. She'd never even seen a photo of the woman. And the car, parked across the street, had been a good fifty feet away, not close enough to provide a good look.

What if she was asked to pick her out of a lineup? Would she pick the wrong woman? What if they went to court and she was forced to stand in front of a judge with her hand on the Bible, swearing to tell *the truth, nothing but the truth, so help me, God*. Would she be able to do it? Could she identify Eleanor beyond reasonable doubt?

"Yes," Claire repeated. She'd do anything to protect her children, even if it meant she had to lie. "I can identify her."

"Okay then." Mr. Mitchell dipped his head in agreement. "Looks like we proceed."

"You'll contact the court?"

"Before the end of the day," he promised. "I'll petition the judge to sign an emergency order preventing her from contacting you. Then the court automatically sets a date for a hearing and—"

"A hearing?" Claire frowned. "Why do we need a hearing?"

"By law she's entitled to an opportunity to defend herself."

"She doesn't deserve a hearing." She heard her voice rise, hitting a decibel nearing a shriek. "She doesn't deserve anything, not after what she did. She vandalized my home. She violated my privacy and my children's privacy."

There'd been a time when she'd actually felt sorry for Eleanor. Granted, they were strangers, but both of them had been betrayed and victimized by Richard. It must have been horrible for Eleanor to have woken one morning and found him dead in bed beside her. And—if the insurance agent had been telling the truth—Eleanor had never known of Richard's double life. She must have been devastated when she'd learned the truth, especially after all the years they'd been married. Eleanor wasn't young. Her children were grown. What was she left with? What would she do with the rest of her life?

Obviously, she'd decided to focus on making Claire's life a living hell. Any sympathy she might have once felt for the older woman had been replaced by a cold hatred when she'd come face-to-face with those hideous, evil words spray-painted across the front of her house and sidewalk. Sophie hadn't noticed, but Dickie had been fascinated by the red scrawls. He'd strained to spell out the letters as Claire yanked him toward the house. "W-H-O-R-E. Mama, what does that spell?"

"Never mind, sweetheart," Claire had told him, hurrying him up the steps and inside.

Sympathy for Eleanor Anderson? She didn't deserve any sympathy or support. No compassion. Not after what she'd done.

"I want her prosecuted to the full extent of the law."

Mitchell jotted a few notes on a legal pad. "If we're lucky, I can convince the judge to sign the emergency order today."

Claire slumped in her chair, flush with exhaustion from the rush of emotions coursing through her. "Why is she doing this?"

He shrugged. "If there's one thing I've learned in my years practicing law, it's that people always have a reason for what they do. Usually, it involves money, power, or revenge."

"Money," Claire murmured, more to herself than aloud. Is that what this was all about? Was Eleanor resentful about the insurance proceeds? What if she signed over the money? What if she gave it to Eleanor? Would that make all this go away? It wasn't as if Claire needed it. She was perfectly capable of taking care of herself and the children. She had a successful career. She could move away, accept a position at another university somewhere else in the country. Florida, Arizona. Somewhere far from Chicago and the memories this city held. She could start a new life.

But what if it wasn't about the money? What if it was about revenge? Who knew what Eleanor might do next, or what she was capable of?

"What about my children? What if she comes around

again?" Claire refused to give in to the fear. It had dominated her life for months, but not anymore. She was done playing the role of a victim.

Never again.

"Call 911," he advised. "And contact me immediately. Meanwhile, I'll follow up with the police. Frankly, though, I have to be honest with you. Unless something else comes to light, no judge is going to sign a permanent order against her. There's nothing to implicate her in this or prove that she's the one who did it... or that she's a potential threat." Slapping the file shut, he lifted his hands in a helpless gesture. "Nothing."

But that wasn't true. Eleanor had left plenty behind. Slanderous scarlet slashes scrawled on the sidewalk for everyone to read, angry red smears sprayed across the front windows and walls of the house. The front walk had been scrubbed and bleached, but the house's vintage cedar shake shingles were another matter. *Spoiled*, the man from the cleaning company had advised. The paint would come off, but the shingles would never look the same again.

Bitch. Whore. It wasn't only the house and sidewalk that Eleanor had spoiled. Claire couldn't wash away the sordid feelings, the sense of dirtiness seared in her soul. Vile, ugly words Eleanor had scrawled for the world to see. Even if everything was cleaned up and put back to normal, nothing would be normal again. How could she continue living in that house? Shopping in that neighborhood? How could she send her children to the same school? Continue her teaching career at the university?

She'd been spray-painted as a scarlet woman. Bad enough that some people knew what Richard had done.

Now, thanks to Eleanor, everyone would assume that she was guilty too. People didn't care about the facts, not in this world of fast-paced social media. If it was out there, they believed it.

Everyone would believe she'd been an accomplice to Richard's sin.

"She did this. I don't care how we prove it, but I know she did this. She's taken away my life. She's taken everything." Damn Eleanor Anderson for putting her in this position. And damn Richard for dying. He must have known what his wife was capable of. He'd left so many questions unanswered... including why he hadn't left her. How could he have stayed married to an unbalanced woman? That wasn't like the man she'd known and loved.

But then again, he wasn't the man she'd thought he was. He'd lied to her, married her without revealing the truth about himself. Richard was guilty of committing the worst kind of sin: a sin of omission.

"You don't have an ex-wife lurking in the background, do you?" Claire had teased him one night. "No ex-wife," he'd promised. "No children, either." And he hadn't lied, damn him. He'd known exactly what he was doing, playing with semantics. Richard didn't have an ex-wife; he'd never divorced her. And there were no children, at least not in the technical sense of the word. His children with Eleanor—their son the lawyer and the daughter who lived in New York—were both adults.

People always have a reason for what they do, Mitchell had said.

Money? Power? Claire didn't care about either of those things.

Did she want her prosecuted? Her jaw clenched.
No, that wasn't what she really wanted.
She wanted revenge. Pure and simple revenge.
And she wanted it *now*.

Chapter Twenty-One

"A NEW SHIPMENT ARRIVED ON THE truck this morning. Finish up with those sheets, and then you can start processing the duvets. We'll need them for this weekend's sale."

The floor supervisor didn't wait for a response. Her heels clicked on the gleaming marble tile as she disappeared around a display of brightly colored towels Eleanor had stacked earlier that morning.

Sighing, Eleanor turned back to the sheet sets she'd been pricing for the past half hour. For weeks, Grayson's had been advertising their upcoming Sizzling Summer Blast in anticipation of Sunday's Fourth of July celebration. They expected heavy foot traffic, and nearly all the sales staff was scheduled to work, including her.

She pulled an armful of sheet sets from the box and stacked them in the glass display cabinets. Last summer, with Richard out of town, she'd celebrated the Fourth with Jeffrey and Susan. They'd driven into the city and watched the fireworks at Navy Pier. The crowd had been shoulder to shoulder, and the traffic home had been insane, but being with her family for the spectacular show had been worth it.

What a difference one year could make. This year, the only fireworks she'd see were the sparkling red-white-and-blue fringed sale banners hanging from the ceilings of the store. If she was lucky, she might catch a glimpse of rocket flares in the distant skies during the late-night drive home. Corporate's decision to keep Grayson's doors open till ten p.m. meant she was on the schedule until the final customer walked out the door. Still on probation, no seniority, and no commission. She'd be selling towels, pillows, and sheets... to no one, of that much Eleanor was certain. Who shopped for bedding on the Fourth of July? Talk about ridiculous. She'd bet her last nickel that the corporate bigwigs wouldn't be shopping during the fireworks. They'd be cruising Lake Michigan on their sleek yachts, tossing back martinis as they enjoying the holiday festivities with family and friends.

Grabbing the empty boxes, Eleanor headed for the back room to find the newest shipment. Unpacking boxes, displaying inventory, and working the floor of the Bedding and Bath department wasn't what she'd had in mind when she graduated college, but someone had to do it. Why not her? She needed the money, and it was an honest job and easy enough. When you got right down to it, working in Bedding and Bath wasn't so bad. Boring at times, but the colorful displays more than made up for it. She loved unpacking new shipments, arranging the luxurious stacks of towels in coordinated displays of lush summer colors. Bedding was different. She couldn't decide which was worse: duvets and bedspreads in their zippered plastic covers or the shower curtains sheathed in plastic. The heavy bedding was a monster to lift, but once on the shelf, it weighed itself down. The shower curtains, however, were slippery and lightweight, and she was constantly straightening the stacks.

Eleanor reached out to adjust a few errant pieces when she spied a figure at the end of the aisle. The woman was half-turned, but Eleanor would have recognized the distinctive crop of carroty-red hair even five aisles away. Anne Kennedy hadn't changed her hair color in years.

"Anne?"

The woman disappeared around the corner.

Eleanor dropped the empty box and hurried down the aisle. Anne probably hadn't heard her. Rounding the display at the end of the aisle, she spotted her friend in the main corridor, heading for lingerie.

"Anne, wait."

Slowing, the woman halted and turned to face her. "Hello, Eleanor."

"How are you?" Eleanor enveloped her in a quick hug. "I haven't seen you in ages."

"I know. It seems like forever, doesn't it?" Pulling away, Anne took a few steps backward. "I've been meaning to call, but the past few months have been so busy. You know how it is."

"I do," Eleanor said with a light laugh, swallowing down the hurt as she realized her friend had deliberately been trying to avoid her. The past few months had been hectic, and she'd been busy picking up the shattered pieces of her life. It hadn't been easy, accepting what had happened. She could have used a friend. Where had Anne been? Probably busy pouring herself another glass of wine.

"How are you?" Eleanor asked, surprised to realize she no longer cared. She'd play the game, wind her way through the niceties of social pleasantries, exactly the way her mother had taught her. She'd get through the conversation and that would be the end of Anne.

"Fine." Her friend managed a faint smile. "And you?"

"Things are getting better every day," Eleanor said, noting as her friend's gaze slid briefly to the *Welcome to Grayson's!* name badge adorning her blouse, then back to her face. Straightening, she plastered a bright smile on her face. Who did Anne Kennedy think she was, to be looking down her nose and judging her for working a tiresome job in some department store? Sometimes life didn't give you a choice. You did what you had to do in order to survive.

And dammit, Eleanor thought, she was going to get through this, even if it killed her. She was a survivor.

As for Anne Kennedy? She could go to hell.

"Did you hear that I moved?"

Anne nodded. "Jim told me that your house had been sold."

Eleanor smiled. "I'm living with Jeffrey and Susan at the moment, until I find a place of my own."

"And all your lovely things?"

"In storage," she said blithely, deliberating choosing not to mention that most of them had been sold. "I'll collect them once I find an apartment. I've been searching, but I still haven't found exactly what I want. I'm looking forward to it. Not that I don't love Jeffrey and Susan, of course," she hastily added, "but I'm used to living on my own. Plus, they need the space. Susan is getting bigger by the day."

"She's pregnant?" Anne's eyes widened. "I hadn't heard."

Eleanor kept her mouth shut. Perhaps if her ex-friend had bothered returning the phone calls and voice mails she'd left, she would have known. "The baby is due around Christmas."

"Do they know yet if it's a boy or girl?"

"They'll find out at the ultrasound next month."

"I bet you hope it's a girl, don't you? Girls are so much fun. Remember how you used to dress Vivi up in those beautiful baby clothes? She was always so pretty." For a brief moment, a flicker of the old Anne appeared. "You were wonderful with children, Eleanor. You put all the other mothers to shame."

"Thank you." Her heart softened slightly as she remembered Anne's misfortune in never having been able to have children. Perhaps if in vitro fertilization had been available when they'd been young, Anne would now be blessed with grandchildren of her own. Instead, she'd kept her trim figure, plus her husband, nice clothes, a beautiful home... and the bottle of vodka Eleanor suspected was never far from a trembling hand. Poor Anne. Everyone was chased by their own demons, and her old friend Anne was no different. People always had their reasons.

The sound of heavy footsteps behind them, accompanied by the electronic squawk of a radio, caused them to turn.

"Excuse me, ladies." He tipped his head slightly. "They told me in the makeup department I should ask over here. I'm looking for Eleanor Anderson."

"I'm Eleanor." Straightening, she faced the officer. Her heartbeat quickened as she took in the prominent silver badge pinned to his uniform shirt, the gold emblem shoulder patch proclaiming his authority as Cook County Sheriff's Police. His belly bulged over his belt, which was weighed down by a radio, walkie-talkie, nightstick, and a big black revolver snapped into a holster. She took a few steps backward at the sight of the weapon.

"This is for you." He pulled an unsealed envelope from his shirt pocket and handed it to her.

Eleanor stared down at it. "What is it?"

"Notice to Appear," he said firmly but not unkindly. "You've been served." He nodded at the envelope. "You'll find the Order in there too."

"Order?" Her heart pounded, and the blood roared through her brain. "Order? What are you talking about?"

"Emergency Order, No Stalking Contact."

"Excuse me?" It didn't make sense. Someone had accused her of stalking? There had to be some kind of mistake. Stalking was a crime... something you read about in the paper or heard about on the nightly news. Mug shots flashed to mind—men with wild eyes and disheveled clothing, obsessed with ex-wives and girlfriends.

Stalking? Why would anyone accuse her of stalking? She might have gone after Richard, perhaps, but he was already dead.

"I think you have the wrong person." Eleanor tried to push the envelope back into his hands. "There's been a mistake."

His eyebrows formed a tent over his hooded eyes. "You *are* Eleanor Anderson, correct?"

She hesitated and glanced at Anne for support. Her friend had withdrawn into the comforting recesses of the pillowy duvets and refused to meet Eleanor's eyes.

Panicked, Eleanor turned back to the officer. "Yes, but—"

"There's no mistake. It's pretty much self-explanatory. The hearing will cover everything."

"But you don't understand—"

"Ma'am, I suggest you get yourself an attorney." Lifting two fingers to the shiny black vinyl brim of his hat, he touched off a salute. "Have a nice day."

"I don't believe it." She touched a hand to her throat, fingered the silk scarf covering the soft, sagging folds of her neck. "I don't understand how this could be happening."

Turning, she saw Anne halfway down another aisle, slipping away as if she feared she might be contaminated by the whole sordid mess. Eleanor watched her vanish, momentarily stunned, though not surprised.

Maybe it was for the best. Anne could be loyal and true, while at other times she was best friends with the bottle. Liquid courage assuaged her troubles, relaxed her discretion, and loosened her tongue. Anne might go home and take to her bed, sleeping off the sorrow and her stupor, or she could be on the phone all night, sharing Eleanor's disgrace all over town.

Someone had accused her of stalking. *You've been served.*

Eleanor stood alone, surrounded by mountains of multicolored towels and linens, blankets and sheets. All those neat stacks and tidy displays of bedding—she'd spent hours fashioning them to achieve the right look...

a casual, yet elegant appearance that invited one to dream that a good night's sleep would make everything right with the world. But that wasn't the way the world always worked. She was living proof. Richard had died in her bed. No matter how nicely you smoothed back the covers, trounced the pillows, or straightened the sheets, bad things could happen.

She fought the sudden urge to rip a duvet from the shelf and wrap herself in it. Layer upon layer circling her body, cushioning her from the ugly disgrace of what had occurred.

"Lady?" A distant voice echoed. "Hey lady, did you drop this?"

She opened her eyes and blinked, staring down at the young boy in front of her.

"This was on the floor." He offered something to her. "I think you dropped it."

Eleanor saw the white envelope containing the official paperwork ordering her to appear in court. Her hand trembled as she reached out and accepted the envelope between her fingertips. "Thank you."

He paused, eying her with a wide-eyed, curious look. "Are you okay?"

Was she okay? She dragged in a deep breath. Every time she thought she was okay, something else happened to mock her hopes that life was improving. She wasn't okay. She was mortified to find herself in this position, and humiliated beyond belief that Anne had witnessed it all.

"Yes, I'm fine." Eleanor choked out the words. "Thank you."

"No problem," the little boy said, and moved on.

No problem? Oh, there definitely was a problem. She stared down at the envelope. Bad enough she'd be forced to live with the knowledge of what she'd done for the rest of her life. Lord knew the embarrassment and guilt weighed her down every day. She never should have done it.

And she never wanted to see Claire Anderson again. But it appeared such would not be the case.

The two of them had a date to meet on Thursday, July eighteenth, in court.

Chapter Twenty-Two

Where was Mitchell? Claire resisted the impulse to check her watch one more time as she shifted on the hard wooden bench outside the courtroom. Her attorney was the one who'd insisted they meet at the courthouse for a brief meeting before the hearing. He was notorious for running behind schedule. Just like him to be late on the day she needed him most.

She hadn't slept at all last night, tossing and turning as her mind played out possible scenarios of what might occur in the courtroom. Would Eleanor sit quietly at the defendant's table, allowing her attorney to refute the charges and rouse the judge's sympathy on behalf of his client? Oddly enough, Claire found herself wishing that would prove to be the case. If Eleanor kept quiet, there would be no outrageous outburst, no stinging accusations from a woman scorned, no talk of a dutiful wife who'd been tossed aside in favor of a younger woman who'd bewitched her husband.

How could Richard have put her in this situation? Eleanor had every right to embrace her role as an innocent victim, but she wasn't the only injured party in his crime. Claire was also a victim, though Mitchell had warned her that the court might not be disposed to see it that way. While the judge had signed the temporary order restraining Eleanor from stalking, they had no guarantee it would be made permanent. What if it wasn't? Claire dreaded the possibility of that happening. She'd be forever looking over her shoulder, fearful for her children, as well as her own safety. Then again, she'd argued silently with herself throughout the night, would the judge have signed the emergency order if there wasn't just cause?

By the time she'd left the house for court, her nerves were shot and her stomach a mess. The heat and humidity blanketed the city like a heavy fog as Claire joined the throng of rush-hour traffic making their morning commute into downtown Chicago. The summer had already made the record books for being one of the hottest in recent history. The scorching heat and muggy weather made life miserable and caused tempers to flare. Steam was rising from the pavement as she surrendered her car in the court's parking garage and quickly made her way into the courthouse. After asking for directions, she found her way to the correct floor. The hallway was empty, with no sign of her attorney.

And that had been ten minutes ago, Claire noted, finally giving in to the impulse to check her watch again. What if Mitchell didn't show up? Twisting her hands in her lap, she leaned her head against the wall, trying to block out the thought of what she would do when she finally came face-to-face with Eleanor Anderson. For all Claire knew, Richard's first wife might already be in the courthouse, tucked away behind closed doors with her own attorney in a last minute tête-à-tête before the proceedings. Was she already in the courtroom? Claire eyed the set of closed doors across from where she sat. Another court hearing was still in progress. Was Eleanor in the room, perched in the back row, awaiting their hearing? Was she as nervous as Claire? What would happen once the doors opened and they found themselves together? Neither of them had any guarantee things would go their way.

She'd never been in court before except the one time six years ago when she'd been summoned to appear for jury duty. Though it had been a different time and courtroom, the man she'd met that day—with the flashing brown eyes, salt-and-pepper hair, and wearing a suit of self-confidence tailor-made for him—was the same man responsible for her courtroom appearance today.

So much in life hung on *what if*? What if she hadn't been summoned for jury duty? What if Richard hadn't been there? They never would have met. She wouldn't be sitting in this hallway, fighting for her own safety and that of her children.

But how could she regret meeting Richard? No matter what he'd done, no matter what sins he'd committed or the emotional harm he'd inflicted, she'd never doubted his love. Yes, he'd betrayed her, deceived her... but he'd also loved her. Richard had been a complicated man. There was no point in trying to analyze his personality. She was too involved, too intimately caught up in the situation to attain the level of detachment required to examine and evaluate on a professional level. She would never understand why he had done what he had.

Her first mistake had been to allow herself to become involved with him. She should have known better. She should have recognized him for what he was. Tulie had been right. Richard had all the classic behavioral symptoms of a sociopath. Witty and clever, charming and articulate, he'd displayed a masterful presence in every situation. Yet he was unlike any other man she'd ever met. His utter self-confidence had drawn her in from the beginning. And it had been his strong belief in himself, the grandiosity that was a natural part of his personality, that had proved part of his allure and had captivated her heart.

Yes, his impulsive behavior, his insistence that things be done his way, that he would be the one to determine the course of action they followed, had occasionally grated on her nerves. But he'd always played it cool, never forceful or over-the-top. Not once had he ever raised his hand against her or the children. He'd never lashed out in anger with his voice or his fist. Maybe if he had, she would have realized there was a problem. But if anything, he'd exhibited the opposite behavior. *Perhaps you're right*, he would quietly state when she questioned him. Maybe she had good reason to doubt, he would say. Maybe she was wrong to place her trust in him. Then he would draw away, quiet and aloof, distancing himself. She couldn't bear it when he behaved like that, giving her the silent treatment, withdrawing his affections. It didn't happen often, but each time it did, she quickly caved to his demands, ignoring that nagging voice inside... the one that warned her something was amiss, that their relationship needed work.

But never for one minute had she ever doubted that he had her best interests at heart. He worked hard to provide a good life for her and their children. Time and again, she'd assured herself that everyone had their off days. Richard was no different. He was only human, and his good qualities, if measured, outweighed the bad. And even his most negative traits—his arrogant manner, his assumed superiority, his determination and drive to succeed—were qualities society admired and valued.

And her human instincts—the intuitive feminine side that he'd encouraged, that he'd nurtured—told her she hadn't been completely wrong in putting her faith and trust in him. He'd given her everything he was capable of giving.

Plus, he'd given her the two things that mattered most. The children were her life. Without Dickie and Sophie, she might as well be dead.

"Sorry, I got caught in traffic," Mitchell said on the phone moments later. "Some guy flipped his car in the middle of the highway, and everything's been shut down. They just reopened the lanes. I'm about twenty minutes out."

Claire checked her watch, catching a sharp breath as she saw the time. The hearing didn't start for another half hour, but traffic in and out of downtown Chicago was always a bear, no matter the time of day or night.

"Don't worry, everything will be fine," he promised. "I'll be there."

He'd better be, for she had no intention of stepping inside that courtroom without him. "I wish you were here now," she confided. "I'm nervous."

"Where are you?"

"Outside the courtroom."

The Other Wife

"Are you alone?"

Claire glanced down the empty hallway. "Yes."

"I'm on my way. Sit tight and wait for me."

It wasn't as if she had a choice, she thought, closing her eyes. What else could she do? Wander aimlessly through the hallowed hallways? Visit with the court clerk?

The sound of heavy footsteps approaching made her straighten. Raised voices quieted as they drew near. Claire opened her eyes, took in the sight of a tall man in a tailored suit, briefcase in hand, sporting features that looked oddly familiar. He halted in the middle of the corridor, tucking a supportive hand under the elbow of the older woman at his side. He glanced at the closed courtroom door, then back to her.

"Excuse me, are you Claire?"

Nodding, she stumbled to her feet.

"I'm Jeffrey Anderson." Placing his briefcase on the floor, he stepped forward and stuck out a hand. "I'm representing my mother as counsel."

His mother? Claire felt the hair on the back of her neck rise as she glanced past his shoulder. Finally, she and Eleanor Anderson were face-to-face. Funny, but Richard's first wife didn't look anything like she'd expected. Her hair was mussed in an odd mix of gray and brown, and she wore a simple beige suit that hung on her frame as if she'd recently lost weight. Her chin sagged, and her face was wrinkled with worry lines.

"You're represented by counsel, correct?" he asked.

Claire couldn't find words as she stared at Eleanor's son... *Richard's son*. It was an eerie feeling, glimpsing the same brown eyes, the slight bump on the nose, the quirky way one eyebrow arched while speaking. It was almost like a much younger version of Richard staring back at her.

She yanked her hand from his and clasped it behind her back. He might be Richard's son, but Jeffrey Anderson was also his mother's son, and that automatically placed him in the enemy camp. And shaking hands with the enemy had never been part of the deal.

"Daniel Mitchell is my lawyer," Claire said, cursing the attorney under her breath. Damn it, where was he? "He was held up in traffic. He should be here soon." And why couldn't she keep her mouth shut? She didn't owe Richard's son an explanation.

He turned to Eleanor, shielding her from Claire's direct gaze. "Why don't we find you a place to sit until the hearing starts?"

Claire watched as he led Eleanor across the hall to a bench some feet away, noting the care he took with his mother, who looked nervous and apprehensive. And with good cause, she mused, sneaking a wary glance at her nemesis. Yet Eleanor didn't look like the kind of woman who'd be capable of thinking such filth, let alone creeping around in the middle of the night, defacing someone's home with ugly obscenities. A person had to be emotionally unstable or mentally unbalanced to do something so dreadful.

And Eleanor didn't look off balance. Nothing about her suggested that she might be capable of vandalizing Claire's property, or of the stalking charge. In fact, she looked like a decent sort of woman. Older than Claire had expected, not at all the type she'd imagined Richard would have been attracted to, even forty years ago. Eleanor had a pleasant enough face, and perhaps when she was younger she'd been pretty in her own sort of way. But the years had robbed her of whatever beauty she'd once had. She looked faded and worn, like someone's grandmother.

Which she was, Claire thought, remembering the letter that Eleanor's attorney—her son Jeffrey, who now stood before her—had sent some months earlier. The letter had included a copy of Richard's will, and the mention of bequeaths to his children and grandchildren. Richard had grandchildren... with this woman. Eleanor was a grandmother. And grandmothers—especially ones who looked like Eleanor, wary, fearful, respectful of the law—weren't normally responsible for committing criminal acts. Not unless they were crazy. And even if she was crazy, could she be held accountable? *Should* she be held accountable? Eleanor was a victim too.

No, I'm the crazy one. Claire closed her eyes, drew in a deep breath. What was the matter with her? This was no time to be feeling compassion, to regret having filed the grievance that had them gathered at court today. In a few minutes, she'd be standing before a judge, asking him to punish the woman for what she'd done. Eleanor Anderson couldn't be trusted. Everyone knew outward appearances could be deceiving. Behind Eleanor's modest and reserved appearance, despite the kindly face and the frightened eyes, was a malicious woman whose heart carried seeds of hatred and revenge.

But what if she was wrong? What if Eleanor hadn't been the woman she'd seen in the car that day? What if she wasn't the woman who'd been making those phone calls, who'd defaced her property and sullied her reputation? And if she was wrong about Eleanor being to blame, didn't that mean that she, Claire, was just as guilty as the person who *was* responsible? Claire's gaze wandered down the hall, lingering on Eleanor's face. The woman's hands trembled as she sat quietly with her son. His arm was around her, and her face was drawn.

Damn it, why did this have to be so hard? Claire turned away, pushing down the fresh swell of sympathy rising inside her. It was a sorry situation for everyone concerned. Jeffrey Anderson seemed like a nice enough man and obviously loved his mother. Claire admired him for that, though she hated herself for doing so. She didn't want to like him or feel sorry for his family's troubles. She didn't want to feel sorry for Eleanor, either. But it was hard not to do so. She blew out a deep breath, trying to gather her senses. Why was she suddenly feeling sympathy for this woman? Yet now she'd seen her, she couldn't help but hope that the court would order Eleanor to get the help she needed. They'd made such rapid progress in the field of behavioral psychology. A comprehensive medical exam and a battery of psychological testing would be the first step. Perhaps Eleanor's chemical levels and her hormones were out of balance. With the proper medication, under the care of a skilled physician and competent psychiatrist, Eleanor might improve.

To do what? Start all over again? The situation would never be rectified. Richard was dead, and he wasn't coming back. Claire was the one who deserved the sympathy. She was the wronged party in this situation. Eleanor was responsible for having put her family at risk. It was Eleanor who'd stalked her in the daytime, who'd threatened the children, her home, and her safety at night.

They had the right woman, Claire repeated silently, turning her back on Richard's wife and son. It had been Eleanor she'd seen behind the wheel of the car that day, parked across the street in her Mercedes, boldly watching and waiting. She'd given Claire the scare of her life that afternoon, and she'd done it in broad daylight. Who knew what kind of desperate act she might consider next? Eleanor had to be stopped before she lost all control.

The woman deserved whatever punishment the judge doled out.

Damn it, where was Mitchell? Claire glanced at her watch. Another ten minutes and they were scheduled to be in court. Her cell phone vibrated. That had better be him, telling her he was parking his car and would join her shortly.

But the caller wasn't her attorney. Claire tapped the screen and raised the phone to her ear. "Hallie? What's up? We're going into court soon."

"Oh God... oh Claire, I'm so sorry. It's—"

Fear caught in her throat. Hallie didn't rattle easily, and the panic level in the nanny's voice was off the chart. "Hallie, what is it? What's wrong?"

"I... I don't know. It all happened so fast. How could she have done it?" She faltered. "They're gone, Claire."

"What are you talking about?" She rose to her feet. "Who's gone?" she demanded. But even as she spoke, she already knew.

"Dickie and Sophie." Hallie's voice broke through her tears. "She took them. They're gone."

"What do you mean, *she took them*?" She heard her voice swelling in panic. Dickie and Sophie were gone? There had to be some mistake. "Who took them?"

"I... I don't know. She wasn't who I thought..." Heavy sobbing flooded the line.

"Hallie, listen to me. Take a deep breath and calm down. Do you hear me? You have got to calm down." Claire choked out the words, trying to take her own advice. "Tell me exactly what happened. Are you sure someone took them? Maybe they're playing a game." She hoped to God she was right, even as every instinct inside cried out she was wrong. "You know how Dickie loves to play hide-and-seek. Have you checked their rooms? Maybe they're outside."

"We're not at the house," Hallie cried. "I took them to the park. They wanted to play... and that's where we met the woman."

The woman. Claire swung round and stared at Eleanor Anderson. How could the woman be responsible when she was here at the courthouse?

"Who are you talking about?"

"The woman with the little boy. He was about Dickie's age. They showed up at the park about five minutes after we did. The kids started playing together. She sat down on the bench next to me, and we started to talk. She was nice. We chatted for awhile, and everything was fine. Then I had to go to the bathroom. I called for the children, but she said she'd watch them."

A low moan escaped Claire's throat. This couldn't be happening.

"Claire, I swear, I wasn't gone for more than five

minutes. But when I got back, she was gone. All of them were gone. The woman, her little boy, and Dickie and Sophie." The tremor in her voice increased. "If it hadn't been for her little boy, I never would have left them alone with a stranger. But she was so friendly, and the kids were having a good time. It never occurred to me that I shouldn't trust her."

Hallie's voice trembled. "And now they're gone. I've looked everywhere, and I can't find them. How could they have vanished like that?" A tremendous sob escaped over the phone. "They're gone!"

She couldn't afford to give in to the panic. "Did you call the police?"

"Not yet," she admitted.

"Hang up and call 911," Claire ordered. They were losing precious minutes. "Then call me right back. Do you understand?"

"Y...yes. I'll do it right now."

The connection broke, and so did something in Claire's heart. She slumped against the wall. Her precious babies gone? She'd already lost Richard. She'd never forgive herself if she lost them too.

"Excuse me." The soft sound of a man's voice made her turn. "I don't mean to intrude. Are you all right?"

No, she wasn't all right. She wouldn't be all right until her children were safe in her arms. Claire stared at Jeffrey Anderson. She didn't want his help. She didn't want anything from him, or his client, either... except for the hearing to be over and a signed court order stipulating that horrible woman keep her distance.

Damn it, where was Mitchell? She scanned the empty corridor.

"Is there anything I can do to help?"

She shook her head. No one could help. Not even Richard's son.

But Dickie and Sophie were Richard's children. If Richard were here, he'd be terrified for them too. And he would turn to any source of help... including his son Jeffrey.

After all, they were related. Jeffrey was Dickie and Sophie's half brother.

"My children," Claire said, hearing the low tremble start in her voice. "Someone's taken my children." She pressed the palm of her hand against her forehead, as if she could clear her thoughts. "They were at the park with our nanny when a woman—"

He stepped forward and offered his arm. Claire grasped it, struggling for composure. A strange buzzing sound started in her ears, and she felt the sting of tears prickling behind her eyes as she allowed herself to visualize the scene. Dickie and Sophie playing on the swings, in the sand, and then... gone.

"A woman took them," she said. "They're gone. Vanished. What should do I do?" Claire lifted her gaze to his. "I don't know what to do."

The buzzing grew louder, and the world started spinning. Then suddenly there was nothing left inside, no legs to hold her. Claire felt herself sinking. Strong arms caught her before she hit the floor.

"Sit down," he said, guiding her to the bench. "Put your head between your legs. Take deep breaths."

Claire sank onto the wooden bench and forced her head down. Closing her eyes, she willed herself to breathe. She felt a faint nudge of something cool and wet against one arm.

"I brought you some water. Try to drink it," a kindly voice urged.

Taking the paper cup without looking up, Claire managed a few sips. Slowly the blackness subsided, and her muddled thoughts began to clear. Maybe it wasn't as bad as it seemed. Dickie and Sophie would turn up soon. The police would find them. Maybe the woman had already brought them back. There would be a reason. There was always a reason.

She took more deep breaths and finished the water. When the buzzing in her ears finally stopped, she summoned the strength to sit up straight and meet the woman's worried gaze. "Thank you."

Nodding, Eleanor stepped backward.

"Have the police been notified?" Though he kept a safe distance between them on the bench beside her, the concern in his voice instinctively assured her she had nothing to fear.

"She's calling them now." A few seconds later, her phone rang, startling them all. "Hallie! Did you find them?"

"No." The young woman's voice exploded in full panic mode. "The police said they're on their way, and that I should stay where I am. But I don't know... I was thinking maybe I should go back to your house. What if this is some kind of mistake? Maybe the woman couldn't find me. Maybe Dickie told her where you lived, and she took the children home."

"The children wouldn't have left the park and gone home… not without you. I think you need to be there when the police arrive." Claire glanced at Jeffrey for confirmation, who responded with a quick nod. "Hallie, do you understand? Stay in the park, and wait for the police."

"Ask her if she knew the woman," Jeffrey whispered.

Claire repeated his question over the phone.

"I've never seen her before." Hallie hesitated, sounding distracted. "I might have a photo on my cell. The little boy… he fell off the slide and started crying, and she ran over to make sure he was okay. Then she started pushing the kids in the swings. They looked so cute, and I took some photos. Let me put you on speaker, and I'll look…"

She paused, then her voice lifted in excitement. "Yes! I found it. I have a photo of her with the kids."

Jeffrey touched Claire's arm. "Ask her if she can send it."

Claire nodded. "Hallie, can you email me a copy?"

"Doing it right now," she promised, her voice crackling over the speaker. "I'll send everything I took. I've got one of her and Richie playing with Dickie and Sophie—"

"Richie?" Eleanor stepped closer. "Are you sure his name was Richie?"

"Yes," Hallie said. "I remember because he and Dickie were teasing each other about their names and which one of them was older. She said her nephew was four…"

With a little cry, Eleanor sank onto the bench. "My God, Jeffrey," she said, clutching the sleeve of his jacket.

"How could she have done it? How could she have taken the children?"

Claire's heart slid sideways in a sickening lurch as she caught sight of the older woman's face, ashen with fear. "You know who has them?" she whispered.

Eleanor nodded, her eyes wide with panic.

"My daughter," she said. "Vivi."

Chapter Twenty-Three

"It's nice to hear your voice, dear. We should talk more often." Eleanor tried to keep herself calm and composed. The last thing she wanted was to tip Vivi off that they were on to her. Together, the three of them had decided that she should be the one to place the call. Eleanor prayed that Jeffrey was right, that Vivi wouldn't be alarmed by a phone call from her mother. Her maternal instincts were running on high as she made the call, and burst into full blown panic when she heard her daughter's voice. There was something eerily calm and simultaneously terrifying about the way Vivi was speaking. Eleanor knew it was important to keep her daughter on the phone, to keep Vivi talking and find out where she was. Eleanor, sitting on the bench, kept her head down, aware of Jeffrey and Claire hovering beside her. They were counting on her to discover where Vivi had taken the children and if they were safe. Everyone was counting on her. Could she do it? Hopefully their faith wasn't misplaced.

"I didn't realize you were in town," she added. "I could

have picked you up at the airport. You should have told me you were coming."

"*Should* have told you?" Vivi's trill of laughter floated across the speakerphone and down the courtroom corridor. "How rich, Mother, and so like you. You've always been good at doling out the *shoulds*. *Vivi, you should have worn the other dress,*' she mimicked in a sing-song voice. *Vivi, you should study harder if you want a better grade point. Vivi, you should have...* fill in the blank," she finished, a sharp edge to her voice that sliced through Eleanor's resolve as neatly as it carved a gaping hole through her heart.

"You don't understand..." Eleanor faltered. How could she have made such a mess of things? She'd tried her best to mother Vivi, but to tell the truth, there'd been times she was secretly scared of her daughter. Since she was a little girl, Vivi had always had a volatile personality. The slightest remark could set her off, and Eleanor had learned to watch her tongue. Richard had always been the peacemaker, the only one able to soothe her spirits and calm her down. Now he was gone, and Vivi was tottering closer to the edge.

God help them all if she took the children with her.

"I didn't know," Eleanor said.

"There are lots of things you don't know about me, Mother."

Jeffrey snagged her attention with one hand, cutting a vertical line through the air. Eleanor nodded. He was right. The most important thing was to keep Vivi calm and centered. "If I'd known you were coming, we could have made plans. I'd love to see you, dear."

"Plans? You mean the two of us having a cozy little mother-daughter lunch somewhere in the city?" Vivi laughed scornfully. "Why would we do that? The two of us have never gotten along."

"Vivi, I—"

"Spare yourself the trouble of trying to deny it. We both know it's true. Don't you think it's time we were honest with each other? You've never loved me, and I sure as hell don't love you."

How could she say such a thing? How could her daughter be so cold and uncaring? Eleanor swallowed down the hurt, blinked back the tears stinging her eyes.

"We're wasting time." Jeffrey tapped his watch. "Find out where she is."

Eleanor nodded. Gathering a deep breath, she prayed her voice wouldn't betray her. "I'm sorry to hear you feel that way."

"Sorry for what? Sorry that I don't love you... or that people will know that you're a failure as a mother?"

"Sorry for everything."

"I don't care, Mother. It's too late."

Something about the way her daughter tossed off the response struck a warning chord in her mind. Too late for what?

"It's never too late," Eleanor quickly replied. "Why don't we meet and we can talk about it. Where are you? I'll drive there right now."

"You can't. I took your car."

"What?" Eleanor threw a worried glance at Jeffrey. Her car had been parked at his brownstone. "How did you get my car?"

"Susan gave me the keys. I told her you wouldn't mind."

"Keep her talking," Jeffrey urged in a low whisper. "See if you can find out if she has the kids."

Eleanor nodded silently, trying to keep herself focused and not lose hope. She had to make things right. Jeffrey's fists were locked tight, his jaw clenched; Claire's body trembled, her face drained of color. Each of them had children involved.

"Of course I don't mind. You can borrow my car anytime you like. That's fine." *Dear God, let that prove to be the case. Let them all be fine.* "Is Richie with you?"

"Yes, he's here. We've been having a wonderful time."

Jeffrey smacked a fist against a hand. "That bitch," he growled softly. "If she touches one hair on his head..."

"I don't see nearly enough of my nephew. He's grown so much since the last time I was in town. I need to visit more often." Vivi laughed. "Susan seemed surprised when I showed up this morning. Seems she hasn't been feeling too well—apparently this pregnancy has been a bit much for her. She was grateful when I offered to take Richie to the park. I suppose you can't call it babysitting since he's not a baby anymore. He's a big boy."

Eleanor closed her eyes. *Dear God, please don't let her do anything stupid.*

"Why don't you take Richie home? I'll meet you both there."

"No, I can't do that. I promised to take him for a drive. Besides, he doesn't want to go home. He's having fun playing with his new friends."

Claire gasped, one hand clutching her throat. "Oh my God. She *does* have them."

Jeffrey wrapped an arm around Claire's shoulder.

"Ironic, isn't it?" Vivi laughed softly. "Richie thought it was so funny when I told him his new friends were related to him. And guess what, Mother? They're related to me too." Her voice skipped a beat. "One brother is bad enough, but it appears I have two... and a sister."

An uncomfortable tightness had wrapped itself around her chest, but Eleanor forced herself to remain calm. It was imperative she keep Vivi talking until they knew where she was.

"I'm glad to hear he's getting along with his new friends. Are they playing together?"

"I already said they were. But as usual, you're not listening."

Her eyes widened at the growing irritation in her daughter's voice. "I'm sorry, dear. I suppose my memory isn't what it used to be."

"What do you expect? You're getting old, Mother. Don't you know that it's the natural order of things, that young people should be the ones with the children? And these three are having so much fun. No need to worry. Richie even shared his little sack of crackers with them. The family that eats together and plays together, stays together," Vivi said. "That's exactly what we are. One big happy family, the way it should be. You should see the three of them. They're so damn cute together. You know, I was thinking that maybe I should contact an agent, see if I could get them in some magazine advertising. Or maybe commercials. There's a lot of money to be made in television advertising."

"This has gone far enough." Jeffrey pushed forward and stuck out his hand. "Give me the damn phone."

Eleanor shook her head. She didn't trust the wild look in his eyes. Jeffrey and Vivi had never gotten along. Better that she be the one to keep her daughter talking than to allow him to rant and rave at his sister, pushing Vivi closer to the edge.

"You need to calm down," Eleanor said, eyeing her son.

"I'm calm, Mother," Vivi replied. "I'm very calm."

"What about the children?" Claire whispered. She clutched Eleanor's arm. "Please. Ask her if they're all right."

Eleanor nodded over the phone, trying her best to convey sympathy and compassion. She herself was scared silly, and she couldn't imagine how this young woman was coping. If some stranger had abducted Jeffrey and Vivi when they were small, she would have been beside herself. She would have turned to Richard. He always knew what to do. He would have taken control and made it right.

But Richard wasn't with them. And these little ones that Vivi had abducted were his. She had to do what she could to help. Her own daughter was responsible for what had happened. No matter what Richard had done, she couldn't turn her back on his children. He would want her to save them. He'd be depending on her to save them all: Dickie, Sophie, and Vivi too.

"You're right, Vivi," Eleanor said. "This pregnancy has been difficult for Susan. It was thoughtful of you to take Richie this morning. I'm sure she thought it was a big help. But what about the other two children? Are you sure you can handle them?"

"You don't trust me?"

"Of course I do," she quickly assured her. "But I was thinking it might be nice if we were all together. Just as you said... *one big happy family*. Tell me where you are, and I'll meet you. Are you at home?"

"Home? How could I be at home? You sold it, remember? Home is gone."

Jeffrey lunged for the phone, ripping it from Eleanor's hand.

"Cut the bullshit, Vivi," he snarled. "Where's my son?"

"Well, if it isn't the High and Mighty Attorney. What a surprise... *not*. I figured you'd be with Mom. You've always been a suck-up."

"Shut the fuck up and tell me where you are."

"Such language," she said, tsk-tsking him with a scornful laugh. "You shouldn't talk like that in front of your son. If you aren't careful, he'll end up with a potty mouth."

Jeffrey's face burned with scarlet rage. The veins in his neck strained against the tight collar of his crisp white dress shirt. "Where are you?" he asked, barely managing to contain his fury.

"Somewhere on I-94. Why should you care?"

"Swear to God, Vivi, if you hurt my son or those other two kids, I'll—"

"Call the police and have me arrested? Put me in jail?" Scorn dripped from her voice like ice cream melting in the hot sun. "What's the matter with you people? I'm just taking the children for a little ride."

"Where?" he demanded. "Where are you going?"

"For someone who's supposed to be so smart, you're quite dense. I would have thought you'd figured it out by now."

"Damn you to hell," he shouted. "Tell me!"

Vivi's laughter floated over the phone. "We're going to visit Daddy."

In the end, Claire went with them.

"You're in no condition to drive," Jeffrey had told her, and Eleanor had to agree. Claire's face was stark white, her eyes expressionless as she stared straight ahead. "Come with us," he urged.

"I can't," Claire replied in a dull monotone. "My attorney said he would be here and that I should wait. But he doesn't know about the children." She turned her head, looking to Eleanor with flat, dead eyes. "How could she have taken my children?"

Eleanor stepped forward and put her arm around her. This young woman was not an enemy. They were all together, joined in a common cause. "Everything will be all right," she murmured. "The children will be fine."

"They're just babies," Claire whispered.

"I know," she said, thinking of her own grandson Richie. He was the same age as Claire's son. If Vivi dared harm any of them... Shuddering, Eleanor pushed away the thought. She couldn't afford to consider the possibility of what might happen. "They'll be fine," she repeated, trying to reassure both Claire and herself.

Choking back a sob, Claire buried her head against Eleanor's shoulder.

Dear God, don't prove me a liar. Please let this turn out all right. Please protect those children… and us too. Eleanor stroked Claire's hair, comforting her as if she were a child, trying not to remember that this was the woman Richard had held in his arms. This was the woman he'd taken for a wife, the woman with whom he'd betrayed her. This was the woman who'd accused her of stalking and the reason she'd been summoned to the courtroom today.

Eleanor pushed away the niggling thoughts, the horrible accusations, the lingering resentments, the desire for revenge. None of it mattered. Not anymore.

"Jeffrey's right," she said. "You must come with us. Vivi won't hurt the children."

But was she right? Even as she comforted Claire, Eleanor's maternal instincts warned her they had good reason for concern. Vivi wasn't a monster. She wasn't capable of hurting a child.

Was she?

If Vivi dared harm even one of those children, she would personally see to it that her daughter went to prison, Eleanor decided as the three of them made their way downstairs.

The heat and humidity outside were unrelenting. The blinding sun had nearly reached its zenith, beating down on them as they waited for Jeffrey to pull the car around.

"Do you think we'll find her?" Claire asked in a small voice.

"Yes, we will... and the children too," Eleanor said. Her hand trembled as she opened the rear door and climbed into the backseat. Riding in the back offered a measure of privacy. She didn't want either of them to see how upset she was.

Or how furious.

Vivi wasn't the only one in this family who might be capable of murder.

"How far is it to the..." Claire shrank further into the passenger seat. "I've never been there," she admitted. "I've never seen his grave."

Eleanor and Jeffrey exchanged glances in the rearview mirror. It would be a race against time and traffic. Lake Forest Cemetery was a good thirty miles from downtown Chicago.

Jeffrey glanced at his watch as he pulled away from the curb. "With any luck, we'll make it before she does."

"But she's already in the car." Claire clung to her seat belt as if it was the only thing holding her together.

"Yes, but we're downtown and closer to the cemetery. She's coming in from Hyde Park. It will probably take her about ninety minutes in this traffic." Scowling, he whipped the car in a sharp turn, muttering an obscenity as a silver Porsche cut him off. "We'll get there before Vivi."

But what if we don't? What will Vivi do? What will happen if... But she couldn't think about those things. She didn't dare allow her imagination to consider the possibilities. Eleanor stared out the window, dully watching as the car inched its way through the grim city landscape, the massive buildings eventually giving way to more open expanses as they merged onto the expressway. As the car picked up speed, she tried to hold back the remorse and regret, the rush of fear she felt for the children, and the relentless waves of anger surging through her. Not for Jeffrey, cursing his way down the highway. Not for Vivi, having taken the children. Not for Claire, having brought the stalking charges. Not even for Richard, having died and left them with this mess.

It was the worst kind of anger... anger directed toward herself. Why hadn't she been smarter? Why hadn't she taken a more active role in her own life?

Why hadn't she seen this coming?

The black iron gates of Lake Forest Cemetery stood open. Eleanor's stomach slid sideways as the car passed beneath the massive Gothic arch. She hadn't been back since that blustery morning last spring when they'd buried Richard. She drew in a deep breath, steeling her nerves for what lay ahead as the car hurtled forward down the spacious tree-lined pathways. Lake Forest Cemetery, with its marble mausoleums, aging stone monuments, and manicured grounds, had been a peaceful resting spot for its good citizens for the past 150 years. Her own parents were buried here, as were Richard's. Not long after his mother had died, she and Richard had purchased their own family burial plot not far from his parents'. At the time, the decision had given her a deep sense of comfort. No matter who went first, things were taken care of and the other needn't worry.

And somewhere not far down the drive was the sizeable granite monument etched with the details of Richard's time spent on earth, which Vivi had insisted on. *Daddy needs a fitting tribute,* she'd announced, and Eleanor had offered no resistance, allowing her daughter to do as she wished.

She'd never seen the headstone, save for the photo Vivi had shown her once the monument was set in place. Eleanor held her tongue at seeing the words *Loving Father and Husband.* Richard had been anything but, especially given what he'd done. But seeing her own name etched next to his, plus the year of her birth followed by a hyphen, awaiting future inscription, left her sputtering. She'd turned away from Vivi before saying something she would regret. She had no intention of spending eternity next to Richard. *Rest in peace*? She hadn't had a decent night's sleep since the day she discovered his betrayal.

And what about the young woman crumpled in the passenger seat? Richard had led her to believe he was her husband too. What were they supposed to do about Claire? Bury her in the family plot, with Richard between them?

Eleanor balled her fists in her lap, fingernails raking the fleshy skin of her palms. She relished every bit of the pain. If she was capable of feeling something, it meant that she was still alive. For such a long time she'd felt dead, buried to the world and to herself. But not any longer. How could she have allowed herself to have morphed into such a complacent, accommodating wife? She'd been nothing more to him than an obedient dog, faithful and devoted, grateful for whatever meager handout he doled out. He'd treated her like a fool, which in some crazy way, was probably exactly what she'd deserved. For isn't that what she'd been? A dull, doting fool, a woman stupid enough to stick around and serve at his convenience whenever it suited him.

Damn him anyway. Never had she suspected that he'd be so cunning and deceitful, so callous about their marriage and family. He'd done a dreadful thing, but she wasn't the only one suffering. Claire was a victim in all this too. He'd made a mockery of both their lives. While she'd hated her in the beginning, Eleanor no longer felt the same. Neither of them was at fault. Richard was to blame.

Damn him to hell. She'd rather be cremated, with her ashes tossed upon the windswept waters of Lake Michigan, than disgrace herself by allowing her body to be buried next to his and carry on throughout eternity the mockery he'd made of their lives.

Whatever had been Richard's final bequeath, hers would be: *No More. No More.*

Jeffrey slowed the car to a crawl, his face grim. "She's already here."

Eleanor stared out the window. Some yards ahead, at the bottom of a grassy knoll, was an imposing white granite mausoleum, with Richard's grave merely a few feet away. Near it stood the solitary figure of a woman.

Vivi.

"Is that her?" Claire frantically groped to unsnap her seatbelt. "But why is she alone? Where are the children?"

Jeffrey's arm shot out, holding her back. "Let me handle this."

"Let me go, dammit!" She wrenched her body sideways, shrinking from his touch. "You can't stop me. I'm going to find my children."

"No." Eleanor suddenly spoke up, surprised at the

firmness in her voice. "Let me do this. I'm the one who should talk to her."

Unbuckling her seat belt, Eleanor reached forward and laid a hand on Claire's shoulder. "Look at me," she urged, waiting for what seemed interminable seconds before the young woman finally shifted in her seat to meet her gaze. "I promise I won't let anything happen to the children. Not your children, and not my grandson. Nothing," she repeated. She reached for the door handle.

"Mom, are you crazy?" Jeffrey yanked off his seatbelt and grabbed her arm. "I'm not going to let you march up there and—"

"Yes, you are," Eleanor said, shooting him a look that instantly silenced him. She shook off his grip. "Listen to me, both of you. I know you're scared. Both of you have children involved... but so do I." She swallowed hard, ignoring the dull, heavy ache in her heart. "Vivi is my child, remember?"

Claire's eyes were huge and hollow. Fear, anger, and apprehension were naked on her face. "Find them. Make sure you find them."

How could she let this young woman down? The two of them had something in common; their love for their children. Eleanor gripped Claire's hand in a tight squeeze. "I will," she promised.

"Five minutes," Jeffrey growled. "You've got five minutes, and then I'm coming after you."

Eleanor nodded. *Grant me strength*, she prayed as she opened the car door; *strength and the wisdom to say the right thing*.

Stepping out of the car felt like stepping directly into a

furnace. The humidity was thick and cloying, like breathing under water. This kind of heat was dangerous, and anyone with any sense would be inside, safe in the comfort of air-conditioning. Eleanor started walking, forcing herself to put one foot in front of the other. Her heels clicked on the pavement, which steamed and shimmered in the scorching heat. She didn't make it ten feet before sweat beads popped on her forehead and chin. Her armpits were sticky and wet, and her suit clung to her like sagging skin.

"Stop right there, Mother. Don't come any closer."

Eleanor halted. Though some distance remained between them, she was close enough to see her daughter's face. Even in the heat, Vivi radiated elegance, not one hair out of place. She stood solitary guard in front of Richard's grave.

"Go away." Vivi raised one arm, palm extended. "And take my stupid brother with you."

Eleanor didn't budge. Something about her daughter's voice triggered an instinctive warning. Vivi had always tended toward the dramatic, but this was different. Her words were flat, her tone queer and curiously detached. Where was the anger? Where was the passion?

And where were the children?

"You don't listen very well. Didn't you hear me? I said *go away*."

"I only want to talk." Eleanor chanced two steps forward.

"And I don't want to." Vivi's eyes narrowed.

Eleanor glanced around the gravesite, past the mausoleum to the surrounding trees. There was no sign of the children. But Vivi had said she was taking them to see Richard. Where were they? What had she done with them?

She wouldn't have done anything stupid, something to hurt them. Or would she? The hair on the back of Eleanor's neck prickled in the heat as she dared another step, then two more before drawing to a halt.

"Vivi, where are the children? I thought they were with you."

"Worried about the children... yes, I suppose you would be. Then again, why should I be surprised? You're so blatantly obvious, wearing your heart on a string, concerning yourself with things that don't matter."

Eleanor stood stock-still. "I don't understand."

Vivi's shrill burst of laughter hung in the dense air between them. "My point exactly. You've never understood, and you never will. But I suppose it's not your fault, since you're not like us."

Like us? Her daughter's words made no sense. Had Vivi slipped over the edge? Every maternal instinct urged her forward. Somehow she needed to find a way to work things out, to fix this before it was too late and they lost her for good.

"Like who?" She chanced a few more steps closer to the gravesite. "Who are you talking about?"

Scoffing, Vivi tossed her head. "Why, Daddy and me, of course."

Eleanor froze, the damp moisture between her breasts suddenly feeling like an icy trickle. "What about your father?"

"You never loved him. And you never loved me, either. Admit it, Mother. It's the truth."

"You're wrong," she insisted. *Hate the sin, love the sinner*. No matter what Vivi might have done, she would always love her.

"Am I?" She laughed. "I don't think so. The proof is right behind you."

"What... what do you mean?"

Vivi nodded past Eleanor's shoulder. "See for yourself."

Muffled footsteps closed in behind her. Jeffrey strode forward with Claire close on his heels. "Where's Richie?" he demanded, puffing in the thick cloying heat. "Where's my son?"

"That's for me to know and you to find out," Vivi answered, wagging a manicured finger at her brother. "But I'll guarantee you this: take one step closer and you'll never know."

"Don't do this," Eleanor pleaded.

"Me? Why is everyone blaming me?" Her voice filled with reproach. "I haven't done anything. You're the one who's responsible, Mother. This is your fault. There's your proof."

Lifting a hand, she pointed at Claire. "There she is, standing right before you. All the proof you need that you aren't one of us. You never were. You never understood what Daddy was all about. But she did. She's the woman he turned to. She's the other wife."

"Screw you, Vivi," Jeffrey shouted. "This is a bunch of bullshit."

Ignoring her brother, she swept her gaze over Claire. "Frankly, I'm surprised. You don't look nearly so good close up as I thought you would. My father had excellent taste. He could have had any woman he chose. I can't imagine what he saw in you."

"I'll kill you," he snarled. "Swear to God, Vivi, I'll kill you with my own hands if you've hurt Richie or either—"

"Oh, shut up and quit whining about those stupid children. Richie is fine, and so are the little mongrels. I assume they're having a good time playing together." A grim smile flitted across her face. "One big happy family."

Eleanor glanced past Vivi's shoulder. The mausoleum and nearby gravesites were sheltered by towering trees, the surrounding grassy areas empty, with no sign of the children. Where were they?

"I want my children." Claire stepped forward, head high, fists clenched. "Give me back my children."

Vivi's eyes brightened. "Ah, you're spirited! Now things make sense. My father loved women who were a challenge, women with minds of their own. That must be what attracted him to you. God knows my mother never spoke up for herself. She never spoke up for anyone. She just sat back and let him tramp all over her."

Eleanor pushed aside the injury. What was one more hurt when your heart was already broken? "Where are the children? You have to tell us."

"Why is everyone so concerned about those stupid little monsters?"

"Because you're insane," Jeffrey hissed.

"None of this is my fault. You want to blame someone? Blame her." Vivi pointed at Eleanor. "She's the one responsible for this mess." Her face dissolved in an ugly scowl as she threw her mother a hard stare. "What did you tell us while we were growing up? *Don't bother your father. He works so hard. He's tired, he's busy.*"

She gave a short burst of laughter. "He was busy, all right… searching for what he couldn't get at home. You didn't have the slightest clue as to what type of man Daddy was. He was vibrant and alive. He wanted passion; he wanted the world. And what did you give him? Nothing." She spit the words at Eleanor, as if they were chunks of spoiled meat. "You dragged him down. You, with your boring books and your drab sweaters, always puttering around in that stupid garden, with dirt on your shoes and underneath your fingernails. Maybe if you hadn't been such a dull old fool, Daddy wouldn't have gone looking elsewhere. Maybe if you'd tried harder, he wouldn't have been forced to turn to other women. He wouldn't have had all those affairs. And he certainly never would have married her," she said with a scornful nod toward Claire.

"That's—" Claire started to speak.

"You think you were the first?" Vivi laughed. "Don't flatter yourself. My father could have had any woman he wanted. He had women all his life, and I don't blame him one bit. He deserved it, stuck married to her all those years."

"What kind of woman are you?" Claire whispered in a trembling voice. "What kind of woman speaks about her mother like that? You are horrid… wicked."

"You think so?" Vivi's eyebrows arched, and a thin smile lined her lips. "I don't believe you qualify for sainthood, either… since you married another woman's husband." Her face wore a look of haughty disdain as she glanced back and forth between her mother and Claire.

"Poor Daddy. He deserved so much better than either of you."

Eleanor blinked away the steamy confusion fogging her mind. She needed to focus on what was important. And at the moment, only one thing mattered. She forced herself to take another step forward. "Where are the children?"

"Why does everyone care about those stupid brats?" Vivi stamped her foot, her blue eyes glittering like ice. "They're safe enough. I locked them in the car." Raising an arm, she gestured wildly behind them, in the direction of the grassy knoll.

Turning, Eleanor lifted a horrified gaze. In the far-off distance, she caught the vague outline of the roof of her aging Mercedes skewed sideways on the tree-lined path. She'd left the children in the car, on a hot day like this?

"Oh, Lord... please tell me you left the car running," she whispered.

"And take a chance that Richie or that horrid little boy would drive away?" Vivi sneered. "I'm not that stupid." Holding up her hand, she jangled a set of car keys between her fingers. "Those brats aren't going anywhere."

Claire gasped. "You left my babies locked in a car with no air-conditioning? How long have they been in there? They'll overheat and die."

"She's right," Eleanor said. "Children's bodies can't handle the heat the same way adults can." It had to be at least one hundred degrees outside, not counting the heat index. She couldn't imagine what it must be like for the children, cooped up inside the car with the windows sealed and the sun beating down on the metal roof. Extending her hand, she pleaded with her daughter. "Give me the keys. Let me help the children."

"I told you to stay where you are." Vivi took a few steps backward.

Eleanor felt the beads of sweat clinging to her face, sticky under her arms, moist between her sagging breasts. Her heart thumped against her chest in an odd, irregular rhythm that frightened her. Her legs felt wobbly, and she wasn't sure how much longer they would hold her up. A mere four or five feet separated her from Vivi. Surely she could manage that. She had to keep trying. She couldn't quit now; not with the children's lives at stake.

"Give me the keys," she urged. "Give me the keys and let me help the children."

"You're in no position to be making demands. Not after what you did to this family."

"I didn't do anything." Nothing was going to stop her... not the fierce pounding in her chest nor the menacing scowl on her daughter's face, or the car keys positioned as weapons between her fingers, poised to strike.

"You destroyed everything." Vivi's eyes narrowed. "You lost the money, you sold our home. You robbed us of our lives."

Eleanor threw herself forward and lunged at her daughter. She tackled her by the shoulders, throwing them both off balance. They toppled to the ground.

"Get off me!" Vivi shrieked.

The hard fall winded her, and Eleanor wrestled to stay on top. She didn't dare let her daughter gain control. Vivi writhed beneath her as they fought in the grassy dirt atop Richard's grave.

"Are you insane?" Vivi screamed. "What are you doing?"

Where was the strength coming from? Nose to nose with her daughter, she tightened her grip on Vivi's hands, keeping them pinned to the ground. "What am I doing? Teaching you a lesson," she panted. "Something I should have done years ago."

"You bitch!"

The gob of wet spit hit Eleanor directly between the eyes just as she caught the glint of metal in the dirt. Her car keys! Eleanor blinked rapidly, never relinquishing her grip as Jeffrey scrambled on his knees and grabbed the keys in triumph. Only when she saw him sprint for the car with Claire close behind did she finally relinquish her hold on Vivi and collapse.

Rolling over on her back, Eleanor stared up at the stark blue sky and brilliant sun. Her breath was coming in short, ragged bursts, hard and labored from the exertion. It was so hot outside. She couldn't remember such a hot day.

Vivi scrambled to her feet and stared down at her mother. Her face twisted in a contortion of revulsion and contempt. "I hate you."

Eleanor lifted a hand and tried to wipe away the spit dribbling down her neck, but the effort proved too much and her hand fell away. It felt as if an invisible elephant had decided to use her body for a couch and settled himself atop her chest. But the discomfort eased at the sight of Jeffrey climbing the hill with Richie safe in his arms. Claire was beside him, a curly-haired toddler clinging to her neck and a sturdy little boy clutching her hand. All the children were crying, and suddenly so was Eleanor. Tears flowed from her eyes, narrow rivers of relief running over her cheeks and down her neck as she lay there in the dirt. She'd done what she had to do. The children were safe.

Vivi tried to dart from the grave, but Jeffrey was quicker. "Let me go!" She struggled against his grasp, trying to shrug him off. "You'll be sorry you did this."

"Screw you, Vivi," he spat out. "You're the one who's going to be sorry."

Eleanor sighed. The mother's heart in her ached for what Vivi would face, but there was nothing to be done. Unlike the others, her own child couldn't be saved. Then the elephant shifted, bringing his full weight to bear, pressing down upon her. She gave a few short gasps, blinking against the heat of the radiant sun as her world exploded in a dizzy haze of brilliance.

"Mom?" Jeffrey's voice faded in the distance. "Are you all right?"

"Call a doctor," she whispered as the light grew brighter. "I think I'm having a heart attack."

Chapter Twenty-Four

"You're making a mistake."

"You already said that," Claire replied, not bothering to glance up.

"You don't have to do this," Tulie said. "Have I said that too?"

"At least five times since you walked in the door." Claire paused at her task long enough to throw her friend a brief smile.

Tulie threw up her hands. "How many more times do I need to say it? I can't believe you're deserting me."

"Don't take it personally. This has nothing to do with you." She pulled a few more books from the half-empty shelves.

"You can't leave." Tulie folded her arms across her chest, watching as Claire continued gathering and stacking books in neat piles around the office floor. Empty boxes stood nearby, waiting to be packed. "What are we supposed to do without you? What about your students?"

"They'll find someone to replace me." A faint disappointment stirred inside as she thought of Sarah.

She'd enjoyed working with the young girl and would miss their sessions together. But Sarah would manage. And if she didn't? Claire took a deep breath, tried to shrug off the stab of regret over leaving her student behind. Sarah would have to find her own way, like everyone else. Sometimes things in life worked out differently than planned.

"I don't get it, Claire. The students need you, the staff needs you. *I* need you. You're my moral support, my sounding board," Tulie wailed. "What am I supposed to do without you? You're the only sane person in this place."

Claire softly chuckled. "I think you're forgetting this is the psychology department. You're surrounded by professionals."

"Exactly my point. Everyone around here needs their head examined," Tulie muttered. She sank into one of the sturdy office chairs in front of the battered desk. "It's not too late to talk to Vilbrandt. He hasn't hired anyone to replace you yet. He'll tear up your letter of resignation if you ask."

"Seriously, Tulie, what would be the point?" She halted in her packing, sitting cross-legged on the floor, tanned legs in a pair of worn shorts, a baggy U of C T-shirt hanging on her thin frame. "There's nothing left for me here. It's a good time to leave."

"But what are you going to do?"

"Play with my children," she replied. "Read more books. Take more walks. Swim in the ocean."

"You're moving to Florida?" Tulie snapped on the words like a turtle on the hunt. "Which university hired you? Florida State? University of Florida?" Crossing her arms against her chest, she stared at Claire with an accusatory pout. "You never told me you applied anywhere."

"Because I didn't," she said, laughing, "and I don't intend to, either. I don't want to think about school, or schedules, or taking on another teaching position. I'm not ready. And someday, if and when I am ready, the right thing will come along." She lifted one shoulder in a slight shrug. "Until then, I'm not worried."

"*If?*" Tulie questioned. "You mean you might not go back into teaching?"

"I don't know," Claire admitted. "Maybe, or maybe not. I haven't decided. Right now I'm open to anything. Life is meant to be enjoyed, and I intend to start enjoying it."

"Sounds like you're going all *carpe diem* on me," Tulie retorted. "Since when have you become such a big proponent of the Seize the Day movement?"

"It's just the way I feel." It was hard to explain. Even if she could, she wasn't certain Tulie would understand. Perhaps no one could, except the three of them who were bound together by the events that had occurred that day in the cemetery. Claire hugged her knees to her chest. Each time she allowed herself to remember that day a few weeks earlier, how easy it had been for Richard's daughter to gain Hallie's trust, snatch the children, and disappear, brought a fresh shiver of fear crawling up her spine. Hallie's panicked phone call, their frantic drive to the cemetery, and Eleanor's fateful confrontation with Vivi at Richard's graveside. The horrific nightmare of racing Jeffrey up the hill and finding their children locked inside that hot car. Her heart had been pounding as they crested the top, but that was nothing compared to the alarm she felt at seeing their little faces pressed against the windows, Richie and Dickie fiercely pounding them with their fists, Sophie crying inconsolably. But save for being overheated and scared, the children had been safe.

But not Eleanor. Claire's stomach slid sideways, recalling the shock of seeing Vivi and Eleanor rolling in the dirt atop Richard's grave. Vivi, with the strength of a madwoman, had lashed out in rage, kicking and screaming at her brother as he pulled her off Eleanor's chest. How could a daughter hate her mother so much? Poor Eleanor. Wrestling with the truth of her daughter's emotional and mental issues had taken its toll. No wonder her heart had given out. How many years had it been under attack, near close to breaking?

Claire never hesitated about her decision to accompany Jeffrey to the hospital. She couldn't let him make the journey by himself. He was Richard's son, and Richard wouldn't have wanted Jeffrey to be alone. She made sure to stay close, sitting vigil with him in the hospital's CVU, keeping the children quiet as they waited for Jeffrey's wife to arrive and for updates on Eleanor's medical condition. A mild heart attack brought on by stress and other contributing factors, the cardiologist eventually informed them. An angioplasty had been performed, a stent placed in one of the arteries. Barring further complications, Eleanor would make a full recovery. After hearing the news, Claire gathered her children and quietly slipped away, allowing Jeffrey and his family their privacy. For her, it was enough, knowing that Eleanor would survive.

"I know I'm not one for getting serious, but I need to

say this, and I need you to listen. I think you're making a mistake."

"Tulie, I—"

"Please, Claire, hear me out. I'm not suggesting you don't have the right to do what you want. God knows you deserve it after everything you've been through."

Claire felt the tug in her heart, tinged with a poignant sadness. She knew her friend only wanted what was best for her. The two of them had forged a tight bond the day they'd met. How could she say good-bye to Tulie?

"When it comes to grief, you and I could quote the medical jargon and textbook theories with our eyes closed. But no matter which doctrine you subscribe to, which professional journal you read, which advisor you consult, all of them give the same advice: don't make any major decisions for at least six months. I'm urging you, Claire, as your colleague and best friend: don't do this. Don't leave. Wait a few more months before you make a final decision. What will it hurt? I'll bet if you do that, you'll find that things seem different."

Tulie was right; a few more months could make all the difference. And that was exactly what she was afraid of. She wanted to keep the grief and pain fresh in her mind. She needed to act on the decisions she'd made... and she needed to act now. A few more months and she might settle back into the comfortable obscurity of the life she'd once led.

And the one thing she was certain of—absolutely certain—was that she no longer wanted that kind of life.

"This might be difficult for you to understand, but I'll try to explain," Claire said. "I've done a lot of thinking since Richard died. I keep remembering what my life used to be like." It was as if she'd been handed a new measuring stick, with her life now divided into two distinct categories: *Before* and *After* Richard's Death. "While he was still alive, the days were always filled with something. Everything moved so fast. There was barely time to savor the sweetness of what we had right in front of us.

"Don't get me wrong," she quickly added. "I loved our life together. But looking back, everything seems so trivial. We were both constantly busy, what with his work and my students, remodeling the house, trying to be good parents. There was barely time for anything. That's the one thing I wish we'd had: more time together. More time as a family, more time to *be*, and to concentrate on the things that were important."

"But it's normal to feel regret when you're—"

"No, that's not it." It was important she make her friend understand. "It's not that I regret anything, because I don't."

But was that true? Claire felt the lump rising in the back of her throat. "I feel like I finally know what I should have been doing all along. I'm not ready to give it up. Not now. Not yet. Dickie and Sophie are still small. My children are the most important thing in my life. They need me. It's important that I be there for them. They already lost their father. I don't want them to lose me too."

"Okay, I get it." Tulie fluttered a long sigh. "As usual, you're the voice of reason. And you're absolutely right. If your heart's telling you this is the right thing to do, then you have to listen. But you can't blame me for trying to talk you into staying. You're the best friend I have. It'll be hard to let you go."

"No matter where I end up, you'll always have me," she promised, unfolding her legs and rising to her feet. "You never really leave the people you love."

"Don't forget you said that." Tulie ventured a smile as she sprang from her chair and caught Claire in a tight hug. "I intend to hold you to it."

Later, alone, as she finished the last of her packing, Claire realized that she hadn't been completely honest. Regrets? Yes, she still had a few lingering doubts, regrets about decisions she'd made in her life.

Perhaps if she'd done things differently… if she'd been more cautious when they first met, if she hadn't been so caught up by Richard's charisma, she never would have gotten involved with him in the first place.

Did she regret it? She'd been over it time and again, remembering the pain and the grief he'd put both her and Eleanor through. They'd been married to the same man, a cheat and a liar. At times she caught herself wondering if Eleanor had any regrets. She must have. She'd lost everything. And if she herself hadn't met Richard, if they hadn't been together, there would be no Dickie and Sophie. She couldn't imagine a life without her children. That would be no life at all. Better to have loved him and lost him than never to have had him at all. Disappointment in the way she'd handled herself? Claire had her regrets and probably always would. But wasn't that part of personal growth? The fact that you could set things aside, learn from your mistakes; that you could move forward, try to make things right?

If not, what was the point?

Somehow, in the coming years, she'd have to make peace with the past. But there would be time. She was determined to make the time.

And there was something else she was determined to do. Something she needed to do today.

Now.

Steeling her nerves, she picked up the phone.

Claire followed the hostess past crowded tables toward the corner booth she'd requested. A little past noon, but the restaurant already was beginning to crowd with hungry shoppers from the mall. Conversations buzzed around her as she slid onto the bench facing the entrance. She wanted to be able to spot her when she walked through the door.

"Your waitress will be with you shortly," the hostess said, placing two glasses of water and menus on the table.

"Thank you." Opening her menu, Claire briefly scanned the contents, though she had no appetite. Her stomach was already pitching at the thought of what the next hour might hold. All the bravado and confidence she'd felt while chatting with Tulie had deserted her. What had she been thinking, suggesting they meet? Why hadn't she left well enough alone? She wasn't ready for this.

"Hello."

Claire glanced up with a start to see Eleanor standing before her. Forcing a smile, she waved a hand at the seat across from her. "Please, sit down."

Eleanor slid onto the bench, tucked her purse close

beside her. She clasped her hands together on the table and regarded Claire with a silent, steady gaze.

Claire took a deep breath. Where to begin? The last time she'd seen Eleanor had been at the cemetery as the EMS crew strapped her to a gurney and loaded her into the back of an ambulance.

"How are you feeling?" She'd been sure Eleanor was dying that day, with her face taut and a ghastly gray. Today, the older woman looked the picture of health. Her eyes were bright and her cheeks flushed a rosy pink. "You look... good."

"Thank you." A cautious smile crept across Eleanor's face. "I'm feeling better. I started back to work this week. My cardiologist says I'll make a full recovery."

"Thank God," Claire breathed, relaxing slightly against the bench. "I'm glad."

"And your children? Are they all right? I've thought about them often since that day." Eleanor's voice quieted. "Such a horrible thing for them to go through."

"Dickie still talks about it some," she said after a moment, "but Sophie is so young. I'm sure she won't remember any of it."

Eleanor shook her head. "It never should have happened."

Claire nodded, weighed down by grief and guilt. If it hadn't been for the grievance she'd filed against Eleanor, none of them would have been at the courthouse that morning. She would have been at home, Hallie never would have taken the children to the park, and Vivi never would have followed them. None of this would have happened.

"It was my fault. I'm sorry."

"Your fault?" Eleanor blinked. "Why would you think that?"

The waitress bustled over to their table. "Ladies, are you ready to order?"

"If we could have a few moments—" Claire started.

"I'm sorry, but I need to be back at the store by one," Eleanor cut in, checking her watch. "I only have an hour for lunch."

"Will this be separate checks?" asked the waitress.

"All on one bill," Claire said. "You can give it to me." She held up a hand, halting Eleanor's protest. "I invited you, remember?" She glanced at the waitress. "I'd like a glass of cabernet, please. The house wine is fine." Something to fortify her, help her through the conversation. Liquid courage in a glass.

"Coffee, please," Eleanor said. "Black."

"I'll bring your drinks and be back to take your order."

"Normally I don't drink at lunchtime." Claire fiddled with her napkin, unwrapping her knife and fork, positioning them at precise angles in front of her. "I'll admit I'm a little nervous."

Eleanor tilted her head with a curious look. "You seem quite brave to me."

"I don't feel brave." The words rushed out of her before she could stop them. "I feel..."

They sat for a moment, eyeing each other.

"Scared?" Eleanor suddenly offered. "Anxious about something that might be said, or how I'll react?"

How did she know? Claire gathered a deep breath, remembering the instant regret and the constant worry that had plagued her after having invited Eleanor to lunch. A crowded restaurant had seemed the safest place for the two of them to meet. Richard's first wife seemed like a sensible woman, but they barely knew each other. With so much emotional baggage between them, who knew which direction the conversation might head or how things would end? What if Eleanor chose to go on the attack and blamed her for everything that had happened?

But what if she didn't? If they never talked, they would never know.

"Want to know a secret?" Eleanor said. "I'm nervous too. So nervous that if I didn't have to go back to work, I'd join you in a glass of wine." A quick smile flashed across her face. "Funny, isn't it? The two of us sitting here together, acting civilized and polite, just as if we were friends who hadn't seen each other in years. Who would believe it after everything that happened? Yet here we are."

She broke off, turning to gaze through the window as if the cars cruising the parking lot for empty spaces held more interest than anything that might be said. Finally she glanced back at Claire. "You said earlier you wanted to apologize. Why do you feel that's necessary? You never deserved any of this. It must have been horrible for you. So let me be the first to say *I'm sorry*."

Eleanor was apologizing to her? "I don't understand. Why would you—"

"Vivi," Eleanor replied. "She's the reason." Her voice gained strength as she continued. "There are some things you should know about my daughter. Vivi was hard to handle from the day she was born. I tried my best to be a good mother, but it wasn't meant to be. I couldn't understand what I was doing wrong. When I learned I was pregnant again, I was ecstatic. All those months I spent hoping and praying it would be a girl. Then Vivi was born, and it was like my every wish came true. I lay there on the delivery table, crying when I saw her for the first time. She was such a beautiful baby she took my breath away. Then they put her in my arms... and she started screaming. Nothing quieted her. Finally they took her away to the nursery.

"We spent four days in the hospital—back in those days, they used to keep you for some time—but I didn't mind. I was scared to leave. She was fine with everyone else—with the nurses, with Richard. But when I tried to hold her, she fussed and cried. It was as if she hated me for bringing her into the world. That never changed through the years." She shook her head. "It's a horrible feeling, knowing your own child hates you."

"I'm sure she doesn't hate you," Claire said. The words sprang from her mother's heart, though the trained psychologist in her suspected what Eleanor said was true. Something was wrong with Vivi... very wrong.

"She's been in the hospital since that day at the cemetery. She'll probably be there for some time. She's a very sick young woman. The doctor said she has bipolar disease. She was diagnosed years ago." Eleanor's face sobered. "None of us knew. I suspect that includes Richard. She lived and breathed for his approval. She would have found it mortifying to admit there was something wrong with her." Her voice faltered for a moment. "The doctor suspects that Richard's death might have triggered some type of psychotic episode in her. If she lived closer, maybe we would have seen some warning signs."

"Jeffrey said she lives in New York."

"That's right. She had a very good job with Grayson's department store."

"Grayson's?" A slight frown furrowed across Claire's forehead. They were at this particular restaurant today because Eleanor had mentioned the time limitations of her job. "Isn't that where—"

"Yes, it's the same store. I work in Grayson's bedding and bath department here in the mall. But Vivi isn't in sales. After she graduated from university, she was hired by their corporate division and moved to New York. She loved her job, and she rarely came home. Richard made New York a frequent stopover when he was traveling overseas, but I never visited. She made it quite clear that I wasn't welcome. When it came to Vivi, I let Richard handle things. He said she was happy, and I believed him. She'd made New York her home. She had a successful career, and she'd settled down, made a life for herself. We knew she was seeing someone. But there was one thing about him she kept secret, even from her father. Vivi was involved with a married man. An older man, nearly Richard's age. The man was Vivi's boss."

Claire took in the news, her admiration for the older woman growing by the moment. It took a great amount of nerve and confidence to confess family secrets and private matters close to your heart. She doubted she had the same kind of courage. "You're sure Vivi didn't tell Richard about—"

"No, I'm positive he didn't know. Richard and I didn't talk much, but... well, something that important, about one of our children, he would have told me." Eleanor looked at her fork, reflecting for a moment. "Vivi's doctor believes Richard's death was the trigger that started her downhill slide. Once she quit taking her meds, she began pressuring her boss to divorce his wife and marry her. In her confused state of mind, I suppose it made sense. Vivi and her father had always been close; then suddenly he was gone. She'd lost her protector, the one man she'd always been able to count on. But things didn't work out the way she planned. After her boss's wife found out about the affair, he broke things off with Vivi. She didn't handle it well. She made a terrible scene at Grayson's corporate headquarters. The company had no choice. Vivi was fired."

Eleanor lifted her gaze to meet Claire's. "I'm not trying to defend my daughter or offer excuses for what she did. Vivi doesn't even know we're meeting today. I've been barred from her hospital room. She refuses to see me." Her face sobered. "I hope someday that will change. But for now I have to trust that her doctors have things under control and they'll be able to help her. God knows she needs it. She did some horrible things. Jeffrey told me that she came to Chicago shortly after she was fired. I didn't know she was here. None of us knew. She confessed to the police about spray-painting your house... although perhaps I shouldn't call it *confessing*. According to Jeffrey, she was proud of what she'd done. And when I think about that day at the cemetery..." She shuddered slightly. "Thank God we found the children in time. I don't think she would have hurt Richie, at least not intentionally. But who knows what was going on in that warped mind of hers? She sees your little ones as a threat—especially Sophie."

"Sophie?" Claire felt herself freeze. "But she's only a baby—"

"That doesn't matter to Vivi," Eleanor said softly. "When it comes to Sophie, she's insanely jealous. You see, your little girl and mine have something in common: they're both Richard's daughters."

Sweet little Sophie. Claire's eyes fluttered shut as her imagination took flight, and she pictured her little girl caught in the snare of a madwoman bent on revenge. Eleanor was right. Anything could have happened. If they hadn't gotten to the cemetery in time and if Eleanor hadn't—

"Jeffrey told me you decided not to press charges against Vivi for kidnapping the children."

"I couldn't," Claire said. "It didn't seem right." The experience at the cemetery had been a mother's worst nightmare. Odd thoughts about it still visited her during the day and returned to haunt her dreams at night.

"I don't expect you to forgive her, or to forget. Vivi was the one stalking you. She damaged your home. She tried to destroy your reputation."

Whore. Bitch. Claire sat quietly, remembering the dreadful words scrawled across her house and sidewalk. The exterior damage had been cleaned up within days. Erasing the emotional scars wouldn't be so easy.

"No one would blame you if you decide to prosecute her on the stalking charge," Eleanor said. "I might do the same if I were you. But as Vivi's mother, I'm asking you—*begging you*—to hold off. My daughter is a very sick young woman. Someday she may be ready to be held accountable for her actions... but not yet. What she needs now is medical help. Please allow her the time to get that help."

Claire stared at her across the table. How could Eleanor sit there and beg for mercy on behalf of her daughter? A daughter who held Eleanor in contempt, who laid the blame for everything that had gone wrong solely at her mother's feet? What if Sophie did something like that? How would she handle it if her own sweet little girl, all grown up, someday suddenly turned on her? What if Sophie spit in her face, or tried to do her bodily harm? What would she do? How would she react?

Things had gone horribly wrong for Eleanor and her child. But what guarantee did any mother have that her child would turn out fine?

None. Life offered up no guarantees. You did what you could for your children. You loved them, and you hoped and prayed for the best.

Exactly what Eleanor had done.

"I'm not going to press charges," Claire suddenly said. She hadn't made up her mind until that very moment. But prosecuting Vivi would only open another sordid chapter in the melodrama into which her life had dissolved. For her children's sake, for her own sanity, she couldn't allow that. How much did a person need to endure before finally realizing it was time to let go?

Richard was dead, but Dickie and Sophie were still alive and so was she. She needed to concentrate on that, on the living. Letting it go, allowing all of them to go on with their lives, seemed the best thing to do.

Not only the best thing, but the right thing.

"No charges," Claire repeated.

Eleanor breathed out a slow sigh. "Thank you."

Claire nodded. "What happens to Vivi now?"

"Jeffrey and I will make sure she receives the medical treatment and the therapy she needs. Once she's released from the hospital, we'll take it from there. Though I'm not holding my breath," Eleanor admitted. "I don't expect any dramatic changes. I'm not a trained psychologist like you are, but I've always believed that people are born a certain way and there's no changing them. It's part of who they are."

"The core personality," Claire murmured. She'd seen numerous examples of people who'd made radical changes in the way they lived as a result of intense treatment. But Eleanor was right. While a person's external behavior, their decision-making process, the way they interacted with others, could often be altered, their core personality remained the same.

"Vivi was a beautiful baby, but her outside never matched her inside. If you'd met her when she was young, you would have thought she was the sweetest child you'd ever known... but only if she found it to her advantage. There was something unpleasant about her just beneath the surface. She thought she was better than everyone else, and she made up her own rules. I think she's always been a..."

"Narcissist," Claire said softly.

"Yes." Eleanor nodded. "I think that's part of her core personality. Richard was the very same. He did as he pleased, and people let him get away with it." She quieted for a moment. "I let him get away with it."

Silence sat between them as the memory of Richard arrived, a late guest at the table.

"I didn't know he was married," Claire said. "He never told me. I didn't find out until after he died. If I'd known, I never would have—"

"You don't need to explain," Eleanor said. "We don't know each other well, but you don't strike me as the type of woman who would allow herself to become involved with someone else's husband."

Claire drew in a deep breath, struggling to maintain her composure. How could Eleanor be so forgiving? God knew she had every right to rant and rail at the situation she'd found herself in after Richard's death. The woman had lost everything—her husband, her house and money... her life. "He managed to juggle things well. I never had a clue."

Eleanor nodded. "It was the same for me."

Kindred spirits, that's what they were, Claire suddenly realized. Women drawn together through circumstances that would test anyone; yet somehow, they had both survived.

"He was gone most of the time. That was difficult, especially because of the children." The words rushed out. "They're so young. But when he was with us, he was *with us*." Claire looked up earnestly. "Do you know what I mean?"

"I do. He always had a way with people." Her eyes filled with a quiet sadness. "I know I'm not an attractive woman. If he hadn't married me, I probably would have ended up an old maid, spending my days in some stuffy, overheated classroom teaching other people's children, going home at night to my books and a cat."

"Don't say that." On impulse, Claire reached out and laid one hand atop Eleanor's own. "You're very attractive."

"And you, my dear, are a very bad liar." Eleanor patted Claire's hand. "I can see why he fell in love with you. You're sweet."

"I don't deserve that," she said softly. "Not from you. Not after what I did."

"You didn't do anything," she reminded her. "It was Richard. That's the kind of man he was. When he saw something he wanted, he took it. And he wanted you." Her face grew thoughtful. "He hated being bored. When I think of the places his business travels led him: Iraq, Kuwait, Saudi Arabia... some of the most dangerous spots in the world. But he liked it that way. He was always seeking a new adventure. He found that in his work. I think that must be why he turned to other women. It wasn't that they were any different; it was the excitement, the thrill of knowing he'd had something he wasn't meant to take. And once he had them, he moved on, satisfied that he had what others didn't, that he was living a life other men only dreamed of."

"Did you know?" Claire asked. "About the other women, I mean."

Eleanor tilted her head, considering, then finally nodded. "We never spoke about it, but I think I always knew."

"Why didn't you—"

"Confront him?" Her smile was bittersweet. "In retrospect, perhaps I should have. But part of me knew that if I did, things would change. He might have left, and I wasn't willing to take that chance. And so things went on. I had my life and he had his. And when all was said and done, he came home to me. Or at least, I thought he did. And then he met you." Slow resignation slid across her face. "I knew there was someone, but I never suspected he had another wife," she finally said. "I think he must have loved you very much. And I don't think there were other women after that."

Claire's breath came in small, soft puffs as she remembered the man who had been her husband... recalling the four years they'd had together, the good times they'd shared, the love he'd poured out to his children. He'd shared his love with another woman too, and another family.

Two women. Two wives. Together, they had tamed him.

"I'm glad we had a chance to talk today," Eleanor said. "Thank you again for dropping the charges against Vivi. That's very generous of you. I hope we can find a way to live in peace. After all, we have something in common."

"The children." Claire nodded. She'd been struck by the family resemblance between her son and Richie when she'd seen them together at the cemetery. Anyone who didn't know could easily mistake the two of them for brothers and never guess the truth, that her little Dickie was Richie's uncle.

"I hope they won't find this too confusing as they're growing up," Eleanor said. Lifting a hand, she fingered away a few tears. "I suppose it depends on the way we handle things. That will make the difference."

Richard had made a dreadful mistake in underestimating this woman. Tears didn't necessarily signify weakness. Often they were the sign of true strength. And Eleanor was strong, of that Claire was certain. She was brave, and she was powerful. Perhaps it had been Eleanor's quiet determination and strength throughout the years that had allowed Richard to flourish and be the successful businessman he'd become. As for the rest, and his personal failures, Eleanor wasn't to blame.

Any lingering doubts she had about the idea that had occurred to her some time ago vanished. It was the right thing to do.

Reaching in her purse, Claire pulled out a sealed envelope. She slid it across the table toward Eleanor. "This is for you. It's a check, from Richard's insurance policy. I kept part of the money back for the children's education. I want you to have the rest."

Eleanor's eyes widened as she stared at the envelope. "That money is yours," she said, making no move to take it. "There was a reason Richard intended you have it. You have small children—"

"I can take care of them. Yes, they're young, but in a way that's a good thing. They won't remember much of this... or of Chicago."

"You're leaving?"

"I'm not sure. I've given up my position at the university. I need to spend more time with my children. I've also decided to sell the house. I expect it will move quickly once it's listed. People are always looking for property close to the university."

The rest she left unspoken. She wanted nothing more

to do with the house in Hyde Park. It no longer felt like home. Memories of Richard lingered around every corner, but so did her questions about the secrets he'd kept. The house was her past, and her future was waiting. She didn't intend to live it in a place filled with shadows.

"Please take it," Claire urged. Dispelling the darkness would begin when Eleanor accepted the check.

Eleanor still didn't touch the sealed envelope. "I don't understand. Why would you do this?"

"Because you deserve it." Honesty was all she had to offer, and it came from her heart. "If Richard and I hadn't been involved, that money would have been yours."

"But—"

"My being in Richard's life changed everything for you," Claire said. "I loved him very much, but it's obvious you did too. Who knows what was going on in his mind… what he thought he could get away with? Maybe if he'd lived, things would have been different. No one goes to bed at night thinking they won't wake up in the morning. He never intended for things to end like this. But they did, and we're left to do what we can."

"To carry on," Eleanor said in a small voice. "Yes, we need to do that."

"I hope Richard knew how lucky he was to have you. You're a very kind woman."

"Me?" Eleanor looked startled.

"I'll never forget your kindness to me, or to my children," Claire replied. "After Richard died, you could have made my life miserable. You could have gone public, and trashed my reputation. But you didn't. And you were the one who reached out to me, remember? You had Jeffrey send me a copy of Richard's will with a letter stating you intended to honor the bequest he'd made to each of his children... including mine."

She drew in a deep breath. "You were willing to do that, even though it came at a tremendous personal cost... something I didn't know at the time. But I know it now, and I'll never forget it. You lost your home because Richard mortgaged it to buy the house I live in. He took you off the insurance policy in order to provide for my children. You lost your house, you lost your life. You lost everything."

"That's not true," Eleanor said. "Yes, I lost the house, but I didn't lose everything. It's taken awhile, but I feel as if I've found myself again." She dipped her head, her cheeks stained with a faint blush. "That must sound like a horrible cliché, but it's the way I feel. It's as if I've discovered the woman I was always meant to be. The woman I might have become if I hadn't married him." She tilted her head, considering. "Someone who isn't scared to break out on her own and try new things. A woman who knows she can take care of herself.

"I've learned that there are some things that I can't do... but there are more things that I *can* do. Things that I *am* doing. I'm beginning to discover that I like who that woman is. In fact, I like her very much. She's taught me quite a bit about myself, about who I am and asking for what I want. And speaking of what I want—" Eleanor regarded Claire with a frank gaze. "There's one thing I would like from you."

"All right," Claire uneasily agreed, though mouthing the words made her stomach flutter like a thousand butterflies had just taken flight. What did Eleanor want?

More money? Security for her future? The envelope lay on the table between them, untouched. What more could she want?

Eleanor reached across the table, ignoring the envelope and the clutter of napkins, silverware, and glasses, to seek Claire's hand. "Maybe not today, and maybe not next month. But someday, in the future, I hope we can be friends."

Epilogue

With the money Claire had given her, she'd been able to purchase a small two-bedroom condo near Jeffrey and Susan. It was the first time in her life she'd owned something outright, and Eleanor found the prospect both exhilarating and nerve-racking. She'd had her misgivings when she signed the deed, officially granting her homeowner status. She'd never lived in a bustling urban neighborhood, let alone in a building with neighbors above and below. What if she didn't like it? What if the noise or the people bothered her? During the few months it took to settle in, Eleanor tried hard to focus on the positives.

It was lovely living close to her family. A mere five-minute stroll and she could be sitting in Jeffrey's living room, rocking her new granddaughter in her arms. Susan never seemed to mind whenever she showed up to indulge herself with a quick snuggle with baby Eleanor. And now that she lived only a few blocks away, Richie often spent the night. He loved his new sister, but babies were babies, and little Ellie was still so small. Eleanor's invitation to spend the night with Grandma was open-ended, and Richie often took her up on it. Many a weekend during the long winter found them cozy and warm, burrowed on the couch under one of Eleanor's crocheted afghans, devouring popcorn and all the G-rated animated films available to mankind, courtesy of her newly expanded premiere cable channels. And once the snow finally melted, Eleanor began taking him to the park located between their two homes. Sometimes she stayed for dinner—pot roast one night, omelets the next. But more often than not, she politely begged off. Susan was a wonderful cook, but she didn't want to pack on the pounds she'd worked so hard to take off. And Eleanor was conscious of not wearing out her welcome. Jeffrey and Susan had their own family. They deserved their privacy.

And so did she.

She hadn't expected to enjoy living on her own so much. Admittedly, there were things she missed, especially once spring arrived. Her flower and seed catalogs had been forwarded to her new address, but a third-floor condo wasn't exactly conducive for a thriving garden. She settled by indulging herself with pots and tubs of flowers strategically placed around the small balcony outside her living room. Often she sat there with her morning coffee or an evening glass of wine, enjoying the sweet little pansies nodding in the breeze, the large colorful azaleas strutting their stuff, the sturdy geraniums keeping the peace. And she had to admit it was nice not having the burden of maintaining a yard, of making sure the lawn was mowed and the hedges trimmed. Plus, the past winter had been brutal with record snowfall and bitter windchill. It was a relief, knowing she no longer need worry about keeping the walks shoveled or the driveway plowed. Looking back, the house in Lake Forest seemed like something out of an enchanted dream. It had been a beautiful home for her family once upon a time, but it was someone else's home now. She had a new place to live, and she'd settled in quite nicely, thank you very much.

There was something to be said for making a life for oneself.

Martha visited often. She'd tried to help with the unpacking, but Eleanor insisted on doing most of it. There was a simple joy and freedom to be found in doing things for herself. Collecting her things from storage, opening each box and unwrapping her treasures, determining the right spot for them in their new home, brought a sweet satisfaction. There was no one looking over her shoulder to tell her she'd done it wrong, that the faded flower watercolor painted by her grandmother didn't belong hanging above the small brick fireplace; that the gaudy carnival glass vase she'd fallen in love with while out antiquing one day, the vase Richard had scornfully labeled as junk, didn't deserve a prominent spot on the mantel. If people didn't like it, that was too bad. She'd spent her whole life trying to please others. From now on, she intended to live her life concentrating on making herself happy.

And that included her job at Grayson's. Jeffrey did his best to talk her into quitting, especially once her financial concerns were no longer pressing. Eleanor made a slight concession by dropping her hours to three days a week. But she had no intention of giving up her position. Much to her surprise, she'd discovered she enjoyed sales and helping people find what they needed. When the bed and bath department expanded to include Homewares, it became even more fun. She'd always loved decorating her home and displaying things in appealing designs. Lately people returning to the store had begun asking for her. Knowing that she was valued for her knowledge and skills was a heady feeling. Plus, she now qualified for Grayson's generous employee discount. She'd tossed most of her towels and linens and indulged in plush new bath ware and bedding. Eleanor smiled every time she caught sight of the luxurious Persian rug on her living room floor. True, it was a knockoff, but the deep rich pile with its riotous colors covered the polished hardwood floors, giving the room a touch of elegance.

She loved her condo. She loved her family. She loved her life. The irony wasn't lost on her. If Richard hadn't died, things probably never would have changed. She would have gone on the way she had for years—sleepwalking her way through the days, weeks, and months; puttering in her garden; lunching occasionally with Anne and watching her friend drown her frustrations with another glass of wine. Yet hadn't she done the same? She'd indulged in baking frenzies and gobbled up the sugary carbohydrates, adding inches to her waist, heaping guilt on already doughy shoulders and arms. But the pounds were gone, and she now was wearing clothes that hadn't fit in years. Without the sugar weighing her down, she felt fresh, clean, alive... it was almost like being reborn.

Perhaps it was the time of year. Spring had always been her favorite season. Throwing open the windows, one could hear the morning lilt of the songbirds returning. The skeletal tree branches no longer raked the sky but burst forth in bud. The flowers bloomed, and the air softened with a sweet, heady fragrance. People smiled more. Or maybe they'd always been smiling and she simply hadn't noticed. When it came to adults, one couldn't be sure. But children offered no pretense, except for in the make-believe found in the stories she shared every week.

Mrs. Ellie, the Library Lady, was back in business. No sleeping in on Tuesday mornings. The children's hour from ten to eleven was a sacred time, one she now shared with Richie. Her grandson proved an eager and capable assistant. He helped with the setup for their weekly craft projects, put out floor cushions and mats for story time, and never complained about cleanup once the hour was finished. She rewarded him by allowing him to choose which of the two stories they would read from the five or so selections she found during the week. Richie loved participating in children's hour, along with the other twenty or so random children, babies through five-year-olds, who showed up each week.

Eleanor glanced at the clock. Five minutes late, but the children were finally settled on their mats, restless and giggling, waiting for her to begin. Pulling a low wooden chair from the children's table, she dragged it to the front of the group and gingerly settled her weight on the seat.

"Mrs. Ellie, you can't sit on that chair!" one of the little boys shouted.

"Why not?" she said, encouraging them with a broad smile. The older children broke out in laughter. She leaned over the chair, checked the rungs, carefully examining the back. "It looks fine to me. Is there something wrong with it?"

"It's too small! That chair is for kids!" they shouted in unison, giggling even louder.

Her eyes widened. "You mean this is a teeny, tiny chair?"

"Yes!" a little girl squealed from the front row. "Teeny, tiny chairs are for kids."

"Who else had a teeny, tiny chair?" she prompted.

"The little bear!" A big boy, probably a five-year-old, answered. "It's from 'The Three Bears.'"

"That's right. Today we're going to read about a teeny, tiny chair in one of our books. It's the story of 'The Three Bears.'" She pulled out one of the storybooks tucked under her arm, holding it up for all to see. Granted, it was an old favorite, and they'd probably heard it numerous times before. But this particular version, newly released, featured rich, colorful illustrations she thought were brilliant and wanted to share. Opening the book, she turned to the first page.

"Once upon a time, there were three bears who lived together in a house of their own. There was a papa bear, a mama bear, and a wee, tiny baby bear." Eleanor turned the book aside in her hands, holding it high in front of her. "See Papa Bear?" She pointed. "Here's Mama Bear... and who's this?"

As she glanced round at her captive audience, the side door creaked open and a woman with little ones slipped into the back of the room. Eleanor smiled at the stranger hanging in the shadowy silence. Sleepy-headed stragglers often showed up late. She gave the woman an encouraging wave.

"Come join us," she urged. "There's plenty of room."

The woman seemed reluctant, but the little boy was having none of it. He tugged her forward and she followed, moving toward the center of the room, a small girl at her side. Eleanor's heart clanged in her chest as she recognized the boy with tousled brown curls, the little girl in the ruffled skirt, the tall, slim woman.

Claire Anderson.

There'd been no contact between them except a card last Christmas, postmarked from Chicago. Eleanor had held her breath as she opened the card and read the greeting. Nothing fancy, a simple Christmas verse stamped in black with a scrawled salutation underneath in a female script: "Claire, Dickie, and Sophie." Who knows why Claire had thought to send the card? No return address, yet the gesture had touched Eleanor's heart. It wasn't much, but it was a beginning.

And now Claire stood with her little ones in the children's room of the library, a story demanding to be read, like the newly illustrated picture book in Eleanor's hands.

Putting the book aside, Eleanor rose to her feet, and clapped her hands together. "Let's play a game, shall we?" she suggested to the small crowd huddled before her.

"Yes, yes!" They rollicked around the floor, little bodies wriggling and squirming with anticipation. "What kind of a game?"

"Shall we pretend we're all bears?" she asked.

"I don't wanna be a bear," one little girl said, her

bottom lip trembling as she began to back away. "Bears are scary."

"You're stupid," a little boy shouted. "Bears aren't scary." He let out a huge growl and bared his teeth, clenching his fingers into pretend claws, causing the little girl to burst into tears.

Eleanor squatted down and wrapped an arm around the child's shoulder. "How about we all pretend that we're little mice?" She glanced around, conscious of the too-bright smile spreading across her face and the all-consuming thoughts whirling through her mind.

Why was Claire here? What did she want?

"What do mice do?"

"Hide!" they yelled in unison.

"Yes, but mice are also quiet." Wrinkling her nose, Eleanor wiggled her fingers around her mouth to suggest a quivering mouse with whiskers. "Let's all try to be quiet as mice, shall we? Now quickly, find a place to hide."

Off they went, including the little girl, her tears now dried, scampering on their knees and scurrying toward corners of the room, into boxes and cubbyholes.

Eleanor turned to Claire, rooted to her spot in the center of the room. A few moments was all they would have before the mice grew rowdy and emerged from their hidey-holes to demand more stories.

"You're very good with them," Claire said.

"I've always enjoyed working with children." A rush of emotions flooded through her, sweeping away every sensible thought in her head. What was Claire doing here? Eleanor knotted her fingers together in a fist, trying to stop the trembling. "How did you know where to find me?"

"Jeffrey told me."

Eleanor glanced at Claire's children on either side of her. It had been nearly a year since she'd seen them, and they'd both grown. Sophie, hanging on her mother's hand, was no longer a toddler but a sweet little girl clothed in yellow sunshine. And as for Dickie and his mop of curls? Eleanor looked up, her gaze darting around the room in search of her grandson. Finally she spotted Richie crouched behind a box, chattering and snickering more like a bushy-tailed squirrel than a teeny mouse. His head sported a fresh buzz cut from just days ago. If it weren't for that haircut, the two little boys could easily be mistaken for identical twins.

"Quite the resemblance," Claire said, following Eleanor's gaze as Dickie pulled free and scampered off toward Richie.

"It makes sense, seeing how they're related," Eleanor said, her heart racing. Knowing the truth about Richard and Claire's involvement was one thing; seeing Dickie again was like a fresh smack in the face with the undeniable proof of Richard's betrayal. She'd thought she was over it and that she'd moved on. Today was a bittersweet reminder that she'd probably always carry a bit of hurt in her heart.

"You're looking well," she finally said. They hadn't seen each other since that day last summer in the crowded restaurant. Though still thin, Claire was a beautiful woman with a luminous inner glow that radiated outward. Eleanor could understand why Richard had been drawn to her presence.

"We're in Chicago for spring break, visiting a friend."

"So you did move?"

Claire nodded "We live in San Diego now. I teach at the university."

"San Diego," Eleanor mused. "That's far away. Do you have family in California?"

"I thought it best if we made a complete break. I had a few offers from different universities around the country, but I decided on San Diego. Lots of sunshine and blue skies. And no snow." She smiled hesitantly, her first smile since their conversation had begun. "I don't miss the Chicago winters."

"I don't blame you." She thought of the harsh winter they'd recently suffered. "It sounds lovely."

"It is. But it's also different. The people are friendly enough, but... well, California isn't the Midwest."

Eleanor nodded. She'd done some traveling in her lifetime, but a vacation was no comparison to pulling up roots and settling somewhere new. Chicago would always be her home.

Claire's gaze swept the room, seeking out her son, as if needing reassurance that he was safe. "I'm not sorry about making the move," she finally said, her face softening. "The children love it. That's the most important thing."

"I'm happy for you." It was the truth. In the year since Richard's death, each of them had found what they needed. She'd settled in, made a new life for herself, as had Claire. What was it that had brought her to the library today? Had she heard about Vivi? Was she here seeking information about her daughter's therapy? Things were going well. Vivi had been taking her meds, but would always have issues. Did Claire intend to revisit the prosecution of charges against her?

"I've been thinking about you lately." The wariness in Claire's eyes slowly receded and her voice gained strength. "I keep remembering what you said in the restaurant that day."

What she said? What *had* she said? The talk between them last summer had been fraught with tension. She'd felt rushed and anxious and had little memory of the actual words shared. But whatever she'd said, she was certain it had come straight from her heart. There was no need to feel nervous. Claire was the one who'd sought her out.

Nothing to fear, Eleanor repeated to herself. *Nothing to fear.*

"We're beginning to find our way again," Claire said. "Life isn't the way it used to be, but I didn't expect it would be. The children and I are settling in, but it's taking time." She glanced at Eleanor. "Does that make sense?"

"Perfectly," she replied. Before Richard died, she'd thought her life was normal, an idyllic, peaceful existence where nothing ugly or upsetting was allowed to intrude. Looking back, she saw what an utter fantasy she'd created for herself. Life in their beautiful Lake Forest home had been like living inside a book woven together of golden fairy tales. But that wasn't what life was all about. There weren't any glittering fairies with magic wands, making all your dreams come true. Life could be gritty and raw and filled with uncertainty. It could throw you down, toss and turn you every which way, beat you up, spit you out, and leave you for dead.

Maybe the Brothers Grimm had had it right all along. Their gruesome collection of classic fairy tales centered around the evil existing in men's hearts. And evil did exist, that much Eleanor had no doubt. But did you allow the evil to destroy you? It was up to each person to answer that question, to find the strength within and make their own choice.

Accepting Richard's death had been difficult, especially when it came to acknowledging and forgiving the wrongs he'd done her. Yet it had only taken a few months for her to learn to rejoice in the things that were right. For Claire, it might take years. But who was to say that what was right for one was right for another? Everyone had their own life and their own way of coping.

Eleanor was certain that the young woman before her would find her way. They were from two different generations; two separate women, unique in their own ways, but they were both survivors.

Richard had not destroyed them.

A teeny, tiny mouse clambered to his knees, pulling at her hem. "Mrs. Ellie, can we finish the story now?"

They glanced down at the turned-up face with the bright eyes and eager smile. In merely a few seconds, they were surrounded by other little mice scampering at their feet.

"I wanted to say—" Claire started.

"Grandma, read us the story," Richie whined, trying to force the book into Eleanor's hands.

"I'm sorry." Claire scooped Sophie into her arms. "You're busy. I shouldn't have taken up so much of your time." She turned toward Dickie, making a grab for his hand, frustration filling her face as he backed away. "Come on, sweetheart, we have to go."

But she couldn't leave yet. Claire still hadn't explained

why she'd come. Whatever had brought her here today had to be important. Richie and the other children would simply have to wait.

Leaning forward, Eleanor gripped Claire's arm before she could escape. "What was it you wanted to tell me?"

"Mrs. Ellie, we want the story. Read us the story!"

Claire's arms were filled with a squirming Sophie, but her luminous eyes and shining face filled Eleanor's heart as surely as if they stood together in a full embrace.

"What did you want to say?" Eleanor repeated.

"Just... *thank you*." Claire's voice was barely audible above the chanting children. "The things you said in the restaurant that day? You talked about being brave and strong, and discovering who you are. About not being afraid to take chances, and not being afraid to love. I've hung on to those things you've said. They made a difference to me. I thought it was important that you know that. That's why I came today. I wanted to say *thank you*."

"Mrs. Ellie! The story!"

Claire snatched Dickie's hand. "We have to go."

"Please stay." Lifting a hand, Eleanor stroked Sophie's blond hair, smiling as the little girl popped a thumb in her mouth and regarded her with wary eyes. When she tilted her head in a certain way, Sophie put her in a mind of a time long ago and another little girl who'd looked as lovely and innocent as this child who was also Richard's daughter.

"I think your children would enjoy the story," she said.

"Please, Mama?" Dickie tugged at his mother's hand. "Can't we stay? I want to hear the story."

Eleanor lifted her shoulders and smiled. "It appears I'm very popular."

Claire hesitated. "You're sure it's all right?"

"Absolutely," she confirmed. Clapping her hands together, she raised her voice above the din, "Listen up, all you little mice. I can't start the story until everyone takes a seat. Scoot around and make room for these people."

She waited patiently as the children scampered for seats. Only after all of them were finally settled on the thick blue plastic mats, Claire with Sophie sprawled in her lap, Richie and Dickie clambering together, punching each other with quick, playful jabs, did Eleanor gingerly fold her legs beneath her, reclaiming her seat on the teeny, tiny chair.

Glancing up, she found Claire watching her. The two women stared at each other for a moment. Then, slowly, a smile began to spread across Claire's face. And then, much to Eleanor's amazement, Claire threw her a little wink.

Eleanor shifted in her chair, fear making it difficult to sit. It wasn't that she doubted the strength of the chair. She knew it would hold her. She was more afraid that the joy bubbling up inside her would interfere with the telling of the tale. How would she get through growling one minute as she assumed the role of gruff Father Bear, then squeaking with the terror of teeny, tiny Baby Bear? Then again, who cared if the chair collapsed? Even if her voice cracked and nonsense spurted from her mouth, what was the worst that could happen? The children would laugh, and things would be all right. Settling back, Eleanor reached for the book. Everything would be all right. She would make it all right. After all, she was also playing the role of Mother

Bear. And, as all children know, when things go amiss, mothers have a way of setting them right.

Mothers might not be able to make all the scary things in life go away. But when they face up to their own fears, they have a way of creating the perfect ending.

Bowing her head, Eleanor opened the book and began to read.

About The Author

KATHLEEN IRENE PATERKA IS THE author of numerous women's fiction novels, including Royal Secrets and the acclaimed series *'The James Bay Novels'*: **Fatty Patty, Home Fires, Lotto Lucy,** and **For I Have Sinned**. Kathleen, an avid royal watcher, is the resident staff writer for Castle Farms, a world renowned castle listed on the National Historic Register, and co-author of the non-fiction book **For The Love of a Castle**. Having lived and studied in Europe, Kathleen's educational background includes a Bachelor of Arts degree from Central Michigan University. She and her husband Steve live in the beautiful north country of Michigan's Lower Peninsula. Kathleen loves hearing from readers. Visit her website at http://www.kathleenirenepaterka.com, and keep up with the latest news, plus access to bonus content and special offers through her newsletter.

Made in the USA
Middletown, DE
24 May 2016